CW00631687

Margaret Burt

Margaret Burt is in her late thirties and has been teaching English, film studies, journalism and media-related courses at further education colleges for the past fifteen years. She lives in Northumberland.

Sweet Dreams Are Made of This

MARGARET BURT

SCEPTRE

Copyright © 1999 Margaret Burt

First published in 1999 by Hodder and Stoughton
First published in paperback in 2000 by Hodder and Stoughton
A division of Hodder Headline
A Sceptre Paperback

The right of Margaret Burt to be identified as the Author of the
Work has been asserted by her in accordance with the Copyright,
Designs and Patents Act 1988.

10 9 8 7 6 5 4 3 2 1

All rights reserved. No part of this publication may be reproduced,
stored in a retrieval system or transmitted in any form or by any
means without the prior written permission of the publisher, nor
be otherwise circulated in any form of binding or cover other than
that in which it is published and without a similar condition being
imposed on the subsequent purchaser.

All characters in this publication are fictitious and any resemblance
to real persons, living or dead, is purely coincidental.

A CIP catalogue record for this title is available
from the British Library.

ISBN 0 340 76663 8

Typeset by Palimpsest Book Production Limited,
Polmont, Stirlingshire
Printed and bound in Great Britain by
Mackays of Chatham PLC, Chatham, Kent

Hodder and Stoughton
A division of Hodder Headline
338 Euston Road
London NW1 3BH

Permissions ∫

For permission to reprint copyright material in this book grateful acknowledgement is made to the following:

Exerpts from . . .

Linda Goodman's Sun Signs appear through the permission of the estate of Linda Goodman, which retains all copyrights and ancillary rights therein except as expressly stated.

Faber & Faber Ltd for an extract from 'Little Gidding V' from *Collected Poems, 1909–1962* by T. S. Eliot (Faber, 1974).

The Random House Archive & Library for extracts from *Killing for Company: the case of Dennis Nilsen* by Brian Masters (Arrow Books, 1995).

Little, Brown and Company (UK) for extracts from *The Stranger Beside Me* by Anne Rule (Warner Books, 1995).

Thames & Hudson Ltd for extracts from *Interviews with Francis Bacon* by David Sylvester (Thames & Hudson, 1975); revised as *Interviews with Francis Bacon, 1962–1979* (Thames & Hudson, 1982).

Chambers Harrap Publishers Ltd for 'Sea Purse' from *The Chambers Dictionary* (1998).

Dedicated with my love to Geoff Yates

Acknowledgements ∫

To Geoff for being so positive and creative when helping me with my novel and my life. To my Dad for all those books and to Ann. To Ros at Edwards Fuglewicz for energy, expertise (and patience!), to Helenka and Joanna, and to Julia for picking my manuscript from the pile and changing everything for me. To Sue and Lynn at Hodder Headline for helping to edit it and to Diane, Sheena, June and Jane for reading it at its worst. To Andrew, Linda and staff at Northumberland College for listening and much more and to my students for constantly reminding me of what it's like to be eighteen. To Dave and PCC for amazingly patient IT updates and to Jane for red wine, kindness and medical advice when I beat up a character. To all friends at the *Bluebell*, to Eric and Alan for hilarious insights into male sexuality and the images I stole, without which Adam wouldn't be half the man he is today, to Susan and friends (for frequent help with the title), to Roger, to Tony and Jane. To the friends who supported me so crucially when I was Helena's age, the friends who support me now and to my lovely Tyne Valley village neighbours, past and present, for their warmth and inspiration.

And to you, my first readers. I hope you really enjoy the novel.

'*Most babies, as everyone knows, were found under a cabbage leaf. A few are carried in that long nappy, hanging from the stork's bill, or were brought to the hospital in the doctor's bag. Not your little Pisces bundle. She came straight from fairyland, clutching a moonbeam. If you look closely, you'll still see the reflection of elves and magic wishing trees in her dreamy little eyes, maybe even a trace of stardust smudged behind her left ear*'

– Linda Goodman's Sun Signs

Let me tell you about how my life changed, about how I got my house, my man, my freedom. Myself. I live in a Scottish tower-house now, looking over St Mary's Loch in the Borders. My father's money paid for most of my tower-house, and my own body, if you like, started the whole thing off.

Well, in between the time I'm going to tell about and now, the way that I viewed my eggs changed dramatically. Completely. I mean, there were plenty of times (and you're about to witness a few of them), when the main point – the whole point, actually – was the orgasm, and not the eggs at all. What eggs? At other times, I would be moved almost to tears at the thought of a tiny, potential Dominic being doomed to drowning down the S-bend, alongside the cotton wool, the blood and the toilet tissue. Desperate. A used condom was a bagful of Dominics, amoeba-sized shoulders and enormous egos, swaggering to the end to escape their sweltering carrier bag of death.

And then there was Carrie's mother's advice (remember the seventies film?): '*After the blood, come the boys*', or something like that. Of course, some of the boys were more than welcome, no doubt about that whatsoever. But one certainly wasn't – you'll hear all about him, as well. The most unwelcome guests are always the most interesting, don't you think? And worrying in his case.

Anyway, it was the eggs that started the whole story off. I was fourteen and I remember thinking that thirteen would have been a more appropriate age. And the curse was blood – yuck! (I'd never dreamed that it would have lumps in it. Caviare? Disgusting! And there was so much of it.) I really envied those fish that can just drop their neat little boxes of eggs (painlessly?) into the sea – nothing neat about this. I mean, it was exciting to be a woman and everything, but I hadn't expected that I'd have to turn myself inside out quite so completely. So the main egg-memories I have of that day were of the pain, the trauma and the mess. The ache. The ache, and then the knock on the door. Worse! Uncle Mark. God knows how he'd got to know about it: I certainly hadn't told him. But there he was, at my bedroom door – with a letter.

I lived with Uncle Mark at that time. Actually, I can barely remember my father, so in some ways I didn't suffer directly from his death. (He was an actor. He died when I was seven.) Because he had a good idea that he was going to die, he'd asked his friend – a solicitor – to sort of take over from where he left off – or, rather, where he would be leaving off. (Sorry.) Uncle Mark was to sort out the financial and practical side of things: private schools, ponies, universities, that sort of thing. The emotional side proved much more difficult (not really Uncle Mark's forte).

I didn't even want to let him in with his stupid letter at first. Between you and me, he's a bit of a pain – certainly takes his 'work' seriously. I thought it was probably another complaint from school. Plus I really did have a hell of a stomach-ache. But I could hardly turn him away so in he came and sat down on my wicker chair, looking at me *very* strangely.

'Helena.' He used his best solemn face and voice. 'You know that your father left me in *loco parentis*.' (See what I mean?) 'Well, what you don't know is that he also left me three letters for you.'

Well, this was altogether more exciting. Three letters! Images of chequebooks and credit cards came instantly to mind. Pity boring old Uncle Mark was involved. Never mind, he was still talking. 'And at his request, the first letter is to be delivered to you today, on the day you come to womanhood.' *Come to womanhood*? I've still not quite got there yet. What century was this man from? Definitely more of your sanitary belt person than your 'Feel the freedom' tampon type and, God knows, I was having more than enough trouble with that kind of thing that day without all of this. Anyway, I concentrated on what he was saying.

'This first letter is to be opened by you, strictly in private. If you need any guidance following the opening of the letter, you must look to yourself, Helena, or to me.' He put on his most reassuring and kindly uncle-esque smile. 'I will leave you now, with your father's words in your hands.' And he pushed the letter right into my fingers.

Well, I didn't really know what to do when he'd gone. No point in looking blasé and flippant if he wasn't there to see it. Plus it was obviously an important letter. My father. I'd been waiting seven years for this. My breathing went all strange. So I sat down and I opened the envelope – after one or two false starts.

The paper was surprisingly ordinary really – big, blue sheets. But what was written on it most certainly wasn't.

Helena, darling,
What can I say? I love you, I love you, I love you, I love you. What else do you need to hear from me?

You've always been the most magical and special child to me. And now I want to be the most magical father to you.

Just think, you'll never see me grow old; you'll never see me use a commode, or dribble; I'll never disgust you by farting in the bathroom and I'll never see you sniff glue (or whatever the current equivalent is). I'll always be young, strong and virile to you (in my dreams!) and you'll always be a beautiful darling to me. I'll never get run down, worn down or mention my prostate gland to you. I'll never invite all of my middle-aged, middle-class, awful friends around for a party, and drink and dance with them, smoke pot and bitch about children while you go upstairs with your awful friends,

> *drink and dance with them, smoke pot (or worse), vomit and bitch about parents.*
>
> *So far so good? And all of your memories of Florida in the sun, Mickey men in mice suits, Disney films and magic tricks will, I hope, stay bright. At the moment, you always want to be Snow White, however hard I try to convince you that Dartagnan is the more dramatic part. Do you remember all that now? You should see your face sometimes, when you're concentrating on something vital, like undislocating Sindy's hip or making fuchsia fairy dresses – you're so amazingly serious (and seriously gorgeous, of course).*
>
> *But the best bits are still to come – of your life and my part in it now. Because now I truly turn into the father from heaven. I get my chequebook out (every girl's dream, and certainly my dream when I was your age) and I place the pile of golden coins in your fingers. So that you can create your own drama, your own magical life, your own self. And I want your life to be as near to the best bits of the fairy stories as you and I can make it.*
>
> *All that you have to do (and it's a big all) is to work out what your three wishes are. I know that in the stories that takes three seconds, but in real life it's the hard bit. What do you want to buy? What sort of life do you want to make for yourself? And, best of all, what do you want to be?*
>
> *When you become an adult, go to see Mark. I hope he's given you all the security in your life that you've needed, young legal hotshot that he is. Listen to his advice (although, knowing you, you'll probably find your own way) and ask him for the second letter. With that letter comes a cheque for £300,000. All you have to do is to work out what to do with it.*
>
> *Until then, never forget that I love you.*
> *Dad*

Yes! Three *hundred* thousand pounds. Talk about all your dreams coming true at once. Money is my very own magician and he can wave his wand at me any time he wants. *Three* hundred thousand pounds! I hadn't realised until that point just exactly how bored I'd been – bored and blind, adolescent specialities both of them, don't you think? And now, three hundred *thousand* pounds. Yes!

I must admit, the bit about ignoring advice made my skin prickle a bit. I've always preferred to find my own way around things and, let's face it, Uncle Mark was pretty easy to ignore. (Hotshot, for God's sake.) He'd done his best, but affection really isn't his thing – sometimes, between the two of us, he tries just a bit too hard.

It was so nice that my father wanted to make all of my dreams come true. Even seeing his big, loopy handwriting was brilliant; I kept touching it, rereading it. His beautiful darling. I'd sort of given up on that type of father, that type of childhood. And I'll never forget his last sentence. It was all a bit too much to take in, really, 'becoming a woman' and 'becoming an adult' all in one day. I could definitely see how my father and Uncle Mark had become such good friends: 'becoming an adult' was particularly rich. I very nearly went down to Uncle Mark and asked him for my cheque there and then. How on earth was I supposed to know when 'becoming an adult' had happened?

2 ♪

'That creature over there making a phone call – is it an electrically charged dynamo? Is it a flaming torch? Is it a bird, an explosion – or is it Superman? Well, practically. It's an Aries male, which is pretty close. Let's hope you know what you're looking for. Should it be excitement, an Aries man will provide it by the bushel, with seldom a dull moment to blur the sparkle.'

'When Aries represents birth in the zodiac, Pisces represents death and eternity. Pisces is said to be a deep, mysterious sea, into which all rivers flow . . . What makes her swim?'
— Linda Goodman's Sun Signs

Helena isn't the only person waiting impatiently for her life to take off. In a square little bedroom, in a boxy little house, not far – geographically – from Helena's, a boy just a bit older than her is sitting at his computer. His story is different from Helena's – different, but connected.

Adam's mother would tell you that he's in a world of his own – he spends most of his time alone up there in his bedroom. His teachers would tell you that he's in a parallel universe. So far as Adam himself is concerned, the best place to look for him is on his own web-site – it's quite extensive. And very individual, he would say (not that he says much). Creative. Copy, cut and paste.

On the wall of Adam's bedroom is a poster. Have a look at the first part of it.

THE LEGAL EAGLE'S COMMANDMENTS:

- *To have freedom from want*

- *To guide others with their consent*

- *To be self-fulfilled*

Aims that any mother would be quite happy for her son to pursue, don't you think? Nothing much for Uncle Mark to worry about there.

Adam and Helena haven't met just yet – but they will. And when they do, you will recognise the moment when their eyes lock.

Back to Helena.

I've never known why Pisces is called the death sign. I'm certainly full of life – born squawking, Uncle Mark's always said. But this letter business gave me the shivers: my first contact with my father for seven years. I'd forgotten how much fun he was. People seem more serious somehow when you think about them after they've died, don't they? Uncle Mark had always tried to keep me informed: 'Your father would have appreciated that', 'Your father was brilliant at that', or 'Your father loved football', etcetera, etcetera (one of the King of Siam's – remember Yul Brynner in *The King and I*? – and Uncle Mark's favourite phrases). And, of course, I'd seen my father's old television programmes and adverts, even, but it wasn't the same as seeing his own words written down on paper. Paper that he had actually touched.

As you know, I lived with Uncle Mark at that time – 'The bachelor girl and the bachelor boy,' he used to say. (That's a joke, by the way, a jokette I call it – a very *little* joke. They're Uncle Mark's speciality.) In fact there were never any signs of women around at that point and I used to wonder if 'the bachelor gay' was more like it. (Sorry, Uncle Mark – my jokette.)

Or perhaps he was a eunuch. (An eunuch?) I knew all about those from the ponies. I certainly never saw his willy, which was a relief. He supplied plenty of biology textbooks for *that* sort of information. Anyway, there was never any competition around from girlfriends, which was exactly how I liked it.

Uncle Mark's house helped me to make a lot of decisions about the type of house that I would have when I was older. First of all, it would have to have thick walls, so that I'd never hear anyone peeing – or worse – again. God, and he looked so civilised! Stomach turner. Secondly, it would have to have a natural garden of some sort – nothing like the 'patio' that Uncle Mark was so proud of, with its Mark-made B and Q BBQ. Yuck! Finally, it would be magical. Not neat. I'd had enough of neat. Uncle Mark's house was a Leech house and every time he opened the door for us, he'd say, 'Home and dry!' Every time. And it had a nice little name: Beech Trees. (Not that there was a beech tree in sight, of course.) So I had my own name for his house: Leeched Dry. Needless to say, I locked that hilarious little jokette very safely inside myself.

So there I was in Leeched Dry with a boring uncle, a promise of £300,000, and no earthly way of working out how to get it. Marvellous. That's adolescence for you. Learned helplessness. I thought and thought about what I could do and eventually I realised I couldn't do anything at all. Not a thing. Except wait – and I've never been very good at that. So I just forgot about it. Sort of. For a while.

And I concentrated on all of the things I could do something about – all the things a fourteen-year-old would concentrate on. Boys. Boys with spots, boys with stoops, boys with stutters. Boys who probably grunted in the toilet in their own sad versions of Leeched Dry. The choice was fantastic. Finding boys with testosterone, regular features and all their own limbs was the problem. It was all there in my novels and magazines, but fourteen-year-old boys were no use at all. I had to look elsewhere.

Luckily at around that time I got a key to my own room, a silver key. A solid silver key. One thing about Uncle Mark, he was never stingy with me. Or nosy. I spent hours in that room, reading my books (developing my scientific knowledge, of course), trying on clothes. Combing my hair.

My room was very important to me at that time – vital, in fact. It was a real waterbaby's room – china dolphins, seahorses and starfish everywhere. And there were lots of paintings and photographs of pools – pooled water and pooled eyes. There were men's eyes, eyes that I dreamed were looking into mine, and also the eyes of beautiful girls, girls who had white-skinned, sliding bones. (And mouths that weren't too big. Unlike my own.) Eyes – eyes, spirals and whirlpools – fascinated me and I doodled them constantly when I should have been learning about zygotes or the difference between a cornea and a retina. There were photographs of my father everywhere. And a window-sized map of the world. (I knew the major oceans and seas off by heart, and a lot of the rivers.) Oh, and of course a few thousand old stuffed toys on my bed – Dumbo, Winnie the Pooh and the rest.

The sea purse was my most recent treasure – a dark, square little box with crab-like hooks at the corners that I'd found on the beach during a 'Romantics Lakeland Tour' with Uncle Mark. (I'd had to smuggle it into my room because of the germs – Uncle Mark's pathetically germaphobic.) Uncle Mark had said that it would have lain at the bottom of the sea, holding a shark's eggs or a skate's. That was when I first became aware of my own stomach, my own ovaries, packed with their swarms of tiny eggs. When would I open my purse? When would I spend my eggs? And with whom?

I always had long hair. Really long hair. I had the usual girlhood fixation with fairy stories: 'Rapunzel, Rapunzel, let down your hair.' (Rumpelstiltskin terrified me!) Uncle Mark called it my 'crowning glory' (told you he was old-fashioned). When I was really little, we had a childminder called Marie for a while and she used to comb it for me. Comb it and comb it and comb it. It's thick and wavy, a sort of browny, chestnutty colour. After Marie had washed it, I had to drape it over my pillow, on a towel, otherwise I'd have been dripping all night. Still, it was sometimes damp in the morning. And I've got a bit of an unbalanced face – very big eyes, very pointy chin, very wide mouth – attractive and quirky, or unbalanced and strange, depending on whether you like me or not. Between you and me, the abandoned child routine could be quite a useful one; I'm sure you pulled the odd dodgy emotional card out from time to time at that age yourself, if you'll admit it. And I did miss having a father. Terribly. Anyway, with my Rapunzel hair, pool eyes, newfound hips and a few other little tricks, things were developing quite nicely.

Clothes were everything to me then: I liked soft things, velvety things, and tight things that clung. Because my new body was like a cat's body – a very soft, very female cat's – and I learned that I liked to stroke it, to feel it. It was much more fun in the flesh than it looked in those biology textbooks. (Did your books have those ovaries in them that look like a starved sheep's skull? I still can't believe I look like that inside. Grotesque!)

With my newly created cleavage and my hip curves, I was my own centrefold. And no spotty boy or boring uncle was going to get my key while I admired the view from different angles. I also liked to feel my new curves and to touch between my legs and rub a bit. That was enough. For the time being.

Best leave Helena on her own there for a while, I think, and have another look at how Adam is getting on. In some ways, he's a little more advanced than Helena in the sexuality area – his tastes are more catholic and his inspiration comes from a very broad range of sources. While his biology textbook is actually identical to Helena's, his collection of pornography is altogether more extensive: he has the whole of the Internet at his disposal, for one thing. Also, he has a sister – a little sister with very sharp fingernails.

Would you like to see inside his bedroom? Really? And *you* were just starting to think *he* was a bit, shall we say, unusual. His house is not much to look at from the outside: it's a grey, pebbledashed, 1960s council house. Terraced. Cheap. Let's go straight in through the pink, thin but clean door – light as cardboard as it swings in my hand. We're in luck. His mother is at work and he and his sister are at school. Up the stairs now – there's his new jacket on the banister. It's an open-plan staircase – so popular in the 1960s – and it meant that Adam and his sister heard every argument that their parents (and their neighbours) had, every blow they exchanged, every insult they spat at each other (and, like Helena, every motion they passed). Here we are, past the neat, sprigged wallpaper to the door marked, 'Keep

Out!' Best shut it behind us, I think. Lucky for us he's out – he's fanatical about his (extremely limited) privacy.

Well, you can breathe a sigh of relief now – there are lots of things here you'd find in any normal, red-blooded boy's bedroom. And it's commendably neat and tidy – unusually, almost clinically well ordered. There are several shelves, one full of very precisely piled magazines (I'll leave you to guess at their content); a row of shelves lined with a less predictable choice of books – poetry, film scripts, art books; a pristine row of CDs and CD ROMs and another of videos. And in the middle of the room, a desk that is completely clear and clean except for the obligatory, state-of-the-art computer and a pile of files, carefully labelled. On the screen at the moment is a 'Wanted' poster of one of Adam's acquaintances – breasts mother-large, waist childless-small, hips baby-smooth, legs African-long, feet Chinese-small. Copied, cut and pasted. Of course in real life she'd fall over, but this isn't real life. This is Adam's life. Internet – BT friends and family. Best friends.

And the walls . . . the walls are even more interesting. And messy. Mouths. Mouths everywhere – jewelled mouths, red mouths, black mouths, distorted mouths, diseased mouths, screaming mouths, laughing mouths, cut mouths, painted mouths. Hungry mouths. And meat. Meat everywhere. The walls are washed in red, pink, purple and black: butchered bodies, pickled bodies, heads in boxes. Lots of triptychs. And all of the triptychs are framed separately – as the artist himself preferred. There are three figures in each of them – three figures, connected but not yet quite completely connected, in their separate but certainly linked worlds. One wall is totally bare, apart from a map of the world and a huge poster of a fire. Consuming. Oh, and there's that poster that we started to look at earlier – no time to look at it now – so much to see in here, isn't there?

Better get out quickly now and back to Helena.

Shakespeare is the all-time literary hero – or so everyone seems to feel obliged to say. And so, of course, Uncle Mark had felt obliged to buy me *The Complete Works of Shakespeare* for my fourteenth birthday – every girl's dream.

I was actually quite drawn to your heroic Shakespearean type, and I'd collected a few props to help the old imagination along. I had seven main favourites – a bit like the seven rooms of my tower-house now – and I would practise various versions of myself through these seven people.

Five of them were women. And the first, the most obvious one, was Cordelia. She always has long hair in the films, doesn't she? And she's young, and beautiful. Plus, there's no mother in sight and her father's out of it, one way or another, for most of the play. So hers was the first part I tried. Mostly, this was a silent piece. I'd be wearing something thin, white and virginal-looking, with just the pink tip of one, very new, breast poking through, perhaps. Kneeling in front of the mirror, I usually went for a tight waistline and a flowing line below, to suggest a womanly abundance. And mainly I said nothing.

'Her voice was ever soft

Gentle and low, an excellent thing in a woman . . .'

Uncle Mark was delighted when I tried it downstairs (normally clothed, of course) but no one else paid much attention to me in silent, righteous and demure mode, so that outlived its usefulness pretty quickly.

Ophelia was another maidenly sort of favourite, and I had a Pre-Raphaelite print on my wall to help me with this one (Lizzie Siddal in the bath, dripping freely). I had a very graceful, bath-time interpretation of my own, with my hair and my nipples floating freely on top of the water.

Even out of the bath, my hair played an important part in this role, all mussed up and strewn with flowers. I loved Gertrude's speech: *'There with fantastic garlands did she come, Of crow-flowers nettles, daisies and long purples'*. The flowers Ophelia suggested didn't seem appropriate (*'rosemary'* for *'remembrance'* – a bit morbid) so I'd go for primroses, bluebells, whatever was in season – delicate, sort of adolescent flowers really. With a few in the pubes to spice it up. (Not that I'd have dreamed of calling my treasured new angel hair anything quite so gross then, of course.) Naturally, I thought I looked gorgeous – white body, chestnut hair, wild flowers. But again, the dialogue let it down a bit, and '*Aye, my lord*' soon wore a bit thin – even at fifteen. When I tired of feminine eroticism and agreeing, I would turn into Hamlet, stamping around and barking, '*Get thee to a nunnery*,' savagely and darkly.

For the most part, I preferred the girls' parts and costumes, but the Macbeths got the transsexual treatment too. I loved Lady Macbeth at first. I'd spend hours vamping myself into her – a black, push-up bra, loads of dark eye make-up (copied from pictures in a magazine), before reading from his letter in a husky voice: '*My dearest partner in greatness*'. Fantastic. I adored the Polanski film, too (set in Lindisfarne Castle which I also loved), despite the fact that they all sleep with their dogs in it. (Uncle Mark was nearly sick.)

But whatever happened to Baby Macbeth? It's all very well being dramatic:

> '*I have given suck, and know how tender 'tis*
>
> *To love the babe that milks me . . .*'

But where on earth was '*the babe*'? Was it alive and kicking somewhere else, or had she and Macbeth really dashed its brains out (as threatened later)? Honestly, there were as many absent parents in my entire Shakespeare as there were in my entire family. Sometimes I felt like a descendant of '*the babe*' myself. And where was Queen Lear?

When I found the Lears and the Macbeths too bloody and self-destructive to take, I turned briefly to Desdemona, but she was even more of a drip than the literally sopping Ophelia – '*pale as thy smock*' – and I wasn't quite ready for the making of the beast with two backs yet. Some of the arguments were good, though, for a bit of trial S and M ('*Down, strumpet*').

My final favourite was Portia. Not really Portia herself, although she was one of the spunkier cross-dressing types. No, it was the idea of the caskets:

'I am lock'd in one of them:

If you do love me, you will find me out.'

Worlds within worlds, rooms within rooms. The chambers of her heart.

This captured my imagination and I began to collect little boxes, chests and caskets of all sorts in my room. I kept everything in them, from tiny bottles of perfume to fruity lip glosses, earrings, ribbons and sweets. I built up quite a collection. Uncle Mark had picked up a really special one for me on one of his visits to some art gallery or other.

Although I didn't know it at the time, that was how I first met Will Jackson – *WJ* – initials on a box. But that's a later story altogether.

As Helena pauses for breath, there's just time to think about the posters in Adam's room. Take a look at the last part of the first poster first:

THE LEGAL EAGLE'S COMMANDMENTS:

• To control the actions of others

• To avoid boredom

• To live life one's own way

Adam's rules, too. Still sound pretty reasonable, don't you think? And then there's the print hanging on the door.

Head VI – a screaming body, trapped inside a square box. Adam Ramsden – a silent boy, trapped in a square room. How would *you* survive?

It's funny, really, but life at Leeched continued more or less as it had done, despite the money. At first, it felt like I'd won – or, rather, was about to win – the lottery. But I was still spending most of my time at school, or in one bedroom, walled inside a three-bedroomed house. And the letter thing was a bit worrying. How and when would I know when I was an adult? And would my father (or Uncle Mark in his place) agree with me when I felt I'd finally got there?

Uncle Mark was, predictably, no help at all. I tried everything to break him down, to make him tell me what he thought my father meant. But whilst he loved the – sadly rare – attention he wasn't letting on at all. 'Everything in its season,' he would say, or, 'When the time is right, you'll know.' Etcetera, etcetera. He irritated me to death. The time for £300,000 is always now, surely?

I dreamed I was in a huge Victorian maze, full of hedges (beech, of course) and locked doors, which my father had designed and Uncle Mark had built. I was wandering around in the middle, with those damned beech leaves cutting me to ribbons. My father was twinkling down on me, with the map of how to get out spiked on one star-like hand and a chequebook on the other. Bloody Uncle Mark was no help, shouting, 'Time heals all,' and 'Father knows best,' etcetera, etcetera, from a safe distance of about a mile away, while he twinkled the keys from his fingertips.

He wouldn't budge.

So I waited. I was very careful not to tell anyone at school about the cheque.

I did have friends, though. I needed them to get out of Leeched Dry occasionally, for a start – and for lots of more important reasons as well.

When I finally came out of the bedroom era, I decided I needed some more exciting props for the outside world, so we'd go shopping, just Diana, my best friend, and myself. Who could ever say that magic doesn't exist? They'd obviously not shopped.

The road to Edinburgh was the chosen ocean to lead us bobbing to our Promised Land – mine and Diana's. We loved the new, antiseptic sharpness of the Waverley Centre and the neat boxes of shops inside. Or we'd browse around Jenners, drinking tea beside ancient Scottish tearoom hags.

Most of all, we loved the back streets – the Victorian parts of the City. Every shop had been created for us, to give us the treasures we needed. Isn't materialism a dream? Plaguing the life out of jewellers was great fun. We'd discovered a couple of narrow, brick-built shops down a dingy street that sold hand-made jewellery. Diana's boobs were altogether more impressive than mine, so she'd sail into the shop first – like the figure-head of a ship – and demand to try on a diamanté, marcasite or haematite necklace, while I lurked in corners, fingering rings or touching glittering earrings to my lobes, like a guilty piratess.

What I particularly liked in the first shop was a collection of jewellery inspired by the Celts. I'd never lost my fascination with spirals – spirals and knots. Back to Uncle Mark's maze in my case, probably – a search for the soul, in Celtic terms. The man in the shop had told me once that the knots were connected to the 'riddle of life'. Riddle was right!

In the back of the second shop, Diana had discovered an absolute treasure trove – literally. The first time I saw it, it lay on the floor, in a corner beside a small window, and a shaft of sunlight was catching it. Perfectly placed. It was a precisely carved, wooden chest, about eighteen inches long and quite deep, made of rosewood, inlaid with cherry, oak and cedar. The lid was domed and, irresistibly, hinged with shiny brass catches. I itched to open the glinting gold clasps, just as I itched to open my second blue letter (and touch that crispy cheque).

The first time I did open it, my hands were shaking as I lifted the heavy lid and looked inside. Other smaller boxes lay within it, connected by tiny wooden corridors, yet locked by little keys. I opened the first box and found a heap of smooth, deep red garnets. There was an explanatory label on top. The next box had wonderful, swirling purple amethysts in it and the third a pile of opals – 'The Rainbow Stone' as the label told me. Each box within the chest was filled with a different, shiny pile of crystals, or brightly streaked stones. I was transfixed as my fingers wandered through them, loving the smooth, cold roundness.

Unfortunately, time was running out that day and I spotted a poster that outlined all of the qualities of the different gems: *Crystal Health and Wealth: The Efficacious Use of Gems and Minerals*. The language more than the content made me buy a poster for Uncle Mark – it was his birthday soon. I had no idea how old he was, but he was definitely the 'efficacious' type. I quickly bought a crystal for him as well – a crysocolla, which I hoped would *'introduce creativity, joy and serenity'* into his masculine heart, to use some of the label's words. (Sadly, the poster later informed him that it was also the *'Woman's Friend'* – excellent for period pains, PMT and other related problems. He didn't display that particular treasurette for long.)

As Diana and I left the jeweller's shop that time, I gave one last glance to the beautiful wooden chest. That was my second, unknown to me, encounter with Will Jackson: the chest had the words *Will J* carved into its right-hand corner.

As Helena waits longingly for her cheque to arrive, would you like a quick look to see how Adam Ramsden is preparing for his fiery future at the moment?

- *Adam sat too close to a small girl on a bus. He was clean but she could smell him. Distinctly. And she didn't like the smell. She was embarrassed but she moved away.*
- *Adam told his twelve-year-old sister that her (slightly odd-looking, one-year-old) breasts were like squashed poached eggs. She told him his bollocks were like peas – frozen peas. He didn't know she knew words like that.*
- *Adam picked a particularly nice, pearly spot in front of a girl in his class. It was a little psychological experiment to see if there was any connection between how attractively he presented himself and how desirable he was to women. His conclusions were rather different to the girl's.*
- *Adam told the girl next door, very quietly, that he could rape her – if he wanted to. She had annoyed him. He said that if she told anyone else, her mother would get hurt. The girl's mother said that Adam was a little wanker. It wasn't worth telling his mother – they'd tried that before – but she would keep an eye on him.*

The girl carried on annoying him, and enjoyed it more, but she couldn't quite forget what he'd said.

- *Adam learnt how to be powerful at school by controlling the other children and the teachers. Especially the women teachers. He got most of the other knowledge he needed from his computer. He had seven heroes of his own to download. And all of them were men.*

Rather more interesting is what he did with his knowledge and power. And we're just about to see how it related to Helena.

Let's get back to her now, as she journeys towards her destination.

Uncle Mark, of all people, introduced me to St Mary's Loch.

It was the term for the Romantics at school, or Château Chillon as we called it. (That's a Byronic jokette, for anyone lucky enough to have escaped the tortures of my private school education.) We'd just moved on from Byron to Wordsworth and so Uncle Mark had decided it was time for a little trip to Scotland's Wordsworth country. I'd had a lot of this sort of thing: he was determined to kill my love of art and literature completely. I couldn't mention the words 'Peter Rabbit' without being spirited away to Sawrey in the Lake District to spot bunnies. So my heart sank when he looked over my shoulder one day and said, 'I think a little trip to Moffat is in order.' Firstly, I knew a 'spot of the extra-curriculars' was on its way, and worstly I knew Uncle Mark adored Moffat.

As Edinburgh was to Diana and I, so Moffat was to Uncle Mark. He loved the thimbley little bottles of whisky, the tartan rugs, the Scottish fudge. The Singing Potter. (Don't ask!) And best (worst) of all, he loved the clans.

The fact that he's not Scottish could have something to do with it. (Nor am I – we moved up here about nine years ago – we're nothing, both of us.) And so Uncle Mark, like most people, has no clan. Unlike most people, he will not let this lie. He torments the shop assistants in places like Moffat in the quest for what I call Clan Leech: the clan that is connected to Uncle Mark and his tedious, obscure family history. Etcetera. Of course, actually finding Clan Leech isn't the point at all: the point is discussing Clan Leech, and himself, endlessly with every shop assistant too slow or too polite to get away, trying to trace Clan Leech on naff computer programmes, and buying ties, scarves and shortbread tins in every type of tartan that *isn't* Clan Leech tartan.

So this was what I knew I had in store when I heard the dreaded word 'Moffat'.

I walked very slowly to his car that morning. Uncle Mark always has an upmarket Vauxhall model but he doesn't adapt to change well so he insists on calling it 'the Cavalier', because that's what he had for about seventy years of his life previously. The Crying Cavalier, I called it, and I dragged my heels into the damned thing as slowly as I could. For once, I was even sorry to see Leeched Dry retreating in the rear-view mirror. I hadn't even been allowed to take Diana along with me for moral support; it was to be just Uncle Mark and me. A treat.

Still, it was autumn and the outskirts of Leechville were looking pretty warm and colourful, so I started to relax a bit. I tried to work out what I could possibly get out of the day, settled on good grades for my forthcoming exams (desperate!) and gave in gracefully and read my Wordsworth as Uncle Mark drove.

After half an hour or so, I started to get more than a bit bored so I was looking out of the window intermittently. I was just thinking how awful the houses looked – I'm not quite sure where we were – when some traffic lights appeared and I looked up at one grey pebbledashed wall. I had a sense of being lost. Marilyn Manson's tortured version of *Sweet Dreams Are Made of This* was blaring out of a window, drawing my eyes up towards the noise.

And there he was. A staring, starving boy held in the square of the white window. His face was just framed in it, like a picture. He was slightly spotty, with thin, straggly brown hair. Stiff-backed. But his intensity – that was the main thing. His eyes were burning with it. And something else, something I was afraid of yet fascinated by: he sort of lit up the window. Everything around him was grey – grey walls, grey pavements, half-poor, grey people, and then two boxed-in, burning eyes in the middle, like the burning of a red, diseased mouth in a fading face. Yet there was also something dead – cardboard or stone

– about him. Our gaze held for several seconds. What was he thinking of as he looked at me? When I looked at him, I thought of winter, of glittering ice.

I was glad when the Crying Cavalier began screeching its way towards Moffat again.

I was in my cousin's room of all places the first time I saw her. I was just doing some research on one of my special men and wanted to look something up on his computer. The Babysitter, I was reading about – meticulously clean he was and very interested in clothes. Most people find his work extremely artistic and moving, me included. Powerful. So I was just thinking of applying a few of his techniques to my current situation, like. Just thinking about it, you know. And about girls at school, especially one – a thin, quiet one with dirty-blonde hair and cute little tits, who can never quite look me in the eye. A bit like my sister.

Above the music, I can hear the traffic outside my cousin's bedroom window as usual and, I don't know why, something makes me go over there and look down. And there she is – I see her at once, in the passenger seat of a Vauxhall. She doesn't see me; she looks bored stiff. Dead with boredom. Lost. Driver looks a bit of a twat, like, an older guy (probably her dad).

Her hair is beautiful, the most beautiful thing I've ever seen. It's October, autumn, and her hair is autumn hair. There's loads of it, moving and catching the light, the colour of shiny conkers. I suddenly realise what a mess my own hair is and I fiddle with it. Just then she turns around, and for a few seconds she looks right at me. Her eyes are fantastic, like a deer's eyes. A hungry deer. And she sees right inside me. An invitation. They are just picture eyes. My dreams could wind themselves around her like a chain of scars around a wrist. Around her wrist.

My life changes forever. It's the magic of her beauty: it changes everything. Leads me to changing a few things myself. I'd been so lonely. Only the black glitter of my work, and my dreams, had kept me going: the sense of something different, richer. Gold.

Now that I've seen it, it's time to turn my dreams into reality. Now.

*   *   *

Excuse me? I seemed to lose your attention there for a second. Can't have that. I was telling you about how I met St Mary's Loch. That day was significant in all sorts of different ways, not all of which I realised at the time.

Well, somehow I survived Moffat intact – again. The girls in the shops had started to recognise Uncle Mark and he was finding it pretty difficult to get served, let alone strike up a conversation, so his clan game was beginning to bore even him. After we'd had our lunch, he wanted to introduce me to some of the literary bits of that part of Scotland. So it was back into the Crying Cavalier again for a ride up to some monument or other.

'They always seem to teach you about Wordsworth, Byron and Blake, etcetera, etcetera, at school, Helena, but I'm going to introduce you to one of the great Scottish writers today: the Ettrick Shepherd.'

Like I've said, Uncle Mark was pretty hot on the Scottish thing. I was only half-listening to him as he gave me a few facts about James Hogg's life, punctuated by the odd (very odd) hammed-up line of poetry. We were heading north of Moffat on a road that was new to me. I'd never seen so many pheasants before, and Uncle Mark had to be unusually skilful with his sturdy chariot to avoid them. I was still counting the near-casualties as we approached St Mary's Loch. Oh, and we had to stop to let some sheep through, with their funny, black, womb-shaped faces and ginger bodies.

When we got out of the car, Uncle Mark was gesticulating wildly towards a monument – a statue of a man overlooking the loch. Total embarrassment! He moved towards it and began to recite the verses engraved around three of its sides:

> *'At evening fall, in lonesome dale*
> *He kept strange converse with the gale.*
> *Held worldly pomp in high derision*
> *And wandered in a world of vision.'*

I was only partly aware of this recitation. Uncle Mark could make the film script from *Trainspotting* sound like a funeral dirge. So I really wasn't at all prepared for how I would feel when I turned away from Uncle Mark, picking a russetty leaf from the ground as I did so, and saw the scene through the statue's eyes.

There's always a sort of sad magic in the air in Scotland at autumn and we weren't far from the winter equinox that week: the time when day and night even out and almost seem to blend into one – half-birth, half-death. I looked over towards the loch and saw two of everything – two lochs for a start, in a kind of figure of eight shape. The big loch was so still that the earthly world above its surface was perfectly mirrored beneath it. Of the two worlds – the one above the ground and the one below it – I really couldn't say which was more real. Parallel worlds do exist. The swans that Wordsworth had promised weren't there then, and if they had been, the effect would have been even weirder: Salvador Dali's *Swans, Reflecting Elephants* was already all around me as it was. The reflections were perfectly coloured too – yellows, browns, rusts and greens right through. Earthily unearthly. The dry leaf in my pocket crackled between my fingers. The sense of otherworldliness and magic was overwhelming but I didn't want to shake it off.

Uncle Mark's poetry reading faltered to its finish. He seemed to sense my feelings, to a degree, and he touched my hand. 'Are you cold? Why don't we go down to Tibbie Shiel's for a coffee? Get your walking feet on!'

I followed the movement of his head to the centre of the figure of eight and saw for the first time the welcoming body of the black and white building gazing over the loch (just as I had been a second before). It was a pub.

It would have been so difficult to explain to Uncle Mark how I'd been feeling, even if I'd wanted to. It was a bit like when I read my father's letter – I felt touched by life, and by a sort of beauty, and by something more than myself. I also felt the strange breath of adulthood on my cheek.

Uncle Mark took me by the arm as we entered the warm pub, and when I looked around I saw that we were surrounded by couples of all ages – lots of figures of eight in slightly different shapes, joined at the centres by their hands. Some of them looked like walkers or climbers; two people swapped the steamy glances of an illicit affair and one couple didn't look much older than I did. For one second, I caught a look on Uncle Mark's face that I had never seen before: he was staring at one of the sicklier-looking couples with regret and longing written all over him. I realised all at once that Uncle Mark's single state could be connected to his role as my guardian rather than his own wishes (or his feeble pulling power). I also realised for the first time how lonely I would be if he were to remarry. The cuckoo out of the nest. My 'bachelor gay' jokette suddenly made me blush.

Not for long. As he ordered two coffees, he mispronounced 'cappuccino' hideously: 'Two capochinas over here, please!' Shame! In his rush to cheer me up, as he no doubt thought of it, he'd overlooked the fact that a Scottish country pub miles from anywhere would be unlikely to specialise in Italian coffee (that's if they were able, by some miracle, to understand what he was asking for).

Magic, mystery and loneliness: those were the three feelings St Mary's Loch stamped on to my heart that day. Spirit. And I thought one thing as we waited for our coffees to arrive: When I get my £300,000, I'm coming back here.

It was six months before I saw that car again. Six months of looking for it – every day. I never give in, not over something like that. Someone like that. And when I looked out of the window and finally saw it, my heart thumped to tell me it was true – it was the car she had sat in.

My bedroom window had a spectacular view of the back of Sainsbury's. I lived in a big town in the Borders and there weren't many big towns around there, big towns with supermarkets. (I'd guessed from the car that they were more of your Sainsbury's type than Kwik-Save, which was where my own cow disease of a mother shopped.)

There have been two false starts with other Vauxhalls before but when I see her dad's again, there's no mistaking it. He's getting out of it, for one thing, and it's a top of the range job for another. He looks even more of a twat than before – middle-class wanker with a bright tartan tie on and a suit.

I watch him go into the supermarket and I get his registration number straightaway. Then I run downstairs and get my dad's old video camera that he nicked from work (before he nicked off himself) out of the cupboard. When daddy, at long last, comes back out, hauling his bags, I zoom in on him from my bedroom window. Some of his stuff is sprouting out of the top of the carriers. It's dead easy to see what he's bought for himself and what he's bought for her, like. So she likes sweet things and candles. My love. I make a note of that in my file, the file I've set up especially for her (kept carefully beside the ones with my men in them – the Mr Muscles, I call them). I know that'll be useful later. It feels almost like serving her, filing away those details for her.

When he's gone, I tap his registration number into my computer and then e-mail my mate who's in the Force. He owes me one. I've soon got the address. Parking fine, the loser. Bob's your uncle, or rather Mark's your dad.

Beech Trees. Sounds nice. I'm almost ready for her.

There was a period of nine months or so, after I discovered my spiritual home, when I felt that I was waiting for something. But waiting for what? For whom? I wasn't sure, but I sensed it strongly enough. Basically, I felt I was preparing for the larger world, the brighter, darker, altogether stranger world that lay beyond the smoothly plastered walls of Leeched Dry. Yet Uncle Mark would still lock me in every time he left the house, as if I were a purse in a safe, while I felt that the precious things were all out there, waiting for me to press them to my budding breasts. Nothing interesting ever happened at school – apart from a couple of crushes too predictable to bore you with – and Leeched Dry was worse.

I was waiting really, waiting for my home on St Mary's Loch; waiting for The One – the holder of the keys. Waiting for my father's next instructions. Waiting for the bonfire of my life to begin.

And the world was waiting for me. With a lit match in its hand.

Now that I've found her, I've got to prepare. Prepare to court her. I'm not stupid, like. I know a girl like that wouldn't look twice at a boy like me. Not normally. A Kwik-Save boy and a Sainsbury's girl. So I know I've got my work cut out: hair, skin and body – they all need attention. Even my name's wrong. Now that I've got her address I can make a start. I've got the discipline. And I know she'll be waiting for me.

The first thing to go is the hair. From most people I demand some kind of reaction, any kind, although I prefer a strong reaction. From her I want a different kind of reaction. Strong, yes, but warmer. She saw right inside me that day. I want to make the outside look right before she sees me again. So I find a good hairdresser and a good chemist and that's the hair sorted out (and the skin on its way). And I step up my usual Canadian Air Force exercises, to lift my body above its normal standard of army hardness.

My sister helps a bit with the clothes. She's already helped in plenty of other ways (not that she always knew, like). I found out a lot about girls' skins, girls' bodies and girls' feelings from her. So that leaves just the inside to go.

For that of course I turn straight to one of my heroes. I know that one of them will have the depth of feeling to express what I feel for my girl with the autumn hair. I find it straightaway. The words are very powerful. See for yourself.

> 'I sat on the edge of the bed and looked at Stephen. I thought to myself, "All that potential, all that beauty and all that pain that is his life." . . . I sat him on the blue and white dining chair. I sat down, took a cigarette and a drink and looked at him . . . "Stephen," I thought, "you're another problem for me. What am I going to do with you?" . . . I lay beside him and placed the large mirror at the end of the bed. I stripped my own tie, shirt and grey cords off and lay there staring at both our naked bodies in the mirror. He looked paler than I did . . . I put talcum powder on myself and lay down again. We looked similar now. I spoke to him . . . I was telling him how lucky he was . . . I thought how beautiful he looked now and how beautiful I looked. He looked sexy but I had no erection. He just looked fabulous,' – Brian Masters, Killing for Company.

Sorry about the length of the quote, like, but it's such a moving passage. Beautiful. Really beautiful. The Lover, I call him. But he calls himself The Monochrome Man.

The other lads at school would have been disgusted at that

quote. Queer, that's what they'd call him – narrow-minded gets. Pure I'd call that love. Did you see that bit about no erection? She'd love that. I know she's a virgin.

Not so sure about the talcum powder but I'm sure a bit of make-up would do the trick. I've seen my sister at work and her skin is very white. Usually. In most places. Or bandages. I've always found bandages most erotic – white, tight bandages and slings.

Within nine months of seeing the car I'm prepared. I've got my first plan down in writing, my plan to get her. And my smile – my open smile – in place. I'm nearly ready for her.

A normal red-blooded male coming to claim his autumn girl.

Well, when my gestation, lady-in-waiting period finally ended, it ended with a bang. Sweet sixteen and never been kissed. That was way behind me. (All of those experiences with slobbering, damp schoolboys, quarters of oranges and even Diana – strictly for research purposes – could hardly be counted, could they?) And finally, with my standards behind me and my highers half-way through, I was ready for the world at large. Very large.

It gave me Dominic. My man. Dominic, Dominic, Dominic Oliver.

He'd been there all the time – looking for me, preparing for me, waiting for me in the wings. Waiting for Uncle Mark to open the curtains and reveal the lovely me as all of Shakespeare's hero/ines at once. Waiting.

As soon as I saw him, I knew who he was. He was laughing with his head thrown back, a distinctive, roaring laugh: his teeth were small and sharp, his hair was fair and his laughter was electric. He had a look of the devil and a god at the same time. Yes!

I was at a party with Diana, a friend's eighteenth, and I wasn't the only girl to turn her head. He was a bit older than my friend Louise whose party it was. In his twenties, I guessed. He was with a group of friends he knew from school. You could tell he'd known them forever – they practically had their own language. Certainly their own humour. I noticed him immediately but there was no way I could have joined them. So I stood where he would notice me for a short while.

And then I moved.

It was twenty minutes before he came closer to where I was standing. He began to chat to Louise, handing her a glass, leaning his head towards her and smiling as he listened to her. Gorgeous! Louise was smiling back at him, nodding a lot, which was alarming. They were surrounded by Louise's birthday flowers, like a bride and groom. Now that I could see him close up, I could see that his skin was marked with tiny scars and open pores. He must have suffered from bad skin when he was younger; there were one or two angry bumps still. Somehow the tiny marks gave him a vulnerability – made me feel protective towards him. Washed me with the feeling. But he was so alive – he was laughing again now, his eyes smiling, and I could feel his energy near me. I could almost hear a tiny buzz. I was *desperately* jealous of Louise. And I knew I could really touch him. Inside.

As he spoke to Louise, his eyes caught mine. Twice. The second time I held his gaze until he looked away. (All of Uncle Mark's deadly cheese and wine parties at Leeched Dry had obviously paid off on the social poise front, if not in entertainment value.) I thought he was going to come over but he moved away after a quick, but worrying, 'See you later!' to Louise. My breath caught in my throat when he turned his back on me.

Ten minutes later I was walking towards the bar and he was there beside me. Looking at me. Looking into me. What would he say?

'You were certainly interested in those flowers.' He glanced at the flowers he had been standing next to. His lips curved; my face burned.

'They're the only things with any delicacy I can see around here!'

His smile wavered only slightly. 'You looked a bit lost. I just thought I'd come and have a word with you.'

Lost? Not the image I'd been after at all! 'Well you can just think of someone else to have a word with.' Arrogant pig! I strode over to where Diana was standing, all legs, feeling Amazonian. I didn't deign to look back at him but joined in the conversation there with as much wit and life as I could manufacture from the air at that second.

It was much later in the night before I saw him again; I'd almost given up on him and I wasn't going to speak first, obviously. I was making my way over to the loo when somebody grabbed my arm and held on. I looked up and it was him. 'I'm sorry,' he said. 'Let me try again.' His eyes creased in the corners when he smiled – he already had some thin wrinkles there – although his jaw was still sticking out like a fighter's and a tiny flicker of doubt crossed his face. Softer now. Much more attractive. His skin was slightly shiny and I mellowed enough to stay where I was. 'I'm Dominic. Dominic Oliver. Louise is a friend of my sister's.' He shook my hand, mock-formally, and then held on to it. Held on to it wonderfully.

'Helena.' I risked the smallest smile.

'I thought there was something Trojan and well-bred about you when you marched away like that.'

I laughed (although I wasn't sure that Trojan was a compliment, particularly) and got my hand back. Then he *really* looked at me. Everything shone – especially his eyes. He focussed on me completely and I knew I was through to the inside now.

We talked for a couple of hours. The party was in Louise's parents' house and he found a little settee in the corner to sit on, just the two of us. We kept to our separate sides, and he didn't make a move, so I was never quite certain of him. But his hand brushed against me a couple of times, accidentally, and I was certain enough about the feelings that caused! Even bringing me a drink was steeped in meaning, in feeling: he looked at me so seriously as he asked me what I wanted. And then the handing over of the wine – like blood in a glass, sanctified blood – feeding me. He made me realise exactly how thirsty I'd been, and for how long.

He was studying law at Edinburgh University, in his final year. His father was in the legal profession too. His parents knew Uncle Mark – I'd probably met them at one of Uncle Mark's deadly Leeched Dry dos. He had a sister two years younger than himself and his parents were apart. Law bored him and he liked to attend lots of different lectures at University, especially medical ones (bizarre), and some arty ones as well (more interesting). He hated lots of things that he seemed to be – the middle classes, students, that sort of thing.

Nothing about him bored me. Dominic. My shining man. I could make him new, make him complete. Especially his scars.

We both drank quite a lot, and we talked more as the alcohol level rose and we became more animated. I was three and a half years younger than him and the fact that I was still at school was apparently an acute embarrassment to him – several of his comments made that quite clear. Such as when, near the end of the night, he brought me a flower, lifted from poor Louise's bouquet. 'A bud for a bud,' he said, in a voice piled high with sarcasm. It was a pink rosebud. Was my virginity that obvious? Probably.

As the party drew to an end, I waited for him to make a date. My handbag nestled snugly beside his wallet on the table; my hands were near to his as we talked – near enough for him to grab hold of, if he wanted to. He wasn't shy, I knew that. And I made sure that he knew I was leaving with Diana, as arranged. But at one o'clock, he picked up his jacket without a word about meeting again. 'I must go, Helena,' he said, and brought his hand up to touch my hair. He looked almost dazzled, but said nothing. He kissed my cheek slowly, once, and looked at me almost regretfully, his hand still touching my hair. Over before I knew it.

And then he left.

3

'The Emerald

'The "Unconditional Love" stone is a deep beryl stone of great power ... This friend to the seeker assists in deeper spiritual insight, introduces the higher self to the divinity within, inspiring love, prosperity, kindness, tranquillity, balance, patience and the power to heal'

– Crystal Health and Wealth:
The Efficacious Use of Gems and Minerals

Dominic Oliver – he left without a glass trainer in sight. It was really hard not to run after him, but I didn't of course, a well-brought up girl like myself. I thought about him all that night, with Uncle Mark snoring his head off through the wall next door. Partly, I wanted to go over everything he'd said – to experience it all again – and partly I wanted to try to work out why he hadn't arranged to see me again. I yearned for him – me, Helena, the golden girl. And I'd always thought that *Measure for Measure's* Mariana in the moated grange was such a drip!

For two days I waited for him, in agony. I wanted him. I really wanted him. But he couldn't want me. Which bit of me did he hate, then? Or bits? What a list that was!

HIDEOUS THINGS ABOUT HELENA

Hair – *old-fashioned? Too long? Too thick?*

Class – *boring middle-class*

Voice – *too confident? Not confident enough?*

Age – *or lack of it?*

Status – *schoolgirl, for God's sake*

Virginity – *definitely a problem*

Height – *too tall*

Boobs – *too small*

Bum – *too big*

Weight – *too much? Too little? (Depending on where you were looking, exactly.)*

Meanwhile, I was constructing a Dominic Diary.

I cross-questioned Uncle Mark at every opportunity about Dominic's parents. When had they split up? How had Dominic been affected? (I even loved saying his name. Dominic. Desperate!) What were they like?

Uncle Mark, with his usual perceptive nature, had very few answers. Dominic's mother was English, 'a bit of a bore', and now lived in the Midlands (where Dominic had grown up). She'd split up from his father 'a few years ago', and the father was 'a bit of an egotist' and 'a smooth operator'. Dominic was 'bright'. Uncle Mark remembered one or two minor problems – 'the usual boyish stuff' as he put it – of Dominic bullying his sister a bit, and staying in his room all of the time playing on his computer, etcetera, etcetera. And that was it.

I put these few, pathetic facts down in my Dominic Diary, and I waited for him. I didn't eat; I didn't sleep; I couldn't concentrate on anything else. I waited. Obsession. I even envied his sister. I dragged Diana to our crystal shop in Edinburgh, regaling her with

Dominic Details for a long, long afternoon. I selected a crystal for him – an emerald, the *'unconditional love stone'*, which would *'inspire love, prosperity, kindness, tranquillity, balance, patience and the power to heal'*. I wanted him. Diana was bored stiff.

It's always a matter of finding a key when you need a little magic, glass trainer or not. *Never* give up. This time, my fingers on the phone unlocked the door. I rang Louise and told her . . . not about the yearning obviously, I had some pride left. But I did tell her (in cool and coded terms) that my blood was a bit warmer than usual. And did he have a girlfriend? Louise thought not.

Why hadn't he found me?

At last I'm ready to find her. Perfect. The Canadian Air Force exercises have done their business on my body; I've stepped up from two sessions a day to four. I passed my driving test – first time – and even managed to con an old Bundy Beetle out of my mother. (It's ancient, but it still goes, a bit like my mother herself, as I said when she finally gave it to me.) Can't have a knight in shining armour on a mountain bike, can you, really? And I've polished it to perfection – the Legal Eagle would have been proud of me.

Is she ready for me, my autumn girl? She's pretty young. But that's partly why I fancy her. Love her.

Time to find out.

My hair is right, my skin is right, and my smile is exactly right. I've rehearsed it often enough, like (alongside various other techniques). And I've rehearsed my route.

I'm finally ready to get into my Beetle and head towards Beech Trees.

At last he appeared. My shining man. The shock was, he was waiting outside Leeched Dry as I came home from school, the day after I'd talked to Louise. (Thank God for Louise.) He was looking to the right of me, so he didn't see me at first. Great – gave me time to arrange the appropriately cool expression – but I could see the discomfiture on his face, a slight shyness, almost: a completely different face from the one he had shown at the party. And another tiny thing. As he waited, I saw him tug at just one knee of his jeans, tug it into place. The jeans looked seven-hundred years old at least, and I don't know if they'd seen an ironing board in the whole of that time, but there was something about that little tug that made my stomach go all warm.

Briefly. He saw me almost straightaway and his front changed altogether. He tilted his head back, full of himself, and kind of swaggered, even though he hardly moved. My soft-scarred angel. Even his fair hair gleamed. He smiled sort of firmly at me. I thought how upset (absolutely secretly) he must have been in his early teens when the first ugly, red bumps appeared; how relieved he must have been when they (almost) disappeared. I smiled back.

My next reaction was acute embarrassment. None of my fantasies about him had included Leeched Dry. He was already grinning unpleasantly enough at my hideous school dress. Actually, he didn't look towards the house at all. 'You're in Edinburgh,' I said. Not one of my wittier openings.

'God, look at that school uniform!' His eyes glittered a bit, and then he looked at my face and blinked something from his expression before carrying on. 'No. I'm at Beech Trees, waiting for you.' Sarcastic roll of the eyes.

'Leeched Dry,' I replied, automatically, then giggled – oh, no, a schoolgirl giggle! – 'the house, I mean, not me.'

'Well, I'm relieved about that.'

Silence held for a few seconds. I touched the pocketed emerald I'd bought for him, and waited, forcing him to carry this forward.

His words punished me for my silence. 'I was chatting to Louise,' he said, 'catching up on the party gossip, you know – who met who, who puked where, who cleaned it up, that sort of thing.' I blushed. Damn blushing. And damn Louise – I had hoped for a *little* more subtlety. 'Look, I've not got much time to chat. I've got something on tonight and I've still got work to do. How do you fancy a night on the town?'

'In Edinburgh?' God, I was being such a child.

'Yes, Edinburgh.'

'But it's miles away.'

'I'll come for you, Friday night.' He gestured towards an ancient Austin Allegro, mustard-coloured, that I hadn't noticed before. 'But I don't fancy the glass slipper routine. See if your uncle will let you stay the night.'

Anxiety, excitement and defiance must have been displayed across my face like a pocket full of photographs, and he laughed then. 'There's a spare room – Sam's away for the weekend.' Sam was a housemate he'd mentioned at Louise's. 'Tell him I'll protect your schoolgirl honour.'

Perhaps he saw the 'Does he fancy me?' fear stamped on my face, I don't know, but he did claim me then. He moved forward slowly, placed the fingers of one hand on my temple, just touching my hair, and looked at me closely. In the daylight, his eyes were even brighter – was I supposed to shut mine? His knuckles brushed my chin and then he moved my face towards his lips with both of his hands. His lips were crisp, defined, but a bit soft as well. Thank God I'd applied some lip-softener fairly recently. As he shut his eyes, I noticed the tiny pink and blue veins on his eyelids before I shut mine, and felt his lips part my lips. Yes. I tasted and felt the skin of his lips and sensed some of the life and energy of him. My body touched his body and I pressed against him. He put one hand on my back and held me tight to his chest, stroking my hair, just once. Then he let me go all of a sudden and smiled. 'Seven o'clock, then.'

He jumped into his creaky old car and was gone in seconds.

It wasn't until I put my key into the lock at Leeched Dry that I thought about Uncle Mark. And staying the night. Glass shoes. What if he wouldn't let me go?

4 ∫

> *'I met a lady in the meads*
> *Full beautiful, a faery's child;*
> *Her hair was long, her foot was light*
> *and her eyes were wild,'*
> —Keats, *'La Belle Dame Sans Merci.'*

That Friday night seemed to run away from me forever. Three days to fill, and nothing to think about but Dominic. Dominic, Dominic, Dominic Oliver.

Oh, and Uncle Mark. I had to plan that one like *The Great Escape* – escape from emptiness. I nearly didn't get away with it. I picked a time when he was in a hurry – getting ready for work – and moved in for the kill. 'Got anything special planned for Friday night then, Uncle Mark?' Dead casual.

'Not really. I thought I'd do one of my world-famous chillis and get a good video in, etcetera. What do you think?'

Quite who would celebrate one of Uncle Mark's mild mince and onion cowpats I couldn't imagine. Certainly not me: I'd had them before. That strengthened my resolve. 'There's an open day at Edinburgh University on Saturday. Dominic Oliver's offered to take me to it.' (Lying never worried me when it was for a good cause. Plus Uncle Mark had locked me in, against my will, for most of my boring life.) 'He's calling for me on Friday night; he's got a spare room in his flat.'

Even Uncle Mark was too sharp for this one: I'd obviously been less than subtle in my search for information about Dominic's family. 'Dominic Oliver? Unusual – an open day on a weekend. Bit late for an open day now anyway, isn't it?'

'Oh, it's an informal thing. You know I've applied to Edinburgh already. You don't want me to stay at Beech Trees forever, do you?'

Uncle Mark had stopped searching for his boxer shorts (his solicitor's jokette) and was sitting down now. He looked so sad and knowing that I was quite taken aback for a second – and I thought he was going to say no. My sympathy was very short-lived. 'Helena,' he started, 'I know that I can never replace your father . . .' I sighed. This was a familiar speech. I saw Uncle Mark hover, searching for the most appropriate cliché. I wasn't going to help him out. 'Don't go losing your heart, or anything else, too soon.' I sucked in my breath, rolled my eyes and tapped my foot, hard. 'Looks like you've already made up your mind.' He put on his jokiest voice. 'Anyway, if you can't be good, be careful.'

Desperate! Contraceptive advice from Uncle Mark. He was thinking about me in bed with Dominic! That was almost as bad as *me* imagining *him* in bed with someone. Almost.

But he'd conceded defeat, resigned himself to double cowpat and an old Arnold Schwarzenegger film, and he let me go (once he'd checked transport facts, times and addresses, of course).

I was on my way.

Seven to seven, Friday night, and I was ready: sexy, but not tarty; slightly studenty, but not bohemian; fragrant, but not overpowering. And definitely not schoolgirl. Just how Dominic would like me, I hoped – two and a half hours of preparation beneath my new and favourite broad black belt of a skirt.

I was upstairs, reading my Dominic Diary (pathetic, I know), when he arrived. Thinking about Dominic's laughter, his teeth, his eyes, his skin, his sharpness, the tilt of his head on his neck. Remembering the feel of his chest, of his arms. The sound of the doorbell gave me a real jolt. Dominic was early. The thought of Uncle Mark opening the door – wooden spoon in his hand, wooden greeting on his lips – was too hideous to contemplate. I ran towards the stairs, grabbing my overnight bag from beside my bedroom door as I went, and was outside, shouting a quick ''Bye!' over my shoulder, before Uncle Mark could put down his pan.

Dominic looked relieved to see me: he obviously didn't fancy facing polite questions about his parents and prospects from my uncle either. I noticed straightaway that he'd used aftershave, or a different shampoo or something (a sharp, lemony smell hung in the air of the Allegro's luxurious interior), and I was really glad that he'd wanted to make an effort for me. But the conversation during the hour of our journey to Edinburgh was a bit strained and I started to worry. Like I said before, I knew he wasn't shy so how exactly was he feeling? *What* was he thinking? I kept holding my emerald – Dominic's emerald – like a talisman and wondering if I'd ever get the chance to give it to him.

He was talking about where we were going that night. The old car was rattling along as we went and it was hard to hear him sometimes. I gathered that we were meeting some people – some of his friends – at one of the pubs in the city centre. 'Then they're off to a night-club, but I haven't decided what we'll do. How does it sound so far?'

How did it sound? It sounded like I wouldn't get him on his own for hours, that was how it sounded. Was that what he wanted to avoid? I fingered the emerald again. 'Fine. Which night-club are they off to then?' Not that I cared a damn. I kept a little chill in my voice and looked away when he answered.

With a clunking clutch, we arrived at his house in a tatty suburb of west Edinburgh and he showed me up to Sam's room, which smelled of Sam (cheap, musky perfume and hair mousse). A girl! The thought of a girl living with Dominic – even if, I prayed, platonically – gave me just the same stab of jealousy I'd had when he'd laughed with Louise. I wasn't used to this. I dropped my bag off, took an irresistible and informative glance at Sam's clothes, family snaps and underwear drawer, and then ran downstairs to meet Dominic. This wasn't turning out as I'd hoped at all, and I left the emerald upstairs with my other things, locked safely in its part of my *WJ*-marked casket, alongside three secretly purchased condoms and the leaf from St Mary's Loch.

The house was quite a shock after Uncle Mark's extreme, air-freshened tidiness: books, magazines and half-clean, drying clothes were thrown all over in the living room. Plus a quick visit to the loo showed that they were obviously strangers to the toilet duck, as Uncle Mark would have put it. The door to Dominic's room was very definitely closed. I knew that four of them shared the house, but I didn't see or hear any of the others.

All in all I was glad to get out of there and breathed more deeply once we'd made our escape, slamming the brown door behind us as we tipped out into the street to walk to the pub.

I felt pretty deflated as we scuttled along the pavement. Even boring Uncle Mark was always mine and mine alone, and here I was, with the man of my dreams, about to share him with God knows how many people. Memories of seeing Dominic, from the outside, with his friends at Louise's party, were surgically, photographically clear. Would I be able to keep up with his friends, intellectually, I mean? Ridiculous! I'd met plenty of undergraduates who were completely brain dead. Still, I was feeling nervous. My mind kept visiting the little *WJ* box, and what was inside it, locked away in Sam's room: the emerald – my talisman – and, more terrifyingly, the condoms. Did I really want them to be used? The tiny secret box, with its puzzling initials; the known and unknown parts of myself that I had half intended to share with Dominic that night – it was all as difficult and intriguing to me then as my father's letters were.

I suddenly realised that it must have been at least two minutes since I'd lifted my eyes from the paving blocks – or since we'd spoken. I turned to Dominic. 'Just how many of your friends do I have the honour of meeting tonight, then?' It was invigorating to hear that gritty sharpness back in my voice, and he looked taken aback and relieved all at once.

'Four. About.' After a pause he spoke again. 'Helena, did you actually want to come out with me tonight?' His head was higher now and he was looking at me questioningly. It was such a triumph that he had no idea how excited I felt just to hear his voice, to hear him say my name. 'Didn't you want to come out for a drink? Or is it the house? I mean, I know it's a bit of a Fred West experience.'

I laughed. 'Well, it is a bit of a dump. More *The Young Ones* than the doomed ones, though.' Didn't he realise, I'd have sat in a public urinal with him for the night, if it was the only way of being with him? (Actually, public urinals would probably have been cleaner than the toilet at his house, anyway.) 'Come on. We'd better get a move on.'

The pub was in a part of Edinburgh I'd never been to before – it was certainly in a separate compartment of the city's jewellery box from the dusty old shops I'd visited with Diana – Rose Street, right in the middle of things. The streets were really noisy and the pub was noisier still. And dark and smoky following on so suddenly from the bright, high sunshine outside.

As we blinked in the new atmosphere, trying hard to spot Dominic's friends (particularly difficult for me), we heard some shouts from across the bar. 'Dom! Dom! In the corner, over here.' The name was one surprise (he didn't look like a 'Dom' to me) and the size of the group was another: there were about eight of them there, as colourful and as different from each other in looks as the twenty pence mix-ups I'd pestered Uncle Mark to buy for me when I was little. I suddenly felt very young and very clean, with my short dark skirt and my long long hair. Did Dominic think that I was old-fashioned? I wished that I wasn't so tall. One of them was waving us over. He had grubby, sinister-looking dreadlocks and a very bright face. Beside him sat a Gothic type who made my private Lady Macbeth impersonations look pretty tame. Her image was from about the same era, actually, but she certainly seemed happy enough. Very happy.

My heart sank.

Dominic touched the small of my back secretly as we pushed through the crowds, but he dropped his arm pretty swiftly as we neared his friends. He found a small stool for me (I would have to watch what my thighs were doing all night) and introduced me to the crowd. I smiled vacantly as I tried to remember – John aka Dixie (the dreadlocked), Delilah, Rebecca, Tom and Sherry (the Goth) – plus a couple more. Then Dominic was gone, heading over to the bar to get us a drink and leaving me alone with them.

A green nose-stone glinted to my left as a lanky, black-haired boy bunny-hopped from his seat to the one beside me – the one that Dominic had put there for himself. Jeremy, I remembered. I wished Diana was there. He grinned at me horribly and I shut my eyes for one long blink. 'You've survived Cromwell Street, then?'

I laughed. 'I wasn't there for long – luckily.' So I wasn't the only one Dominic had shared that not-so-special joke with.

'Just keep clear of the bog. There're rats down there.'

'Don't worry, I noticed.'

The girl with the Gothic head leaned towards me and smiled. 'So which highers will you be sitting, then?'

Schoolgirl status. The politely interested expression on my face froze.

At that moment Dominic reappeared with our drinks, elbowing Jeremy out of the way, putting down a white wine for me and a beer for himself. I looked beside the Goth's hand. Of course – a pint of beer. She smiled wider. 'Actually, I'm right in the middle of deciding about university for next year. That or full-time work.'

I smiled sweetly, relaxed a bit, and turned my attention to Dominic, who looked quite amused. Jeremy made it immediately apparent that he was not so easily dethroned.

'So, Helena, will you be off clubbing with us later or is it to be a romantic night in with Dom here?'

'Shut up, Jem!' Dominic's tone was a surprise and I remembered the forcefulness of his elbow as he'd pushed Jeremy out of his seat earlier: I'd lost a good inch of wine. The frost melted after a few seconds. 'We've not decided yet – see how Helena manages with you animals over the next couple of hours.'

Actually, I was starting to enjoy myself. The sparring of their conversation was entertaining enough. In addition, the memory of the condoms, lurking in their *WJ* box, was starting to disturb me. What did you do with them, for one thing? How did you put them on? When did you put them on? Would I have to touch one? I remembered the trouble I'd had following that tampon diagram. And were male sexual bits as different from my – now well-thumbed and discarded – biology textbook as the female sort had been? Night-clubbing was rapidly starting to look attractive.

From time to time, their talk wandered off to university life. Dixie-the-Dreadlocked was doing the same course as Dominic, so there were references to criminal law, forthcoming exams, property law, lively or deadly lecturers, and so on. I drank more wine at these points and, once or twice, forgot what my legs were doing. My skirt was shorter than usual for me and, as I didn't have to worry about sneaking 'soberly' past Uncle Mark's bedroom door for once, my sips of wine were longer.

Jeremy-the-EverReady was extremely observant at these

points, referring to the 'legs that launched a thousand ships' more than once. This went down about as well with Dominic as Jem's earlier comments had done and he wasn't shy in letting Jeremy know. 'For fuck's sake, Jem, haven't you ever seen a woman's legs before? Go and salivate over somebody else. Please.'

Eleven o'clock approached and an ever-so-casual hand (guess whose?) on my knee made Dominic decide. 'Right – enjoy yourselves, then. We're off.' There were groans from the crowd – which was much larger and drunker now – amongst which I heard a quiet, 'Don't keep her up too late,' from Sour Sherry. Jem tried one last kiss on my cheek (probably more to wind Dominic up than anything else) and then I was off, hauled right out into the refrigerated air of the street outside.

'I'm sorry about Jem: he's a lecherous git. He can't seem to resist that sort of thing.'

'"That sort of thing"? Thanks a lot.'

'Oh, you know what I mean. Anyway, you seemed to be able to handle him well enough.' He shook my arm slightly. 'And Sherry, she's all right really.' A group of hooting girls, with paint on their faces and lethal-looking medical instruments in their hands, distracted us and briefly forced us off the pavement. 'You didn't want to go night-clubbing, did you?'

'I might have done,' I said, teasing him.

'Well, I can always walk you back there, if that's what you want?' Dominic stared ahead. Easily offended!

'Don't be stupid,' I said. 'I wanted to talk to you.'

He turned his head to me and looked into my face. 'I've been wanting to talk to you all night. Next time we go out – if we go out – we'll go somewhere different. I just wanted you to meet them, though.'

Dominic smiled at me so sweetly that I almost forgave him the 'if'. I also realised that he must be well over six feet tall to smile down at me like that. (I had clumpy rubber heels on.) 'Careful.' He put his arm around my shoulders as my ankles wobbled slightly. 'You're cold.' I hadn't thought about the nightly temperature drop when we'd left Cromwell Street and my top was quite thin. 'Here.' He took his jumper off. It had seen better days, but when he pulled it over my head it smelled vaguely of fresh washing powder and his skin. Fantastic. I breathed him in. Pulling my hair free of the soft neck of the sweater, he said, 'Your hair's so heavy . . . it's brilliant, Helena.' That was one worry crossed off my Hideous Helena list. He turned towards a shop window, still holding me, and kissed me. My hair was still in his hands. His big, bony nose rubbed against mine and he said, 'You smell great. Let's get away from this mess.' We walked on.

The brown door of Cromwell Street looked much more solid and reassuring than it had done a few hours earlier as Dominic nudged it open. The house was Georgian – must have been quite nice, once. I didn't even mind the peppery, dusty smell of socks and dogs that tickled up into my nose as we walked in. Someone was obviously in – doomed music thumped from up the stairs – and Dominic grunted something about Eric and his heavy metal habit as he ran to the toilet, leaving me to wander into the living room alone.

I curled up on the old Dralon-covered settee, chilled now that the wine was wearing off, and lifted my knees up to my chin. I could hear Dominic flushing the vermin away, then he bounded down the stairs and into the kitchen. Rather him than me. I was relieved to hear a kettle buzzing and the chink of spoons in cups. Boiling water gets rid of most germs, doesn't it? I laid my head against the nasty brown Dralon, and dreamed: emeralds, condoms, sex and tenderness. What did I want to happen next? The music from above thumped hypnotically as I repeated the options to myself. I didn't even realise that I'd closed my eyes. Five glasses of wine! Uncle Mark would have had the stomach pump out. Eric must have left the gas fire on before retiring to his room, and its buzz joined the buzz of the kettle and the strange music. Electricity.

Dominic was beside me all at once, with two mugs on a tray, and biscuits, milk and sugar as well. Setting the tray down on the floor, he climbed on to the settee alongside me with his back on the armrest. It was pretty cramped on there and the brown Dralon itched at my legs. His arm squeezed in around me. 'I forgot to think about where my legs were,' I said. I was very sleepy.

'They're gorgeous legs.' Dominic's hand was stroking them –

they were all crooked up – from the backs of my knees to the tops of my thighs. He stroked and stroked. 'Helena.' He said it very softly. Did he like saying my name too? He stroked some more. Then he moved one of his legs to the floor. 'Coffee. Do you want milk and sugar?' I remembered how carefully he had served me with the wine at Louise's and nodded. 'Baby,' he said, half-mocking me.

Dominic stirred it in, left his own mug on the floor and moved back on to the settee. Then he lifted the mug to my lips, his arm around me again, one hand holding all of my hair away from the liquid. I took the mug off him after a few sips. He touched the insides of my thighs lazily with his long, lovely fingers. This was too nice. I sat up, started to worry and shook off some of my sleepiness.

'Eric,' I said. Help, I meant.

Dominic looked at me, put my mug back on the floor and kissed my lips. His eyes were so unguarded and gentle. Then he looked up towards the ceiling, asking me: Upstairs? I hesitated, then nodded, but I'm sure that some of the fear was still showing on my face.

As I walked up the stairs behind him, I noticed how tired I was. I'd looked forward to seeing him so much that I must have used all of my energy up doing that. Plus it was late. When we got to his door, he whispered, 'Get your things,' and went in – leaving the door open for me.

I braved the toilet first and sat there thinking. What if he wanted full sex? What sort of sex would he want if he didn't want full sex? What did sperm taste like? What did willies feel like? What if I wanted full sex and then changed my mind? Would I sleep with him, after whatever sort of sex we'd had? Would an orgasm be different with him? Would I have an orgasm? (Men *always* have orgasms, sometimes without meaning to – even I knew that!) I was in there for a full five minutes, Eric's mood music thumping away at the door the whole time.

Time to go. I poured some shampoo and a few other female-looking chemicals down the loo in the futile hope of staving off disease, brushed my teeth (but left my make-up on), picked up my bag and things from Sam's room and pushed open the door to Dominic's.

A broad male back was turned towards me as I entered the room and his muscles were sort of set. Tense. As Dominic turned to meet me, he flicked his head back, caught my eye and then smiled. The room was lit by a lamp, but I could still see the faint marks on his skin. He looked young. I dropped my bag, remembering guiltily that Uncle Mark had bought it for me, and put my jewellery – including the secret condom carrier – on to his table, alongside his law notes and his computer. There was some skin cream there too, which was a surprise to me: I'd never connected men, and skin, and cosmetics before. Seeing me look at the white bottle, Dominic glanced away himself, quickly. His occasional shyness always surprised me. I thought of the emerald and dropped my head, tired.

Then he was beside me, lifting my head and kissing my lips, parting them, touching the inside of my mouth lightly with his tongue, and a slightly metallic tinge came through. Silver fillings? I touched back with my clean tongue: thank God I'd brushed my teeth. He held me very close to him – my best bra was pushing right into his chest as he put his arm around my shoulders and lifted me up from the knees with his other arm, carrying me easily towards the bed. Bliss. Once we were there he held me against his chest, cradled against him, nuzzling my hair and face with his cheek and lips. Don't you just love men's strength? I held him back, pressing my face close to his, wanting to join with him. Although I hardly knew him, I knew that I *could* join him; I knew that for certain. He laid me down on the bed then and took his shoes off, mine too – which was a relief – and stroked my toes, ankles and calves slowly. Then he fingered the thin skin of my thighs again, lightly touching them inside, at the top. Almost strumming, if that doesn't sound too gross – and it wasn't at all gross. It was innocent. Completely. And it made me jump. 'You're really sensitive there, aren't you?' he said, smiling a bit into my face. 'I knew you would be.'

I hadn't a clue which bits were the most sensitive – most of me felt pretty highly charged at that moment. Dominic lay beside me, moving his hand to my breasts, outside my T-shirt and his sweater. I stroked his chest then, as I'd pictured myself doing all night, enjoying the feel of the relaxed muscles there through his clothes. Yes. His head was close to mine on the pillow of his bed.

I felt the skin on his face, slightly oily and bumpy. His eyes shone and I touched his fairish lashes, his biggish, bony nose.

'Helena?' he said. I nodded. 'We don't have to do anything. You can stop any time you like. Any time.'

'I've brought some condoms.'

Dominic laughed, a surprised roar. 'Great. But we don't have to use them. Do you want to just sleep with me?'

Hoping my relief wasn't massively obvious, I nodded.

Dominic pulled my T-shirt and his jumper off and I wondered, as I unravelled my hair, if he meant what he'd just said. His fingers stroked my boobs through the silky material of my white bra and he made a noise in the back of his throat.

'They're too little?' I was worried.

'They're lovely, Helena. I love them.' His teeth glinted – they were so white – then his head went down to kiss my almost-cleavage while his hands stroked my nipples, really gently. He breathed against my skin, and I stroked his fine hair with its longish, silky fringe. I liked him playing with my breasts, and held his head there. How come he was so much better with my own body than I was myself? I'd lived inside it for eighteen years, unlike him.

After a few minutes, Dominic pulled his head up to face me again, kissing my face, smelling of my skin. I pulled his T-shirt off this time, and stroked his bare chest. I kissed one of his nipples shyly and stroked the tip with one finger. (Was that right?) He just smiled, slowly. My skirt only just covered my bum and I was on my side, facing him. I felt his hand between my closed legs and he rubbed there – the same way that I had rubbed in my room at home. 'Is that nice?'

Yes. 'Definitely.'

He laughed again, surprised but pleased, and felt me really carefully with his long fingers. I was wearing tights, which was desperately embarrassing and unglamorous, but he didn't seem to mind – he just rubbed and rubbed at the tight material, and a high sweetness built up between my legs. My bum and breasts were warm and tingling too. Were they supposed to swell? They felt as if they were. I was playing with his chest and touching his nipples occasionally, which were hard all at once. Should I do something with his willy now? I was more than a bit unsure.

Still looking at me, he pulled away slightly and took off his trousers and socks. He looked tall and strong and broad (steak-fed bones his flesh couldn't quite match) but a bit ungainly with nothing on but his brief, black underpants. He wasn't even vaguely shy now. Then he sat on the bed, and pulled my tights down and unbuttoned my skirt. I looked at him nervously, feeling very cold and bare and girly in my white bra and pants.

'Get into bed,' he said very quickly, and then he followed me in there himself.

The bed smelt of mice – the sheet was clean but the duvet cover wasn't. The sudden coldness calmed me down, but I nuzzled myself against him. I thought of the emerald, in its box, blessing us. I touched the front of his underpants, which were very clean and cotton. It felt bigger than I'd thought it would, which was a bit, more than a bit, alarming. Dominic sighed suddenly and said, 'Helena, what am I going to do with you?' and he pulled away from me slightly. He arranged my hair on the pillow, but I still wanted to touch him, and I turned to his lovely hardness with one hand while stroking his chest with the other. 'Wait.' He wrapped both of his arms around me. 'Feel.' And he laid his cheek on mine. One hand held my bottom close, very close, towards him, pushing the lips of my sex into his erection. Into him. The other hand cradled my back and stroked my hair.

'I've never done this. I'm not sure. Of anything now.' Why did I feel little, all of a sudden?

'I know, darling.'

The 'darling' was wonderful. I repeated it to myself, knew that I would write it in my Dominic Diary later.

Dominic rubbed and rubbed his big hardness against my new softness. My silky knickers began to feel damp and a definite heat built up between my legs. I made a funny noise. 'Shhh, I know. It's all right.' I wanted to rock. I started to rock, to move my hips. My bum wobbled hideously, but he seemed even to expect this and just held me tightly to him as I pushed my full-of-feeling breasts into his wide-boned chest. It was hard to breathe but I loved his closeness, and I wrapped my arms tightly around his neck so that he couldn't see my face. His breathing was getting faster and faster and I rocked harder. The bed creaked, but Eric's softly thumping music reassured me that he could – probably

– hear nothing. The heat and tension between my legs were building up unbearably and I didn't know quite what to expect. 'Dominic.'

When I said his name, he came with a cry, and so did I, shaking, with a high, sweet feeling and a loud sound from my throat I certainly hadn't planned on making. For seconds, this strong pulse beat and beat between my legs and a wetness at the front of Dominic's underpants showed me for sure that he'd come too. But his arms held me to him still. 'Lovely, lovely Helena. Sleep now.' He stroked my hair and my eyes, whispering to me for minutes until I finally did.

I woke twice in the night. The first time, Dominic was taking my bra off. Eric's music had finally stopped. I was very sleepy. He pulled my pants off, and some cold air came in beneath the musty quilt. He sort of arranged me – my legs, my arms, my hair – like a doll, then he moved my waist slightly until I was just right for him. It was a bit strange, so I kept my eyes shut. He stroked the little curves between my legs, just once, and kissed my brow. I opened my eyes then, for a second, and he was watching me. I smiled and slept again.

I dreamed of flying. I dreamed of St Mary's Loch. Of course, I dreamed of Dominic.

The second time I awoke, Dominic was asleep and I desperately wanted to give him the stone. The idea had woken me up. I got out of bed, silently, fetched it for him, and slipped it under his pillow, smiling at his closed eyes. He never moved. We both slept then.

I get to sleep, easily enough. I've been working the muscles in my chest, my arms, my legs, ready for her. But it's hard to stay asleep. I wake up thinking: My time is now, my time is now. I'm finally ready. Over and over again in the night, I wake up with a hard on I have to rub away. On my own. Thinking of her – her lips, her deer eyes, her hair.

The moment has come.

Morning was less magical. Thirst and the urge to use the loo came first, waking me. I forgot where I was, for a second, then I saw Dominic. Fantastic, was my first thought. How do I look?

my second. My face felt gritty with old make-up, my mouth was dry and ruggy, and my breath stale. Really attractive! Luckily for Dominic, he was still asleep.

I swung my legs over the side of the bed quietly. The baggy green curtains were closed and the room was gloomy, but I found my bag and dragged out my dressing gown and some cleanser.

There was no sign of Eric in the loo. (Had he heard the creaks last night?) So I could pee in peace. Then I took my make-up off and washed my face, and some other, lower, bits of my body. It was 10 o'clock. The toilet was evil – lime green and strange-smelling. I flushed it, and then remembered the shampoo, as it frothed hideously up the sides. Can you break toilets? It smelled like a cross between a public toilet and a chemist's counter. Disgusting. My toothbrush was still there from last night, so I used it, alongside a wooden hairbrush someone – one of the girls, probably – had left lying in front of the black-spotted mirror. Drinking water from the tap refreshed me, although I sprinkled some on to my hair accidentally. (No cup available, of course.) I looked semi-human now, but my eyes were still a bit puffy. I scuttled back to Dominic's room quickly, not wanting to meet Eric like this.

Dominic was awake now, lying on his back, watching me as I came into the room. I'd thought his eyes were blue before, but they weren't – they had lines of green in them, and at that moment looked worryingly thoughtful and preoccupied. Detached. I remembered the emerald underneath his head and smiled at him as I walked through the door. He smiled back, briefly, coolly really. Then turned away. Ow! My heart thumped inside my ribs. While he had his back to me, I went to get some clean knickers and pulled them on, then got back into bed beside him. I remembered how I used to crawl into Uncle Mark's bed when I was little, at Christmas, in the early hours of the morning, to unwrap my presents – how he'd always turn towards me. I almost wished he was there. Almost.

But it wasn't Christmas, Uncle Mark wasn't there and Dominic was talking. 'I must have a wash. Do you want a drink or anything?'

His voice was unnecessarily casual, I thought, then he was up, with his back to me, pulling his old T-shirt and some (thankfully) new underpants on. Didn't he want me, now that I'd slept with him? No, it couldn't be that – far too nineteenth-century. What would I do if he was bored with me all of a sudden? His footsteps were heavy as he walked down the stairs to brave the kitchen and I wondered: What is he feeling? What questions is he asking himself?

At last Dominic came back, with a mug full of water in his hand – the mug that I'd used just the night before. Pushing it into my hand without a word, he sat on the bed beside me, his face averted. 'Dominic?' It was so different from when I'd said his name last night, and I remembered how his body and his spirit had reacted then. He flinched now – jumped almost. At least he looked at me but his face was blank bar a slight but definite resentment. Definitely more than a mundane, bad morning mood. 'What do you want to do today?'

'I've got work to do. My exams are coming up.'

'Work? On a Saturday?'

'Well, in the afternoon at least.'

I was quiet for a minute, not knowing what to say. I pulled my dressing gown tightly around me. This was getting me nowhere. 'I'll get dressed, then.'

'Fine.'

I retired again to the bathroom with my things and dressed, thinking all of the time. It dawned on me suddenly that I still hadn't seen a man's willy (although feeling one had been quite good). Maybe I never would. Or maybe I'd never see Dominic's, at any rate.

My patience with Dominic was wearing thin now. I remembered how I'd felt, waiting for him to contact me before. The yearning. Why hadn't he made a date with me at the party? There was no way I was going to go through all of that again. He *must* like me – he couldn't have acted the way he'd done the night before unless he felt a lot for me: 'lovely' Helena, his 'darling'. Time to follow my intuition – believe in magic, make it happen. I put a bit of make-up on – 'war paint' was just the word – working out my strategy as I did so. A direct attack was deserved, I thought: I had nothing to lose but a bit of pride. And everything to gain.

The hard back faced me again when I stalked back into the

room. I moved around to his side of the bed so I could see his face. Why were his eyes so angry, so bitter? Narrowed. What had I done? But I wasn't in the mood for defensiveness. 'Dominic, why did you wait so long after Louise's party before contacting me?' My clean clothes and painted face had brought some vital confidence back to me. I was glad he was still lurking away in bed in his grubby T-shirt. Maybe *I* didn't want *him* anymore. My energy level rose, hearteningly.

'Men normally fall in love with you instantly, then, and collapse at your feet?'

I sighed and sat down on the side of the bed. 'I'm not talking about men in general – I'm talking about you, or trying to.'

He moved on to his back, turning his face away from me. 'Maybe I just wasn't as interested in you as the rest, then.'

The sharp heat of tears hit the back of my eyes – just what I didn't need. He looked up at me at exactly that second. 'Shit. I don't mean to be such a tacky bastard.' The bed creaked, and his arms were around me at once, warmly. 'Sorry, Helena.'

I refused to cry or wilt. This was a more infuriating puzzle than the Mark-made maze of my dreams. But I loved hearing him say my name and luxuriated in his wonderful embrace for a full minute. When I knew my eyes were back to normal, and my make-up was safe, I pulled away and faced him again. Round two.

'What then?'

'You were so lovely last night . . .'

'But?'

'But you're young. You're so young.' His arms came up sharply. 'You're younger than my sister, and she's *really* young. You've got school and exams to think about. Then you'll be off to university, shagging anything with a pulse for a few years, until you get that out of your system.

'And sex. What about sex? I can't have sex with an eighteen-year-old schoolgirl. It's ridiculous. You're not a real woman at all yet. I bet you've never even seen a completely naked man before, have you?'

'*You're* ridiculous. One minute I'm going to sleep with every student in the country, the next I'm the eternal virgin. Which is it to be, Dominic?'

'Neither. You're not ready for a relationship yet, end of story.'

I knew from the set of his face that I could lose him, right there.

'Maybe *you're* not ready to start a relationship,' I touched his lovely, stony, oily face, 'I already have.'

Everything depended on this. The horrible quarry of loneliness that I'd glimpsed at St Mary's Loch was in front of me again. I wanted Dominic more than any 'real' woman in her twenties ever could. I looked into his eyes, desperately trying to read them. I loved his eyes – the whites were very white, they shone. He shone.

'No, it's not that. It's just . . .' he waited '. . . it's just that last night, I realised exactly how ready I was. I was really narked with Jem, and he's a mate. Jealous – I've never been jealous like that before. And you. Even when you're asleep there's something magical about you.' He thought for a few moments. 'I couldn't pull away from you if I tried. That's what's wrong with me.'

He didn't touch me. His head was rigid on his neck. Desperate. My castle was crumbling into its moat. How was my red-blooded rescuer going to reach me now? Time for Rapunzel to install a lift. 'Get dressed.' I wanted him, and I had to show him that. While he found his various bits of clothing and put them on, I reached down below the pillow and pulled out the emerald.

Eventually we sat on the bed, facing each other, self-respect partially restored to both of us. The emerald was hidden in my tight, battle-balled fist.

'Dominic. Darling. I bought this for you.' He smiled properly at the 'darling', for the first time that day, and then looked down at my unfurling fingers. I kissed one eyebrow. 'It's an emerald. It's a symbol of patience, healing, kindness.' I wasn't ready to mention love, but I tried the word tentatively in my own mind. 'It's our talisman. We have to swear an oath to each other. Swear. Swear that we'll never hurt each other, that we'll look after each other, that we'll bring out the best in each other. We both have to write that down and keep it. And you keep the stone. Forever.'

So we swore, we wrote it down and he kept it – I don't know about the forever. Only the very young can make such promises. I never dreamed that I would betray his trust.

*   *   *

I got up after that sleepless night and I started to get ready: ready for putting the first part of my plan into action. Ready to meet her at last.

I switched off my computer and adjusted my pile of CD ROMs, then checked my books and my notes. The stories of my seven heroes are locked inside my head anyway, my other personal computer. I practised my open smile in the mirror, brushed my teeth and combed my hair. I locked my door, went downstairs and reminded my mother that she was not, under any circumstances, to enter my room. (My sister didn't need reminding, like – not after the last time, I thought.)

I checked the Bundy Beetle over for fingerprints. It was shipshape. I'd already checked my route, done a reconnaissance drive.

Within thirty minutes, I'm at Beech Trees. It's hot. I wait in my car. I wait behind a wall. I wait at the doorway of her house. I don't even get to see her father.

I feel hopeful at first, waiting, watching – an army exercise, looking for clues. I'm sure I can see her room on the right-hand side of the first floor. It's all greens and blues, like the sea or a bruise – whichever I prefer. I think about her lying in bed, on her own, for a while. And I wait, wait and wait.

At 2 o'clock the sun is high. Burning. I pick up a bright stone from her drive – my first treasure. I'm sweating. I know my face gets shiny, like. I'm not looking my best for her. I check that my new trousers aren't creased. I've just gone back into my car to wipe my face when another car pulls up.

She gets out. She's got loads of muck on her face, but she's still beautiful. Her hair is made up of all different colours – the sun brings them all out. My autumn girl with the sun in her hair now.

There are no Beech Trees. There is no autumn girl. Not today. Not for me.

How can I say this? Hard for me to face. She's with a bloke. With him. His car is tattier than mine and so is his face. I've got plenty of time to look at both of them – the knackered old car, the scabby old face. What is she doing with him? She kisses him; she waves goodbye to him. She never even sees me.

I drive home. A weaker man would have cried, but not army hard Adam – no way.

When I finally get home, I find that my instructions – my very clear instructions – have been disobeyed. My sister's been in my room, reading one of my books. She's moved it. She's dirtied it. I can't believe it. She's too fucking stupid even to understand my cataloguing system. I remember what my dad used to do if I touched any of his things. I reckon she gets off lightly.

I walk into *her* bedroom. Stupid boy bands all over the walls, as usual, nylon teddies on the bed. Feeble-minded, tinsel-toothed little bitch. She's sitting on the floor, reading a magazine. 'Adam.' She looks up, nervous, guilt in her eyes and a gormless expression on her face. I crunch one of her CDs deliberately as I walk across, so she knows what's coming, like.

'You don't touch my things. You never go in my room. You're not worth wanking on. Is that clear enough?' I mean, I'd never talk to my autumn girl like that, but you haven't seen my sister.

Her usual dead stare makes it worse and I can hear my mother running up the stairs. Slap in her stupid white face, a nice back-hander. Blood on her lip. I flash it through my mind first, then relish the enactment. Fresh red blood on her nose, instead of her lip – she can't even get that right. I like to redden her face, liven her up a bit. Then she's blubbing, as usual, and my mother is nagging – stereo fucking hysterics. Back to my room.

I calm down a bit, like, after that. I feel better. Time. I've still got time. Time to get her away from him and to practise for when I do.

And I've got his registration number.

5 ∫

'You're fairly safe in risking an unchaperoned trip to his rocky cave, because the typical lunar man is the soul of gallantry with women. He'll usually be a gentleman until you stop being a lady'
– Linda Goodman's Sun Signs

'Next time we go out – if we go out – we'll go somewhere different.'

This time, I had a definite date. Where would Dominic take me and what would we do?

I had to wait a whole week. There was no way I would tell him how much that hurt. (The next night would have suited me.) I'd already given quite a lot away that emerald Saturday, emotionally speaking, so I'd just smiled coolly when he'd suggested a date a week ahead, saying, 'Fine. I'm quite busy next week myself.' But by Friday night I was ready for him. Ravenous!

Uncle Mark was no longer a problem – well, not in the way that he always had been before. I could hardly invent another open day so I opted for my own version of the truth – Edinburgh being a long way away, Sam's room being empty again, Dominic avoiding the breathalyser. But he was a pushover. He barely even tried to make me feel guilty: there was a very short sermon, followed by, 'Just remember my earlier advice.' Who could forget? So I was free.

Seven o'clock and I was there, at the door, ready. I'd gone for tight and black – not quite up to the Sour Sherry standard, but close. If Dominic was worried about my age, I'd show him I was more wild than child. Wet Ophelia was sunk at last.

It was obvious Uncle Mark was raring for some scintillating conversation with Dominic and I couldn't stomach that. He hadn't even started on the chilli yet, he just sat in the living room, looking at his watch and twitching, like a nervous athlete on the blocks, cracking the odd jokette. I had to go and sit on the step, sure that he planned a sprint for the door as soon as Dominic arrived. Luckily it was a warm night and as soon as I heard the 'vroom' of the Allegro, I was off and out with a window-wave, before Uncle Mark could do a thing about it. When I looked back though, and I saw his face, looking at me beseechingly through the glass of Leech's double-glazing and the smeared window of the Allegro, I felt a real pang of guilt.

The old plastic car seat creaked when I settled in. 'Oops,' I said. 'Where are we off to, then?' It was actually quite hard to sit in those black trousers.

'Wait and see. It's a magical mystery tour – about the right era for this heap of shit.'

Certainly Dominic's Orient-not-so-Express looked desperately old and unhip, but there was nothing tired about a magical mystery tour! 'Just the two of us?'

'Just the two of us. Until we get back to the house. The girls are at home this weekend. And Eric. Not that any of us see much of him.'

'I noticed.'

Things were much easier in the car this time and we chatted – about my uncle, Dominic's sister, my Diana, Dominic's Dixie, plus plenty of other friends of his that I'd not heard of before. He touched my knee once, at some traffic lights, and smiled at me at the same time. Just the touch of his hand made me jump, and he really smiled then, with his eyes as well as his gorgeous lips.

After forty minutes or so, the road looked less familiar and I realised we weren't heading into Edinburgh. This worried me a bit. I hadn't known Dominic for long and the only address Uncle Mark had was for Cromwell Street. I looked at Dominic sideways, not wanting to voice my schoolgirl fears, and he laughed. 'I told you we would go somewhere really different. Wait and see.' I still wasn't sure quite how far I wanted to go, in all sorts of different ways, but I didn't have much choice just then, over the direction at least.

Hills and fields surrounded us, and the scenery was becoming more and more desolate and sparsely populated. This notched up the electricity between Dominic and myself even more as we drove through the quiet countryside – a potent mixture of wariness and lust, on my part at least. Eventually we came to a really steep hill and the Allegro chugged its way upward forever (I didn't know how much the poor thing had in its boot at that point) and then suddenly stopped, inexplicably. There was nothing at the top. Nothing but some ancient shrubbery and a few pieces of rubbish, all crowned by a teetering, tottering, derelict old tower-house.

'Dominic . . .'

'I know. You have to wait. Stay here – and don't look out.'

I waited a full ten minutes as he marched to and from the boot of his wounded car to the battered tower-house. I was starting to feel depressed and cold. The hot sun of daytime was changing into a much cooler mood, more suitable for the evening.

At last Dominic came round to my side of the car and opened it, viewing my dismal expression like a visitor in a zoo might view a caged animal. 'Come out. And don't look like that.' He took my hand and pulled me from the car. It was the first time he'd held my hand and it felt right, reassuring – and more.

We went downstairs first. Some old tramp or other had obviously been staying there at some point: there were ashes in the grate and cigarette cartons littering the fireplace. It was one huge room, with jagged stone walls – cracked and damaged in parts. 'We're upstairs.' Dominic pulled at my arm impatiently. I suppose my distaste was still showing. There was a tiny, cramped, winding staircase, with very steep, smooth steps. 'Careful,' he warned, unnecessarily, as he looked back at me. Soon he came to a doorway and I saw a flicker of light through the opening.

This room upstairs was big too, taking up almost the entire floor. Dominic had lit a fire; lots of twigs were crackling away happily in the old stone fireplace. There was a fair amount of smoke in the room too; there were probably some old birds' nests in the chimney. Great. I'd smell like an old Arbroath Smokey for hours – very seductive. He'd placed a huge candelabra, candles flickering away like mad, beside the fire, and saw me looking at it. 'Nicked it from my sister,' he grinned, quite pleased with himself.

On the floor, in front of the fireplace, was a big old rug. On that, he'd laid a real feast – dusty purple grapes, Brie, crusty bread, cherry tomatoes, olives, pears and little slivers of smoked salmon. Finger food of the very finest kind – a snackette with style. And it was brilliant to see a bottle of champagne and two glasses standing beside the food. I laughed out loud at it all. Ridiculous! Wonderful. 'Sit down,' he said.

There was a big cushion at the side of the rug, to the right of the fire, and I crouched down, glad to be near the noisy orange and yellow flames. Dominic sat beside me and put his arm around me, but as soon as his fingers touched me he jumped up again. 'Almost forgot.' There was a tartan blanket warming beside the fire. 'I knew you'd be cold. Get warm first, then I'll show you the best bit.'

He arranged the blanket around my shoulders and hugged me at the same time. I was torn between enjoying the attention and the warmth and security of the blanket, and the urge to display my new vamp image. Lady Macbeth never wore a blanket – in fact the only character I could remember who did was Poor Tom the Bedlam beggar, and that wasn't quite the effect I was after. Still, his arm was around me and I soon stopped thinking about Shakespeare. Dominic was talking. 'I don't even know what you like to eat. I had to guess.'

'It's perfect. Excellent.' In fact, I always did like lots of little things to eat.

'Are you warmer?'

'A bit.'

'Come and have a look, then.' He led me over to a glassless window and leaned out of it. 'Down there. See?'

I looked down towards the ground. There was an old shrubbery – gorse and dead rosebushes and so on. But past that, at the bottom of the hill, was a tiny loch. The sun was still fiercely pink in the sky and the tiny loch glittered in its light. My skin prickled. I thought straightaway of St Mary's Loch and its doubling magic. I shivered. 'What are you thinking?' he asked, and I turned my back on the window, facing the inside of the room instead. The orange light from the fireplace and the cracked old walls made it look like a cave – a cave softened and warmed by Dominic for me. Especially for me. I turned to him, let the blanket fall to the floor, and kissed him, in full Lady Macbeth mode, almost violently, pressing myself into him.

I felt his response instantly – it pressed back, pretty definitely – but he pulled away and stroked my hair. 'Steady.' I felt anything but steady, but I let him guide me back to the fire and we sat down again. He stroked a breast once and rubbed my ear with his nose. 'I want you to eat. I want to talk to you.' What excellent invitations!

I could be steady for a while.

The spirit of St Mary's Loch was singing in my ears as the branches sang in the flames. My future was beaming out from the fireplace.

Dominic asked me what I would like to eat, cutting cherry tomatoes in half so that I could avoid the little green, hairy navels that I'd told him I hated, tearing off pieces of bread and giving me sips of champagne from a cold, beaded glass. He didn't eat much himself, and I had the feeling that if he kept a diary about me, my nutritional needs and preferences would be noted down on the very first page.

While we ate, I told him of some of the magic of St Mary's Loch (though I carefully left out my dread of loneliness). He told me stories – of people that he knew and places that he'd been. Troubadour. My senses seemed to swim, to change. Then we were quiet and my limbs were so relaxed that they were liquid, joining him as only liquid can join itself. So it came as a shock when he finally circled my waist with his arm and spoke. 'Helena.'

'Dominic.' I smiled up at him.

His arm tightened. 'Tell me about yourself – all about you? Really tell, not just the chat, the outside. The inside. What about the inside?'

Big question. My smile started to slip. 'What do you mean?'

'Well, what do you hope for? What are your secrets? What do you dream of? Have you ever been in love?'

I was used to keeping my dreams to myself. My secrets? I hadn't told anyone about my biggest secret – my £300,000 –

under Uncle Mark's strictest ever instructions, not even Diana. I dreamed about Dominic, Dominic and St Mary's Loch, but that would sound stupid. So I settled for a truthful reply to the last question. 'I've never been in love. Not even close. Until I met you, I never even wanted anyone to kiss me, not really.'

He smiled with his eyes. 'And what about now?'

'Now it's different.'

I hoped that he would leave it at that. I'd lived alone, really, for so long; Uncle Mark had read my hopes and needs very studiously – still, my dreams were my very own, very private bedside book. But Dominic was continuing. 'And your parents. What about your parents? Why do you live with your uncle? Tell me why?'

I couldn't. It was too direct, too raw. Anything I said would sound superficial, would *be* superficial. The spirit of Cordelia Lear, another motherless sister, came down to join me. I shook my head.

'Nothing.'

'Nothing?'

This was getting ridiculous. I smiled automatically with my mouth, and then clamped my lips shut.

'I can't, Dominic. I just can't. Don't ask me.'

'You can't talk to me?' He tilted his head, with a half-smile.

'Not about that.'

'I talk to you. I can tell you about my parents, their divorce.' He had touched on these things. 'Why can't you talk to me?' The smile was gone.

Because it's painful. Because it's been too lonely and too hard for too long. Because I can't.

I looked down. The magic of the room was evaporating. Useless tears were threatening the remnants of my painstakingly applied Lady Macbeth make-up. 'I just can't. Don't.'

He'd turned away from me so he couldn't see my face. 'All right, then. Let's go.'

Go? I didn't want to go, but all of a sudden I knew I didn't want to stay. It was growing chilly, and Dominic was chillier still. He started to pack away the food and the plates. A stabbing glance was thrown my way over his shoulder as I walked behind him to the now black doorway that was our exit. His torch wasn't massively helpful and so it took us forever to pack up the boot of the Allegro fully, putting the candelabra and the remains of the champagne in last.

The car was freezing when we finally climbed into it. I deliberately didn't look out over the little loch again, knowing how close I was to crying anyway. It took three starts before the engine gulped into life again, and then we were off, down the dark and bumpy track.

'How long will it take us to get back to Edinburgh?' I asked, after a minute.

'Are you sure you want to go to Edinburgh? I can always take you home.' Thanks! Why did he always punish me, with his silences and then his words? I wasn't used to it: Uncle Mark's idea of punishment was a homily that took three and a half times longer than usual before it came to its meandering conclusion of 'Do unto others, etcetera, etcetera', to create a boredom-induced submission. I didn't know how to cope with Dominic at all, so I wrapped my arms around myself, hugging my silence in. He could decide where to take me; I wasn't going to say a word.

Sure enough, after about twenty long, long minutes we pulled up outside Cromwell Street's dismal door. I was feeling pretty brown myself as I followed Dominic into the familiar dingy living room. The dusty Dralon reminded me of our passion of the week before so I sat on the floor instead, leaning my arm on the unmatching chair as I did so. Dominic lit the lethal-looking gas fire, put a couple of lamps on, and then went into the kitchen, where I could hear him making coffee. He hadn't even asked me if I wanted anything. My bag was still on the back seat of his car and there weren't even any spare rooms available if things got worse. What should I do? I nipped the nasty armchair and then headed for the rats' nest to check my make-up. Actually, it felt good to spend two minutes in there free from Dominic's air of doom. A sudden clatter announced the arrival of his housemates below: Eric, Sam or Jen – which of them would it be? I took a deep breath (unwise), coughed, emerged and walked downstairs.

The room was fairly full when I got there and my seat beside the fire was taken. They were all talking away, so I smiled around and then sat down stiffly on the left-hand side of the settee –

right where, the week before, Dominic had stroked my thighs so tenderly and had fed me with coffee. Might as well have been last century! I wondered if he had even bothered to make a cup for me now.

'You must be Dominic's new friend?' A lively-looking girl with bright, plum-coloured hair and a vaguely Liverpudlian accent was speaking. Sam. I recognised her from the photos and immediately felt guilty about the underwear investigation.

'Yes. Helena.'

'This is Jen, Angus, Doug and Olivia. Oh, and I'm Sam.'

Still no Eric. At that point, Dominic walked through the door – at least there were two coffees in his hands. Not for long. 'Coffee, coffee! Dom, you're a hero. We just need five more cups.' And he was dismissed again into the kitchen, without having even looked at me once. Sam was now enthusiastically slurping away at my mug. 'Foul! Sugar. Never mind.' Suddenly, I was glad that they'd arrived and I brightened up. I wasn't looking forward to being alone with an angry Dominic later, but I'd face that one when it came.

'Where've you all been?'

'Oh, just to see a film. We asked Dom if you both wanted to come, but he was too busy setting up the Passion Castle for you.' My face turned pink but I was glad he'd talked to them about me. Sam laughed. 'Don't worry. We're used to Dom and his romantic enthusiasms.' She turned to Jen then and began to talk about the film again, not realising how her comment had sliced into me. Why hadn't I asked Dominic a few questions of my own while I'd had the chance?

Then he was back with a trayful of mugs. Eager hands reached out for them and he saved mine until last, saying abruptly as he handed it to me, 'I'll just unpack the car,' and then he left. I wondered if he would bring my bag in for me – a return to Leeched Dry wasn't an attractive proposition but I definitely wasn't going to ask Dominic about his plans. Meanwhile the discussion about the film continued, punctuated by the aggressive banging of the car boot and slamming footsteps on the stairs behind us. The general conclusion was that the film was 'a bag of shite' but some of the more pretentious comments hinted that a couple of them might be media or film students, or something –

phrases like '*film noir*' and '*mise-en-scène*' were 'casually' scattered occasionally. Not having seen the film, obviously I was excluded from the conversation. My back nestled into the Dralon, my legs curled underneath me (no need to worry about getting it dirty) and I drifted into my own thoughts.

Sam must have taken pity on me. 'Are you coming up for Dominic's twenty-second party later, Helena? It should be a really good night.'

This was the first I'd heard of his birthday. 'I'm not sure, Sam. I haven't thought about it.'

'It's not for ages. We're all getting different costumes for it. It'll be great. I'm going as the Queen of Hearts.'

'The tart with a heart, Sam,' interrupted Doug, 'the perfect part for ye.'

'Fuck off, Doug,' she retorted, totally without malice. 'What are you going as? A gas chamber?' They all laughed. 'Doug's got a bit of a wind problem,' Sam explained.

'Well, ye don't even need tae get dressed up – just come as ye are. Sam-bam-thank-you-mam – the purple-headed warrior.'

Sam was just summoning her breath and her wits for the next thrust at Doug when Dominic re-entered. 'Enjoying yourselves?' he asked, dryly.

'We were just asking Helena about your party, Dom, trying to decide on a costume for her. She could come as an ostrich with those legs – they're about twice as long as mine,' moaned Sam, wriggling her own – admittedly stumpy – legs. I watched Dominic's face carefully. He pointedly avoided my eyes, saying only, 'Your legs are fine, Sam,' which hurt me as much as the fact of his ignoring me did.

Then he sat down on the opposite side of the room from me. Did he think about last Friday night as well, every time he looked at that awful settee? Probably not. Jen suddenly remembered half a bottle of Southern Comfort left over from another night and they all cheered up when she went to get it from the 'food museum' (kitchen, I guessed). 'A night-cap, a night-cap.'

'Doug, you're not allowed any. There's already enough methane in that toilet to power a battleship. Someone actually tried to clean it last week. Was that you, Helena? Are you the domestic type?'

Dominic could see that I was stuck for words and he moved across the room to me. 'I don't think so, Sam. She didn't make a very good job of it.'

His back pressed against the front of my calves when he sat down. Whatever his mood was, he didn't seem to like anybody else teasing me and I was pleased he'd stuck up for me against Sam, even if it was over a very minor issue – cleaning toilets obviously wasn't a point in your favour in this house. An image of the pine-scented toilet duck hidden in my bag, which I'd secreted away from Leeched Dry that afternoon, jumped guiltily into my head.

Jen reappeared then, handing round variously sized and well-thumbed glasses of golden elixir. If I did a bit of forensic work on those glasses, I'd probably get fingerprints on Dominic's last ten women at least, I thought. I sniffed at my glass sceptically at first – it smelt of methane and cherries before you even drank it: I really hoped Doug would decline, especially if he was going to stay the night. He didn't, of course, just lifted his glass towards Sam with a jaunty salute and a 'Cheers!' before downing it in one. I put my nose into my glass again and took a tiny sip. Fire! How had Doug drunk his down like that? Dominic noticed my reaction somehow, turning around and saying very quietly to me, 'Leave it if you don't like it,' but I took a few sips more before placing it on the floor beside him.

Sam decided it was time for toast: 'Better get something dry into Doug, before there's a major explosion.' He illustrated her comment with a proud, blasting fart, amongst groans of 'Too late!' then he got up to follow Sam into the kitchen. Dominic made the most of the diversion by grabbing my hand and pulling me to my feet, and we headed for his bedroom as Doug and Sam headed towards the toaster.

Even the mouse droppings quilt looked comforting as we entered the room. I was relieved to see that my bag was there and went to get my cleanser and night-shirt out of it. The spotty dog on the front of it (a Christmas present from Uncle Mark) suddenly looked ridiculous and I stuffed it under a pillow quickly. Too late, though – Dominic had seen it and pulled it out again with his surprised laugh. 'What the fuck's this? 101 Dalmatians? I didn't know you were a Disney fan, Helena.' His mockery was softened by the fact that I could see the emerald sitting on the table beside his bed.

I went into the bathroom to cleanse my face and brush my teeth and re-entered Dominic's room looking at least four years younger and five shades paler. 'What are you doing?' I asked. He was looking through my bag, which I thought was a bit odd, yet he didn't appear in the least bit guilty. What was he hoping to find?

'Nothing,' he said, dropping the bag and moving towards me at once. I hoped he hadn't got as far as the toilet duck or last week's condoms.

We sat on the bed together and Dominic broached the subject of his mood. 'I'm sorry I was a bit heavy before there. Can we forget it?'

'Definitely. Is that normal for you?'

'Well, I just felt you were pushing me out.' He was still a bit huffy.

'What were you looking in my bag for?'

'I didn't think it was a big deal – just trying to get to know you, I suppose.' Dominic thought differently from me about so many things. Were all men like him? He spoke again. 'Sam was right about your legs – they're fantastic.' Not too tall, then. My legs were almost as long as his were, although he was a good four inches taller than me. Taking my arm, he began to caress an inch of wrist with great concentration, rubbing one circle of skin rhythmically, like a little dance. 'You look better without all that make-up. Do you want to talk to me now?'

'Not really.'

Not at all. I lay down full-length and pulled him towards me on the bed. I kissed him full on the lips and then kissed his temples, stroking his hair. He focussed still on my arm, and I'd never been so aware of all of the nerves in that one tiny area of my body before. Round and round his fingers went. 'You must be a Taurus, then?' I asked, meaning, 'Invite me to your party, now.' Also, it would explain the love of food.

'No, Cancer. My birthday's not for weeks.'

'The crab – that explains a lot.' (Actually, I didn't know much about Cancerians except that my mother had been one. My father was Aries: fire and water.)

Dominic laughed. 'Do you want to put your Dalmatian nightie on?'

'No, thanks.' I pulled away from him in a mock-sulk of my own.

'Well, I want to take these off; I've been wanting to all night. Lie still.'

Actually, he made no move to unbutton my trousers but knelt down beside me (I was lying on my back) and ran both hands slowly up the outside of my legs, feeling my shape, almost as if he was measuring my silhouette. Memorising it. The expression on his face was suddenly serious. When he reached my waist, his fingers squeezed in then he moved back down to my ankles. His fingers circled one and then he kissed the anklebone, holding my foot gently in both his hands. 'Your feet are so slim, considering you're so tall.'

'Too tall?'

'Never.' He smiled. 'Lie on your front. Let me massage you.'

'What if I fall asleep?'

'If you fall asleep, I'll put your Dalmatian nightie on you, tuck you in and fall asleep beside you. Don't worry.'

Reassured, I lay on my front and lifted my arms up on to the pillow, beside my head. 'Little girl,' Dominic smiled, with only a hint of mockery. He arranged my hair first, drawing it away from my face and laying most of it over one shoulder. My black silk top must have been hideously creased. Then he held his cheek against mine so that I could smell him – a funny mixture of Southern Comfort, lemony soap and coffee. His skin smelt a bit like that crackly smell there is in the air before it rains sometimes – a slight sharpness and freshness mixed. When he moved his head down and started at my ankles again, I knew that there was no chance whatsoever of falling asleep. His concentration seemed to bring all the nerves of my skin right to the surface. I felt his hands on the back of my calves, smoothing and soothing, until he came to the crooks of my knees. He touched me so gently there that it tickled and I wriggled. 'Sorry.' He kissed the back of my neck, resting his hands heavily on my thighs as he did so. Then he rubbed me from my knees to my thighs, over and over again, so rhythmically, so thoroughly, that a sigh came out.

For a few seconds then Dominic stopped and I could feel him

looking at my legs as clearly as I had felt his touch before. I hoped my bum wasn't looking its most colossal. Nothing happened for a minute and then he touched between my legs, right where my trousers had been rubbing at me, teasing me, all night. His fingers were electric. If he wanted to have full sex with me that night, I knew I wouldn't be able to say no, but I opened my eyes and frowned a bit, thinking about it. He noticed at once and lay down beside me. A big hand cupped the back of my head. 'It's all right, Helena. You decide. We don't have to do anything you don't want to. Ever. Do you want to sleep?'

'No. It's lovely.'

'Lovely,' Dominic repeated, rubbing at the line where my buttocks met my thighs, and then at the creases between my legs. He knelt over me and pushed his face gently between my legs, while he continued to stroke my legs and buttocks. I was shocked yet excited at the thought of him looking at me so closely, and worse – smelling me. But he reassured me straightaway. 'You smell gorgeous there. Not a baby – a woman: a woman and a baby all at once.'

Dominic moved away for a minute and I heard him undressing. He got back on the bed in just his underpants and lay beside me. As I faced him, he untucked my silk top and pulled it over my head. Then he unhooked my bra and I wriggled a bit awkwardly out of that too. Moving down the bed, he put one hand on each side of my body, feeling the sides of my ribs with his long fingers and looking at my breasts. 'They're so pretty.' His head moved in to nuzzle between them and then he gently took one breast in his mouth, sucking the nipple.

I hadn't expected this at all, and jumped, but the shock was a nice one, and I could feel that the nerves in my breasts were connected to the ones between my legs somehow. How many times has he done this? I thought, as he began to stroke the tightest part of my trousers in unison with this gentle sucking. I held his head, stroking and stroking his brow and fingering his delicate eyelids. He rubbed his erection against the front of my leg for a second, and then he drew away, holding the breast he'd kissed in his hand. He kissed my lips then and looked at me closely. He smelled of me – of girl's skin, and very slightly of my perfume. 'Helena?' I nodded. 'I want to pull your trousers

down. I want to see you in nothing but your little panties.'
Yes. I nodded again, pleased that I was wearing my newest
and skimpiest undies for him. When he took my trousers off
quickly, I heard his breath catch in his throat when he saw the
tiny silk knickers. 'These are gorgeous. You're gorgeous.' Then
he laughed his surprised roar. 'Uncle Mark didn't buy these,
did he?'

'How did you guess? I bought them. For you.'

'Turn around again. I've been dying to see your bum all
night.'

His fingers traced the lines where the edges of tight silk touched
my buttocks and he made a low noise in his throat.

'Too big?'

Dominic slapped my bottom. 'Maybe a bit curvy. Stop asking.'

Cold touched me instantly and I turned on to my side. He saw
my face. 'I don't mean it, Helena. Every woman thinks their bum
is too big. It's fine – it's lovely.' I said nothing. 'Are you cold?' I
nodded. He got off the bed and lifted the quilt away from me,
then held it high, like a tent opening. 'Come in then.' I crawled
in alongside him. 'Look.' He grabbed the emerald from beside
his bed. 'I swear – I swear on the emerald that Helena's bum is
not too big. I swear. Okay?'

I laughed, sort of. 'Don't joke about the emerald.'

He smiled and put it back down. 'I know. Here – lie here.'

Lying on his back, he pulled me on top of him so that my
head was resting on his chest. I breathed in his smell – I would
know it anywhere, always. 'I love your smell.' I had the strangest
sensation of hearing him say, 'I love you,' in return, but he
hadn't, I knew he hadn't. And yet I'd definitely heard him with
a part of myself.

Forgetting my curviness for a while, I lifted myself and put my
hands to either side of Dominic's head, looking down on him. 'I
adore you.' I looked into his eyes so intensely I felt I could feel
his soul, hear it buzzing. His eyes shone, as if no one had ever
said that to him before. Maybe no one ever had, so I laughed
and said it again. 'I adore you. You're gorgeous.' I lowered my
hips, so that the tiny silk knickers touched his erection. That felt
good. Dominic cupped my buttocks with one hand and gentled

my breast with the other. He looked almost helpless and I guessed that he was close to coming, as I was too. His hardness thrilled me – it was mine, and I rubbed against it regularly, until his breath was rough and mine was catching on itself. Then I moved down to cradle his head in my arms, as all of the feelings began to run through me. I kissed his temple and whispered, 'I adore you, Dominic,' a third time, which made him come at once, crying out, with his hands wound up in my hair.

Afterwards, Dominic didn't move or speak for several minutes: he just held me. Maybe even he was a bit embarrassed by the intensity of his responses. I loved it that I could make him come, just with my words, that I had that power over him. After a few minutes, he looked down towards me and smiled a very small smile. 'Are you all right?' His hand touched my face.

'Great – what about you?'

'I don't know.' He looked so open.

I smiled at him. 'Are you tired?'

He nodded, but got up anyway. 'I'll just get a wash.'

Grabbing a T-shirt and some clean boxer shorts, he disappeared into the rats' nest for a couple of minutes.

I changed into some wholesome cotton undies while Dominic was gone, and was lying waiting for him when he came back and got into bed wearing just the boxer shorts. We still hadn't seen one another completely nude. He turned around to me and touched my breast, just once, then noticed the knickers.

'Those are pretty too. Are you putting the Dalmatian on?'

'What, after all the stick you've given it?'

'Go on. Let me put it on you.'

Dressing and undressing me seemed to please him. He pulled the nightie from beneath my pillow and stuck it over my head, pulling my hair free and laughing. 'You look about six.'

'Wonderful.'

'It is. Let me hold you while you go to sleep.'

But I held him in the end, stroking his face as he slept, cradling his head, 'Maybe a bit curvy' keeping me awake, refusing to go away.

6

'Try to understand him. These aren't changes of personality. They're simply lunar moods, moving across his consciousness, here today, gone tomorrow. Both during and between each mood, the Cancer man is true to himself'

– Linda Goodman's Sun Signs

The next morning, Dominic's mood was completely different from that of the week before. He woke me when he came back into the bedroom from the bathroom. 'Hi.' He got back into bed and kissed me slowly. 'You're covered in bed smells.'

'Mmm.' I was all sleepy. It was me who felt sad today – curvy, not so little me.

'What time is Uncle Mark expecting his puppy back at the kennels?'

'Get lost.'

'Really. What time?'

'I haven't said. Just some time this afternoon.'

I'd guessed he would still be worried about his exams and I had my highers to think of (occasionally).

'Get dressed, then. We'll do the town.'

Smelling of toothpaste and medicated soap, he was ridiculously cheerful as he pulled the mousey quilt off me, making me shriek, and then he left, saying, 'I'll get you some toast and coffee.' I'd decided that I wouldn't even mention the curvy jokette to him or show in any other way that I was hurt by it. It frightened me that he'd gained so much power over me in such a short period of time and I didn't want to make him any more aware of it than I had to. I would eat his damned toast, supposing it came with half a pound of lard on it.

I dressed slowly – a skimming skirt and a baggy T-shirt – and made my way reluctantly to the rats' nest. No one else was up yet – it was about 9 – and I'd heard the others leave, or go to their bedrooms at about 1. The hairbrush was Sam's – it was full of short, spiky purple hairs now – and there were a few fine fair hairs woven amongst them. I wove in a few chestnut hairs of my own and then went to work on my face.

When I returned Dominic was back in the bedroom, sitting on the bed. 'Here's your toast.' He watched me pick it up and start to eat, then looked away, and his thoughtful expression made me guess that, on one level at least, he was quite aware of how his 'curvy' comment had affected me. I was quite surprised that the toast was spread with creamy, fresh butter, and the bread was fresh too – thickly cut, with poppy seeds on it. I'd half-expected Wonderloaf and rancid butter after the 'food museum' comment the night before. But food was obviously important to him.

Still, the coffee was a shock. I wrinkled my nose up immediately and Dominic clarified the situation for me. 'I know. It's Sam's – I've run out. I've been taking the piss out of that chicory shit she buys for months now, but she says it stops the others from nicking it and swears she likes it. It's disgusting, isn't it? I'll get you some more in Edinburgh.'

Within ten minutes I was organised and packed up, and we were in the Allegro, chugging towards the city centre. 'What are we going to do?' I asked.

'Anything. Bookshops, craft shops, art galleries, cafes, food shops. Everything. What do you want to do?'

'I don't mind.' I just wanted to be with him. Pathetic. I tried to shake off my miserable mood, assess the situation. I could always lose weight if I really needed to; it wasn't a life or death issue. I sat up straight and took control. 'Coffee first. I need some after that enamel stripper at your house.'

It didn't take us long at all to reach the city centre and park the Allegro – car theft wasn't one of the more obvious hazards facing Dominic in Edinburgh. Then we headed down into the packed, noisy streets to explore.

I dragged him into one or two of the more special cosmetics

shops. Although he bellowed, 'Not more make-up!' on being forced into Crabtree and Evelyn (or Crab Apple and Adam, as he called it), he bought me a little bottle of geranium-scented shampoo, whispering, 'I'll wash your hair with this next time you stay with me – get the stench of Cromwell Street out of it,' romantically (?) in my ear afterwards. He loved bookshops, and I bought a copy of Keats' poems that included *The Eve of St Agnes* because he said that Purple Porphyro (back to 'long purples') had given him the idea for the feast of the night before. And we drank coffee together. He *could* pronounce 'cappuccino' (and 'espresso') which was a huge relief. Afterwards, I was tricked into a Disney shop to see what other Dalmatian delights could be found, and finally he turned towards The Mound and the National Gallery of Scotland, towards the bottom of Castle Hill. He laughed slyly, saying, 'I'll be very careful to avoid reference to your bodily parts, Helena,' as we approached the street sign, earning an almost crab-like nip for his comment.

I love art galleries, despite the fact that so many visits to them in the past have been too much a part of Uncle Mark's educational routine to be enjoyed, and I was really looking forward to being able to amble around one unencumbered by his comments. A poster advertising a visiting exhibition caught my eye, promising: *Will Jackson – The Secret Wood.* A half-formed image of the garden I wanted to make when I was older leapt into my mind, and although I didn't know why, the name Will Jackson attracted me too. I pulled Dominic forward. 'Let's have a look at that.' And we went towards the room that held the exhibition.

The poster at the doorway informed us that Will Jackson was a young Scot who worked in wood. (I'd figured that much out myself.) He was an ex-paramedic, and his pieces were '*unique and original, contemporary, yet referring back to the exquisite workmanship of the 1920s and 30s.*' So far, so predictable.

We moved inside the room to see the exhibition. As soon as I saw the smaller pieces – tiny boxes – I understood the *WJ* of my jewellery box that Uncle Mark had bought me, and the *Will J* of the treasure chest in the dusty jewellery shop. Many of the pieces were small, cleanly finished boxes ('*with the crispness of a Charles Rennie Mackintosh*' – I was considering acquiring one of those posters for Uncle Mark). They were inlaid with different shades of wood, such as maple, cedar and redwood. When I looked closer, I saw that they all had trademark secret doors, corridors or circular chambers, but these pieces housed all sorts of treasures (not just crystals) such as notes, original poems, or tiny rings. The hidden sections were carved into softer, rounder shapes than the crisp, masculine lines of the outer boxes, providing a gentler, petalled effect: *'secret roses'* as the sheet informed me. Apparently, this gave his work a sense of *'fruitfulness and generosity'*. This fruit and flower theme carried on into his furniture which varied in size and scale from a child's stool, bordered by a chain of cherries, to carver chairs that were more like thrones, their high, rounded backs edged with stylised walnuts, fir cones and apples.

I was in love with these treasures, touching the bigger items when the security guards couldn't see. I felt the beautifully smooth, carved wood and I appreciated the fact that a man could combine the masculine and the feminine, the hard and the soft, so seamlessly. Dominic interrupted me after a bit. 'Come on, I feel almost jealous. You never look at my law notes like that.'

'Bloody law,' I laughed, in his voice. I'd finished looking at the exhibition anyway so we wandered around a few of the other rooms before walking back outside into the sunshine.

'We'd better get back soon.' I'd sensed that this was coming, and I nodded – trying not to look too depressed. Dominic grabbed my hand and kissed my cheek, and we went to find the Allegro for the unhappy journey home to Leeched Dry.

It wasn't until I'd waved Dominic goodbye, and unlocked the door to Leeched, that I remembered something vital. Dominic hadn't mentioned his birthday party to me again.

7

'Pisces woman

'The hardest lesson she has to learn is to overcome her . . . doubts'
– Linda Goodman's Sun Signs

What do you think was the first thing I did when I got up to my
bedroom in Leeched? I know – I'm so predictable. I measured
myself. I knew how tall I was, of course. You don't get to 5' 10"
at fourteen without encountering the tape measure more than
once. (I'd dwarfed Uncle Mark's Snow White measuring stick
at about nine.) I knew I was a size 10 or 12 in clothes, so that
should have meant, according to the labels, that I had a 34-inch
chest and 36-inch hips maximum, right? Wrong. I was a 35-inch
chest (which sounded okay), 24-inch waist (so far so good) . . .
and what about the curvy area? Thirty-seven inches. More than
an inch for every year of Jesus' life. Desperate.

Desperate and disproportionate. My rib cage made up about 34
of the 35 inches of the chest. Could I lose two inches from my hips
without developing a chest that was completely concave? Probably
not. Damn Dominic Oliver. I bet *he* never got the tape measure out.

Exercise was one option – walking on the floor on your
buttocks. Wouldn't that just flatten and widen them hideously?
Could it widen them much more?

I stripped off and had a good, honest look in the mirror. Was
there really a problem? I jogged up and down a bit, watching
my marathon-cum-model routine in the mirror. It was fine
until I turned around. My God – had Dominic seen that? All

of it? No wonder he'd commented. Exercise was too slow – I needed exercise, diet and a major miracle, urgently. And then some surgery. Before the arrival of the Gemini/Cancer cusp, I wanted to be in the shops, choosing my 'party frock' (Uncle Mark's cash card permitting) with the type of slinky body that would fit into anything. (I know – I was very young.) I had eight weeks. I consulted a few magazines that afternoon, made a list, and stuck it on the fridge at Leeched.

LEGAL

Fruit – good for skin

Vegetables – not fried

Potatoes – not chips

Chicken – free range

Fish – any

Bread and eggs – in moderation

Low-fat cheese and spreads

Crispbreads

ILLEGAL

Chocolate, crisps, butter, sweets, red meat, pastry

Fatty cheeses

Curry, chilli

Anything fried

Most other things

The list was the first thing Uncle Mark saw when he got in from work that night. He did do most of the cooking, after all, so it was best to let him know. He was looking curiously pleased with himself. And he was not pleased with the list *at all*.

'Oh, I've been expecting this for ages. I read all about it in my *Adolescent Anxiety* book—' his favourite reference book '—eating disorders: anorexia, bulimia. Even royalty has succumbed: *The Disease that Devoured Diana*. There's a whole chapter on it. I know all about it.'

'Uncle Mark, I'm going on a diet. I'm not about to turn into some sort of stick insect.'

'Helena, you're fine. You're just a big girl, that's all.' Sensitive as ever. He saw my face. 'Tall. You don't need to diet. Look what happened to Princess Di!'

'She didn't wear a seatbelt, then she got into a car with an alcoholic. It's not up for discussion. I can cook for myself, if necessary.' (A complete lie, as we both knew.)

'Not with your highers just around the corner, you can't. I'll have a look at it.'

He winced visibly when he saw his venomous chilli outlawed and his shoulders drooped. But as he headed back into the living room, I thought there was a slightly springier bounce to his step than usual. Then he whistled. I was immediately suspicious. 'Where have you been today?'

'Oh – just out.'

'Out where?'

Slightly sheepish. 'Totty spotting.'

'*Totty spotting*?' I was aghast. I didn't know he knew words like that. 'What did you say?' Complete role reversal. It was the first time I'd played Goneril. 'Totty spotting? You can't.'

'Why not? You've got your own life – university applications, Dominic Oliver, diet, etcetera.' He caught my Gonerilish eye; a diet was hardly a life. 'Well, I've only been looking.'

It was getting worse. 'Where, for God's sake?'

'Singles' club in Edinburgh – *Dinners for Dates*. It was *Lunches for Lovers* today, actually, an exclusive club. Quite a good selection.'

Uncle Mark actually smiled. I couldn't believe it – Dominic and I might have seen him. I was appalled! 'How old are you?' I never could quite remember.

'Forty-two. What's that got to do with it? I'm quite eligible, actually.'

Forty-two. I'd thought he was older. Certainly, he seemed older. I felt guilty when I considered why that might be.

'So I thought I'd go again next week. You'll be off out, of course.'

'Of course.'

'You never know – it may not be long before I've got a lady of my own to share my Friday night chilli with. Might spice it up a bit, too.'

What a disgusting thought. This little jokette sent me rushing upstairs to start my exercise routine, utterly nauseated.

I lay in bed at Leeched that night, between my clean, colour co-ordinated sheets, thinking about it all: here I was, Saturday night, in the springtime of my life (etcetera), and I was full of terrors. Dominic was out, God knows where – I never asked him where he was when he wasn't with me, and he never said; Uncle Mark was probably trimming his moustache in preparation for his future lunch lover. And I was lying in bed – stomach aching (I couldn't even hit the right body part) – thinking, What if Dominic leaves me? Then, What if Uncle Mark leaves me? What if one, or both, of them finds someone else altogether more interesting than me instead? Where would I go? What would I do?

All in all the next week trailed by listlessly – I was definitely in *Measure for Measure* Mariana mode again. I had no idea what I wanted to do after school, so I'd half-heartedly applied for a few university courses in subjects that vaguely interested me: psychology, literature – subjects that were a natural progression from school. But I had a whole new sense of urgency now about which university I went to and which degree course I followed. I had to get out before some kind of a hideous Auntie Markette moved in.

Uncle Mark must have been aware of how I was feeling because a couple of days after our 'totty spotting' conversation, I found a card pushed under my door when I got home from school. It had a good quality print of some earnest Renaissance painting on the front and inside he'd written:

> *Dearest Helena,*
> *You will always be my primary concern. There will always be a place*
> *for you here at 'Beech Trees' with me.*
> *Your affectionate,*
> *Uncle Mark*

Ungrateful, I know, but the repetition of that 'always' made me feel even worse.

A further complication was that I'd already applied for a place at Edinburgh University (BD – Before Dominic) to do business studies. I hadn't the remotest interest in business studies (faint ideas of Richard Branson-like adventures with my £300,000 had made me choose it) but now, all of a sudden, I wanted to gain a place at Edinburgh more than anything else in the world. Worse still, their offer was pretty high, which meant that I would have to work harder than I had ever done in my life before. Reading the list of the subjects I'd be studying, if I did get there, made an Uncle Mark poetry reading seem like a tobogganing trip in Switzerland. All of this suddenly came into very sharp focus.

And then there were my curves – still. I'd weighed myself several times. Nine stones twelve pounds. Nine and twelve, twenty-one. Coming of age. And nine stones twelve pounds was dangerously close to ten. Ten stones was unthinkable, that huge, fat zero, coming right after that skinny, Sherry-shaped one. Ten Ton Tess. Unbearable. I'd consulted a height to weight chart, which stated that my weight was 'acceptable' for my height, but I didn't believe it. I'd never felt less acceptable in my life. So I had my brains, my body and my soul to work on.

One thing did – momentarily – stop me from falling into the moat completely. On the Wednesday night I was deep (or trying to be deep) into Scottish history when I heard the phone ring. Uncle Mark's standard 'Could you hold the line, please? I'll just go and get her' (sometimes he even gave his office number automatically) brought me tearing downstairs – any kind of diversion was so welcome at Leeched Dry – and I grabbed the receiver from his fingers.

'Hi, Helena speaking . . . Dominic!'

Uncle Mark's face was swamped in disappointment when he heard me say the name. He knew he'd missed the chance of an interrogation – again. I wondered how Dominic had got my number; he'd not asked for it. Plus Cromwell Street had no phone. He was in a call box, his voice tinny. 'What are you up to, Dominic?'

'Legal cases, legal cases and more legal cases. I'm almost dying of boredom. What about you? Did you read your Keats?'

'I understand why you want to be Porphyro.' (Purple, pouting, pouncing Porphyro. Peeping Porphyro.) 'I'm less keen on Madeline. Supine? She's like a wax dummy. I don't fancy her part at all.' His laughter crackled through the wire. 'Where did you get my number?'

'Louise.'

Of course. There was a long pause. I glared at Uncle Mark, who was earwigging enthusiastically from his peachy Dralon throne. His concentration was so strong, I could almost hear it. He retreated to the kitchen, mumbling and bumbling as he did so. I heard him slap at my food list waspishly as he made himself a cup of tea.

'Sorry about that. I had to stare at Uncle Mark.'

'I wish you lived a bit nearer. I'd love to see you tonight, just for half an hour, even.' I immediately thought of my place at Edinburgh – and the grades I needed to get there – and groaned. 'Thanks a lot.'

'Sorry, Dominic. I was just thinking, I'm not going to get anywhere unless I do really well in my highers.'

'What grades do you need?' I rattled them off. 'That doesn't sound too bad.' Not to the next up and coming legal hotshot, perhaps.

'I'll need to do better this year than I did last,' I said. 'That's all.'

'Ah, right.'

I told him – quietly – about Uncle Mark's 'totty spotting', not bothering to keep the scorn out of my voice. Dominic roared again, much louder than before.

'Life in the old dog yet. He'll be buying Dalmatian nighties for a whole new litter of his own soon.'

'Don't!' I was horrified. Would Uncle Mark's sperm still work? Unthinkable.

'Listen, can we make it Saturday night instead of Friday this weekend?' Very casually, he was breaking our arrangement. Why?

'I'm not sure,' I said

His voice acquired a harder edge. 'Have you got something else on?' he asked.

'A tentative arrangement.' Lying – trying to suggest that everybody wants Helena just now.

'Break it.'

'What if I can't?' I put some steel into my own voice.

'If you can't, you can't. I'll see you on Friday, Helena. It's no big deal. It's just it's getting a bit predictable, that's all.' His voice was very sharp now.

Predictable, curvy, no big (and no little) deal me.

My head ached from studying, my stomach ached with hunger, and my thighs ached with stretching. And everything ached with sadness, sadness and the predictability of my rows with him.

'Right then. I'll see you Friday.'

I didn't mean to dismiss him, but I did.

I couldn't wait forever. Well, you wouldn't, would you? It's a muscle, you know, and my Mr Muscles have always been strong. I thought I'd perfect my technique so that, when I did get her (and get rid of him), *all* of me would be ready, like, and I'd be able to get all of her ready. So I got myself two pets: the dirty blonde (remember her?) and a little rat.

The dirty blonde is the easier of the two to work out. I've picked up more about women from those cunts at school than they realised. So I picked up one that looked ignored, got her a few garage flowers (about the same price as one of my magazines and about the same purpose) and started to practise on her. Guns and Roses. I'm not going to keep her, obviously. Dirty.

The rat I feel pretty affectionate towards, just now. I'm feeding it up and up and up so that it'll trust me. Then things will change.

Black-head boy has got a clean licence – about the only clean thing about him. So I'll have to use another method.

8 ∫

'Cancerians care deeply about the hungry, and they feel a responsibility towards every empty stomach in the world'
– Linda Goodman's Sun Signs

I suppose I knew what to expect that night when I got into the Allegro. Ice. Pure ice. If I'd touched him, my fingers would have stuck – freezer burn. So I didn't. I kept remembering what Sam had said about his 'romantic enthusiasms' so I joined in with his silence, joined in until it became embarrassing. Until it became unbearable. Until he won – because eventually I had to chip the ice.

'What have you got in mind for tonight, then?'

'Nothing much. There's a special party on tomorrow night – that's why I wanted you to come then instead.'

Right, there'd been no hot date lined up, then; I was off the hook. But I could see that I was stuck with the Ice Man for quite a while yet and I absolutely wasn't going to let him know how I'd been feeling.

'Why didn't you say that instead of saying I was predictable, then?'

Dominic looked genuinely surprised and glanced away from the road for a second. 'I didn't say that.' He obviously couldn't remember his comment at all; it had been a purely reflex reaction. My soft-scarred angel. Frozen angel. How could I press the 'defrost' button? Never easy with Dominic, as you'll have seen by now.

'Am I predictable?'

'You? I've never met anyone less predictable in my life.' Dominic thought for a minute. 'I never know whether you're going to wag your tail or bite my hand.' He laughed. 'Have you got your nightie, then?'

'Yes, a different one.' A *real* woman's nightdress. One that I'd bought myself.

'Oh, no – the death of the Dalmatian! Will Uncle Mark ever forgive you?'

Not if he saw the nightie I'd just bought, no, I thought.

Dominic had relaxed a little, but I knew that he wouldn't relax completely until my (non-existent) tentative arrangement had been discussed and I really wasn't ready to air it. I needed to keep the upper hand, from time to time at least. Sam's comment and my curves lay heavily between us. A mound. But he still wouldn't look at me properly, and his shoulders were up, so I stroked his thigh – wagged my tail just a bit. He looked at me then, quickly, but deliberately didn't smile.

'Where are we going then?' I asked.

He answered my question with one of his own, one of his crabby lawyer's tricks. 'Do you like Indian food?'

'Love it.'

'In fairly basic surroundings?'

'Don't mind.'

'That's where we're going, then.'

I should have guessed it would involve food. I'd hardly eaten all week and I'd had my first almost-fast the day before. (There'd been no avoiding a bit of one of Uncle Mark's daily lows – the 'high tea'.) My foresight meant that I could eat whatever I wanted now and still lose some of my mass of flesh. And I was definitely hungry – starved, in fact. We dropped my bag off at Cromwell Street, breathing in the smell of warm skin, warm socks and again, inexplicably, dogs – the emerald was still there beside his bed, and then we were out on the scary streets of Edinburgh again. 'It's within walking distance,' Dominic explained, as we left the (so far) trusty Allegro outside his house. The thud of a bass guitar drew my eyes to Eric's window, but there was no sight of him in its empty square. We walked on. Then Dominic took my arm and drew me behind him into an off-licence and shop. 'I'll just get us a bottle of wine – the restaurant's got no licence.' He moved straight towards the red wine section. 'Red all right or do you prefer a girly white?'

'Red's fine.'

But when I made to draw away to look at some magazines, Dominic held my arm even tighter. I was puzzled but stayed beside him until we reached the checkout, feeling like a toddler.

'Sorry, Helena,' he said, tucking the litre bottle of wine under his arm, as we left the shop, 'it's just I've seen some really mad bastards in that shop, that's all.' He slung his arm around me.

'Where is this place?' I asked him as we walked.

'It's just around the corner. The luxurious Gorgie Balti Palace. It's great. Really basic, all wooden benches, and you eat the curry with your fingers. You'll love it.'

'Is it clean?' It was out before I could edit Uncle Mark.

Dominic made his delighted roar. 'If you've survived Cromwell Street, you'll survive the balti house. Yes, it's clean.'

A red and green beacon of a restaurant – somewhere between a palace and a shack – appeared in the distance like Brigadoon. We'd arrived. It was hot and steamy inside as we waited for our table. There was a fair sprinkling of students (their tables marked out by empty bottles, full ashtrays and tortured – sculpted – cans) but there were also quite a lot of middle-aged types in there as well. Dominic almost read my mind. 'We could come here on a double date with Uncle Mark and his new totty – when he finds her.'

'Desperate. And then take them back to Cromwell Street for a night-cap?'

'Perhaps not.'

A waiter, whose waist was about the size of my wrist, showed us to our seats at a rickety table in the centre of the restaurant. A sigh puffed out of my still fat stomach – fatter than usual, actually, that night – as I sat on the same side of the bench as Dominic before settling down to read (or count, in my case) the menu. They were playing an Abba track in Hindi or Urdu and the high notes were manic, making it hard to stay depressed. I leaned sideways towards Dominic's ear. 'No one seems to be eating much.' Several of the tables were bare of food.

He looked at me above his menu. 'No. It gets a bit chaotic here at weekends sometimes.'

A few puffs of smoke were emerging from the badly curtained-off kitchen. Then a strip light blew. Student types were swigging lager, beer and wine rabidly as they waited – chattering, laughing and lively. My stomach rumbled deafeningly above their voices, making Dominic laugh. 'We'd better get our order in quickly. Doesn't Uncle Mark feed you?' If only Dominic knew how hard he tried.

We decided upon papodoms and pickles and chutney to share, and then Dominic ordered a chicken balti and I chose a vegetable and chickpea one. And a house special nan.

'Their nans are like duvets,' Dominic explained.

'A bit cleaner than yours, I hope?'

'Thanks. Actually, I've given it its termly wash, ready for your whiter than white body.'

'Great.' I was genuinely relieved.

The waiter uncorked the wine, Dominic poured it and I sipped at the fruity, tinny taste, licking at the residue on my teeth. Actually, I did prefer white, but I didn't want to be too teenage. Dominic went quiet again and I thought I detected a fresh touch of frost about the lips. Silence. 'Where's this party tomorrow night then, Dominic?'

He couldn't resist it. 'Isn't your "tentative arrangement" more interesting?' he asked before looking away from me, feigning boredom but reeking of resentment. I wanted to enjoy the rest of the night, appease him, yet avoid complete 'bottom dog' status. Difficult.

'I don't ask you about your arrangements when we're not together, do I?'

Dominic thought for several seconds. He decided. He had to drag it out of a part of himself that was so low down, his voice changed. 'I don't have any arrangements when we're not together – tentative or otherwise.' A crab-like addition was irresistible. 'Because of my fucking law finals, for a start.' Followed by the Return of the Ice Man.

My fingers curled around his long, unwilling hand. 'Dominic, next time you want to change a date, just tell me why. The only arrangement I had was with a bit of hurt pride.' He, of all people, should understand that. Throwing back his head, he looked exactly as he had the first time I'd seen him – entirely, obnoxiously, pleased with himself. I almost regretted my concession. Then he remembered about me and his face fell as he thought back.

'I'm sorry. I've been a wanker, haven't I?' A little smile. 'I was revising legal communication that night as well.'

'It's okay. I could have lots of arrangements, any time I wanted.' I wasn't going to withdraw all of my fishy little hooks in one go.

Bending slightly to nuzzle my cheek, he whispered, 'I know, Helena, I know that.' Then he looked directly into my eyes and I relished the vivid white and green for a second before he kissed me on the cheek, saying, 'You look gorgeous.' My stomach rumbled again – thank God I hadn't burped. 'Very romantic!' He jabbed my ribs, laughing.

'I can't help it – I'm absolutely starved.'

'I know. It shouldn't be long now.'

I'd had one glass of wine before our papodoms and pickles arrived, and another glass before I tasted my first balti. It finally arrived, steaming away like a party: a huge wok with elbow-sized handles, filled almost to the brim with glistening red, orange and green vegetables and dotted with creamy chickpeas. A distinctive waft of coriander hit my nose. Bliss. Taurus rising. I was lost in balti for a good five minutes before I heard Dominic's strange burst of laughter.

'What's the matter?'

'It's your hair.' Dominic combed it back from my face. 'It was just about to go for a swim.' He laughed again. 'It's great that you enjoy your food. I hate girls who're always on a diet.' Terrific. He'd just turned me into one. But he was looking at me kind of sharply, and I guessed that he'd remembered his curvy comment. I slowed down a bit, nonetheless, and took a big sip of wine. He sat back, looked at me sideways, and smiled, wiping a bit of sauce from my cheek. Then he arranged a morselette of his chicken on to a tiny pad of nan bread, grinning as he put it into my mouth. 'It's the Dalmatian on her duvet.' He fed me with three or four more pieces, then I went back to my own bowl, which was just slightly spicier than his. It tasted earthy, garlicky and fresh – soul food, I kept thinking, as I gave up completely on worrying, counting and stomachs and ate almost the whole bowlful, cramming carbohydrates and fat in like somebody starving. Wonderful!

Exams took up too much of the conversation – Dominic's and mine. Hideous revision timetables worried at us both. Coaxed, he talked about his mother. She'd remarried, briefly and badly, which hadn't gone down well with Dominic and his sister at all. He moved on quickly, saying again that law bored him; he wasn't certain about staying in the profession at all, long term. I noticed that he was very careful not to ask me about my parents this time.

By now we'd both finally finished eating. 'Would you like a sweet? You'd love their ice cream.'

'No, thanks.' It was getting hard to breathe. That one meal had had more calories in it than I'd eaten all week. (The only sweet thing I'd eaten recently had been my daily Uncle-Mark-administered Haliborange vitamin tablet – I'd nearly grabbed the whole packet out of his hands at times.) Dominic went to the counter to pay the bill while I picked up my jacket.

We were both quiet as we wandered (waddled) home. I was thinking of my faithful antique condoms in their shrine. If I kept my eggs to myself as long as I'd kept those condoms, my children would be shrivelled pensioners at birth. Would it be third time lucky for me tonight? Would it hurt? Would I bleed? (Surely not – all those ponies.) How many other girls had he slept with? I thought again of Sam's comment.

Still, he was with me now. Best concentrate on that. 'What're they up to at Cromwell Street, then? I saw Eric's light on before.'

'Yeah. Eric's being Eric. Sam and Jen're over at Doug's – I don't know whether they'll come back or not. Sam's having a hot romance with him.'

'But she was *horrible* to him the other night.' I was really surprised.

Dominic nodded, his eyes amused. 'Of course. That's part of her seduction technique.'

'What about Jen? Won't she feel like a lemon?'

'Not at all. They're a pair: Doug just has to put up with it.

He'll probably feel more of a gooseberry than Jen.' He laughed. 'They'll torment the life out of the poor bastard, which he deserves, of course.'

We were nearly at Cromwell Street and I was glad to sit down in the grubby living room – I'd eaten so much that I was exhausted. I took my shoes off and curled up in the big old armchair (dusting it surreptitiously first). Thankfully I was wearing quite wide, loose trousers. Dominic had brought some of the wine back from the restaurant with him and he went into the kitchen with it. 'Do you want a glass of wine or a coffee?' he was asking, from a distance.

'Just some cold water, please.'

It was a warm night. Still, I was feeling very hot. The thump of heavy metal music was coming down to me through the ceiling. My head was thumping vaguely, too. I rested my cheek against the stale-smelling back of the chair.

Then Dominic was standing in front of me – a glass of wine in one hand, and a cup of water in the other. He handed the water across to me and sat down gingerly on the arm of my chair, drinking his wine. I could smell it, and suddenly the smell was inside me as I swallowed a mouthful of water. The cold water slipped into the hot cup of my stomach and lay there, waiting unpleasantly.

'Are you all right? Not like you to be so quiet.'

'Yes. I think I've just eaten a bit much, that's all.' Stupid – to eat next to nothing all week and then stuff myself. Stupid, stupid.

'Well, you did trough a fair bit down in there.'

'Sensitively put.'

Stroking my hair back from my face, he felt my brow. 'You're hot.'

The scent of red wine rose from his fingertips and a sudden fist of sickness hit me. I *had* to get away. 'I'll just go to the loo.' I tried desperately to look cool and unhurried (not easy) but once I got to those stairs, I ran up them. *No!* It was locked. No, no, no. Eric. I'd thought he was in his room. I knocked – battered – on the door.

'Hold on, I'm in the bath.'

Unthinkable. I didn't know whether I was going to puke, have diarrhoea, pass out or all three. But I knew something terrible was going to happen Now. I knocked again, really hard, not knowing what else to do.

Dominic was at the bottom of the stairs. 'What's going on?' Couldn't I just die? I leaned against the door as he ran upstairs to me.

'I feel awful. And Eric's in the bath.'

'Eric, get out!'

'I've only just got in.'

'Come into my room, Helena.'

'I can't.'

God, no, diarrhoea would be the worst. I sat on the floor, just within the doorway of his bedroom. My insides finally turned, the smell of red wine and curry was in my nose, and a loud, horrible noise came out of my throat. 'I'll get you a bowl.' He ran downstairs but it was too late. My stomach clenched, I couldn't breathe, then hot splashes of acid were coming out of my mouth. All over Dominic's carpet.

A chipped and depressing bowl appeared beneath me and Dominic's head was by mine. 'It's all right. Don't look like that. Don't sit down there.' It wasn't all right at all. I was freezing; I had sick all over my clothes and I still felt deadly. Stupid. I couldn't look at him. 'Come and sit in the chair.' I shook my head; I knew I was going to be sick again. Fingers touched my face and I could smell red wine on his skin again. My stomach heaved and I vomited horribly, violently, from my nose as well as my mouth this time. At least I managed to get most of it in the bowl. 'I'll get you a towel.' Thank God it didn't look like it was going to come out of the other end. And I heard Eric finally coming out of the bathroom, grumbling away. I was mortified. My stomach was hurting and I wanted to go home. More than anything, I didn't want Dominic to see me like this. But he had. He was wiping the stringy vomit from my mouth with a towel. I bolted for the bathroom and just about made the toilet bowl.

Behind me, Dominic stood in the frame of the door. 'Are you all right?'

'Leave me alone. Please.'

'I can't. How can I leave you like this? I have seen people being sick before, you know.'

'Please.' My voice was harsh. Uncle Mark wouldn't have humiliated me like this – he would have given me some time to 'compose' myself, and returned half an hour later with a cup of tea.

'I'll leave you for a bit, if that's what you want.'

Dropping the towel there, Dominic went back into his bedroom. I immediately locked the bathroom door then he was outside it again, banging and banging against the flimsy wood. 'I'll leave you alone, if it really makes you feel better, but *don't* lock the door. It's dangerous.' He was annoyed now and my eyes filled up. I unbolted it, but left it closed, and waited behind it until I heard him walk back into his room. He was cleaning up in there, going up and down the stairs, then scrubbing. The whole house would stink of second-hand balti! Would they all know it was me? Putting the towel down against the door meant that at least Dominic couldn't barge in on me.

The sudden waves and blows of nausea carried on for about twenty minutes. After about ten of those minutes, the buzz of the television told me that Dominic had settled downstairs. Pleasure at my newfound privacy was followed immediately by gloom. Didn't he care how ill I was? There was hardly anything left in my stomach now, and there was a bowlful of calories in the rats' nest. I washed my face really thoroughly, managing to leave most of my eye make-up on. My skin was a horrible greeny-yellow colour; I looked about seventy.

The television noise died. I was just cleaning my mouth, with toothpaste-on-a-fingertip, when the last wave came. I made a dry, retching sound into the toilet bowl, similar to the first noise. It must stop now: there was absolutely nothing left. I sat on the floor. Bits of dried sick were crusted on to my clothes and it was probably in my hair too. The carpet stank of old pee – no sign of the toilet-hugging rugs so beloved of Uncle Mark. My sides hurt so much I was scared, and I was too tired to stop the tears then. I put the crooked plastic toilet seat down at last and laid my head on it, sniffing. There was one really loud thud on the door. 'That's it. I'm coming in now.' The door jerked open, and then Dominic kicked hard against the towel. 'This is ridiculous.' He was furious – I'd never seen him like that before.

'Jesus.' He was in front of me. I turned my head away from

him and just cried, as quietly as I could. 'Helena. No, no.' He dropped right down on to his knees, in the middle of all the crusty bits on the floor. 'Come on.' He took my arm; I pulled away from him.

'I don't want you to see me like this.'

'So I gathered.' But his voice was gentle and he rested a hand on my head for a minute. 'Has it stopped now?'

The sickness had, but I just couldn't stop the crying. 'Everything hurts . . . my throat, my stomach, my ribs. Everything. I want to go home.'

'No, don't go home. I'll look after you – stay with me. I want to look after you. You don't understand . . .'

When Dominic's hand pulled away from me, I thought he was going to leave. I cried some more. I was shaking with cold and my nose was running. But he bent down and picked me up in his arms like he had before. Pushing the doors open noisily with his foot, he laid me straight down on the bed this time, keeping one arm round my shoulders. 'Really, do you want me to take you home now?'

That started me off again. Mutely, I turned away from him and curled up on the bed. Returning from the bathroom a second time, with some more towels, Dominic lay down behind me and I thought, So much for the condoms, and sobbed even harder. I was sick of myself now, and couldn't breathe properly, but I couldn't stop. Dominic's warm arms pulled my stiff body towards him and held me close.

'Jesus,' he said again, 'you're absolutely freezing.' Cold air wafted between us for a second as he pulled off my sicky top, then he moved away and returned with a big, old, clean jumper which he pulled over my head. My cheek was on his chest and I was so relieved that he couldn't see my face; he just held me, rubbing me, trying to get me warm. 'Don't cry, Helena. I shouldn't have left you there on your own like that, whatever you said. I'm sorry.' A towel nudged itself into the space between us and I blew my nose on it. Dominic didn't even seem to mind snot – just carried on holding me close. My breathing calmed down some. His chest pulled backwards as he tried to look at me, to talk to me, but I said,

'I can't. My face, my hair.' I couldn't bear him to see me, so he held me close again and soothed me until eventually I settled a bit. A funny hiccupy noise came out and then I blew my nose, and wiped my face with a clean corner of the towel. Dominic was still holding the back of my head with his big hand, making little noises, like, 'Tshh, tshh,' to a baby. When I finally stopped, he said, 'Good girl. Let me look at you, Helena.' And I pulled away from him slowly. The pads of his fingers touched my temples as he combed the hair back from my face with both his hands, nodding at me slightly. His fingers caught in a bit of old curry and my eyes filled up.

I said again, 'My hair.' I was usually so proud of it. 'I have to wash it.'

'No way, Helena. You're freezing. And shattered.' He touched the sides of my face. 'You're still shaking. Look at me.' His eyes were always intense, enchanting even, and he looked into mine, so deeply, so greenly, that I felt healed. Partly. Suddenly realising that I *was* absolutely worn out, I relaxed. 'There.' He almost whispered it. He stroked and stroked my temple, still looking at me intently. 'I just want you to calm down.' My breathing slowed more. 'Let me do your hair and face. Where are your things?'

'Over there.' I could barely move my arm to show him.

'It's okay. Just wait.'

I closed my eyes, and heard him move around between the room and bathroom for a couple of minutes. Then he was lying beside me again. 'I've seen my sister do this.' Holding my hair from my face, he put some cleanser on the back of his hand then rubbed it clumsily into my cheeks, my nose, my brow, my chin, my eyelids. It was hypnotic, and so tender. Uncle Mark had never touched me so tenderly, even when I was a child. Because I wasn't his child. No one had ever touched me like that before, not in the parts of my memory that I usually visited. A little thrill went through my nipples, which surprised me. Then he wiped all of the cream off with my cotton wool and with it the tears, the sick, the make-up, even some of the humiliation. I smiled at him, but he was serious. 'You're fine. You don't need to worry.' He reached to the side of his bed, and then I felt him press the emerald into my hand.

'You kept it,' I said.

'Of course I kept it. Don't worry.'

Closing my eyes, I felt the firm bristles of the wooden bathroom brush on my scalp. Bliss. 'I'll get it clean; you'll be able to sleep, and then tomorrow I'll wash it.' He brushed and brushed, properly, holding the hair by the handful when he came to a knotty bit and working through. 'Are you always so violently sick?'

'No, I'm never sick.' It was true.

'What happened then?' The regular brushing and brushing continued, warming and soothing my scalp.

There was no way that I was going to admit to it – the starving, destructive chewing inside that set in now whenever I even thought about the future, and about him, and about how dependent I was becoming on him. 'I don't know. I must've just overeaten.'

'You're tall; you're young. You need to eat a lot.'

'I don't usually drink red wine.'

'You didn't drink that much. My fault, I shouldn't've taken the piss. Are you all right now? Do your sides still hurt?'

'A bit.'

Stopping brushing for a minute, Dominic stroked my ribs through his jumper. 'Do you want to get changed?' I nodded. He brought a T-shirt of his, and some fresh, blue cotton knickers of mine with tiny green fish on them. Immediately, I thought of his eyes. He pulled his sweater over my head as I unclipped my bra, and then he pulled the T-shirt on, quickly. I shrugged out of my bottom things and pulled the knickers on. It was the first time he'd seen all of me, in the light. He put his whole hand over my sex, almost protectively. 'I love your little cunt.' Even the way he said that sounded tender. Closing my eyes, I felt the emerald in my palm, like a rosary bead. I watched him then, thinking, I love you, I love you, you are The One. I love you. I knew it was in my eyes, but I wasn't ready to tell him. What could I tell him then, to let him know how precious he was becoming to me? He was smiling at me as he brushed my hair some more, saying, 'Helena,' quietly, twice, three times.

'He's dead,' I said. 'My father. He's dead.' Tears prickled at my eyes again. 'No one's ever touched me like you have. Ever.' Then, stupidly, 'Uncle Mark – he's not my father.'

Dominic's hands were smoothing my hair, touching my scalp now. 'I know, Helena. I knew it already. I'm your family tonight.' He put the light out and we lay together in a close embrace – an embrace that would suffocate me now. 'Sleep now.' I breathed against his skin, rocked slightly against the beat of his heart, and fell asleep almost at once.

The rat was a complete mistake, like – ungrateful bastard. I fattened it up until it was all self-satisfied and sleek. It got pretty tame around then. Then I starved it a bit – just to let it know who was really boss. Kept thinking of my dad. One day, when I'd nicked some paper from school, he'd been all pally. The next time I did it, he broke my tooth. Instant. He was like that. See how the rat fucking liked it.

It tried a soft look for a while. I'm sure it was a woman. So I'd stroke it, play with it a bit, then push it back in its cage. The second day it was getting wary of me, like. Learning some respect. Nipped my finger once. Only once. Then, this morning, I woke up and it was gone – gnawed its way out of the cage. Don't know how it got out of my room.

So I'm thinking, I need something on the softer side, a bit more loyal, like. I put my best open look on, comb my hair and take myself off to my friendly local animal shelter. Slavery bastards.

Funny way to protect things. A puppy would have more sense than that lot. I come out with a kitten – well, half-cat, half-kitten, really – a leaflet, and the promise of a 'home visit'. It doesn't look like it expects much out of life, so I reckon it's come to the right place. It reminds me of her sometimes, the way it holds itself on a good day. (Not that it'll have many good days. Last one didn't last long, so to speak.) It's definitely a girl – I checked this time. I put it in the rat's cage. So I have a little fiddle around with her every now and then – just practising, like – partly because I'm bored with it, and partly to show it who's in charge.

I don't bother with the feeding up routine this time. (I've found you don't always need the flowers either, do you? Not if they're desperate enough and ugly enough, and this pussy would be both, before long.)

She won't look like my autumn girl for many days. I know

you'll be interested in my plans. But I'll keep that side of things to myself. For now.

Dominic didn't wash my hair the next day. My body had really gone for gold and in the morning it turned itself inside out again. Luckily, my womb went for the low, dragging ache of early contractions (as I imagined them), rather than the full-blown, exploding labour pains which it was also capable of when it shed its eggs. I envied again the sharks with their sea purses, their neat and separate egg boxes. Clean. By the time I got to use those condoms they'd be perished, I thought.

We were still wrapped up together when I woke up. A familiar ache, too familiar, made me open my eyes. I wasn't sure whether it was the ructions of the night before that had caused it or not, at first, so I staggered to the rats' nest, armed with my bag, to find out. The nest was looking pebble-dashed and unpretty. I spent as little time in there as possible. I felt odd, actually. Everything seemed unreal, there was a sort of background music ringing in my head and my colour hadn't improved at all either.

Clutching my bag, I returned to the bedroom, waking Dominic at the same time. He leant up on one elbow and looked at me questioningly. 'What are you doing? Christ, you look awful.'

'Thanks. My period's started, that's all,' I told him. He groaned, and sat up fully. 'I know. I've hardly been every man's dream date this weekend, have I?'

'I don't mean that. Get back into bed. It's just that it's the last thing you need today, isn't it?' Dominic pulled back the quilt for me. 'Are you feeling better at all?'

'Sort of. I feel funny, really. Not sick or anything – just unwell.'

'No wonder. I bet the bathroom looks like a war-zone.' He laughed. 'Poor Eric.'

'Don't.'

'You must be really dehydrated. Do you think you dare eat anything?'

'I don't know. What do you think?'

'I'll go to the shops and get you something. What do you want?

What about hot chocolate? And toast? And soup – aren't you supposed to drink soup when you're ill?'

'Dry things, I suppose. Toast sounds good.'

Dominic jumped out of bed. 'I'll be back in a minute. Then I'll sort the bathroom out.' I groaned then, feeling sick all over again just at the thought. 'I know, it'll be a first.' He started to get dressed.

'I need a bath as well.'

'Okay. I'll put the immersion heater on.'

I heard the whirr of an ancient boiler after he'd reached the bottom of the stairs and then the slam of the horrible brown door. I never wanted to move again.

Ten minutes or so later, Dominic was back, thumping up the stairs. He pulled open the curtains then sat on top of the bed, pulling open bags like Santa. 'Look – I've got everything.' There was yeasty-smelling brown bread with sesame seeds on it, and he'd been to the chemist. 'This is to replace minerals and salts and all the things you lost through the puking.' Do chemist's powders have calories? 'And here are some pain-killers in case your tummy gets sore.'

I laughed. 'Tummy's a Dalmatian word.'

He smiled. 'And here's some bubble bath. And magazines. All girls like magazines. And chocolate, for when you feel up to it later.' He pulled out a bottle next. 'Lucozade. Always makes you feel better.'

'I'm going home later.'

'I was thinking about that. You know I can't normally see you all weekend, what with my revision and everything – and yours, really?'

I hadn't known actually but I just said, 'Yes.'

'Well, why don't I shed the party tonight? You're not going to revise anything today, are you, the state you're in?' Subtle. 'You could ring Uncle Mark. I could revise there, at my desk, beside you all day. And look after you. If you felt up to it, we could go out tonight, then I could take you back to Leeched tomorrow. How does that sound?'

Dominic was right, really. I'd only planned to do a couple of hours' work in the afternoon anyway. And I liked the idea of being beside him all day, watching him while he worked.

Family-esque. 'Well – I suppose you have bought all those magazines.'

'Great.' He was grinning – a very young, wide grin. 'Go and ring Uncle Mark now. Get it over with. I'll walk you to the phone box. It's just up the street.'

The phone call was soon over with and later, after much cleaning, cursing and energetic action, I smelled a sweet, drifting scent. Bath time!

My mind drifted as I lay among the bubbles, soaping all of the sickness out of my skin and hair. Lucozade . . . I hadn't been ill much, before. The last time I'd been really ill had been when I'd had 'flu – proper 'flu, where you can hardly walk and everything hurts. Uncle Mark had come into my room – knocking first, of course. 'I've brought you some vitamin C, lemon drinks, etcetera, etcetera.' He'd laid them on my bedside table. 'And this.' A great concession – *Smash Hits*. (Uncle Mark thought it was 'teenage rubbish'.) And then: 'I nearly got you some Lucozade, but I thought you were too old for that now.' I was twelve. He knew I loved Lucozade, even when I was well. Was he waiting all that time ago for me to grow up, to be old enough to leave? Waiting until I was old enough to let him pick up his life where it had left off when I was seven? Eleven years was a long time and he was a good man; I couldn't expect more of him. But I'd needed more – needed more still. The way Dominic had accepted me so completely the night before had made me aware of my need in a way that I never had been before. Dangerous.

I could hear him now, in the kitchen downstairs, making quite a lot of noise really, moving, muttering, swearing and clashing occasionally. God knows what he was up to. The rats' nest was steamy and hot. The clouds of steam were loosening some old dirt, which was trickling down the walls towards my water now. Having a bath had never tired me out like this before. I was lying back, with my hair on the surface, like a sleepy mermaid, drifting. Lucozade, bubbles, baths, water, floating. Dreaming.

Really loud bang on the door. 'Helena! Helena!' Dominic. Damn. I jerked myself up uncomfortably. Wetly. Had he knocked before?

'I'm coming out.' I jumped out instantly and made a grab for the towel at the same time. My head sang suddenly, and I fell back against the corner of the bath and the wall with a heavy bang. Double damn.

'What's that? Open the door!' Dominic's voice rang with annoyance. I wasn't having this argument again and I really wanted to be in bed. I didn't have the energy to match his. Another bang decided it and I unclicked the peeling silver bolt, pulling the towel around myself at the same time. 'Jesus! You are a fucking liability. Have you hurt yourself?' He pulled his dressing gown up around my shoulders, over the towel I was clinging to, and put his arm around me. 'Bed. Now.' I was marshalled to his room.

I sat down on the side of the bed, pushing my hair out of my eyes, and then remembered my period. Triple damn. 'I need the loo.' I grabbed my bag.

'For Christ's sake, hurry up then.'

Sure enough, the towel had a round, scarlet mark on it. I sorted myself out, then staggered back to the bedroom where Dominic was waiting for me. I got into bed in his dressing gown, pulling the towel, clean side out, in with me. Apart from the 'becoming a woman' speech from Uncle Mark, periods, blood, pain and mess had never been mentioned at Leeched Dry – any inappropriate stains had been dealt with very much when Uncle Mark wasn't around.

What should I do?

I tucked the towel in, to one side. 'I'll just take this home with me.' Dominic's eyes were questioning for a moment, then sharpened before a slow shaking of the head.

'Helena, Jesus fucked, which century are you living in?' He was really annoyed with me and I didn't understand why.

'What do you mean?'

Sitting down hard on the bed beside me, Dominic picked up the towel before I could stop him and shook the stain to the top. I blushed bright red. 'Women who can have babies bleed. Sam bleeds, Jen bleeds, my sister bleeds. You bleed. It's normal. It's right.' He put his hand on my stomach. 'I accept it. I accept you. Completely. It's the same as last night. People are sick sometimes. It's called being part of humanity. I don't want to go out with a fucking robot. The towel can go in the wash; the bathroom can be cleaned up; it's nothing. It doesn't matter.'

'It's not appropriate.' Etcetera. I was miserable. Predictable.

'Not appropriate?' He grabbed my arm, reddening my skin. 'Not fucking appropriate? I can't stand this. None of us are appropriate. That's not the point. We're big, we're complicated and we're messy. We eat, and shit, and puke, and live, for God's sake. And we live in skin, in bodies, with hair and holes. You have to accept yourself. And we have to accept each other. The differences are part of the point.'

He held his hand to the fresh circle of a bloodstain, and some of the red wetness transferred to his fingers; I was appalled and twisted my head away. His other hand touched my face and his voice softened suddenly. 'Helena, look.' He looked deep into my eyes – understanding me, reaching me. His eyes were bliss. 'Look.' Gesturing with his raised palm, his bloody fingers. 'Touch.' An invitation. I touched his hand with my hand. His eyes were intense. 'We all bleed. One blood.' My own blood was transferred back to me, my fingers, my palm, and I felt a tingle, like an electrical charge, go through me. Like a blessing, but more definite than anything that had ever happened to me in church. 'The differences are one part of the point, and the similarities are another.'

'The differences are embarrassing.'

'Not now. Not now that you're with me, now that you're a woman. It's a new time. Don't you see?' He laughed. 'Bloody Uncle Mark's got a lot to answer for.'

'I'd've been in trouble without him, Dominic. He's always been good to me – always.'

'Sorry. I know. And he made a better job of looking after you than I have. Did you hurt yourself getting out of the bath before?'

'No. I'm fine.'

'You're not. You should rest. I'll just get you some breakfast.'

I was glad of the chance to calm down as Dominic rushed around downstairs, making toast. I was especially glad I'd been able to avoid the food museum so far. It was probably more of a war zone than the rats' nest. The warm bath had soothed my stomach some and I was beginning to feel a bit better.

Dominic was balancing an enormous tray on one hand when

he came back into the bedroom. 'Good. You look almost human again. It's because you've been resting. You think too much.'

'You talk too much. And shout too much.' I wasn't used to the shouting at all.

Dominic's laugh roared out. 'Sorry. I keep forgetting that you're still a puppy.'

'Cheek. And you think you're the Lion King.'

The tray was dumped on to the bed and he grinned. 'Look what I've got for you.'

The tray held warm toast, hot chocolate, a tablet and some water. 'Eat now, while it's all still warm.' He handed me a piece of toast. 'Eat it slowly and you should be okay.'

'I do know how to eat.'

He raised his eyebrows, a wicked expression on his face, but at least he held back from saying the obvious. I ate one piece, a toasted quarter of a bun, and then another. I still felt all right. Relief. I swallowed a tablet and lay down. 'Will you brush my hair? Like last night?' I asked him.

His eyes smiled. 'Sure.'

I felt him brush my hair gently until I was almost asleep and then he lay down beside me and rested one hand on my stomach, warming the soreness away. I was naked beneath the dressing gown. Cancer, I thought, as I drifted, the sea crab, the deep sea creature from the watery womb of the earth. Loving damaged people. Loving scars. Dominic touched the side of my cheek with his lips and his nose, warming the skin there. 'Sleep now. It's all right. Sleep.' I fell into a doze at once.

'Sleep. Sleep. Macbeth doth murder sleep.' I remember that line from school, don't you? Most state schools do *Macbeth* because it's the shortest, and it's got action for both sexes in it – so the teacher said. Sounds good. So I wait until my kitten is asleep and claim a bit of action of my own. Dozing in the middle of the day. And I've got work to do.

She's in her cage, but I can get to her between the wires. She smells different – different from me and from the little blonde. I tickle her between the legs. I've been there before. She doesn't even seem to mind that any more, so what's the point then? I'm drinking coffee and eating some toast my mother's just made.

The coffee is minging – fucking cheap chicory stuff. I've told her about that before. No class. I pour the hot coffee right over the cage. Laugh. Get a hard on. Give kitty a buzz and me, all at the same time.

Perfect. I'm ready for the next stage.

I could hear him working as I slept. My hair felt wet and tangled but I felt safe within his room. I could hear him typing at the keyboard: clatter, clatter, clatter, clatter, and the noises came into my dreams. And then I could hear him moving stuff around – I opened my eyes and tried to focus in on him.

'What are you doing?'

Just getting my room ready, like. Making sure my mother and sister finally get the message. Marking my patch. I do like to leave my mark.

They only had four signs in the shop, but I've always been inventive. So I make the most of the four. Put *Do Not Disturb* on my bedroom door, and then *Disturb, Disturb* and *Disturb* underneath it. Told you they were stupid. And *Private* at the bottom. *Enter* I save for over the bed to impress the dirty blonde, if she ever gets that far. Plenty more *Private* parts inside – all the things I've told them over and over again never to touch: my books, CDs, CD ROMs, clothes, special magazines and specialist equipment. My drawer with my autumn girl's stone in it. My chair, my wardrobe. My bed. And almost the last sign inside, I've arranged especially for kitty – *Pet's Corner*.

He was arranging things – my things. 'What are you doing?' I said.

'I thought I'd put a few of your bits and pieces about, so you'd feel at home here.'

My cleanser was on his worktable, a couple of my little boxes were on the bedside table, and a book I'd brought was lying beside him. 'They're my things. You should ask me if you want to go in my bag.' It felt wrong.

'Sorry. Didn't think.' He shook his head slightly. 'Do you want your stuff around the place or should I put it back?'

'No. Leave it all where it is now. But don't forget to ask, another time.'

That made Dominic laugh then. 'Yes, ma'am. Can we forget it now?' I nodded.

The rest of the day and evening passed calmly. I rested and read – poems and magazines, magazines and poems. Dominic worked, read, wrote, swore, tutted, read, wrote, sighed and swore some more. In between all of this, he brought me tiny platefuls of food (some of which I ate), until I felt stronger and stronger. Almost back to normal. I slept again, then woke up all of a sudden.

'What time is it?'

Dominic was still at his desk, quiet now. 'Seven o'clock. How are you doing?'

'Better. I must be better: I'm bored.'

'Good. So am I. Do you want to get up?'

'Definitely. Are you finished?'

'More than finished. Stale. More than stale. Almost dead, really.' He stretched himself and put his pen down.

'Let's go out.'

'I'll get you some clothes.'

I brushed my hair (which took some doing) while he selected my clothes, then I slipped to the nest in my dressing gown to put my make-up on. Dominic shouted through the door, 'Your clothes are ready. Go easy with the trowel.'

'Get lost.' I lavished more mascara on. Definitely back to normal.

I returned to the bedroom.

'Do you want to meet up with the crowd who are off to the party? I know you probably won't feel like going to the actual party, but we could meet them for a drink beforehand.'

'Ugh! I couldn't.'

'A soft drink, then? And a chat?'

'Who'll be there? Whose party is it?'

'It's one of the lads from my course – a friend of Dixie's. So he'll be there, and Sam, Jen and Doug. And Sherry. And Jem. A few others as well. It'll be a good crowd.'

'Okay then. I'll just get dressed.'

The clothes that Dominic had laid out for me were an interesting combination and I examined them closely: a black bra and tiny black knickers (the private clothes) and a red silk top and longish, slim black skirt (the public clothes). He was watching me. 'Don't want to show your curves off too much. Especially if Jem's going to be there.' Curves. Again. I kicked him on the ankle – quite hard, actually. He howled and then tilted his head back, laughing.

'You deserved that.'

He laughed more. 'You know I don't mean it.'

Did he mean it? In fact, what with the puking, dieting, and tiny, half-eaten meals that day, I did feel noticeably thinner. One way to kick-start some weight-loss. I'd be under nine stones soon. I resolved to stick to mineral water that night. I pulled the clothes on quickly and, sure enough, they were slightly bigger on me than usual (apart from the underwear, naturally).

We were off to a different pub this time: the party was on Cromwell Street's side of Edinburgh, so we decided to walk to it. At first, I was feeling much better. Dominic was asking me all about my choice of degree course. Would the fact that I had £300,000 coming my way fairly shortly affect the way he felt about me, if he knew? I wondered. He was enthusing about Edinburgh. 'It's a great place to live. You'd love living here. And it'd be much easier for us to see each other, wouldn't it?'

'Unless I got a car, and carried on living with Uncle Mark.' I'd just started driving lessons at the time. Well, Dominic didn't like this idea. (Neither did I much, but that wasn't the point.)

'Why would you do that? No offence, Helena, but living with him doesn't seem to be exactly thrill-a-minute time. You'd have a much better time living in the city centre, or near it.'

No offence? Infuriating! 'I don't criticise your parents, do I? You've never even met him. He has his good points.'

'Well, that's another thing – he might have met someone to share his good points with by then: you said he was on the lookout. You don't want to be in a Jen situation at Leeched Dry, do you?'

'I thought you said that it worked well between the three of them?'

'You know what I mean.'

I'd had enough of being in victim-mode for one weekend. 'I

might go to a different university altogether, anyway. Or not go to university at all.'

'Stay Uncle Mark's little puppy forever?'

'If I want to.'

'"If I want to." I told you you were young, didn't I?'

The 'told you' made me bristle more than anything. 'And I said you talked too much, didn't I?'

At this stage we reached the pub so I was spared his response. Why was he so caring at some times and so critical at others? He seemed to think I was *his* little Dalmatian puppy. I didn't need his advice all of the time. 'I'll go to the bar,' I said, deciding.

'Okay, if that's what you prefer.' Ice Man again, instantly. He pointed at one of the pumps. 'I'll have a pint of that.' And he was off.

I felt suddenly awkward, left on my own in a strange pub. I hadn't been eighteen for long. What if the barman questioned my age? I couldn't stand any more humiliation. But my height served me well and so did the barman (a sparkle in his eye and a diamond in his tooth – zirconia, probably), and with mineral water and beer in hand(s) I was soon swinging around to find Dominic.

'Helena!' Sam saw me before Dominic did. (He was engrossed in a conversation with Dixie-the-Dreadlocked.) They were all dressed up, looking more of a mix-up than ever. Dominic hadn't mentioned that. Sam waved me over to the seat beside her, several seats away from where Dominic was sitting. My heart sank until I remembered his latest puppy comment, then I straightened up and smiled brightly, pushing his drink over towards him cheerfully. He gave a neck-cracking nod, and then Sam was engaging me in conversation with her usual subtle approach. 'Eric said you had a bit of an explosion in the bathroom last night. Rather you than me. OK now?'

'Fine, thanks.'

'Got Dominic clearing the bathroom up, anyway – amazing. Well done. Was it too much wine?'

'Amongst other things.'

Sam was wearing a short black tunic, black stockings and a dog collar. Her purple hair sprouted above all this incongruously.

'Vicars and Tarts,' she said, noticing my stare. 'Didn't Dom mention it?'

'We're not going to the party itself – we just came out for a drink.'

'I didn't dare come as a tart – Doug's such a bitch. You could have got your legs out again, though. Had all of the men fighting over you.' Her eyes twinkled, and I laughed.

'I'm not sure about that.'

I looked around at all of their costumes. Dominic was sand-wiched in between Dixie and Sour Sherry. Dixie was wearing a priest-like robe with a big chain around his neck, which his dreadlocks were touching ceremoniously. Sherry had 'got her legs out', right up to the dark stocking tops. Vampire bat. Her sharp knees were nudging right into Dominic's thighs. She was wearing a very tight black crop top, and her boobs looked rounder and very inviting. Bigger than mine. Cute rather than dangerous, Jen was dressed in a pencil skirt and high heels, and Doug, who was sitting beside her, was a fairly rounded, self-important-looking vicar.

Just then, Jeremy and his twinkling nose bounded across from the bar. 'Helena, why aren't you dressed up?' He pulled a seat up to me, a look of sheer delight on his face because Dominic was too far away to do anything about it. 'I bet Dom didn't tell you, did he? And I was really looking forward to seeing those classical legs again.'

'What are you?' I asked – a fair enough question. Jem was wearing a lot of black eyeliner and very tight trousers.

'What do you want me to be, Helena?' His eyes glittered wickedly, emphasised by the sooty blackness around them. 'Your pimp or your rent boy?'

I laughed. Jem was as irrepressible as ever. 'Neither. What a choice!'

'That's a coward's answer.'

Something about the set of Dominic's jaw spurred me on. 'A rent boy, then – I don't fancy being pushed around by some old pimp.'

'As you wish. Am I pretty enough for you, then?'

'Just.' I couldn't help laughing at him. Dominic's jawline looked more rigid still. His face was all bone and tension.

He deliberately didn't look towards me. This strengthened my resolve. He wanted me to live near him – to leave the sort-of-security of Leeched Dry and Uncle Mark behind. Let's see if he was prepared to put himself out, see if he was strong enough to meet my many needs. And strong enough to resist Sour Sherry's thighs, which were still pointing towards him at a threatening – or inviting – angle.

Jeremy was still talking. 'A fantastic opportunity has been missed here tonight, Helena.'

'What do you mean?'

'You, of course – you. In whatever guises you might have wished to present yourself.' He lifted my hair. 'Helena the tart of Troy obviously.' He considered me. 'Or Alice in Wonderland – with a few optional extras, perhaps.' And finally, 'Definitely a sex kitten with style – a bit of supple, feline splendour of the first order.' He bowed to Sherry's laughter. 'Now, how do you see me?'

I could feel a crackle of tension coming from both sides. Sam was listening intently – one eye on Dominic and one eye on me – while he had given up the pretence of chatting to Dixie altogether, despite studiously appearing to ignore me. Difficult. Go for a relaxed approach. 'Oh, I don't know, Jem. Isn't it something like rent boy runs off at the mouth, or pimp without a purpose? You tell me.'

'So young, and yet so cutting.' He looked mock-wounded. 'Rapunzel with razor blades – beneath the wig. It is a wig, isn't it?' He tugged at my hair lightly, not perhaps realising that he was pulling at Dominic's emergency cord as he did so.

'Enough, Jem.' Again, I heard the low voice that Dominic rarely used. He wasn't looking at me, but he held Jeremy's gaze with a threatening sideways stare. Silence surrounded us.

'Dom by name and Dom by nature, eh, Dominic? Why don't you let the lovely Helena speak for herself?' The lightness of Jem's tone belied his words. The silence crackled, then waited. Waited for me to speak.

'Come on, Jem. Act the professional – a cheap and cheerful approach and then on to the next conquest.' I tried a tentative laugh.

'Cheerful but never cheap, Helena. Don't underestimate me.'

He got up and bowed toward me. 'I'll be back soon. Would you like a little wine to help you through this duel?'

Dominic's fists clenched and I said quickly, 'No, thanks, not so noble Jeremy. I've got a drink here.' I smiled to soften the words. He bowed again, and was gone. Sam got up to follow him, her little tunic bobbing simultaneously with her purple head. I couldn't hear most of what she was saying, but the word 'arsehole' drifted back clearly enough at one point.

Empty seats lay to either side of me now and I felt suddenly exposed. Then Dominic was sitting beside me, startling me. 'Can I have a word, Helena?' He moved his stool back from the group slightly, forcing me to follow. He looked right into my eyes – hard. Ow! Was that a technique they taught would-be lawyers? It wasn't an expression I'd seen before: intense yet cold, harder altogether. 'If you *want* Jem, then go with Jem. Now. But don't put me through this. Just don't.'

I was alarmed but defiant. 'Then don't tell me what to do. And don't ignore me. Anyway, you know I'm not interested in Jem.'

Dominic looked surprised for a moment, then thoughtful. He glanced away, and then looked back at me – intense again but closer somehow. He nodded. 'Understood.' He pressed my arm and looked at me once more before moving back to sit beside Dixie just as I heard Jem and Sam come back from the bar and settle in beside me. Sour Sherry repositioned herself immediately, almost nuzzling Dominic and whispering something in his ear that I couldn't quite hear. I felt tired suddenly. Dominic focussed on me directly across the table. 'Are you all right, Helena?' he asked, seriously.

I nodded, and Sam chipped in, 'Of course she's all right, Dom,' and began chatting to me once again, blocking Jeremy out of the conversation completely. 'I was desperate to come as a tart, you know, but Doug can make such predictable comments.' She was deliberately speaking loud enough for him to hear. 'Of course, he's been a complete slapper in the past – haven't they all? – but that's different. How he managed it, I don't know, with his bowel problem. It must be one of the lesser-publicised fetishes with women – the Fart Fetish.'

'That's all ye know, Sam,' Doug retaliated. 'Any real woman

can see ma attraction, Helena – pure animal magnetism.' His broad Scottish chest inflated, despite the deafening stereo hooting of Sam and Jen.

'The costume's right anyway, Doug. Father Fart to a T,' said Jen, and they hooted again. Doug was obviously pretty difficult to deflate.

'Girls, girls,' interrupted Jem. 'How is the male ego to survive this onslaught?'

'The male ego has had its day, Jem.' It was for his ears and Dominic's.

'It's as full of wind as Doug's lower bowel,' cackled Sam, and Jen joined in again. Doug joined in the noise with one proud blast.

A couple of minutes later, as I was idly listening to more banter, Dominic appeared at my side, hunkering down so that his face was level with mine. 'How are you doing?'

'Fine, thanks.' I smiled at him.

'Do you want to go back soon?'

'No, I'm enjoying myself.' The conversation was lively enough, and I'd been cooped up in one room all day.

'I'll get you a drink, then.'

'Just mineral water.'

'Why don't you try some fruit juice? Get some vitamins at the same time.'

This amused Jem, still sticking to my side. 'Doctor Dom,' he laughed. 'I'll buy you a vodka and orange, Helena. The vodka'll do you more good than the vitamins.'

'No, thanks, Jem.' I wanted to defuse this one at once and smiled at Dominic. 'Mineral water would be great.' Fruit juice had calories in it. Dominic headed towards the bar.

Sam was still engaged with Jen in a character assassination of Doug, so I tried what seemed like a fairly safe topic of conversation with the ever-ready Jem. 'I've still not seen Eric out of his room at all yet. Is it because of his exams?'

'We're all in the middle of exams, but Saturday nights are sacred.' He bowed towards Dixie. 'Eric spends just about all of his time in that bedroom. I dread to think what's lurking below the floorboards in there.'

Dominic reappeared then with the drink and made to pull

up a stool beside me but Sherry shouted, 'Dom!' and patted the seat beside her. 'Dixie doesn't know what to do about his holidays – America in a sports camp or France in a camper van.' Her stocking tops pointed at Dominic. He smiled at me over his shoulder, returning to his former seat. I smiled back, determined not to let her see that she was getting to me, and resumed my conversation with Jeremy.

'We could meet at midnight tonight,' he was saying, 'leave everyone else at the party and wait until Eric was asleep, carry him into Dom's room, put some heavy metal on in the background so that he'd feel at home. We could prise up the floorboards, open the cupboards, search for his trophies and uncover his innermost secrets.' He was triumphant. 'Then we could search for *your* trophies, and uncover *your* innermost secrets.'

'Thanks, Jem, but I'll keep my secrets covered up and my trophies to myself for now.'

'Spoilsport,' Jem sighed. 'No sense of adventure. Well, let me know if you change your mind.'

'No, Eric can lie safe in his bed.'

'It wasn't Eric's bed I was thinking of.'

I laughed and turned to Sam, who rescued me with some Eric stories – records he had supposedly broken: longest time spent alone in a bedroom, ever; longest time spent in the bath, ever; longest time spent at Cromwell Street without speaking to anyone, ever. I don't know how much of it was true, but all of it was funny.

At about 10 o'clock, I suddenly started to feel really tired. Dominic came over to my side, stopping Sherry mid-sentence (which was gratifying, not to mention an achievement in itself), pulled up a stool and put his arm around me. 'You look done in. Let's go back.' I nodded and we said our goodbyes amidst descriptions of what we would be missing and so on.

What do you think was the first thing Dominic said when we got out into the street? 'I could've cut Jem's balls off tonight.' It was almost exactly what I would have predicted.

'He was only flirting, Dominic. He was doing the same with Jen later. It's best to let me handle it; it was nothing.'

Dominic nodded. 'Okay. It's just I've got a bit of a short fuse about that kind of thing, that's all.'

'You don't say?'

We both laughed, and he relaxed and wrapped his arm around my shoulder. 'You seem a lot better, anyway.'

'Yes, I feel great. Just a bit more tired than usual.'

He bent down and rubbed my ear with his nose. 'I'll carry you upstairs to bed then, when we get in.'

'Sounds good.'

'I've been thinking about your bum and your little cunt in those black knickers for hours.'

'Dominic!' People wandering between pubs surrounded us, but no one seemed interested in what he'd said, if they'd heard. 'Did you spare a thought for Sherry's knees? Or Sherry's thighs? They've been resting against you all night.'

'What?' He looked nonplussed.

'Nothing.' I let it drop. But his head tilted and I realised he was pleased that I was jealous of Sherry. 'Maybe I was mistaken. It is hard to imagine.'

He tilted his head back more, then, and gave out his roaring laugh, his teeth shining. 'Cheek!' He laughed again. 'Shit, I've picked up one of your Dalmatian words.' We walked on, and his arm stroked my shoulder through my jacket. 'Speaking of which, what've you brought to wear in bed tonight, now that the Dalmatian's finally been put down?'

'Something short, sexy and feminine.' I was teasing him, enjoying the fact that I knew what excited him. He groaned loudly. 'And chosen especially with you in mind.'

We'd reached the terrible door and I half expected Dominic to carry me upstairs and throw me on the bed there and then. But he started to lead the way into the living room first. He caught my glance, his own eyes alive. Turning all at once, he lifted me off the floor and literally ran upstairs to the bedroom with me in his arms, laughing. But when he put me down on the bed he was careful and said almost shyly, 'You get changed. I'll just get a glass of water.'

I went into the loo and then changed straight into my new nightdress, glad that I was feeling so much better – in every way. It was thigh-high and firmly waisted, midnight blue, with tiny slits at the sides. I hoped my legs looked more inviting than Sherry's had: I mean, they were definitely longer.

There were so many things I didn't know about, physical things, and lying curled on the bed waiting for Dominic I cooled, beginning to worry about some of them. I wound the quilt around myself protectively. An urgent thudding on the stairs showed me that Dominic hadn't cooled any. He burst through the door with a glass of water in his hand and got undressed while I took a sip of the cold liquid.

Dominic jumped into bed, wearing just his underpants and T-shirt, but when he saw my face, he looked worried too. 'Do you feel sick?'

'No.'

'Are you sore?' He felt my stomach with his hand.

'No. It's not that.'

'What then?' My stomach rumbled slightly beneath his hand, as if in reply. 'You won't be sick now. Should I get you something to eat?'

'No. I'm not really hungry,' I said (although I was, a bit, but I didn't want to have to hold my stomach in even more).

Dominic thought for a minute, looking at me – the crab, searching below the surface of the sand. Then he smiled. 'Not hungry, not sick, not sore, yet not speaking. Let me guess what you're going to say. It must be an Uncle Mark-type worry about something . . . something completely inappropriate. And absolutely unmentionable.' He barked his laugh.

'Patronising pig!'

'But not wrong?' Fish-like silence. 'What might you be worrying about?' He pulled the quilt away from me. 'There's quite a choice. What if I bleed over Dominic? It wouldn't matter. What if he makes me have full sex, despite the fact that I think my own blood is disgusting? You know I wouldn't do that. What if I change my mind, because I don't feel sexy because of my period? Is that it?'

'Amongst others.'

'Well, I might have a bit of an ache for a while, but it wouldn't kill me, and it wouldn't be the first time. Is there anything else?'

'I think you've got it just about covered.' I hauled the quilt back up to my chest, tucking it tightly around me.

'For fuck's sake, stop worrying.' He pulled his T-shirt off and the quilt down. 'Let me see you properly.' Dominic ran his hands over my bare shoulders and down my sides, nipped my waist tightly between his long hands, then his mood mellowed visibly. 'Your bones are so fine.' Still holding my waist, he played with one nipple, mouthing through the silky material, then looked upwards to my eyes. 'Did you really think of me when you bought this?' His voice was quiet, serious.

'Yes.'

'What did you think?' Dominic's beautiful eyes were seeing right into me.

'I thought, What would Dominic think was sexy? What kind of fabric would his fingers like to touch? Which parts of my body would he like me to emphasise?' I thought of Sherry, briefly. 'How much of my legs would he like to see?' I touched his nipple now, caressed his slightly hairy chest with its wonderful muscles. 'That sort of thing.' I placed my hand over the front of his underpants. 'You feel really big and strong there.' I rubbed him slightly. Greenish eyes were locked into mine, but when I touched his cock they closed and he tilted his head back, making a deep noise in the back of his throat. Then he focussed on me again.

'Helena – don't touch me there. I've wanted you for days; I'll come in seconds if you touch me there.'

I kissed his chest, moved. 'That's all right.'

'But what about you?'

Jumping off the bed, he pulled me to my feet. 'Just stand up – all tall and lovely.' I held myself rigidly, not knowing what to expect. Kneeling on the floor, he buried his head in my stomach briefly, bringing the image of my sea purse flooding into my mind, and then he stood beside me. 'I want to look at you. If you weren't so fucking squeamish, I'd look at you everywhere. Never mind.' I felt self-conscious yet excited as he examined me, thoroughly yet lovingly, seeming to note me down in his memory.

Gentle lips touched my shoulders and neck first, in tiny, poppy-petal kisses. Then he turned me around and felt my spine and shoulders through the slippery material, kissing my neck again, the back this time, squeezing my waist, almost measuring it. I was glad I'd lost a few pounds. Then he drew his long fingers up the inside and back of my thighs. I felt his tongue and lips on the backs of my knees. 'I like to see your legs. Right the way up.' Then he pulled the nightdress off over the top of my head, and when my hair fell down, he lifted it over the front of my shoulders. He fingered the tops of my thighs for minutes, touching and exploring, and then I felt his fingers on the – now highly charged – silk-skimmed piece of flesh between my legs. His hand stroked my sex through the silky knickers until my legs felt weak.

Turning me around to face him, Dominic pulled me on to his bare chest. I smelled his skin and hair and pressed into his muscles, fingering the base of his spine. Long arms held me to him, with one hand covering the small of my back and the other pressing my sensitised bottom to him. I knelt on the floor and pressed my lips to his cock, through the white fibre, and grazed my teeth along it. Enamel and cotton, hard and soft. Then I held him around the hips and rubbed my nipples against the swell of his lovely cock, trying to show him that I appreciated his body as he appreciated mine.

'Helena – don't. It's wonderful, but don't,' he said, drawing me up to face him, and then he lifted me up from under my arms, making me wrap my legs around his waist like a monkey. As he stepped back into the big old armchair, the bulge of his penis was pressed against the area between my legs. I enfolded his thighs in my thighs, put my hands on the chair arms, and enjoyed the feeling of his cock growing between my legs. His thumb rubbed my clitoris and I felt a red warmth there. I lifted slightly, so that he could massage the whole area with his hand, and so that I could reach him inside his underpants. I rubbed firmly and rhythmically with my fingers. My legs strained. The feelings his fingers were making were really urgent and intense, more so than ever before, and I kissed his face as overpowering feelings warmed and then shook me, right to the centre of my stomach, breasts and sex. I fell against him, squeezing him harder than I'd meant to, and again I said his name. I *loved* saying his name. 'Dominic.' Twisting, he cried out once and came instantly, holding my sex to him with one hand and the back of my waist with the other.

Several minutes passed as we lay entangled in each other

in the old chair. Then I opened my eyes and looked at him, wondering. Did it feel as intense, and wonderful, and definitely right to him as it did to me? I touched Dominic's face and he opened his eyes. I tried to ask him with my eyes, to ask him how he felt. 'You are gorgeous. Absolutely gorgeous.' His eyes flicked down towards my stomach briefly. 'And didn't bleed once.' I turned my face away from his and his hand guided it back at once. 'Sorry, Helena. I keep forgetting your Uncle Mark squeamishness.' Putting both arms around me, he whispered through my hair, 'You are absolutely beautiful. I love making love with you.'

'I didn't do anything.'

'That was more than enough. Just looking at you practically made me come tonight. And you know just how to touch me.'

I nuzzled against him. 'Maybe you'd like to touch all of me next time. Inside as well.' I touched his now tender cock. 'Properly.'

Dominic's eyes smiled as he brushed back my hair. 'Helena, that would be brilliant – but I can wait until you're ready. Until you're certain.' He carried me into bed, snuggling me into him when we got there.

'Maybe next time,' I whispered, and I stroked his bony, beautiful head through his hair until he fell asleep.

How would you feel if I told you that I slept soundly that night? That we lay curled against one another, cocooned by a powerful mutual trust? That the last thing I thought before I fell asleep was that I could sense the steady pulsing of Dominic's soul, coming through his skin and connecting to my soul? A bit strong, I know, but that's how it was.

The point at which I started to really trust him, to *stop* worrying, is perhaps the point at which you *start* to worry about me. A man who can almost read a woman's mind – a very young woman's mind – and allay her fears is a dangerous man. A very powerful and seductive type, of course, which I enjoyed, but I'm sure you're aware of the potential problems. Have you noticed, I'd almost completely forgotten about the money and the second letter? Almost.

Wordsworth's two swans glided into my dreams that night, swimming across the surface of the loch, mirrored clearly in the water. Their souls were buzzing gently to one another, in an atmosphere of complete peace and repletion. Such rare peace. There was no sign of a little duckling with black, spiky hair, big boobs and lacy stocking tops, squawking to the big swan from the shore in my dreams that night.

I had no idea of what danger was lying in wait for me – both outside and inside Dominic's arms.

You're there, then? Ignorant get. Thought you'd forgotten about me altogether. You do want to know what happened to kitty, don't you? I mean, I'd hate to bore you, like.

In fact, it was all a bit of an anti-climax. Kitty was saved. I'd had a brilliant idea, involving a firework and a very sensitive area of kitty's anatomy, like, inspired by the leaflet from the animal shelter, which I thought was a pleasingly ironic touch.

Then, just when I come in with all of the stuff, kitty disappears. Like the rat. Bit of a coincidence that, don't you think? I know who the animal freedom fighter is when I think about it, like. My mother. She never got over what I did to the dog before, even though it was dead and everything.

She's never had a clue about me, my mother – no idea what to make of me. The worst thing about our house, street even, is that there's nobody with any life in it, apart from me, I mean. Grey, stone-smashed walls, and grey, stoned, smashed people. A deadness. *'Nothing is a problem for me,'* as Damien Hirst says. We've all got our ways out – mine is the Internet, my books, my pictures, and my heroes. My plans. My sister's is dense boys, cheap clothes and other people's snotty babies; my mother's is telly, cigarettes and men. The last one she tried to move in looked like he'd swallowed a beach ball – fucking fat bastard. Not that he was the one doing the swallowing, like, from what I could hear. So now it's just the telly. Wherever you are in our house you can hear it droning on – the whine of soap opera arguments.

School's supposed to be the way out: fifteen minutes with the careers' officer to sort out your life. I suggested film director, scriptwriter, artist. He looked bored stiff and suggested a modern apprenticeship. Slavery, the most ancient apprenticeship in the world. Who was the fucking apprentice, me or him? I had more vision in my last little finger joint than he had in the whole of his body.

The only growing trade around where I lived was DIY off-licences in people's front rooms, selling cheap, smuggled booze and fags to school kids – polluting the little bastards for good. The school buildings looked like something out of Bangladesh – mobiles stinking of mould, damp paper and piss. Smoking Suzie dragged out of the science cupboard and the 1950s, with her jam jar lungs filled with tarry cotton wool – teacher made sure to pass the cotton wool around so that we could all get properly contaminated with the forty-odd-year-old fag fumes. Very considerate. Just like home. Except at least at home there were CD Roms, and science programmes where you could turn into a particle of nicotine, get inside a vein and shoot around some poor fucker's diseased heart, having a good look. The whole of school was one big diseased heart – I spent as little time there as I could. I preferred a hi-tech, Pic and Mix approach.

There are ways of being poor that are different, like in *Living in America*, the Bronx. All those braziers. A kind of black, alive poverty. I could hack that. Now when my dad used to come home sometimes, it was different. Then you got energy, electricity, a kind of crackling blackness – a jolt into life. I hated the bastard – fucking hated him. And I still can't stand the smell of drink, like (his way out, not mine). But at least you knew you were alive and I think I got kind of addicted to that.

That's what kitty was going to plug me into. Maybe my mother enjoyed her mercy mission. Anyway, the cat's gone for good now.

The firework will come in handy for another time.

9

'I made another world, and real men would enter it and they would never get hurt at all in the vivid unreal laws of the dream'

– Brian Masters, *Killing For Company*

I'll gloss over the next few weeks. A lot of time was taken up in exam preparations, and you don't want to read about those, do you? (Bad enough having to do the things.) Anyway, we worked towards our exams and our relationship grew.

The promised penetration didn't happen the next time. (Don't worry – I won't gloss over *that* bit.) Oddly, it was Dominic who seemed reluctant to initiate it. Perhaps it represented a more complete commitment to him, I don't know, or maybe penetration itself isn't so important in the British post-baby boom of the crowded new millennium. Still, there was an awful lot (almost everything) for us to explore without that, so our repertoire was building up nicely.

I enjoyed most of it actually, proving to be very *un*squeamish when it came down to it. The only thing I didn't fancy was oral sex (me to him – fellatio – ridiculous word). I didn't like the thought of all that sperm in my mouth, although I was quite happy with the penis itself. Dominic just laughed, said it wasn't surprising really, given 'Uncle Mark, etcetera'. (He did quite an impression, having met him by this time.) Then, more thoughtfully, that he wasn't sure if he'd like it if he was a girl – hard to breathe, for one thing. So that was okay.

My diet progressed, although I never mentioned it to Dominic.

The funny thing was, he usually made a point of watching what I ate when we were together, so I sensed that he knew I wasn't eating. Plus I was thinner. Yet every now and then – rarely, admittedly – he would make some kind of a curvy comment that would keep the whole thing going. As my emotional dependency grew, my body shrank. That was how it worked.

One thing that helped a lot with the shrinking was the change taking place in Uncle Mark's life. He'd had a few 'hot dinner dates' (jokette) over those weeks, and Leeched was a flurry of after-shave and new ties. I was relegated to the role of dresser and advisor. Uncle Mark immediately discovered he was an extremely eligible 'bachelor boy' and – much more slowly – worked out that his 'hot shot' legal job was the main attraction. This was a massive blow to his ego, obviously, and he soon – sort of – followed his own advice to me and played down his work and his salary. Anyway, the last thing on his mind was whether or not I was eating, so I was soon down to eight and a half stones. I felt good, strong, and I did look slim in just about anything. Getting below that weight was the problem.

Although Dominic would still sometimes ask, I continued to by-pass most questions about my parents. One night immediately after my exams were over there was a crescendo of questions too loud to ignore. Catastrophe.

I was feeling really excited that weekend – there was a lot to look forward to. It was the end of June and I'd been seeing Dominic for weeks. Months. My exams had finished just a couple of days before: I wasn't sure whether I'd got the grades I needed for university or not, it was down to Edinburgh or York, but I was hopeful. And, although I was being pretty cool about it, I was keen to go to Edinburgh – usually – to spend more time with Dominic (who planned to do his Diploma in Legal Practice there).

Life for Dominic was altogether more stressful. He had one exam left to do, and it was a big one, apparently. Medical Jurisprudence. Yuck. When I'd suggested waiting until his exams were completely over before meeting again, he'd been very definite. 'Just one night. I have to see you just once, or my week's going to be too fucking depressing for words. I'd never survive it. I'll work around it, around you. One night off will give me something to keep going for.'

So I felt very new and bright as I stepped on to the train to Edinburgh that night. Uncle Mark had bought me a new set of clothes to celebrate the end of my schooldays, and I'd gone for a short, narrow skirt, a very soft, silky black jacket and some spiky shoes. My hair was braided into a long rope, held high on my head and swinging down my spine. The train itself was far from glamorous but, for the first time, I was aware that the movement was somehow erotic. It seemed to be chanting to me, a familiar chant – Dominic, Dominic, Dominic Oliver – and even the bumping up and down was really quite pleasant. Plus there was the added edge that I was wearing stockings for the first time.

It's funny how you can feel eyes on you, isn't it? I mean, at first I was aware of several men's eyes on my legs, men being pretty predictable animals. The smeared glass of the window to my left suddenly seemed interesting, alternating with the glossy magazine I'd brought with me. But then I felt a new feeling – almost a charge. I turned my head round to look up into eyes that I'd seen before – eyes that were totally focussed on me for seconds before they pulled away. Where had I seen him? He was locked into a part of my mind I couldn't get to just then. I only knew that he'd looked different the last time I'd seen him.

There was something wooden about him and, strangely something strong and attractive too. It was odd seeing the gleam in the eyes within that wooden body; he was an animated ventriloquist's dummy of a man. And he was sitting beside a girl. Despite his woodenness, or perhaps because of it, he was the one in control while she was a limp rag doll, white and beaten, with a worn-looking bruise around the eye nearest to me. Two dolls I didn't want to play with. And I didn't feel they should be playing with each other. I was sure they were together, yet they joggled as separate toys on separate thighs of the train's lap. I was glad that I'd be getting off the train shortly. I turned away from them and moved my mind's eye back to Dominic.

His aim was a first-class honours degree and he was putting himself under massive pressure to achieve that. His father had 'taken' a first, and Dominic had a very strong sense that, for him, anything less constituted complete failure. Have you noticed how some men 'take' charge of everything? Even filling a car with petrol is an act of mastery! The twenty-second birthday party was looming ahead unmentioned and I still hadn't met any of Dominic's family. Despite his annoyance when I'd been reluctant to talk about my parents, I didn't know that much about his. From what Dominic had said, his father seemed pretty forceful.

Consequently for Dominic that weekend at least ten years of ambition was building to an inescapable head, whereas my champagne bottle had popped and I was ready to drink from the glass. I'm sure you could make a few predictions now but I was just eighteen and reacted to pressure very differently from Dominic, so I was still innocently looking forward to a good weekend.

As I walked into his arms from the train, I thought, not for the first time lately, that I was close to leaving behind Leeched Dry and its antiquated attitudes for good. I hugged Dominic, breathing him inside me appreciatively. Need. The train journey had been my idea – an unusually selfless gesture to give him some precious extra revision time before meeting me. My heels clicked on the concrete as I stepped back and looked into his face, expecting him to be pleased to see me, but no. His smile was a movement only – somewhere between the dreaded Ice Man and normal flesh and blood.

'Congratulations,' he said. He kissed me and handed me a parcel, so I knew then that his mood wasn't deliberate or personal – more a culmination of the tortures of studying for four years towards a top degree in a subject he didn't enjoy.

'What is it, Dominic?' I turned the shiny parcel over in my hands.

'It's a Helena's-Highers-Are-Over present.' The second smile was a bit better. My Dominic. 'Come on, let's get out of here.' His arm drove me forwards. 'Train stations are fucking depressing.'

Not having seen each other for a week, we'd arranged to go somewhere quiet so that we could talk. I put my present under my arm and we headed for the higgledy little streets near the Castle where Dominic had found a tiny, tucked away pizzeria that had just changed hands. He kept talking about his exams as we walked, while I was feeling very slim, shiny and smug in my new clothes, with my own exams way behind me. I mentioned Uncle Mark's celebratory generosity to Dominic briefly, hoping that he would comment on my new clothes or appearance – I'd spent *hours* getting ready. (Plus, it was the first time I had worn a short skirt since the curvy comment, but I was confident that, at eight and a half stones, most parts of my body were pretty acceptable.) Dominic's reply was fairly abrupt, though. 'Celebrate the end of your highers? Uncle Mark *will* be celebrating. He can really go for bachelorhood now, can't he? What with you at university and him at his *Luncheons for Lechers*, or *Dinners for the Desperate*, or whatever.'

My face fell. He hadn't even noticed what I was wearing. And my feet were starting to hurt. It would be better in the restaurant, I reasoned, when we could talk to each other properly and relax a bit.

But Dominic didn't relax. He was bloody. He talked about his finals, and kept returning to his dread that he would get a 2:1 (which sounded like a good enough degree to me – Uncle Mark had got a 2:2 and he'd done all right, but I wasn't going to mention that). Black worries were interspersed with repeated statements about how sure he was that he *would* get a first, and lists of all the assignments and exams in which he had *already* achieved a first. Riveting stuff.

The silver wrapping paper around my present shimmered at me and I tried to lighten the atmosphere at our table as we waited for our food to arrive by opening it. Great. It was a glossy hard-back book all about Will Jackson – his life, his background and his work. I was genuinely entranced, remembering our visit to the art gallery of all those weeks before, but Dominic's gloom would not shift. 'I don't know why I bought you that. I could see how taken you were with him that day – I don't want to be traded in for an arty joiner. Christ, why did I do law?'

'Shut up, Dominic – you just did!' I was getting impatient with him now. 'And you've only got one exam left. It's a lovely book. Thank you.' I kissed his rigid cheek.

The food arrived then but he refused to have his mood lifted. Every song that was played in the background seemed to affect him. I sighed, knowing I was in for a long night. The house white was really acidic – more of a salad dressing than a drink – and I swallowed a glass or two suspiciously, while Dominic worked his way through the rest at unusual speed. He kept looking away from me, listening in to other people's conversations and watching the waiting staff critically. The couple beside us had a lengthy conversation about the girl's mother, who just 'wouldn't let go', and Dominic's face soured even more as he listened. I was gamely trying to eat a small amount of pizza and a filling amount of salad, almost wishing I hadn't come, when he turned his vinegary attention back to me. 'They think they've got problems. I'm seeing someone who doesn't even seem to *have* a mother – the Immaculate Conception with a sex change.'

Enough! I slapped his face – hard. 'You miserable bastard!' It didn't sound like my voice. Dominic's neck cricked – both the words and the slap were new to him; in fact they were new to me (not very Dalmatian at all). There was an angry red mark over his cheekbone and heads turned towards us, but I was past caring. Didn't he realise how awful he was being?

'Helena, I . . .' But I was off, leaving him with his ungraciously given present and the bill to grapple with as I made for the station with a mouth full of salad and a heart full of hate.

I got to the end of the street before he caught me up. I was appalled at his words, but also appalled by the fact that I'd hit him – my Dominic.

'You made me do that. You made me hit you. How could you say that, and how could you make me hit you?'

'I know, you're right. I'm sorry.' His hands spread in an apology. 'I was getting rid of a whole load of crap that wasn't anything to do with you.' I thought he was going to let it drop, but no. 'It's just, I don't understand. It's such a basic thing – your mother, your parents. Why can't you just talk to me about it?' I turned to him, blazing, my anger snaking out in waves around me.

'Listen to me this once. Basic is the right word, Dominic – it's a basic human desire to have parents, a basic human need. There's nothing simple about it, though, if that's what you mean. It's almost impossible, growing up without parents; it's difficult all the time. That's why I don't talk about it, don't try to put it into pointless words. When I want to talk about it, I will, but I don't talk about it to anybody.'

Dominic backed away. 'I've never seen you so angry.'

'Well, I've never seen you so callous. Or insensitive.'

I walked away from him again, although I was heading for Cromwell Street this time, and didn't say a word to him until we reached the ugly brown door. The Ice Woman's first appearance. Slow footsteps behind me told me that Dominic was starting to feel ashamed.

Sam and Jen were talking in the living room with some friends when I got in so I headed for the stairs and went straight up them to Dominic's room with him still trailing behind me. As the bedroom door closed behind us, I heard Sam's laughter ringing out and remembered her 'romantic enthusiasms' comment. I rounded on Dominic. 'Besides, why should you be the one person that I talk to about this? For all I know, I'm just one of a chain of girlfriends you've had in this room – on that bed.' I gestured towards it. 'You want me to turn myself inside out for you, just to satisfy your curiosity. Well, I can't open and close myself like a book.'

'No, Helena.' Dominic bent into the chair, let out a breath, and angled his head towards me. 'Look, I know I've been a bastard tonight, you're right. Hitting me I can take – you've got to hit somebody. Fairness is hardly the point when you've been left without either of your parents. What I can't take is that you won't talk to me about it all. Surely it's healthier to talk about things – especially something as important as your family?'

My anger was dissipating gradually. I walked over to his desk and rested my palms on it. I could see the messy piles of books and files there and his joyless revision timetable pinned to the wall. 'Helena' was pencilled in for Saturday night, with a big ring around it, and I sighed and sat on the bed facing him.

'I have talked about my father a bit with Uncle Mark, in the past.'

'And what about your mother?'

'Stop it!'

'You really never talk about all of this with anyone, do you?' Shock froze his features. Then he spoke again, very quietly. 'What the hell happened?'

Neither of us spoke for a couple of minutes. There were bursts of laughter, and wind, from downstairs, and the usual morose music thumped through from Eric's room. I went and sat on the arm of his chair. 'I can't. Leave it.'

Grabbing me, Dominic pulled me on to his knee and my new skirt rode up over my legs – the first public appearance of my stockings – but he didn't seem to have noticed. Wrapping one arm around my shoulders and the other around my legs, it was my eyes that he looked into. 'I'll leave it for now. But later you'll tell me – when you're ready.' He stroked my legs until a stocking top surprised his fingers. 'You look brilliant tonight – you were so happy when you got off the train. I'm sorry for upsetting you.'

'You mustn't try to bully me into telling you things. Or anything else.'

'I know. I try not to. I want to look after you, not hurt you, but sometimes,' he looked down, 'the two of them seem to get mixed up. Maybe I hurt you so I can look after you afterwards. I'm sorry.' His long fingers were caressing my legs again, soothingly, steadily.

'Well, I'm sorry for hitting you.' I stroked his face. 'I've never hit anyone before.'

'I know. You're really gentle, aren't you?' Dominic kissed my cheekbone, right on the spot where I'd hit his. 'Normally, I mean. It's me who always gets worked up about things, not you.' He looked over towards the mound of books and files with disgust. 'It's these fucking exams.'

'I know. We could have left it until after you'd finished.'

The intensity of his eyes was wonderful. 'The only thing that's kept me going this week is you, knowing I was seeing you.' He drew his hand down the heavy rope of my hair and his expression fed me. 'You're not a link in a chain, Helena. Not at all. I have had other girlfriends, obviously. But not like you.' His fingers touched the edge of a stocking top. 'I can't stop thinking about you.' He smiled. 'I'm obsessed.'

'It's not just sex?'

He barked his surprised laugh. 'We haven't had sex.'

I wriggled in his lap. 'You know what I mean.'

'No – not just sex, although I have been thinking about that a lot this week as well.'

'Good.'

Dominic smiled widely and scratched an eyebrow. 'Constantly

actually. I'll probably get a pass degree for law and a first for Helena's body.'

'Which bits have you been thinking about?'

'Your legs, obviously.' He looked down. 'Jesus, you look fucking gorgeous in these.' He outlined my thighs with his fingers, appreciating their length and new slenderness, until he reached bare skin. I stopped him.

'Dominic. Get undressed.' We both stood up as I undressed rapidly to my underwear, and he was soon standing before me in his proud yet awkward nakedness. I touched his fuzzy chest. 'I want to lie in your lap again but I'll be able to smell your skin now. I love the smell of your skin.' He bit his lip and pulled me on to his knee, sitting down in the same movement. His long fingers skimmed up and down my stockings again. I curled into him and whispered in his ear, 'Every time I've crossed my legs tonight, I've thought about you. About you touching me.' I held my hand over his enormous erection. 'Which other parts of me have you been thinking of?' I asked. He slipped his hand inside my knickers but he never took his eyes off my face.

'Your hair,' he said, running one hand down my braid and, in a lower voice, 'Your lovely little cunt.' He pushed one, long, middle finger right inside me. I jumped, and then lay still for a few seconds, getting used to the new sensation. It felt invasive and strange, yet exciting. And big. God – what would a willy feel like?

'No one's ever done that to me before, Dominic. No one's ever been inside of me before.'

Shutting his eyes, he said, 'Jesus. You always do that to me, Helena. Just the way you talk nearly makes me come. I've been desperate to see you.' I nestled into his chest, kissing the skin and just holding my hand over his erection, warmly and gently. 'Let me concentrate on you,' he said. 'Let me find out what you like. Don't even touch me.' He moved my hand and began to play inside my body, rubbing my clitoris in a circular way with one thumb, while pushing his finger inside me deeply, forcibly sometimes, making a different sort of excitement there. Dominic was feeling me, exploring me, playing me, and I felt like an exquisite and expensive instrument, held in his lap. My arms were loosely around his neck. His fingertips touched my nipples occasionally, lightly. I loved the feeling of my silky-swathed bottom pressing firmly against his strong thighs too. I pressed my lips to his chest and shut my eyes, but he checked me. 'No. I need to see your eyes so I can tell how you're feeling.'

'I feel like I'm going to wet myself.' It was true. It was hard to work the muscles out.

Dominic smiled. 'Don't worry, you won't. And even if you did, it wouldn't matter.' He kissed my head. 'You're with me.'

I had to feel his cock then, to press it. He looked at me with such passion that tears came into my eyes, and he mouthed, 'Shh.' He escalated the jabbing of his finger, until it was hurting me and pleasing me all at once. I passed into a world of feeling, moving in his lap, rubbing his penis with both of my hands as best as I could in the tiring tangle of limbs. My lips were against his shoulder, and I was moving rapidly towards my release when I felt him insert a little finger into my bottom. I made a noise and bit into his shoulder, rocking and rocking into him, with my back arched like an animal, the tension building up inside my bottom, as well as between my legs now. I was soaking, and a little noise kept coming from my throat as the sensations of orgasm shook me. I had no control, and I looked at Dominic for reassurance as I gripped his penis, and that made him come too, throwing his head back violently.

We lay knotted, and increasingly uncomfortable, for several minutes. Now that he had touched me inside – really touched me – I didn't want him to pull out of me, and he seemed to sense that; he kept his finger inside my sex. Then he squeezed my shoulder. 'I'll have to move.' He pulled his hand away and shifted himself, lifting me a little as he did so and then he cradled my buttocks in his big hand, murmuring to me, 'I loved pushing my finger into you. It's all tight and hot and private there. Intimate, I suppose I mean. I love your passion, and your tiny noises – even your shyness, when you almost daren't say something and then you do.' He rocked me for several minutes until I was lulled, softened against him. 'Are you sleepy?' His voice was hushed. It was only about 10.30, but I'd had a long and nerve-wracking week altogether. I nodded. He kissed my head. 'Come on, then.' And he picked me up and carried me over towards the bed. Just before he got there, he stopped. 'You're lighter, aren't you?' His arms moved slightly, weighing me. 'I thought you looked thinner before. How much do you weigh?'

'I don't know.' The pizza I'd eaten lay solidly in my stomach and I was tired. I didn't feel light at all at that minute. Dominic laid me down on the bed and took off my underwear, bit by bit. I could feel him looking at me so I moved away from his gaze, curling into and under the quilt.

'You *are* thinner. I'm going to weigh you tomorrow. Fucking exams. Are you hungry now?'

'God, no.'

It took him a couple of minutes to clumsily unravel my rope of hair, then he switched off the lamp and curled up behind me, warming the backs of my thighs with the fronts of his. He stroked my side once and stopped, surprised.

'Shit, Helena – I can really feel your ribs.'

'Let me sleep.'

A last kiss touched my shoulder. 'For now. But we'll have to talk about this tomorrow.'

Cold shoulders woke me up in the night – my own. I'd been dreaming erratically about my father, my father and the sea. When he was quite young he made an advert, an advert for aftershave. My father strolls on to this gorgeous beach and stands on the sand, looking out to sea, while the music washes about quietly in the background. (He looks quite hunky in this one.) His eyes move from the waves of the water to the wavy shapes of the sand. Suddenly he catches his breath, the music builds up, and he swoops right down below a long curve of sand and emerges with this amazing woman in his arms, and they roll just once together on the sand, in a sort of molten movement. Just at the point when the two of them are lying there, looking into each other's eyes, their faces freeze and they both turn into glass. Then the shot changes to an image of a people-shaped glass aftershave bottle, half submerged in the sand.

I've had one of the bottles since I was little, and the video of the advert; they're two of my favourite bedroom treasures. Glass parents, I thought. Half-submerged. I shivered a bit then slept.

It's like a dream.

I'm on a train. And I see her – my autumn girl – I see her

again. She was the last person I expected to see on that old nail on a Saturday night. I'd not even been thinking about her as much, either, what with the dirty blonde and the other animal experimentation.

She looks thinner. Like a younger deer – an excited younger deer. That's the first thing I notice. And she's got the same gorgeous hair. But there's something different about her. She's wearing a really smart jacket and a short skirt, but she looks sort of less pure. He's done that to her – she's got a gleam in her eye and a bulge in her thigh, so to speak – suspenders on under her skirt. I can see the bump on my side whenever she moves her legs. She still looks spectacular. She's got her hair done into a rope, like a whip moving down her back. Her eyes are as alive and soft as ever. She's so thin, I can see the tendons in her hands – puppet strings: strings I want to pull. But she barely looks at me, in a world of her own, dreaming, and crossing and uncrossing her legs. Fucking gorgeous legs. I want to see them all the way up. I'm not the only bloke looking at her. I hardly take my eyes off her the whole journey.

If I hadn't been with the dirty blonde, I'd have gone across to her. I'd have gone across anyway if I hadn't guessed he'd be meeting her when she got off the train. She looked so perfect, delicate, like china – a china vase I could've picked up and carried away easily, or smashed with my hands.

There was a world of difference between her and the dirty blonde, Vikki. Vikki was a good six inches shorter, for a start – and I'd never let her wear suspenders, not in public (and she never kept them on for long in private, like). Vikki looked especially nasty that night – purple love bite on the one side of her neck (mine) and black eye on the other (also mine, of course). Her nipples were sticking out like the lit buttons on a fruit machine – but her clitoris was the reddest button of the lot. *Press here*. Any time. *Hold. Shoot*. Glad to. *Exchange*. Any day. She'd been quite pretty when I'd first started seeing her. She looked dead now. I was ashamed of her. She wasn't altogether dead, though. Women are fucking sly. It was her who'd insisted that we go out – to meet some abortion-faced wanker of a cousin of hers.

That was the last time I went out with her, the dirty blonde, come to think of it. Fucking bitch went off with the cousin, and my wallet, the next day. I used to make her try to suck all of the tension, all of the anger, out of me (until her mouth shook like kitty's did). But I could never quite get rid of it all. Haven't yet.

There's something about the look on her face – autumn girl's – that really annoys me as well. Upsets me. She's thinking about him, not me. That's what it is. I know she doesn't mean it, but it's cruel, isn't it, ignoring me like that? It makes me want to do something really extreme, something I've seen often enough in my specialist magazine collection – I want to take her over my knees, there and then on the train, lift her smart skirt and smack her little arse, hard, kinky underwear and all. Not to really hurt her. I mean, I still love her and everything – seeing her again brings all those feelings back – just to leave a few artistic fingerprints here and there. Make my mark, so to speak, like a painter on his canvas. Make her think of me instead of him. Ever had that feeling?

Once I'm home, I keep running that scene through my mind again and again, creating and directing a film, zooming in on different bits all of the time. *Tease on a Train*, I call it. I'd been good at making videos at school, artistic, like. Made a few at home before, too. This one will be a part of a whole series, a series of seven. And the title of the series will be *Alchemy* – turning metal into gold. I can spin my golden dreams into reality, when the time is right.

Why don't you unlock the door to my world and your own? Just picturise my world. Take a look at my first work of art.

Alchemy One
Tease on a Train, Shooting Script

Zoom, long shot, Helena boards the train, looking gorgeous but vulnerable. Zoom, Close up, she sees me. Smiles. Reassured. Longing shows in her eyes. Zoom, long shot – the other passengers' faces, blank, dull, unsuspecting. Dead. Zoom, medium shot, my ambush, her surprise, our struggle. Zoom, medium shot, my strength, my power, wrestling her over my knees, easy military precision and rehearsed movements. Admirable.

Zoom, close up, my strong hand in the small of her back, my other hand holding her long, stockinged legs down, her knickers, tiny, black, silky, the cheeks of her arse raised over my hard knees, very white, girlish, smooth. The ultimate invitation. Zoom, close up, her face, upset, embarrassed, frightened, all at once. Extreme close up, her deer eyes, wide. (That's the best bit.) Zoom, my big hand (bigger than in real life) coming down, hard, flat on her silky arse. Repeat, repeat, repeat. Zoom, her legs, her thighs, kicking helplessly. Her little tits hanging down. A glimpse of black bra and cleavage. Zoom, close up, my hand, pulling her knickers down, hard, my other hand pressing into her back. Zoom, her lovely face, close up, humiliated, exposed, ashamed. Trapped. Tears in her eyes. One for sorrow. Recognition of my superior strength dawning all over. Her lips trembling. Fear. Respect. (I kept replaying that bit.) Zoom, close up, her bare arse, red raw now, knickers halfway down those thighs. My arm coming down again and again, strong, manly, muscles flexed. No sign of tiring. Zoom, extreme close up, more tears. Beaten. Mascara everywhere, losing control, thrashing. Zoom, close up, my face: strength, mercy, kindness, humanity. Complete control.

Medium shot, my hands, pulling her knickers up, pulling her skirt down. Patting her backside, fatherly, like. Long shot, passengers' faces. Alive now. Fear, awe, respect. Envy, definitely. Medium shot, her sitting on my knee. Restored to order. A little doll. Mercy. Love. Me, wiping her mascara away, drying her tears, arranging her hair. Microphone – first words: 'Thank you, Adam.' Very nicely. Not really hurt.

Fade out.

Just imagining her voice saying my name gives me a hard on that aches. She's so feminine. She'd say it so gently, so lovingly, whisper it, like. I'd look after her after that. She'd be so grateful. My dad's beltings never hurt me, did they?

He meets her at the station – Edinburgh, same as us. Ugly as ever. He doesn't look very pleased to see her, miserable bastard. The lion and the lamb. My lamb. He looks a bit thinner as well. Maybe they've some kind of a sick anorexia pact going. He gives her a present – looks like a book. Has it got the same sort of pictures in it that mine at home have? I wonder. Bet she'd like to see them.

I follow her for a few minutes, dragging the dirty blonde behind me until she complains too much. And by the time I've left them to their cosy Italian, I understand: I understand one thing as clearly as if she's told me it herself – her and Vikki have got one thing in common. No mother, I can tell. Partly because I've seen her dad doing the shopping, like, but more the way she looks: gorgeous, but a bit neglected, a bit delicate, especially around the eyes, now that she's thinner. I love scars – scars and silence.

She's perfect for me.

I learn a few other things from their conversation too. She's called Helena, like Helen of Troy. And he's called Dominic. He's sitting his finals in law. Middle-class wanker.

I've typed my script up and set up a separate file for her – in my computer and in the secret drawer in my room, a drawer that is now especially for things relating to Helena (containing the stone and this shooting script). If the series is called *Alchemy*, then that makes me The Alchemist, I reckon. Sounds good – a transformer of power and a creator of precious things.

The rest will be a doddle. I can sleep easy in my bed now.

Clinking cutlery woke me next. It was very bright, and for a few seconds I couldn't remember where I was. Then I saw Dominic standing over me with a very full tray in his hands. Force-feeding. I think I sighed. Still sleepy, I struggled to sit up.

'What time is it?'

'Half-seven.'

I definitely sighed then, but I knew he had to revise, so I smiled at him. 'My train's not until twelve but I can read my book or something while you work this morning.'

He put the tray down and sat on the bed. 'No. I've decided I'll take you home. I don't want you sitting on your own on that dismal fucking train. We'll just have to set off a bit earlier, that's all, so I can get back to revise.'

'Haven't you finished your revision?'

'In a way. I just want to keep looking over my notes, checking my plans, that sort of thing, you know.'

I knew. 'I don't mind the train.'

'I mind.' Dominic looked towards my new stockings which lay discarded on his side of the bed. 'You could be sitting there, all gorgeous, thinking about me, and some other bloke could think you were looking like that for him. Anyway, I want to talk to you.'

I knew, roughly, what that meant, and I also knew that there was no getting out of it. Or the mound of food that lay at my side. Best just to front-load the fat and starve it off later.

'That looks nice.' A complete lie: it looked like a pile of calories, and my body still had some pizza left in it from the night before. But his face relaxed instantly, and I was so glad that I'd said it that I almost meant it.

'I thought you'd be hungry. You probably haven't been eating so much because of your highers.' Guilty face.

'Probably.'

'There's a bit of everything.' His forefinger pointed out each separate chipped but clean plate. 'Grapefruit, croissants, cheese, boiled eggs, those little tomatoes you like, with the green bits cut off. And coffee.' He smiled. 'Lots of coffee.' The coffee smelled strong and rich. He poured me some from his chipped cafetière – he knew I loved good coffee and somehow he always found the money to buy the little things I liked (if not a new cafetière). He passed me a milky mugful – my sugar habit having stopped weeks ago – and I inhaled the aroma right in, before taking a sip of it. 'What do you want first?' I wondered how much Dominic knew about calories. Not much, I guessed. Time to find out.

'That grapefruit looks really cold and refreshing.'

He handed it to me. The flesh had been, fairly inexpertly, cut and prepared. There was a bit of sugar on it, but never mind. I managed to get away with half a grapefruit, one egg, lots of little tomatoes and one (small) bite of croissant. No cheese. The conclusion was that I'd eaten about 200 calories of food and Dominic Oliver didn't know what a calorie was. It was a lovely breakfast, and I escaped almost completely without bossing because he could see that I was eating quite a lot. And I knew, from his relieved expression, that he'd be able to revise without worrying about me.

Breakfast over, Dominic went downstairs with the tray and

I nipped into the nest to give my precious stockings a wash. When he returned from the kitchen, I was clean-faced and minty-mouthed, hanging my stockings over the back of his desk chair to dry. Coming up behind me, and putting his arms around my waist as I bent, he said, 'Leave those here, will you, Helena? Don't take them home. They'll remind me of last night.' He stroked one of them. I laughed.

'There'll be more of my things here than at Leeched soon.'

Dominic kissed the side of my throat. 'Good. Anyway, I don't want anyone else seeing you in them apart from me.' I turned to him and put my arms around his neck. 'Your legs are enough to make any normal, red-blooded man lose control of his senses.'

'Or any abnormal red-blooded man?'

'Exactly my point.'

'So which are you, then? Do all normal men like to keep their girlfriends' underwear lying around their desks, so that they can fondle it when they're bored with their essays?'

'I don't know about all men. I only know about me.' He gently pushed his fingers into the split of my bottom, feeling me through the cotton of my dressing gown. 'And you.' Redness flooded right through my face and neck and I turned away from him, beginning to collect some of my other things together. I heard his now familiar laughter break out, and then he slapped my bum once. I whirled around, redder still.

'Dominic!' He tickled my sides.

'Well. You can't be a Dalmatian all your life!'

'I can if I want.'

'"I can if I want"? You sound younger than a Dalmatian now. Careful, Helena – you're regressing! You'll reach puppy embryo stage soon.' I poked his ribs with my fingers and he lifted me up and spun me on to the bed. 'That reminds me.' He darted out of the room and knocked on Sam's door. I couldn't think what he meant until he returned with some bathroom scales in his hand. His expression was half-serious, half-teasing.

'No.' I was definite.

'Why not?'

'Just no.'

'No scales just now then,' he said, 'but I'll ask Sam what you should weigh, she'll know.'

'Don't you dare.' This was incredible. I was too thin now! 'I'd be really shown up.'

He continued as if I hadn't spoken. 'If I weigh twelve nine or so, I suppose you should weigh about nine or ten stones. You're not much shorter than me but your bone structure is much finer.'

'You'll be buying a calorie counter next!'

'Not a bad idea.' His brow puckered and at last he changed the subject. 'I'm going to have to take you home soon.' He looked down at the carpet. 'I'm dreading this week.'

'I know. But imagine Friday.' The day after his last exam I was going to stay with him for a while.

'If I can last that long. What if, by Friday, I've cocked up my exams? A 2:1 is so fucking mediocre.'

'You'll never be mediocre. Exam results have nothing to do with it. You've got nothing to prove.'

'I do.'

'Who to?'

'Myself, my dad, you. Everyone.' Dominic's eyes flickered away from me, impatient with himself. 'My dad calls people who have 2:1s and 2:2s "second-class citizens".' He rolled his eyes. 'Just his little joke.'

I wondered if Mr Oliver had ever cracked that particular jokette at one of Uncle Mark's cheese and wine dos. I doubted it. 'Does he have many jokes like that?'

'A few.'

'Uncle Mark used to do something similar when I was little. I was quite bright when I was younger, but I could never live up to my father. What I mean is, if I was second in the class at something, Uncle Mark would say, "An excellent attempt, Helena. Almost a chip off the old block. Your father was naturally brilliant. See if you can't be first next time. Go for gold." I still hate that expression.'

'So how did you react?'

'Well, it was pretty direct. I stopped trying. I hate being counted, and being counted and found lacking is the worst feeling of all. So I tried to stay in the top part of the class but I stopped trying to win altogether. Because it seemed I never could.' I returned to Dominic's problem. 'But you're his son –

his only son. Who cares what degree you get?'

'My dad does, and I do.'

'Listen. Really listen. I don't care if you even go into that stupid exam on Thursday; in a way, I'd be glad if you didn't. I can see you. I know you, inside. That's the important thing. A first or a second is a number, not a person.'

'It's proof of a mediocre brain or a sound brain.' He said it automatically.

I frowned. 'Is that you speaking?'

Dominic's laugh was like a dry cough. 'No. Pure Nick Oliver.'

'Look, for me, please – stop torturing yourself. In four or five days the whole thing will be over.'

'I'll try.' Doubt still distanced his eyes. 'It does help – the way you are. You don't seem ambitious either for yourself or me.'

I felt guilty, remembering how pleased I'd been about his earning potential when I'd first met him. I'd even written it down in my Dominic Diary – I'd have to be very careful that he never saw that. But what I'd really wanted was someone to protect me, and I knew now that money was only one part of all that. Still, I couldn't imagine finding a dustbin man sexy. I tried to respond honestly.

'I suppose I respect your ambition, but I don't want you to hurt yourself with it.' (And I definitely don't want Nick Oliver to hurt you with *his* ambition, I thought, but didn't voice.)

'I'm probably making my dad sound worse than he really is.' Doubtful, but I appreciated his loyalty. Dominic still looked really low and we were going to have to go. I stood up and held the emerald in my hand. I took his hand in both of mine, with the emerald pressing between our palms. 'Remember what you said about periods?' I pressed harder, so that the emerald was digging into his skin. 'One blood. We're the same, despite the differences. I promise you, I won't think any less of you if you get a third, any more than you'll think less of me when my grades come out lower than yours did, which they will.' (Dominic had sailed or, more probably, steamed, stewed and sweated his way through his exams with top grades, of course.) I said more firmly, 'I promise.' He looked back at me, pain, passion and intensity in his wonderful green eyes.

When he looked at me like that, I knew that magic was alive and well.

'Thanks.' Dominic wrapped his arms around me and kissed me really hard, as if we were both going to die within the week, then broke away. His eyes told me that we would have to leave.

The journey home was quiet. Having truly exhausted the issue of my weight, Dominic actually said little and was preoccupied and unusually quiet. I read my Will Jackson book, stroking its glossy cover with my fingers. He had Chinese hair. Half-gypsy, half-silk. Every time I looked at a photograph of a box or a piece of furniture, I thought of a different part of my own body: folded secrets, smooth curves, dark corners. I'd never thought wood could be so erotic.

Then we were outside Leeched – the land of square rooms, clean corners and tidy beds. Or so I thought.

Saying goodbye to Dominic was always hard, but that day was just impossible; I felt like I was sending him alone into the arena with slavering lions. Best to keep it brief, for both our sakes. I grabbed my bag from the back seat and my book, and kissed his lips softly, touching his pocket where I'd seen him put the emerald earlier. 'Four days,' I whispered. 'Good luck, darling.' A mute nod and a semi-smile were my reply. Then I was out of the car and into Leeched – an hour and a half earlier than Uncle Mark had been expecting me.

Two sounds were in my head as I opened the door with my key, the loud roar of Dominic's engine (which always reminded me of his laugh) and the muffled sound of Uncle Mark up in his bedroom. I put the kettle on, laid my precious book on the shiny pine kitchen table and ran upstairs. 'Uncle Mark, I'm back. Dominic gave me a lift home.' I knocked on the door. 'Uncle Mark?'

'I won't be long, Helena.' Uncle Mark's voice sounded funny. Sort of formal. Public, even. 'I've just got out of the bath. I'll only be five minutes.'

'I'll make you a coffee.'

'Good idea.'

Sitting back at the shiny pine, I turned over the pages of my book but I was dreaming, really. Dominic, Dominic, Dominic Oliver. When would he tell me he loved me? I hoped desperately that he was falling in love with me, as I definitely was with him. It was such a relief not to have a revision timetable nagging away in the back of my mind. Poor Dominic. Then I had a brilliant idea: I could write to him. At the University. I knew he had a pigeonhole there – he called it 'the bore drawer'. How wonderful for him to go to his post and find a letter there from me, when he expected some tedious law document or circular. I'd have plenty of time over the next few days, now that I'd broken up.

Broken up. Coffee break. Cold coffee. Funny, Uncle Mark still wasn't there. I went to the bottom of the stairs. 'Uncle Mark. Your coffee's going cold.'

Two figures appeared at the top of the stairs. Two bodies. Uncle Mark cleared his throat. 'Better make that two coffees, please, Helena.'

'Uncle Mark!'

I scuttled back to the kitchen, my cheeks burning. Then they were in the kitchen too, before I'd had time to think what to say. I couldn't even move, let alone speak. Totty – in *my* house. I sneaked a look at her. *Old* totty, thirty-five at least. She was wearing a sort of upmarket cardigan, a short, blonde, neatly curled hairdo (not rollers, please?) and pointy, toe-curling shoes. The shame. She looked almost as embarrassed as me. If she hadn't been so well seasoned, I bet she'd have shinned down a drainpipe to escape me, like in the old Laurel and Hardy films. She'd probably seen all those films first time around – entry price a couple of empty jam jars.

'Helena, this is Lisa. Lisa, this is Helena.' We both nodded automatically in true, Leeched Dry cheese and wine mode. 'Well, it's about time my two girls met one another.'

'My' 'two' 'girls'??? I was his *only* girl. She was a geriatric! This was getting more and more obscene. Uncle Mark busied himself with her coffee. (It was obvious that I was in no fit state to do it.) For a second I wished Dominic was there, then remembered the roar of his engine and cancelled that idea.

She – Lisa – was sitting at the table, looking at my Will Jackson book, touching my book. She seemed quite at home, pretending to be a normal human being – how many times had she been there before? 'I like Will Jackson's work. He lives not far from me.' She smiled, but I could neither smile nor speak. I nodded blankly, then picked my book up.

'I'll just go upstairs and unpack, Uncle Mark.' Let me out.

'Helena, stay and drink your coffee. Chew the fat with Lisa and me.'

'Chew the fat'. I logged his latest expression down – useful for days when I was finding it difficult to stick to my diet. Disgusting. Then another thought occurred: hadn't he said he'd just got out of the bath? He wouldn't, would he?

'I'll not be a minute.'

Dashing up the stairs with my bag, I headed straight for the bathroom. Sure enough, there were unusually sweet smells all around. Plus – massage lotion. All those wrinkles! Cardigans and condoms. Stomach turner. Just like me and Dominic, only twice as old. At least. Just when I was discovering that sex was so intimate, so exciting, so special – so much – I had to discover that Uncle Mark was doing it as well. Hard to believe he'd even think about it, let alone do it. And so quickly! I couldn't get my head around it at all. I unpacked as slowly as I possibly could. I was saved from further trauma – and fat chewing – by the sound of the door opening.

''Bye, Helena!' she called up the stairs. At least she was tactful. I had to be more grown up, more Leeched about this.

''Bye, Lisa.' A start.

'We'll have a chat another time.' The door closed. An established relationship, then!

My feet thudded ominously on the stairs as I walked down to join Uncle Mark in the kitchen. 'Sorry about that, Helena. Wasn't expecting you back so soon.' Obviously not.

'You don't have to hide from me or anything.'

'Well, you do look rather shell-shocked.' Uncle Mark actually laughed, then stopped when he saw my face. 'I didn't want to embarrass you.' With anything inappropriate, etcetera.

'How long have you been seeing her?'

'Two weeks and three days.' His smirking lip lifted his moustache slightly. Counting the days.

'I'll get my coffee.'

Uncle Mark followed me around the kitchen, obviously

preparing for a mammoth fat-chewing session that I knew I wasn't up to. 'Would you like something to eat? A nutritious snack?'

'I've just had lunch.' It was almost automatic now, the food lie.

'How's young Dominic? How's his revision schedule going?'

'Fine.' A sudden thought occurred. 'She's not married, is she, Uncle Mark?' I needed reassurance that he hadn't sunk into complete debauchery. Plus I knew better than anybody did that there was a soft lip beneath the crisply-groomed black moustache.

'Good God, no. Divorced.' He puffed out his chest, Doug-like. 'I'm the first.'

'What?' The oldest virgin in town?

'The first man.' Uncle Adam and Lisa Eve. Gross! Except it was me that was about to be expelled from peachy paradise. I looked at Uncle Mark quizzically.

'The first man since her divorce,' he explained. 'She hasn't courted anyone since 1989.'

Courted? Weird. I did a quick calculation – Thatcher government and Madonna. Back to virgins.

I got away with about ten minutes of chewing, two cups of coffee and three warnings about Dominic and diets before I could escape upstairs to my Will Jackson book, my letter and my crowded thoughts. Uncle Mark's last words echoed a previous theme. 'There'll always be a home for you at Beech Trees, Helena. You're my responsibility and I take my responsibilities very seriously – you'll never be pushed out, by Lisa or anybody else. Don't go rushing into young Oliver's arms too quickly. Take your time.'

'Take your time'? Massage lotions and bedrooms after two weeks and three days? Jaw-dropper. Still, he was trying to help – I knew that. And now I was in a rush to write my letter. I knew I'd have to post it that night if Dominic was definitely to get it before the dreaded Medical Jurisprudence. I took out the lapis lazuli that I used for inspiration and began to think.

Sunday Night

I held the stone in my hand, I sat at my table and I thought.

How could I start? The stone alone didn't do the trick, so I turned to my book, my favourite book. Thought about all the preparation and art that all of the people I admired put into their work, like. Looked at a few pictures. All I needed was a strategy.

Then I had it. I'd go to the University and have a look at all of the notice boards and pigeonholes there. There couldn't be that many Dominics who were in their final year of doing law there, and if there were, I'd just have to follow them all through until I found the bastard. It'd be worth it. I'd have to work through him to get to her. I made a few calculations. Wednesday. That was the best day.

Sunday night
Hi,
I bet you're surprised to hear from me. How can I start? I'm clutching my lapis lazuli stone (I know – ridiculous) and my Will Jackson book for inspiration, but it's still difficult to begin. I wish I was as good with words as WJ is with wood. Never mind.

The biggest news is about Uncle Mark. You won't believe it, but when I got in tonight he was upstairs, wait for this – with totty. Old totty. Lisa, her name is. And they'd been in the bath together. Shocking. I still can't get over it. And he looks so pleased with himself, the old stud dog. It's unbearable.

I wonder how you're feeling as you read this? Better than the last time I saw you, I hope. I know how difficult your work is, and how important it is to you, but you really must try not to get obsessed. My feelings for you will be just as strong whatever happens to you. And don't dwell on your dad's so-called jokes and put-downs. I know I shouldn't criticise him. Just remember I'm thinking of you, and will be there for you whatever.

What have you got in mind for us next Friday? I hope you're going to take me somewhere really special. I've got some money – I guess your allowance will be close to running out now (or even your mega-loan). I'd rather it was just the two of us, unless there's something really good going on.

Are my wonderful stockings still in place on your chair? I love to think of them touching your back as you sit at your computer, caressing you in my place. I keep thinking of the train journey yesterday as well. I was so excited, imagining your hands on my

> *legs the whole time, feeling every bump of the train. I'm still*
> *excited now, thinking of how your hands were later. And the*
> *rest. I'm going to buy some new underwear to bring with me on*
> *Friday – I'll have plenty of time to shop with Diana now that*
> *the dreaded highers are over. I'll get something really sexy so*
> *that we can celebrate your freedom in style. Who knows – you*
> *could be the one to end my everlasting virgin state, although*
> *I loved the way we sort-of had sex on Saturday as well. I love*
> *feeling the strength of your arms when you lift me or touch*
> *me. I love the muscles in your chest and arms. I can't wait*
> *to see you.*
>   *Your own Helena*

That was all I had time for – I was meeting Diana later. I'd post my letter on the way. I started to get ready to go out.

I start to get ready to go out. It will take me just an hour to get to Edinburgh (in the Bundymobile) and I've planned my route precisely – even know where the law school is. It's just a matter of time.

I look at every notice board, every student common room and every pigeonhole in the place. I've come especially dressed as a scruff to fit in there, using Dominic, the lanky bastard, as my role-model. In fact there are three Dominics – Dominic Cairns, Dominic Kirby and Dominic Oliver. I take the post for all of them straight home and back to my bedroom.

The third one is him and there are three things of interest to me: an invitation, a note and a letter. The note doesn't say much.

> *Hi, Dom*
> *Just a line to wish you luck. Hope you survive Thursday. See you*
> *Thursday night.*
> *Love Sherry*
>
> *XXXXXXX*
> *XXXXX*
> *XXX*
> *X*

That pathetic little pattern of kisses. I wonder if the dirty bastard's playing away. The invitation is altogether more interesting.

You are invited to an end of exams bash, June 30th. All at 37 Gadsby Street, AKA Cromwell Street, welcome.
  Love, Delilah and Co. XXX

Cromwell Street? Maybe I *have* got something in common with the lanky bastard after all.

And the last – the letter. It nearly breaks my heart at first, until I think about it logically, like. No one's ever sent me a letter like that. Not until now, I mean. I know she wrote it for him, sort of, but it is *my* letter. The spotty bastard's never going to see it for a start. And so much of it applies to me – nearly all of it. I put it in her drawer, alongside the stone from her drive. And I put a second version of it on to my computer. I use *all* of her own words, every one. I just take a couple out, and then I can see exactly what she wants to tell me. She knows me so well – it's almost psychic. Definitely psychic. I keep looking at it over and over again.

Hi,
I bet you're surprised to hear from me. How can I start? I'm clutching my lapis lazuli stone (I know – ridiculous) and my Will Jackson book for inspiration, but it's still difficult to begin. I wish I was as good with words as WJ is with wood.

I wonder how you're feeling as you read this? Better than the last time I saw you, I hope. I know how difficult your work is and how important it is to you, but you really must try not to get obsessed. My feelings for you will be just as strong whatever happens to you. And don't dwell on your dad's so-called jokes and put-downs. I know I shouldn't criticise him. Just remember I'm thinking of you and will be there for you whatever.

Are my wonderful stockings still in place on your chair? I love to think of them touching your back as you sit at your computer, caressing you in my place. I keep thinking of the train journey yesterday. I was so excited, imagining your hands on my legs the whole time, feeling every bump of the train. I'm still excited now,

---

> *thinking of how your hands were later. And the rest. I'm going to*
> *buy some new underwear to bring with me on Friday – I'll have*
> *plenty of time to shop with Diana now that the dreaded highers are*
> *over. I'll get something really sexy so that we can celebrate in style.*
> *Who knows – you could be the one to end my everlasting virgin state,*
> *although I loved the way we sort-of had sex on Saturday as well. I*
> *love feeling the strength of your arms when you lift or touch me – I*
> *love the muscles in your chest and arms. I can't wait to see you.*
> *Your own Helena*

See, it makes perfect sense now, doesn't it? Gives me several
facts to put down in my Helena file too. I start a new page. As
she says, my work is difficult and I'm obsessed with it.

- *Lives with uncle – both parents presumed AWOL/deceased*
- *Current partner lives at 37 Gadsby Street*
- *Current partner out on Thursday night (with a different girl),*
  possibly with other occupants of the house
- *Stockings placed close to desk and computer, presumably in current*
  partner's bedroom
- *Definitely a virgin*

The last fact is perhaps the best of all.

I've got two letters now – a real one and a virtual, personal one:
both of them extremely intimate and artistic. Dominic Oliver's
got nothing. And I'm going to get those stockings next. My
stockings. I put a copy of my letter under my pillow.

Now I can think of her every night, as I direct my plays, my
dreams.

If real life is less real than a dream, then how alive are we? Is
imagination more important than reality, fiction truer than fact?
Questions I've not answered yet.

I was full of doubts before I fell asleep. How could I find a way
into Dominic's heart? What was the best home for my own heart,
my own body? And I thought of my father before I fell asleep,
opened my eyes and he was there.

I was walking across the tarmac to a tiny, private plane –

very exciting. The aluminium steps leading up into the inside of the plane were beckoning me, and my father was standing behind the steward, smiling at me widely. I started up the steps towards him and suddenly the steward put out his arm, barring my way.

'I need to board the plane. My parents are on there.'

'No, madam. Your father is on the plane. You have no access to your mother. You may not board the plane.'

My father moved down the steps and pushed the steward to one side. His smile broadened as he pulled me past. 'Helena, darling.' I looked into his eyes and I awoke.

'You have no access to your mother.' What was all that about?

I woke up really early that Thursday morning – about 5 a.m. – keeping military time, of course. Ready for action.

Not that getting the stockings was any big deal, like. It was one of the easier bits. A lot of things are easy to me. People like Vikki – the dumb blonde – make things so hard for themselves with their weaknesses, their fears. It must have taken a lot of nerve for her to nick my wallet like that. She must have hated me, I know that now. Well, I hated her. Every time I fucked her I hated her, it just took her a long time to work it out. So that was us even. I saw her out once with her bastard cousin – glued to his knee. Pure suction. I wasn't going to go after her, obviously. But I was going to go after my autumn girl's stockings.

When I want something, and the time is right, well, I just go out and get it. I do things people like you only dream about. I plan it sometimes, but I don't worry about it – ever. When I see something inviting, I take it. Or touch it. So watch out in crowds (and out of them). Watch your back, especially if it's invitingly curvy. I enjoy taking people's power away from them, taking the remote controls of their lives right out of their hands and switching to my channel.

I spent most of the day arranging my room, reading my books, cataloguing various goods. I had a part-time job at that time, in a crappy little chemist's shop, so I had a lot of cosmetic goods around (no video cameras in the storerooms, stupid wankers). I was arranging them, and a few other items. There was no need to work on my plan; it was simple enough, and it was all in place really. I'd got so many clues from his pigeonhole. I'd be returning there.

The only trouble was, I didn't know what time he'd go out – miserable bastard – so I had to be outside his house by 6, to be on the safe side. Lives in Gorgie – a right dump. There's a TA centre near where he lives, not that I think he's seen the inside of it, like – Salvation Army's more what he needs and there's one of them as well. A street map led me to his spot, so to speak, and now that I'm here it's just a matter of sitting in my car, waiting. You can tell which one is his without even looking at the number, the front door's that scruffy. Fucking students. Dirty, bean-eating, yoghurt-knitting, lardy farty little bastards. It's obvious there's nobody in that house with a military background. And there are lots of comings and goings – a whole group of them are obviously meeting up there before a party or something. So I wait.

About 8 o'clock, I see a punky type – mushroom face and common, dyed hair, must be 'Sherry' – go in, then a white Bob Marley look-a-like. Then it's music, lights off and on, and laughing. I start to think they're there for the night and I get pretty bored then. But at 9 o'clock, somebody lets them out of their cage, the Rasta man first and then the rest of the zoo. Lady Luck is on my side, as usual: it's still light. And what a collection of deadbeats, fucking losers the lot, including him – 'Dom' – with not enough money to pay for Helena to go out. Autumn girl and winter boy – what is she doing with him? Not to mention he's walking along the street all linked up with mushroom face, definitely 'Sherry', I hear the name, looking very cosy. Obviously playing away.

I get out of the Beetle, very casual, and look around the house from the outside. Cat man. There are lights on in just one room – the front bedroom – and heavy metal music is pounding out from there. A heavy hippie this time. No competition.

I walk straight into the house and go upstairs. If heavy boy emerges from his pit, I'm a friend of Big Dom's, just dropping by to pick up some notes, not sure which room is his, sorry and all that. Like with the pigeonhole, it's third time lucky – two girls' rooms first. I can tell them straightaway like, by the smell. Hair lacquer, make-up, underwear and perfume. (Speaking of which, the toilet was fucking stinking. I know why they call the place Cromwell Street, filthy gets.)

The third room is his – toxic dump – notes and files all over. And spot cream, not surprisingly – same type I used to use. And the stockings are there, just waiting for me. I don't take anything else – don't want him to get suspicious, or even halfway streetwise and intelligent, and start locking doors or anything.

Then I'm off. Heavy boy never even came out of his room. And those stockings are going exactly where they belong – over the back of my chair, caressing me, touching my back, just like she wanted in the letter. My own Helena. Touching me.

Obsession.

Dominic. Dominic, Dominic, Dominic Oliver. Obsession. Friday took forever to come, as always.

Dominic rang me on Thursday night at about 9.30; he'd just left Cromwell Street. He'd taken to ringing me a couple of times a week by then and I had Uncle Mark trained – he would go into the kitchen to 'mooch about' etcetera, and dream about the lovely Lisa, presumably. Of course the first thing I asked Dominic about was his exam and he was full of that. 'How did it go?'

'Good, but I'm not sure how good. I'll just have to wait and see. We're in the Enzine Ewatt, celebrating. Thank God they're over, anyway. I can't believe I've finally finished – until the Legal Practice course, that is. Still, that's months away.'

He told me a few yawn-inducing facts about Medical Jurisprudence (which he liked actually – Doctor Dom) and I could hear the familiar buzz of the pub in the background. I noticed he hadn't mentioned my letter.

'Anything interesting in your post this week?'

'Not that I can think of.'

Puzzle. 'Not even in your pigeonhole?'

'Definitely not. Why?'

'I sent you a letter; I posted it on Sunday night. Didn't you get it? I wanted you to read it before you sat your exam today.'

'Shit. Sorry, Helena. There was nothing.' He thought for a few seconds. 'I wonder if someone's moved my stuff by accident? Sherry said she'd left me a note in there the other day as well, but I didn't get that either. I bet Damien Oliver's grabbed my post by accident – that happened once before.'

'No!' Mega-blush, instantly.

'Why? What did you say?'

'It was a bit personal, actually.'

Dominic barked his laugh. 'I bet you're really blushing. Lucky Damien Oliver – it'll be the steamiest letter he's ever had. He's about four foot ten with glasses.'

'Don't!'

'Sorry. It'll probably turn up.'

'Where are you off to now?'

'A party – one of Sherry's mates. We're all going. Speaking of which, I'd better get back to them all, Helena. They're baying for me. It must be my round.' I could hear them all, howling in the background. One wolfish howl sounded distinctly higher and hungrier than the rest. 'I'll come for you tomorrow – as soon as I get up, which won't be early. I'll see you at about twelve. Oh, and bring some extra clothes with you, and some trainers or something.'

And that was about it. He hadn't even asked me how I was, but I didn't worry about that for long, with the acid bubbling away in my stomach and the memory of a greedy female howl in my ears. Sherry. Sweet and sour Sherry: sweet with Dominic and sour with me. Now why should that be? Sherry's thighs, Sherry's notes, Sherry's little smiles, nudges and comments. All for Dominic. Tonight. I was glad he hadn't got my letter.

Maybe I'd been wrong to promise myself to him.

10

'They told her how, upon St Agnes Eve
Young virgins might have visions of delight,
And soft adorings from their loves receive
Upon the honeyed middle of the night'
– John Keats, *'The Eve of St Agnes'*

I'm so glad I've got her letter to keep me company. And the stockings, of course. I'm building up quite a collection – soon, I'll have as much of her stuff with me as she's got at Beech Trees.

A man can get lonely waiting for his woman, waiting for the right time. The perfect time. In the meantime, I've got the stone, the stockings and the letters – her home, her body and her heart. There are plenty of dreams I can weave around those three. Dreams are often better than reality, don't you find? But, as you know, I make my dreams come true – even the strange ones, the illegal ones. Marilyn Manson's twisted face is in my mind. Sweet dreams. It'll not be long before the fantasies in my head (including, maybe, the one in my drawer) become my own, very personal, private filming sessions. With Helena and The Alchemist as the stars.

And there's a second script in my drawer now as well, *The Bandaged Bride*. It's a shooting script too, so to speak, and it's linked to the last item on my list – the list you saw before. The item I keep thinking about more and more. This script is much more avant-garde than the first one. That's how it goes with me, like. It gets more and more extreme as it goes along.

Francis Bacon, another of my Mr Muscles, inspired this – The Mouth Man. And nuns. There's a bit of a religious feel to it.

Take a peep, by all means. Just pictureeyes my world.

Alchemy Two
The Bandaged Bride, Shooting Script
Fade in.
Long shot of Helena, looking very elegant and together, coming into my flat. Long black dress, little handbag and all that. I'm holding the door open to let her in. Next, close up of her face, confident, smiling, subtle make up. Hair all clean and shiny. Any red-blooded male would want her, would envy me. Next, medium shot, Helena sitting down, laughing, chatting, nodding. Two for joy. She looks just right on my black leather settee, in my flat – very stylish, all three of them.

Next, long shot of me, walking into the kitchen, laughing over my shoulder – open, like. Next, medium shot of me, fixing some drinks. Next, foregrounding, some white powder in a little dish, my big hand pouring the powder into her white wine. I know she'll like white wine. Next, long shot, me, returning to the living room with the drinks on a tray. Next, close up, she sips her wine, camera lingers on her lips, slightly reddened. Inviting. Next, medium shot, she sips her wine, laughs at one of my comments. Nods. Smiles up at me. Next, close up of her face. Buzzing noise, maybe some electrical music or maybe that music from The Hunger. *Camera goes in and out of focus as the opiate takes effect.*

Next, extreme close up, her deer eyes as she starts to lose consciousness, or to change consciousness. Next, very artistic shot, long shot, me, The Alchemist, picking her up in my arms. Her dress draped all around her, almost touching the floor. Her limbs, elegant, her face, relaxed. Medium shot, her head, moving around, dazed but conscious. Feeling, but not knowing, not capable of being really hurt. That's the point.

Next, long shot, my bedroom. Massive four-poster bed, of course. Me, laying her down gently on the bed. Next, long shot, me undressing her. Her protesting, moving her limbs around helplessly, but strangely, terribly slowly. I sprinkle the bed with poppies and poppy petals. Beautiful. I whisper in her ear. Troubadour.

Foregrounding, rolls of bandages at the side of the bed. 'What's next?' hangs in the air. Soft focus now. Next, long shot, she's completely naked, like a baby. She's lying on her back, on the bed, crying gently, half out of it – doesn't really know where she is. Very soft focus, I wrap her up in the bandages, slowly, lovingly, protectively. Very tight at the neck, waist, knees and ankles. Almost like a corset, showing her curves, her curves and her slenderness. Next, close up of my face, concerned, manly.

Next, my hands at work, skilful, masterful, a bit of the military paramedical touch. I know a virgin, a nice girl like that, wouldn't want any man's cock in her, not at first. I'm looking after her, it's written all over my face. Next, another, very special shot. Long shot, her body, tightly swathed in bandages, her head, her eyes, almost everything covered. Arms wrapped individually, legs wrapped together, tight. Lily white except for the red and black scattering of the poppies. A beautiful mermaid. Just one strip bare – the bit I want most – her little vagina. The whole scene shifts to black and white, but the vagina is in colour, pink and pearly beneath the fine, chestnut hair, the vagina and the mouth. Masterly touch, don't you think, the colour?

Next, long shot, me, naked, moving over to the bed. Stroking the tightly wrapped body. Feeling her. Measuring her. Light coming through the window, which is arched, paned. Black diamonds on her body; black poppy petals against the bandages. Close up, she kind of jerks her head back, but the movements are drugged. She can't be hurt, won't feel a thing. Next, close up, my cock, long, strong, superb (longer than in real life). Rubbing against where her forehead is. There's a slight gap in the bandages below there, her reddish lips are showing through, pouting. Her head turning away. Suffering, but not too much. Next, medium shot, my hands pinching her tiny waist, pinching the places where her little tits are. Hard. One nip with my teeth. Slowly moving down to her vagina.

Camera cuts from the vagina to the reddish lips and back again. Resting my hands on the side of her hips, looking at her. Really looking at her. Next, close up of her head. Still. She's either completely unconscious or she's ready for it.

Next, close up. Sharp focus. My cock, her cunt. Her cunt, pink, glistening, through the chestnut fuzz. Looks even more moist and warm because of the whiteness and tightness of the rest of her. The ultimate invite. Presenting herself to me. Next, extreme close up – I jam two fingers into her, hard, my middle fingers. To see if she's ready. They come out wet. She barely moves. Next, extreme close up. My cock, extremely hard and manly, straight into her, I'm holding her by the hips. In, out, in, out, in, out. Tirelessly. She twists once, sharply, pained through the drugs. Me, very masculine, holding her slender body to me firmly with my strong hands. Heroic. I come, with a particularly dramatic thrust. Extreme close up, I withdraw. A little blood, very red, staining the white bandages. Artistic. Next, close up, my face. Concern, mercy, humanity, tenderness, masculinity, love. Next, long shot, I unbandage her gently. Her lovely head falls to one side. I brush her hair. Wipe the blood away. Close up, I kiss her tenderly. Wrap her elegantly in the sheet this time. She wakes up; opens her eyes. Microphone – first words: 'Thank you, Adam.'
   Fade out.

There have to be some connecting features – it's a series, you know – and I like that one:
   'Thank you, Adam.'
   Fade out.
Francis Bacon mouths howl around me in my room all night, calling me to recreate them.
   Next time, I'm going to share the action out.

I was well under nine stones but it was really difficult to stay there. All that week I'd been eating just fruit or raw vegetables all day and a little meal with Uncle Mark (and Lisa, twice now) in the evenings. My skin was looking fantastic (all that fruit) and my bum was just right, really high and tight. Exactly how I wanted it.
   The top half looked dire, though. I had to spend three hours getting ready for Dominic, working out how best to present each bit, and as I'd promised in the letter, I'd bought some new underwear – a very tight black Lycra body with six tiny pearl buttons between the legs. The top half looked like a

normal, if skin-tight, black T-shirt, but you could feel the little buttons pressing into you the whole time. It felt like a restricting, sexy corset. That was why I'd bought it – Scarlett O'Hara mode. I'd teamed it with body-painted black jeans. The jeans looked great, but in the cruel light of Leeched Dry's mirror, my chest and arms looked terrible: the skin was pulled really tight around my collarbones and ribs; my always minimalist cleavage had gone and my breasts themselves had practically disappeared too. Still, the material of the body felt silky and Dominic would love it – the little buttons and everything – so I finally decided on a petrol blue lambswool jumper to pull over the top of it all. The softness of the wool and the wavy mass of my hair complemented each other, and my legs could still be relied on to launch ships, thank God.

The other drawback of being so thin was the effect it was having on my brain: my emotions were as starved as my stomach. Somehow, this felt right – if all of my security was being scraped away, well then, scraping the flesh off my bones was one way of expressing that. And I was angry with Dominic for feeding me with doubts about my body, about Sherry, about his feelings for me. Starving myself was the best way I knew to show my anger in a 'lady-like' and 'appropriate' form. Blazing rows were never heard at Leeched Dry.

Dominic arrived bang on time as always and I threw my bag and jacket into the back of the Allegro. He put his arm around me and kissed me straightaway, looking really relaxed. 'You smell nice!' I was freshly bathed, ready for him.

'Where are we going?' I asked.

'Surprise. A big surprise.'

Dominic looked really happy, not his usual, cool self at all. He was hardly ever that relaxed. And he headed in the opposite direction to Edinburgh altogether. I'd wondered when he'd mentioned extra clothing if he had a night away somewhere planned, so I was instantly excited.

'Go on – tell me where we're going. Are we staying somewhere? Overnight?'

'Wait and see.' He looked at me out of the corner of his eye. 'First, we're stopping for lunch.'

'Oh, I've just had some.' Automatic.

'Well, we're stopping anyway.' Definite.

'I'll share yours with you.'

'Okay.'

But when we did stop later, at a wooden, roadside café, the smell of bacon made my mouth water. In fact, he insisted that I order something and I got away with a salad, which wasn't really breaking my diet anyway. Dominic made me eat half of his baked potato but I managed to scrape all the butter off. It was difficult not to tell him all about what I was or wasn't eating, what I weighed, how I felt, what exercise I'd done, because I was thinking about all this the whole time. But I never spoke about it to anyone (a bit of a habit with me, as you've seen).

Then we were back in the Allegro. We reached Selkirk and headed south, then the landscape started to look familiar to me, although the road didn't. And Dominic was chatting away about the party the night before.

'I was pretty knackered after my exam, so I didn't stay long. We left at around midnight.'

I didn't want to ask directly about Sherry. 'Did everybody else have a good time?'

'More or less. Dixie still has one exam to go, so he left with me. Sam and Doug had a row – a real row. Neither of them knows what they're doing now they've finished their degrees, so the stress levels are getting to them a bit. And Sherry finished her exams yesterday as well, so she was in a bit of a state.'

'Really?'

'Yes. She was sick, actually.' Dominic laughed. 'I thought she was harder than that. It wasn't quite as spectacular as your display but she still made a fair mess.'

'So you had to mop her up?'

'Dixie and me. Both of us.'

'How did she get home?'

He looked at me sideways again. 'We dragged her there, between us, then left her to it.'

'Right.' Not right.

Then I looked out of the window and squealed – very puppyish. That was why it was familiar! The edge of St Mary's Loch was swimming into view. We'd approached it from a different direction, that was all.

'Dominic! How did you know about this?'

'The tower-house. Don't you remember? You told me about it that night. I've had it planned for weeks.' He was delighted with himself (and possibly me), smiling straight into my eyes. I thought he'd crash the car for a minute. 'We're staying two nights at the pub – the Tibbie Shiel's. I'm going to concentrate on you for three whole days instead of stupid, boring law exams. You've been so patient with me – I wanted to treat you.'

All of my doubts disappeared – for the time being. 'Pull the car over.' The view of the loch at that second was spectacular.

'Why?'

'Just do it.'

Dominic obeyed, laughing. I threw my arms around him and covered his face with kisses, pressing him against the Allegro's window.

'It's really exciting. I love it! I've been dying to stay here.' I hugged him and he laughed louder, teasing me.

'There's no need to be quite so Dalmatian about it. It's only a pub.'

'No, it's not. It's magical.'

Within minutes we were pulling over on to the crossover of the figure eight where the pub lay and I jumped out of the car. Dominic picked up my bag and his own; we ducked into the porch and then into the whitewashed bar. He collected the keys (I even loved hearing him say 'Dominic Oliver' to the man behind the bar,) and we were shown into our room – a plain, double-bedded room upstairs. 'The bathroom is for your use only, Mr Oliver,' the man said, showing us a large bathroom with a spectacular (if netted) view of the loch. Then he left us to it.

Dominic unpacked a lot of our stuff while I scavenged about the room examining every little thing: the old fireplace, the coffee cups, the biscuits, the view. Then I looked at what Dominic had brought with him, glad to see the emerald glinting on his side of the bed. I kept going back to the bathroom to look over the loch and Dominic shouted through to me, 'We are here for three days, you know.'

'What are we going to do first?'

'How about a walk around the loch? It's about five miles all the way around, apparently.'

Great, lose half a baked potato straightaway. 'Brilliant. I'll just change my shoes.'

The day was blue, bright blue, brighter than my jumper, but as I stepped out of the pub towards the loch, I still felt the power of the hills all around me – a dark, forceful power, belittling almost. When we walked around the loch, hand in hand, our rolling walk brainwashed us into peacefulness, like mechanical, nightshift soldiers. When we'd walked for about a mile and a half, absorbing the strange, carved out scenery and the atmosphere to the full, I was starting to feel really breathless and tired. Usually I was quite a strong walker but the depletion in calories had obviously drained my energy, so we sat down on the sandy, tussocky bank of the loch and began to talk.

For the first time, I really broached the subject of Dominic's mother's remarriage, and in his new, relaxed, post-examination state of mind, he began to unbend a bit.

'My parents' marriage was hard enough. They took one each in a way – my father concentrated on me, and my mother on Jane. My dad would take me out walking or to a rugby match or whatever, and my mum took Jane shopping or skating.

'But it didn't work out. I mean, we weren't particularly jealous of each other, or anything, but Jane missed my dad on those days and I suppose I missed my mum. Besides that, the pressure my father was piling on top of me was pretty heavy, even then.' Dominic fingered his face unconsciously. 'That went on for a couple of years and when they finally did split up, we both went with my mum. No discussion.'

'That must have been hideous. Did you miss your father then?'

'Not really. To be brutally honest, I was relieved. My dad was at his most critical. I can remember coming joint first in a history project one year – the Tudors or some crap – and not wanting to tell Dad because being *joint* first wouldn't be good enough for *his* son. I hid the prize, I was so pissed off with him. But when he found out at a parents' evening, he went mad. Said I'd shown him up.

'Then things with my mother were a bit of a mess. I'd felt

pushed out by Jane for so long. I suppose I was a bit of a bully. It's better now but even so, if I'm honest, things are still a bit ropy there at times.

'But the worst bit of all was when my mother remarried. I was about fourteen. It was quite quick. He was younger than she was and I thought he was a bit of a gold-digger. Anyway, it was a disaster.' Dominic thought for a moment. 'I hated him, loathed him. Wished him dead – and told him so.' Grimace. 'Like I said – fourteen. I don't expect I was much fun to live with exactly.'

'How did your mother react to all that?'

Blue-green eyes were angled towards the loch. 'Suggested I went to live with my father.' Dominic was silent for a minute and I bit my lip, imagining his reaction. 'She couldn't stand to live with the nit-picking bastard but I was supposed to manage somehow.'

The eyes narrowed; the old bitterness was scarring his face. 'But in the end I had to stay with her; my dad said I couldn't live with him. Too busy. I still found it hard to forgive her.' Looking down, he scraped at the soil with his nails. 'I can't even now, quite. Her new husband left her three months later.' Awkward pause. 'She never forgave me either.'

I slipped my arm around his waist, not knowing what to say to him. 'How awful for you.' My Dominic.

He lifted his head as if it was heavy. 'For all of us, really.' He paused. 'I wasn't exactly the perfect step-son, son or brother at that time.'

I winced. I realised I was witnessing the birth of the Ice Man: Ice Boy made his first appearance on the film screen of my mind. 'At least I always had Uncle Mark to myself. Until Lisa, that is.'

'Lisa?' Of course. The letter having gone astray, I hadn't told him about it all. He listened serious-faced, evidently equating Uncle Mark's relationship with his mother's second marriage. 'Does it make you feel pushed out then, now that he's definitely got a girlfriend?'

'Yes, a bit. Uncle Mark tries to say it won't affect me – he's very sweet – but the truth is, it does. I feel my stay at Leeched is . . . sort of finite now. About to reach its sell-by date.' Jokette. I tried to laugh, but it was true. Dominic hugged me warmly and I felt a bit better, saying, 'I'll be at university soon, anyway.'

'Do you think you'll opt for Edinburgh, then?'

I still wasn't ready for this. 'Not sure.' I began to talk about my forthcoming driving test and we walked on for another thirty minutes or so.

It was really hot by then – mid-afternoon in late-June – and I pulled off the big, woolly jumper as I walked, enjoying the warm but slightly breezy air on my skin as I did so. I tilted my head to the sun, unwinding completely. My lungs were full of the grass-scented air; even my skin seemed to absorb it as we walked around the loch together. I had thought we were walking in a companionable silence but when I turned to Dominic, to say something, I saw that he was looking at me hard.

'Helena?' Big question in his voice. He took hold of one of my wrists and turned me towards him slowly, taking the other as well. I smiled.

'What's up?'

Green eyes moved slowly, coldly down, examining my body. 'You.'

My smile faded. I waited.

His explanation was brief. 'Sam's chart says for your height nine stones nine to ten stones three is the best weight.' His fingers circled my wrists tightly, gripping them now, making them seem even bonier. Then he pulled both wrists into one of his hands and touched a collarbone and then a rib with the other. And, worst, one tiny breast. His eyes were fixed on mine. 'What's going on?'

The unfairness of it made my eyes sting. 'I don't know, Dominic, you tell me. Am I a little curvy or am I a little thin? Which is it? When was I just right for you, then? I don't seem to remember that bit!'

'When you ate when you were hungry. Is that too much to ask? When you didn't look starved. And miserable, sometimes, when you thought no one was looking.' He shook my wrists for emphasis. 'This is my fault. I knew you were losing weight and I didn't do anything about it. And it wasn't your exams at all. You look worse than ever.'

My new clothes. Three hours getting ready for him. I wrenched my wrists away. 'Thanks a lot.'

'Well, you do, Helena. *And* you lie to me. You hadn't eaten this morning, had you, when I asked you about lunch? You were starving. What's going on?' Dominic asked again.

'No, don't turn this around to me. You started it. You couldn't quite let it drop, could you? Little comments. Not often, but often enough – just enough to hurt me. You knew the effect it was having on me. Why did you do that?'

Dominic let my wrists fall and I rubbed them; the skin was pink. He sat down again, dipping his head, and I noticed for the first time that he looked a bit thinner. Fucking exams, I thought. Not me. I waited.

'You're right.' His head lifted, very slightly. 'I did know what I was doing. I knew exactly what I was doing.' His face was stained, darkened, with guilt but I wasn't softening any.

'Well, it might be a good idea to tell me about it.'

'I tried to stop it. You were never fat in the first place – that was obvious. I tried to stop myself. You can't stop ideas coming to you, but you can stop yourself from doing something about them – or saying something. I stopped myself, nearly every time.

'Every time I took the piss out of your weight – every time – I tried not to. I knew I was upsetting you. I used to do the same to my sister in a different way, to make her smaller. To stop her getting the attention.'

'You wanted to stop me from getting attention?'

'No, not with you. I just wanted to protect you. I hate it that you're so thin now – you'll get ill – but I've always liked your delicacy, your sort of fragile bones. Maybe I wanted to make you little so that I could build you up again.' He grimaced. 'Save you, just in time. Bring you back to life.'

Dominic thought some more. 'Maybe I wanted to turn you back into a little girl so that I could make you a woman, with warmth instead of . . . Uncle Mark's concern. Is that so bad?

'I tried not to upset you. I would never let anyone else hurt you. *I* would never hurt you deliberately. I stopped myself nearly every time.' He saw my face and his words dried up.

'You wanted to hurt me so that you could heal me? Break

me so that you could restore me? Like a piece of china or an ornament. *Make* me a woman?'

'Helena, don't. I'll never do it again – not in this way or any other. I'm not evil, not bad. I'd never hurt you.'

I knew he was thinking of the emerald. I stepped back from him, crushing the soft grass. 'Maybe you need to find someone new to destroy. I'm not sure I want to get any closer to you – or stay close at all.' I meant it. 'Why don't you *make* someone else? Try Sherry, if you want.'

'Helena, don't. Really, don't.' Dominic was looking around, desperate for inspiration, for the right words. I was pleased to see the distress on his face – he'd hurt me enough. 'I want you to be strong, to be happy. You know that.'

'Just leave me alone for a bit, Dominic. I need to think.'

I marched quickly ahead of him, back to the pub, and was glad that my legs were long and strong – Trojan, even – that they could carry me in style.

But by the time I actually got to the pub, the changes in my body were worrying. It wasn't just that I was very breathless, it was also the heaviness. Why did I feel so leaden? My legs were dead. I dragged myself upstairs. Damn. The bedroom door was locked, of course, and he had the key. I slipped into the TV lounge I had noticed earlier and sat down to recover. I began, almost against my will, to cool down.

Double damn. Because I knew I'd colluded in it, creating Dominic's power by trying to turn him into my mother, father, brother and lover so quickly. Everything. Responsible for my happiness. And really, the compliments and reassurances had far outweighed the criticisms, which had been few and far between. Someone more substantial might not have noticed them at all. It was my own uncertainty that gnawed at me. Guiltily, I remembered locking Dumbo in a toy suitcase when I was about six and battering him about my bedroom before nursing the poor thing back to health, bandaging his woolly little limbs. And didn't I enjoy Dominic's strength, my delicacy, in exactly the same way that he did? His 'shit', my 'cheek'; his lion, my Dalmatian; his scars, my white skin; his arms, lifting my legs from under me? His weight, fifty per cent more than mine. Doctor and patient. But was all of that healthy? Was it right? And if not, whose fault was it exactly?

My thoughts were interrupted by the distinctive sound of his steps, loud, heavy and irregular, walking past the room, up to the bedroom. I thought about his mother's remarriage, his compliments, his booking of the room (probably in a precious break from revision) and his skin. His slightly shiny skin. Soon a different sort of pain – a hot pain for Dominic – came into me. A couple of minutes later he ran downstairs, his steps as heavy and as clumsy as ever, past the television room and outside, where I could see him through the window, looking over the loch: looking for me. I watched him for several seconds. His head went down and he came back inside. It was only then that he tried the door to the television lounge.

'Helena!' He was perplexed, annoyed, unhappy – all the things he always was when he was concerned.

'Dominic.'

'I don't want Sherry, you know that.' He stared at me from the doorway.

'I don't know. I don't know anything. You never tell me how you feel.'

'I don't want Sherry,' he repeated. His voice had become slightly gentler.

'What do you want?'

Dominic thought for a while. 'A lot of different things. The biggest thing – for you to eat. Normally.' After a further minute of reflection, his voice was gentler still. 'For you to feel better.'

I walked across to him and wrapped my arms around his neck, tight. His arms moved around my back, holding me. Clumsily, unusually nervously, he guided me down towards the settee and we sat down together, still one.

'Look, Helena, truce. You eat properly for the three days we're together here, and afterwards, and I promise I'll *never* tease you about your weight again.'

'I don't know if I can promise that.' Self-destruction is a strangely addictive habit and I was sucking at its nipple.

'Okay then, promise to try?'

'Definitely.' I hated feeling like I did then. 'How come I feel so much heavier when I'm over a stone lighter?'

'Over a stone?' Dominic swallowed. 'Maybe your muscles have wasted – if you don't eat enough, your body uses fat and then muscle.'

'How do you know?'

'Sam's diet book. That's how I knew what you were doing. When you ordered a salad and then scraped all the butter off that potato, I knew for certain. Not to mention you look so run down.' His eyes creased in concern. 'The muscle can't always be replaced.' Doctor Dom.

'So you know what a calorie is now?' I laughed.

But Dominic's face looked more serious still. 'A unit of energy, like you, like me. Only you don't have enough at the moment.' One blood. 'I've booked a table for us to eat here tonight. Is that okay?' He stroked my hair.

'Fine.'

Dominic put both arms around my shoulders and I turned towards the lounge, with its magazines and books that nobody would ever read, and its old TV, before looking back into his face. 'The way I feel about you . . . you said I didn't tell you.' His hair was messy from the walk; his eyes were clear – searching. I waited. 'I love you.' *Totally* unexpected. 'I love you. That's how I feel.' *Totally* wonderful. I drank it in. I'd been holding so much back for so long, I almost didn't know what to do with it all. I jumped on top of him, tightening my knees around his sides. It's a wonder that old settee survived.

'I love you, Dominic. Dominic Oliver.' I bit his neck. 'I really love you. Let's go to bed.'

'Helena!' Dominic's bark was even more surprised than usual. His arms gripped my waist. 'I love you with sex or without sex, with sort-of-sex or without sort-of-sex, fat or thin. All of that.' He touched my brow. 'Do you understand?' Yes, I understood: he didn't want to confuse the emotional and the physical, the spiritual and the sexual. What about a combination of all four?

Apparently not possible – not just then. We went upstairs but Dominic didn't carry me, didn't stroke me, and didn't mar the purity of his love for me with a physical gesture. He loved me, he loved me, he loved me, he loved me. But he wanted to show me that he could be gentleman-like too.

For a very short period of time, luckily, I could wait.

The more I think about her lately, the more I think about how I can prove my strength – of character, body, feeling – to her in a physical gesture. And how I can prove to myself and the poxy world around me that I'm alive. Really alive.

Up and down the streets I went today, trying to walk my energy, my anger away. Everywhere I went, I could tell that other young blokes were trying to get rid of something, somehow as well: dog shit smeared into the pavements, 'Tac sold here' on the doors, and blasting music coming out of all the upstairs windows of all the crappy cardboard council houses. Middle of the day, like – no school, no work, no life.

Getting back to my room was a relief. All right, it was flowers, fag ash and soap operas in every other room, but my room was always mine, wherever we were living. Clean. And that's where I turned to one of my Mr Muscles to help me out, to inspire me, like. There he was – on every wall, all around me: mouths, meat and heat. Crying mouths under bandaged eyes, screaming mouths, bloody mouths, distorted mouths. Red heat. Electricity.

I'll give you a few of the master's words to get you in the mood.

> *'I've always been very moved by the movements of the mouth and the shape of the mouth and the teeth. People say that these have all sorts of sexual implications, and I was always very obsessed by the actual appearance of the mouth and the teeth … I like, you may say, the glitter and colour that comes from the mouth, and I've always hoped in a sense to paint the mouth like Monet painted a sunset.'*

I'm just planning my very own recreation of Monet's bloody sunset and my plans are almost complete. Me and Francis, we've got the same aims:

> *'We nearly always live through screens – a screened existence. And I sometimes think, when people say my work looks violent, that*

perhaps I have from time to time been able to clear away one or two of the veils or screens.'

One screen is about to lift.

Lying on my bed that evening, I read my Will Jackson book for inspiration as I waited for Dominic to finish his bath. I read about how Will's work as a paramedic was related to his work as an artist – the smoothing of the wood and the calming of the flesh, the patience, the love, and the creation or recreation of something beautiful. I stroked my own little box where it lay beside the bed. (Thought about the secret oval box of eggs that lay inside of me.) There was a photograph of Will Jackson inside the front sleeve of the book, looking younger than I'd expected – late-twenties perhaps. His hair was so black and shiny. I felt the gloss of the page beneath my fingers. His eyes looked back at me, looking less intense actually than his comments within the book had led me to expect.

The Dominic who emerged from the bathroom at last was the playful, very lively one I hardly ever saw. Almost a male Dalmatian, in fact. Grabbing the book from my hands, he threw it to one side.

'Dominic!'

'I've seen enough books for a lifetime – well, until October at least. Let's go.' He shook both of my arms, joggling me.

'Where to? There's nowhere for miles around here.'

'There is. I saw another pub back there: the Gordon Arms. We'll go for a drink, and then come back here for dinner.'

So we were off.

The Gordon Arms Hotel was a big, black and white building that lay at a crossroads. Dominic headed for the back bar and ordered a beer and a glass of wine, taking them to a round table in a corner of the bar beside a fire where we sat down. A big, shaggy-haired dog ambled into the room to greet us. I ran across to it, delighted. 'It's a bearded collie, isn't it? I love these. Diana's Mum's got two of them.' I stroked its big, heavy head. The man behind the bar answered me.

'Aye, it's a beardie. We've got five of them here. D'ye want to see the new puppies?'

'Five? That's brilliant. I'd love to see them.'

He left the room and I said to Dominic, 'I always wanted a dog. Uncle Mark doesn't like the hairs, the germs, the licking . . .'

'The shit!' Dominic interjected – and barked out a laugh that would have done a beardie proud.

'Well, it must have been hard enough to look after me at times, without a dog as well.'

Two brown and white fur balls were rolling their way into the room. Dominic was on his knees at once, wrestling with them and teasing, howling when they bit him with their needle teeth. They were aggressive with each other too, opening their jaws really wide, like tiny hippos, though they didn't seem to do each other any damage. I felt very only-child – not used to the horseplay, dogplay even – but they were adorable, with a sharp, puppy smell and beautiful but strangely psychotic eyes. I stroked their soft fur, whenever I got a chance in the flurry of play. Even that was enough to over-excite one of them, and it got its snapping teeth entangled in the arm of my blue jumper, halfway through a bid to lick my face.

'Dominic!'

He laughed out loud for a full minute before rescuing me, parrying the other puppy away to do so. Then he played with them both, rolling them towards each other, copying them, and making low half-human, half beardie noises for them in the back of his throat. He looked up at one point, his arms full of puppies, like wriggling babies. It was a strangely sexy second. Two of the older, dreadlocked, dogs looked on like exhausted grannies watching their charges being happily occupied in a playground.

'Come on,' Dominic said. 'We're going to be late at Tibbie.'

We gulped down our drinks and launched ourselves into the Allegro, trundling back towards the pub and our meal.

'I love dogs,' Dominic said, unnecessarily, as he steered his way back around the loch. 'I'm going to have five at least, just like that.' He looked really happy.

'I could hardly handle them one at a time.'

'You were fine, considering you're not really used to them.'

He turned away from the view and the road to look at me for a second and laughed. 'They were a bit of a handful, weren't they?'

Tibbie appeared like a friend around the corner, and we rushed towards her and into the little side room. 'I'm starved,' said Dominic, claiming a table. 'What are you going to have?' He pointed at the blackboard. Somewhere between the solid and the starved was where I needed to be. Difficult. I certainly wasn't ready for chips.

'Grilled trout with almonds, salad and new potatoes,' I read from the board, and smiled at him: 'Health rather than heart attack.'

'Sounds good. I think I'll have the same.'

He ran to the bar to order and came back a minute later with an unopened, dewy-cold bottle of yellowish white wine. 'Chardonnay,' he read from the label. 'Do you think you'll like this?'

'Bliss.'

He took it back to the bar, and a waitress soon appeared with the bottle and two glasses. Dominic poured immediately. 'A toast!' He grabbed my waist and lifted his glass. 'To Helena – health, happiness and a life of heated passion. Oh, and no more highers.'

'To bathos,' I said, clinking my glass against his. I was delighted when Mr Straight As didn't get my jokette and whispered 'Anticlimax' in his ear. A middle-aged couple at the next table smiled, eavesdropping madly. I took a sip of wine, and then clinked his glass again. 'To Dominic Oliver – may you achieve exactly what you desire from life: five bearded collies, one fat girlfriend, oh, and no more fucking exams!'

The couple smiled more widely and Dominic laughed like a gunshot, then whispered in my ear, privately, 'Hardly fat,' tightening the grip of his long hand around my rib cage.

The food arrived then: the Yarrow trout was a very strong, river-swimming fish, smelling surprisingly sea-like, savoury and fresh. Wonderful. We ate in silence for a few minutes – food worries made me a bit subdued and I was really keen to avoid any conflict over eating that might spoil the evening. I ate the salad first, forking the coleslaw to one side because of

the mayonnaise. But I decided I could eat all of the trout –
I wanted to steal its strength – as long as I peeled the nutty,
butter-speckled skin away first. The shellfish-coloured layers of
light flesh were so delicate and appealing that I ate almost half of
it in one go, then sat back suddenly, feeling quite full. Dominic
put his fork down and laid one hand on top of mine, saying
quietly, 'Don't eat too quickly, Helena. That's what happened
before, after the balti, I think. Sam says your stomach shrinks
and then when you eat a lot, you throw up. She says you're
to build up gradually.'

I pulled my hand away. 'Sam's about as sensitive as you are.
This is private: you shouldn't have discussed it with her. You
shouldn't have discussed it with anyone.'

'Well, she's always on a diet so I knew she'd know all the ins
and outs of it. You're right, I didn't know what a calorie was.'
I smiled in spite of myself. 'And you're right about her level
of sensitivity, and mine maybe. But she was really concerned
about you as well. She won't say anything to anyone – she
said that straightaway.'

'You know I don't like to talk about this sort of thing.'

'This sort of thing – food, parents, plans, feelings sometimes. It's quite a long list, Helena. You have to trust people
sometimes.'

I thought about the money and blushed.

Dominic laid his knife and fork down altogether then and took
my hand again. In the nosy cosiness of the dining room, his voice
was very low. 'Look, I don't want to be a pain. Just eat what you
like. Try some more salad and some potato. Maybe the fish is a
bit rich for you.' He prepared a forkful of food: a piece of potato
and a few squares of beetroot salad. 'Here. It's a cubist painting.
Or a sculpture.' He fed me with it and then gave me three or
four more mouthfuls before I began to eat more myself, picking
a few pieces from the trout's translucent bones until I'd eaten
quite a lot of it. Then I really was full, and sleepy suddenly.

'Are you tired?' asked Dominic. 'Do you want to go upstairs?'

'No, honestly, you finish your meal.'

'I'm full anyway.' Apart from some salad and bones, his plate
was clean. His gaze followed mine. 'Not keen on that; I don't
know how I'd manage on a diet.'

'Ask Sam for some advice – I'm sure she'd be very discreet.'

'Shit! You're not going to start worrying about Sam now, are you? Start thinking I'm secretly lusting over her?'

'I'm ahead of you there – I've already done that one.'

He laughed. 'Well, if we've got nothing to argue about for once, we might as well go to bed. Unless you want another drink down here?' We'd finished the wine.

'No, thanks, I think I've had enough.'

As he put his hand on my stomach again, his eyes glinting, I knew he was thinking about the puking incident, but he showed great restraint and said nothing apart from, 'I'll get the bill.' The keys appeared before me. 'You go upstairs.'

In the chilly bathroom I took my make-up off, staring out over the loch as I did so, wide awake now, naturally. Then I brushed my hair, and washed my hands and feet. Apart from that I remained fully clothed, sitting on the bed, curled up, waiting for Dominic to arrive. Then he was framed in the doorway, looking tall and strong and dazzling. He always seemed so alive. Electricity. He jumped straight on the bed in front of me, putting his hands on my sides. 'These are brilliant,' he said, handling my jeans. 'Are they new?' I nodded. 'Let me feel them.' He ran his hands right up my legs and hips, 'Mmm,' then flopped down beside me. 'You must have thought of me when you bought them?' Smug look.

'No, actually.' I wanted to shock him out of his complacency. 'I thought about all those men on the train who were looking at my legs last week.' I glanced at him sideways. 'I felt like feeding their bizarre fantasies about me.'

Dominic rolled on top of me, serious suddenly. 'Don't, Helena. I hate to think of anyone hurting you.'

'Apart from you, you mean.' I couldn't resist the dig.

His lips kissed mine, softly. 'I've said I'm sorry about that. I'll help you to get back to a better weight – feel stronger.' Long fingers stroked my sides and I knew from the frown of concentration that he was thinking how prominent my ribs were, but he pushed the thought away. 'This is nice too. It's all silky.'

'I know.' I leaned closer and whispered in his ear, 'It goes all the way down. Tiny pearly buttons between the legs.

Silky everywhere. And I *was* thinking about you when I chose it.'

Dominic was both pleased and intrigued, his eyes creasing. He lay down beside me. 'A leotard?' he said, questioningly.

'*Leotard*?' I teased him. 'It's called a body.' I could feel the tiny buttons; had felt them all night, pressing into me.

Dominic repeated, 'A body,' and stroked the top half of it thoroughly, then touched my nipples very gently with his fingers. 'Helena, I won't go on, but don't lose any more weight. I can carry you upstairs just as easily at nine or ten stones as at eight. I can't imagine you being anything less than totally feminine, even if you were much heavier.'

'Don't go on. And I am more than eight stones, actually.'

'Not much.' He nuzzled me. 'You're always gorgeous, though.' He kissed the inch of skin to the side of each eye, then my nose. He looked deep into my eyes. 'I do love you. I really love you.' One soft kiss on the lips. 'I love your lips, your eyes, your hair, your gentleness.' He placed one hand heavily on my stomach. 'It's awful – everybody thinks they want to fall in love like this, but it gives the other person so much power over you – gives you so much power, Helena.'

I stroked his big, hard head with both of my hands. 'But I can use that power to care for you, love you. You don't have to feel vulnerable.'

'Vulnerable?' Dominic repeated, snapping his head away. 'I can't imagine my father ever feeling even vaguely vulnerable.' He dropped on to his back and I dragged him on to his side to face me and pulled his head down to rest between my breasts, stroking his hair, stroking his eyes closed. Feeling the slight bumps on his skin.

'There are plenty of ways to be a man. I love it when you're sensitive; I love the depth of your feelings. It sort of makes you more masculine, not less. It's a strength to let yourself feel something intense, not a weakness. One blood, remember?' My insides were soft with love for him.

He looked up into my eyes again. 'I've never felt like this about anyone before.'

'Neither have I,' I murmured, both hands in his hair.

'We're both virgins, then?'

I laughed at that. 'In a sense, I suppose.'

He rolled back on top of me again, holding his eyes close to mine and letting me feel his breath, his life, on my face. 'I want to make love to you now. Completely.' His fingers felt between my legs, and I felt again both electricity and the sense of a blessing. 'One blood,' he said.

'I know. I want to make love to you as well. I want to feel all of you, inside of me,' I said.

Dominic's beautiful eyes searched mine. 'I won't hurt you. Maybe one of the pushes will hurt, but I'll try to make it so nice at the same time that it doesn't matter.' The buttons between my legs dug in pleasurably as he stroked and stroked between my legs through the tight jeans.

'I know,' I said. 'Don't worry.'

'Just don't close your eyes. At all. If I can see your eyes, I'll be able to understand you, to see you inside, to feel your feelings, inside.'

I nodded my head, looking up at him. He was so beautiful – and so strong. I felt his penis through his jeans: young and strong and going right inside me. Yes.

Sitting over me, one knee on each side of my legs, Dominic began by examining the silky body. His hands felt bigger than ever, running up and down the tight black Lycra. Then he fingered my nipples through the material, his caresses creating a tingle between my legs as they always did.

'I think you could make me come just by doing that.'

Dominic smiled and sat back up over me, his head held high, proud of the control he had over me in that intimate way. He pulled his T-shirt off, then held both hands tight around my waist. 'Let me just see your legs in these before I take them down.'

Raising himself, he turned me with his hands until I was on my front, my arms to either side of my head. Again, he stroked the body first – my shoulders, my spine. It felt good to be so tightly enclosed, restricted almost, by the black clothes: I felt like a Victorian bride, dressed to disrobe (except I was well aware of my clitoris, amongst other erogenous zones). Dominic's hands touched my bottom next and the tingling started between my legs again. Then he surprised me – he put one whole hand down underneath me, between my legs, holding my sex, and lifted my bum up a few inches. My jeans were cutting into me, splitting me. I felt as if I was presenting the most secret parts of myself to him for inspection – exposed, embarrassed, humiliated almost. But very hot. Dominic massaged me quite roughly with one hand, and little noises started to come out of the back of my throat. He knelt over me and whispered in my ear, 'You have the most beautiful behind I've ever seen.' I blushed bright red and he laid his cheek on my face. 'Don't be embarrassed. I want to see all of you – know all of you. Feel all of you.'

Dominic got off the bed and I heard him take the rest of his clothes off. My eyes were closed. Then he was on top of me again, lifting me up so that he could unbutton my jeans this time, pulling them down roughly. The breath caught in the back of his throat when he saw the rest of the body. It was tiny, and so tight from top to bottom that it made my legs look even longer than usual. It was cut very high over the thighs and buttocks, and I could feel his eyes concentrating on the tight black triangle that made up the lower half.

'God, Helena.' It was the charged, low voice that I now recognised as coming from the part that was most privately him. Again, he put his hand below me and gently lifted me, making a little noise as he did so. I could feel him looking at the tiny, pearly buttons, then he shifted, raised my behind higher, and kissed and nuzzled the three-inch strip of material that encased my sex, over and over again, while keeping one warm hand on my bottom. Everything was being stimulated then; even my breasts were pressing into the bed, hotly. I felt like an exquisite and beautiful object – Tiffany's Jack-in-the-Pulpit vase, being reverently touched by a loving collector. This went on for minutes, and I was moving, murmuring, saying Dominic's name in a kind of drugged dream. Then he fingered my clitoris once. My body angled towards him of its own accord and he knew then how excited I was. He lowered me and again I heard the deeper, private voice. 'Turn over, Helena.'

My body was open to him, like the golden vase, as I lay on my back, facing him, my thighs turned out very slightly. My Dominic. He could do anything he wanted with me now, anything at all. He put his fist between my legs, where I knew

I was soaking, aching, and then his hand touched my shoulder. 'This is great, it's like a little corset; it makes you seem even more of a girl – it's holding your body, your waist so closely.' Dominic's eyes looked down at me – they were wide with pride. 'I feel like you're displaying yourself to me.'

I smiled. 'I am. I knew you'd love it.' I fondled his broad chest and ran the other hand right up his cock, from the fuzzy, fleshy base to the wet, tender tip. Yes. Over and over again.

A flicker of worry crossed his face and I knew exactly what he was thinking. 'Come here,' I said, and he lowered himself until his chest was touching my breasts and his erection was on my thigh. I put both arms around his neck, looking into his lovely, frowning face. 'Don't worry about coming too early: it's not an exam. It doesn't matter if everything isn't perfect.' I smiled, remembering. 'You're with me.' I held his head between my hands. 'I love you, Dominic. I adore you, you know I do.'

'Helena, I don't want to come until you do.'

'Okay.' Slipping my hands around his back, I felt his spine and then fingered the sensitive crease between his buttocks. 'I won't touch you at the front then, until you really want me to.'

Dominic's head moved down and his eyes returned to the area between my legs. 'It's like a little locked door or a purse.' A mermaid's purse, I thought. Then I thought of a poppy seed head, packed full of those tiny, whole new lives. Dominic knelt in front of me and carefully unclicked the pearls, one at a time. The body sprang up, exposing my sex to him completely and instantly for the first time that night. He laid his cheek against my warmth there for a moment before moving back above me, a look of sheer love and contentment on his face. I loved the openness of his expression, his trust. Honest trust.

'Let me take this off.' Dominic finally pulled the body right over my head, so that I was completely naked. 'I want to make love to your whole body, your whole soul, not just those few inches – even if they are very erotic inches,' he smiled. 'I must touch you there, though.'

Despite the warning, when he rubbed my clitoris, I really jumped, making him touch me more gently, less directly then. 'Sorry, Helena. Don't forget, you have to look at me so that I make sure I don't hurt you.' I nodded; I didn't want to bleed on the sheets, amongst other things. Dominic was creating surges of new life, new waves, with his magical fingers, opening the secret lips slightly all of the time. His green eyes were drawing me into him, almost hypnotising me at the same time. 'It is wet there, isn't it, sweetheart?' he asked. Despite my nod, he moved slightly, and I knew that he intended to kiss between my legs to make sure that I was wet enough to take him. It reminded me of childbirth, of a man looking between a woman's legs, waiting for his baby's head to show. But I couldn't bear him to move his face from mine.

'No – stay there, Dominic!'

I needed him and he felt it, touching his lips to the skin above my right eye. I lifted one hand to his head and held his hair in my fingers. Dominic's big hand gentled my head, my hair, while his other hand continued to play with my clitoris and tease the soft lips of my opening. My breath started to sound ragged, impatient, and I was lifting my hips up to meet his fingers, my skin aware and alive. Just at that point, he turned his wrist and pushed two fingers inside of me, quite hard. I flinched, but he continued rubbing at my clitoris. Even his fingers felt big, invasive inside me, and I knew how long his cock was. 'I want to stretch you, just a little bit. Does that hurt in a horrible way, or a nice/nasty way?' I smiled, a bit nervously, at his reversion to Dalmatian words.

'Nice/nasty – just.'

Dominic nodded and continued more gently. Then he replaced his fingers at my clitoris with his cock, which grew rapidly harder with each movement. I loved his hardness but guessed he didn't have long, so I touched his penis then looked into his eyes, willing him to enter me, to be blessed by my love and my body at the same time.

Reading my face, he nodded and reached to the side of the bed. 'New condoms.' I hadn't realised he'd brought any. Dominic smiled and started to put one on (while I had an Uncle Mark moment and glanced away). I felt him finger the enervated skin of my clitoris and the soft lips around it, and the heat was building up there unbearably. I felt weak, like water almost, and stopped moving for a couple of seconds. Then he held my hip bones in his hands and, looking right into my eyes, pushed about an inch of his penis into me. It went in, but it seemed to catch on some skin, somehow, and I made a little cry. Dominic moved out at once. 'Okay, okay, Helena. Sorry.' Caressing my clitoris again, he touched the skin of my cheekbone at the same time, then pushed into me once – firmly but slowly. 'Jesus, you're tight.'

Dominic's body was still, allowing me to get used to the feeling of being so completely filled by him in that way. He felt very big and very sensitive inside of me like that; I was a tiny mouth around him. My left hand was flat against the wall of his chest, while my right hand remained tangled in his hair, gripping him. I began to move against him then, drawing him inside of me bit by bit. 'You feel strong, really strong inside me.'

Despite the discomfort, I pushed myself towards him, loving his big cock opening my small tightness wide, and the regular movement of his hand against my red-hot clitoris. I moved against his tender hand and hard cock, increasing the vibrations caused by his fingers. I thought of my own sea purse, my own store of eggs, hidden within my body. But it was Dominic who would have to discard his tiny seeds so soon, and I was glad that it was my body that had the magical purse inside of it where a child could be formed. I felt I was moving into a different state, almost moving outside of myself, all feelings, all softness. My hand cramped hard around his hair. A pulse of pleasure was beating in my body, and I packed my other hand against my mouth – anchoring myself – while the rest of my body shook. 'I love you, I love you,' came out of me, and Dominic threw his head back, his back arched, his cock almost completely buried in my skin.

Limbs, weight, feelings and skin-smells engulfed me afterwards, as Dominic lay heavily on top of me. My breath gulped, and he seemed to come back into himself and remember where he was. Lifting himself up, he said, 'The condom, angel – I've got to pull out.'

'Okay.'

A few clumsy movements later and he was beside me, saying, 'Come here.' He lay on his back and drew me towards him so that I was on my side, facing him, with my head up on his shoulder.

'Did I hurt your head?' I asked, looking down to my cramped

fingers, where a few fair, fine hairs were lodged. 'I pulled, didn't I?'

'Don't worry about that.' He hugged me to him. 'Are you sore?'

'A bit.'

'I don't think you bled.' He touched me between my legs very gently and lifted his fingers back. 'Just a tiny bit. I didn't realise.' His red finger painted a tiny crescent mark on his chest. 'One blood.' He smiled. 'Any guilt? Any Uncle Mark related trauma?'

'Not at all. Just a bit worried about how much I feel for you. And tired.'

'I know. I feel the same.' He kissed me. 'But I feel really happy as well.'

I reached over and put my hand on the lamp switch. The emerald glinted at me from the side as I did so. I picked it up and stroked the hard stone along Dominic's cheekbone, then held it in front of him. 'Look.' His eyes smiled. I slipped the stone under his pillow, where it belonged, and he held me to him, looking into my eyes one last time. I stroked his temple. 'Sleep now, baby.' And he closed his eyes at once.

I lay in bed that Friday night, that Saturday morning, thinking, thinking and thinking. I couldn't close my eyes. No matter how hard I tried to kid myself, like, I knew she'd be losing her purity. With him. And probably that night. What normal, red-blooded male could turn down an invitation like that?

'Who knows, you could be the one to end my everlasting virgin state, although I loved the way we sort-of had sex on Saturday as well.' Look at the effect it had had on me – I knew that bit, and more, off by heart. My own Helena. She sounded so innocent.

But as daylight gradually dawns, and I know she's soiled herself with him, my anger turns from black to blue – a fading bruise. I even feel a kind of love for the greasy bastard. I mean, we're connected in a way – man, woman, man – connected through blood, her blood; we've both shared in the shedding of her blood.

Then a different sort of feeling grows, a different idea for a film script – the third of my series of seven. The feeling's not like the pure, absolute love I had for her before, when I cared for her, and was merciful, and restored her. Saved her. She's had that, like, now. Still my feelings are strong, more like the feelings I had for the dirty blonde, maybe – hot lust and hate mixed – but it's more passionate, because it's connected to her. My autumn girl. There's more than one way of losing your virginity and the Mouth Man had shown me the way.

So my third script is a definite progression from the other two; I surprise myself sometimes. Of course, a few of the ideas came from my dad, but not all of them by any means. This third one is different in two main ways, the first one being the way I think of the stars – it's me and my victim now, as opposed to me and my lover, co-starring, before. And I'm stronger than ever, showing hitherto unrevealed aspects of character. Her lips started it off in *The Bandaged Bride*: reddened, inviting. My third, and best so far, is called *The Parting of the Lips*. Nice, gentle title. One for the girls.

Alchemy Three
The Parting of the Lips, Shooting Script
Fade in.
Establishing shot, click. A scruffy, ordinary street in Gorgie, the West End of Edinburgh. Me, walking down the street, looking purposeful, righteous, angry. Medium shot, click, the dirty brown door. Me, bursting through it. Long shot, click, me, running upstairs – big, strong strides. Medium shot, click, the door to his bedroom. Me, kicking it in. Martial arts movements. Big thigh movements. Over the shoulder shot, click, the view of his room – messy, disorganised, contrasting with the military precision of my earlier movements and my smart appearance: the sharp and the sloppy juxtaposed. Camera follows me into the room. Locates evidence of their impurity, his attempted destruction of my love for her. Close up of my face, click, pain in my eyes. But my jaw – in control: strong, determined, manly. In search of justice.

Long shot, click, I move into an alleyway. Dark, secluded. Grey light, very artistic. Film moves from colour into black and white. Wait, wait, wait.

Foregrounding, click: an old brick, with one sharp, broken end, resting beside my foot. Tension building. 'What happens next?' in the air. Several people walk past. Point-of-view shot, click. Victim's head and shoulders appear, walking past, completely unaware.

Close up, click, my face in profile. Total focus. Total control. Superb concentration. Long shot, click, I pounce, brick in hand. My arm around the victim's throat – very sudden. Brick hits victim's chest. Extreme close up, click, blood seeps through victim's clothing, chest area. Replay, replay. Long shot, click, a fight, a struggle, a dramatic display of my superior strength. Victim's knees crumple. Face collapses: pathetic, vulnerable. Pained. Frightened.

Three for a girl. Triptych.

Black and white still – very dark, very moody. Long shot, click. Victim lying on the floor, alone. Foetal. Boxed in. Legs curled into body. Erotic. I could do anything with that body.

Extreme close up, click, point of view shot, the victim's lips, in colour now, parted, reddened – beautiful. The mouth in colour. Crisply cut. Exactly like before – the ultimate invitation. Close up, click, my leg – one kick at the prone victim's face. Just one. Mercy, not maiming. Minimal scarring; just enough to remember me by. Lips redden and swell, mouth distorted, ready. Long shot, click. Me, stepping back, touching my jeans. Close up, click, victim's beautiful face, lips bleeding, mouth red, rest black, and white. Lips bleeding; eyes wild.

Microphone, first time, hear my jeans unzipping. Point-of-view shot, click, victim's face out of control, weak. First words, 'No, Adam. Please, no.' Close up, click, my face, strong, controlled, army hard. Contrast with victim. Extreme close up, click, click, my cock, emerging from my jeans. Thicker than in real life. Long shot, click, me, kneeling down to victim. Close up, click, my cock, entering the crimson cushion of the victim's lips, seeking the redness, the bleeding – redder and more intimate than those of the vagina. Deeper. More room for a big man like me. More vulnerable, painful, personal this time. Almost choking victim. Victim in a different world – breathless, helpless, semi-conscious. Medium shot, click, in, out, in, out, in, out. Strong thrusts. Extreme close up, click, my cock, covered in victim's blood and slobber.

Long shot, click, I step back, unmoved. I kick the little behind on the floor. Zip up jeans. No further attack on victim. Mercy. Strength. No cleaning up of soiled site or victim. Victim spent. Last words, 'Thank you, Adam,' as before. Victim's voice, lower, changed, strange.

Fade out.

The difference with this film, though, is that it never will fade out. That's the other big difference between this and the first two – I'm going to make this one happen. Pictureyes it.

I'll give them more than seven days for their world – a more generous time than God had. After that, they're in my kingdom. My father's kingdom.

Necropolis.

Utopia.

The next week was the happiest of my whole life, especially the two remaining days at St Mary's Loch: we blessed our love in its beauty and we blessed each other with our love, our bodies.

The next day I woke up before Dominic, and jumped into the bath while he was still in bed. I looked through the nylon-net-framed window as I dried myself. Lazy vapour trails lined the sky. The loch was glittering at me in the new blueness of the day; it was really calling me to go outside. I ran back into the bedroom and kissed Dominic awake. 'I love you, I love you, I love you. Come outside and see.' Very Dalmatian. Dominic smiled before his eyes even opened, then I pulled him up. 'Let's have a look at the loch before breakfast.'

Within five minutes we were dressed and out there, breathing the life into our lungs from the new air. This time, we started off walking to the left of the loch (I definitely didn't want to relive the darkest bits of the day before), before sitting down on a grassy section overlooking the water. Some travellers had probably been there before us, had shared this spectacular view: the ashy remains of their fire sat in front of us and we breathed in the smell of the charred wood as we talked.

It was almost time to go back to Tibbie for breakfast when Dominic fell silent for a minute. I stood up, and was taking his hands to pull him up too when he looked up at me, and said, 'Sit back down again for a minute, Helena. There's something I've been wanting to talk to you about.' What could it be? He certainly looked serious. I felt small, scrabbling back down beside him again.

'Don't look like that,' he said, taking my hand. 'It's nothing

like that. It's just my birthday.' His party, of course. Sigh of relief.
'It's the week after next,' he went on.

'It's fancy dress, isn't it?' Why hadn't he asked me before?

'Yes. It's also a Nick Oliver special.'

'What do you mean?'

'Well, most people have a big do or something on their
twenty-first birthday, don't they?'

'I suppose so.'

'My dad's a bit different. He decided I would come of age when
I graduated – with my first-class degree, of course.' Dominic
pulled a face. 'I should have my results by then. Imagine if I
get a 2:1?'

Imagine. How awful. But I couldn't say as much.

'So, what has he got organised?'

'Nothing much – a marquee in the grounds of one of the
poshest places in Edinburgh. A champagne toast. Seventy-five
'specially selected people – half of whom I invited; the other half
friends or colleagues of his. People he wants to impress. People
he wants *me* to impress.' Dominic sighed and looked away. 'I
shouldn't be like this about it. There's one thing you can say
about my dad: he's certainly generous.' Guilty, I thought, and
controlling. But I kept my mouth shut. 'Anyway, I'll get to the
point.' He looked directly at me, the liquid colours of his eyes
more beautiful, if possible, than those of the loch in front of me.
'I thought it would be a good way for you to meet my dad. And
my sister. My mother's not coming.'

Stirring the grey ashes with a charred stick, I let the idea
sink in. It was obvious that this wasn't a party to be enjoyed
– endured, more like.

Dominic continued, almost reading my mind. 'I know it
sounds like a bit of an ordeal, but I promise, he'll be absolutely
charming to you. I wouldn't suggest it otherwise. He's always
saying how much he likes women.' I flinched although there
was no conscious irony in Dominic's voice. 'He'll think you're
beautiful. He'll love you.' What about you? I thought. Will he
love you if you've got a 2:1? Dominic seemed to hear me. 'It's
me he'll be hard on if I haven't got the first. But he'll keep that
to a few witty or caustic comments. I can cope with that.'

That's why you've been so worried about it that you didn't

ask me until today then, I thought. So worried that you never mentioned it or discussed it with me before. So worried that I don't know whether I should go – to watch my Dominic, struggling to keep whole his pride, his heart. Twenty-two years of pressure was building up to a very thinly stretched party balloon, floating up above his head now.

'Do you want me to go? Do you think it's a good idea?' I asked.

'You don't have to go, not if you don't want to.'

'That's not what I asked.'

When Dominic looked at me, there was a confused fourteen-year-old boy in his eyes. My soft-scarred angel. 'I'd love you to go. It's a massive night, in a way. I'd like you to be there because it's a kind of initiation, I suppose. My dad wants to show the world that I'm a perfect specimen of manhood.' He lifted his eyes to the sky. 'And I want to show . . .' he thought for a minute, '. . . I suppose I want to show that I can take whatever he can give. That I'm up to it, whatever it is. And I mean, I'm just about free of the whole thing. After my Legal Practice year, I won't need his generosity. I'm going to get a summer job, anyway, which always helps a bit; I've never been totally dependent on him financially.'

So, Dominic wanted me to see his success, the glory of his graduation, degree-wise and man-wise. But what if his graduation wasn't so glorious? He wouldn't want me to see that – he needed me to see him in lion-mode, with his big head thrown back, all strong. Still, his father wasn't exactly a monster; there was more than enough emotional generosity inside Dominic to prove that his parents had got quite a lot of it right. Old Nick wouldn't go in for public humiliation, surely? I imagined that asides were more his speciality. Soliloquies. A solution.

'I'll go. I'll buy some spectacular clothes, put my hair up, show off my social graces and make your father wish he was my boyfriend.' It was the perfect thing to say; Dominic responded at once with a laugh. 'But I'll sit with Sam and Dixie and so on.' Not him. If he's humiliating you, and you want me to stay away, I will. But if you need me, Dominic, then I'll be there. I would think of it as work, work to pay for the love and the trust that we normally shared, shared to maintain his pride, his lion's pride, and his lion's heart. My heart. More of a play than a party, but I was used to that sort of thing from Uncle Mark's legal dos, and I could stand being the bright shining young thing that brought light to the event. Occasionally.

'That would be great. My dad's put a lot of effort into it, so I was a bit worried about the chatting and so on. That was why I didn't mention it at first.' One reason. Dominic kissed me. 'I'll ring him at the office after breakfast and tell him you're going to come.' He'd spoken about me to his dad, then.

'Good idea. Now, let's go and have some breakfast.'

The work done, for the next two days we cemented our love through the feeding rituals, the lovemaking rituals, the union with nature. The words. The rightness of our love for each other, proven again and again. I couldn't believe that anybody else had ever felt like we felt about each other, had ever shared themselves in such a liquid way, so that I really wasn't sure where the edges of Dominic's happiness, Dominic's soul, joined mine. The sheer scale of the beauty around us seemed connected to the scale of our love. Vital as life. Maybe more vital than life, really.

Then it was time to go back – not to Leeched Dry, but to Cromwell Street. It had been arranged with Uncle Mark that Dominic and I would spend several days together, prior to Dominic's visiting his father for a couple of days to finalise arrangements for his party. Dominic would drop me off at Leeched the following Sunday night, spend one night at Cromwell Street alone, and then go on to meet his father the next day.

Well, he did meet his father shortly, but in very different circumstances.

11

∫

'Sea purse: a small whirlpool formed by the meeting of two waves at an angle, dangerous to bathers'

— Chambers Dictionary

This time I went straight up to his room. I'd guessed he'd be out a lot, end of exams, that time of year, like, so I just watched from outside. It seemed like only one of them was in, a little girl with bright purple hair in the living room, watching TV. She looked around quickly when I walked in.

'Sorry about this. Dom's left something in his room for me. OK to go up there and get it?'

'Fine.' Stupid purple head swings back to the telly.

I reckoned I'd got a few minutes to look around. Found what I wanted at once – revision timetable-cum-diary thing, hanging on the wall, with the dates of when his exams had been on, when he was away, when he was seeing Helena, when she was staying with him. The lot. I took it with me and I worked out from that exactly when she'd be there, when his room would be empty and when they'd be walking back into it.

When I could make my move.

Even so, there's more hanging around this time than before. There's only one occasion, according to the timetable, when I can get my victim alone. Sunday night. So here I am, the stink of whisky in my mouth. (Vital part of the chemistry of The Alchemist – a magical mouthwash, turning fantasy into fact, turning me into my father, as the smell fills me with his filth, his hatred, his energy. His life.) At 8 o'clock, I'm walking up and down outside that shitty front door again. Vigilante. My car's parked around the corner, ready.

There's less coming and going this time; I think a couple of them must be away. The heavy boy's in his room the whole time, like, same as before, and the purple girl is in the living room. No sign of the lanky bastard or Helena just yet, which is just as I expected.

At 9.15 the purple girl goes out, leaving just heavy boy to worry about. I'm outside the door in seconds. I know it won't go exactly like the script, but I'm ready for a bit of ad-lib. I expect that. And here's the remake. Come to the pictures with me – my treat. Enjoy.

Until the end.

Alchemy Three
The (Second) Parting of the Lips
Fade in.
Establishing shot, click: a scruffy, ordinary street in Gorgie, the West End of Edinburgh. Almost dark. Me, walking to the door, looking purposeful, angry, righteous, strong. Medium shot, click, the brown, dirty door. Me, opening it quietly. Long shot, click, me, running smoothly and quietly upstairs, like a panther: big, long, silent strides. Medium shot, click, the door to his bedroom. Me opening it. Hushed. Clean, precise movements. Over the shoulder shot, click. Light switch, the view of his room – messy, disorganised, clothes everywhere, contrasting with the military precision of my earlier movements; the sharp and the sloppy juxtaposed. Camera follows me into the room. Close up of photograph on the table – Dom and Helena. Extreme close up, his skin, scarred, worse than mine. Soiled. Scan. Evidence located for the first time – bedside drawer, woman's black underwear, box of condoms, close up, click – opened. Close up of my face, click, pain in my eyes. But my jaw is strong, in control, manly.

Microphone, first sound, pulsating heavy metal music. Threat of discovery. Switch to my eyes, click, wary, worldly, judging risk. Long shot, click, me running down the stairs, out into the street, head turning around, urgent, keen-eyed. Long shot, click, I move into the alleyway. Dark, secluded. Not quite black and white. Yellowish light from streetlamp. Artistic.

Break for refreshments. Nothing happens. More whisky. Fire water. Long wait. Long, long wait. An hour and more than an hour.

Click back into action. Extreme close up, click, electronic watch, lit in the alleyway. 10.45pm. Foregrounding, click, a brick, with a sharp, broken end, resting beside my foot. Tension building – 'What happens next?' hanging in the air. Long shot, very swift, primary victim walks past, alone. Long shot, hero follows, long, strong strides. Expert attack, jumps on victim, very sudden. Unexpected. One scream, very shocked, very loud. Instant reaction, hero, drags victim into alleyway. Surprisingly hard fight, blows exchanged, kicks. Total focus. Total control. Hero picks up the brick. Hits victim, hard, in breast, from short distance with brick. Victim screams, again, very loud. Danger of observation. Victim knocks against hero, bangs hero's head on wall. Stunned. Brick in victim's hand. Victim bloodied. Looks into hero's face. Hesitates. Three for a girl. Fatal.

Hero punches victim in face. Victim falls. Medium shot, click, hero kicks victim hard in ribs. Replays, replays, replays. Blood seeping through victim's clothing. Face collapsing. Pathetic. Vulnerable. Cornered, down. Dark. Hard to see. Hero bends. Close up, click, victim foetal, long legs curled into body, face protected. Erotic. Artistic. I could do anything now. Hero kicks once, in side of face. Loud shout. Victim's lips, bloody, battered. The ultimate invite. Shared blood. Softer than the vagina. Mashed. Open. Swollen. Sound of feet running, hardly registers. Hero, total concentration on face, in eyes. Close up. Hero kneels in front of victim's face. Unzips. Pushes cock towards victim's face. Victim really screams. A reaction. Alarm. First words, 'No, please, no.'

Cut. Sharp brick hits my back, my shoulder. Spin around, damaged. Shit! Rasta man, purple girl, side by side. Brick hits my shoulder again, surprisingly strong, focussed. Fucking bitch hanging on my back, biting. Pulling hair. Military man out-manoeuvred. Outnumbered. One option. Elbow girl. Run. Fast. They stay with victim; hero returns to car. Escape, with brick. Escape, escape, escape.

Fade

There are all sorts of ways of losing your virginity; I didn't realise that until then. And that was the night I really lost mine.

I was in my own world, really, walking along the street, in the dark. Calm, peaceful, unworried. Sunday night. I was thinking about something so stupid, so ordinary – a job, maybe, now that my exams were over. And how that would affect the time I could spend with my love. And making plans, plans for my life, as if I was in control of its direction as usual. Normal.

And then I'm in his world. Entirely. Seconds, that's all it takes, and I'm in his dream. His masturbatory dream – that's the very worst part.

Steps, quick and sudden behind me. Trouble. Real trouble. Maybe escape? A shocked scream comes out – not what I'd have chosen. Strong arms on my back. No escape. Switch of colour. Shock. Then yellow, dead skin. Surreal. My nightmare; his weird and wonderful wank. Brighter. And I can smell him; I don't like the smell. Whisky. I don't know what he wants of me, but I'm not going to let him take it.

I'm doing all right for a while, holding my own, at least, and then a pain – a hard pain. Hard over my heart. I scream, scream for my life then. Think he's going to kill me; know he can kill me if he wants to. Does he want to? Half fall, half knock, up against him. I bang his head – lucky – stun him for a time. Grab the brick, and look at him. Shadowy, but I can see him better that way, see his mood, somehow: young, brown hair, not bad-looking; then I see his skin. Marked with scars. Familiar, and the yellowy light. Everything else is different. Thin skin, over chips of cheekbones. Poor-looking. Polluted. Stinks of whisky. Hard. Dead and alive. One of his front teeth is grey, the other crowned – badly. All of these ideas of him are recording in the video of my mind. I hesitate. Weak, weak, weak – fucking stupid.

One second is enough. He punches me in the face, the eye; that slipped second was enough. Lost it. Fall, curl up. He's kicking me in the ribs, hard, body thudding, jerking, against itself. Sick. The alleyway is filthy. Stinks of piss. I try to protect my face, my head, my eyes, with my arms. Almost useless. He sort of kicks down into me from the side, my face. No! Please, no. Did I say it or just think it? Did I say 'please' so quickly?

Everything is slow, really slow. Blood in my mouth; my teeth feel wrong, loose, on the side. I think again, He's going to kill me. Teeth, death. No. Shout, absolutely consciously, and as loud as I can. His skin beside mine then, intimate, close, too close – and the worst thing, the very worst thing. His zip. Creaking itself down. I stare at him through my curved, curled arms. If I'd seen those eyes before, I'd have killed him with that brick. Ice Man. The Ice Man.

Cock. Someone else's cock. Next to my face. I can smell his skin. And those eyes. Pure pleasure. I've had it now, had it completely. One last scream: really my last chance. 'No!' Definite.

Thank God – sound of feet. Sound of voices. A fight. Lots of noise. Sam's voice; Dixie's voice. Thank God. Then Dixie there, beside me. Thank God. Dixie.

'Dixie.'

'It's a bloke, Sam. All right, mate, it's all right. Sam, get an ambulance.' But she's stuck. 'Here. It's all right.' Dixie's touching my shoulder, pushing a jacket underneath my head. 'He's gone.' He doesn't recognise me, even though I've said his name. My mouth's all funny anyhow.

It takes ages to turn round. 'Dixie. Thank God.' Everything hurts. Creaks almost.

'Jesus, Sam! It's Dominic.'

Sam's crying now, really crying. 'Dominic . . .'

'Get an ambulance, Sam. Get an ambulance. He needs you – he really fucking needs you! Go on.'

I hear her run off. My eyes ache but I've never been so glad to see anyone in my life. 'Dixie.'

He moves my hair back and I realise that there's blood everywhere, especially on my chest.

'Dom, what a fucking mess.' His arm on my shoulder.

'I thought he was going to kill me.' I don't sound like me; my mouth is wrong. Don't feel like me. A tooth is loose.

'I know, I know. I saw his eyes.'

'Dixie, he had his cock out . . . It was like being in a film. Really. He had his fucking cock out. He was going to do something to me!'

'Sam's getting you an ambulance. You'll be all right.' No.

'Dixie, what was he going to do? I'd never even thought of a

bloke doing that to me.' He puts his other hand on my shoulder.
'What the fuck was he going to do? Don't tell Helena. Don't tell
anyone. Don't ever tell Helena.'

'No one'll know, Dom. No one will ever know. He's gone,
mate. No one knows. I won't say anything.' His hand is on top
of mine. 'He was a nutter – not your fault. Don't even think
about it. Don't. Did he break anything? Anything else?'

'My face, my chest, my ribs. It hurts to breathe. One of my
teeth is all loose – at the side.'

'Shit. You have to push them in. I've read about it. Definitely.
Straightaway.' I just lie there. I feel like I'll never move again.
'Here, Dom. Let me have a look.' Dixie comes around to the side
of my head and lifts my top lip away from my teeth. It's really
fucking battered in there, and I shout again. 'I know. I'm being
as gentle as I can, I promise. It's this one here, isn't it? I'll be
really quick.' Dixie holds my mashed face away from the tooth
and pushes it firmly back up so that it's more in place. Carefully.
It's a horrible, horrible feeling, and it doesn't seem quick at all.
It makes a noise. Dixie's got blood all over him. Water comes
automatically from my eyes. Can't I just die now? Even my nose
runs. Big Dominic Oliver, the hard rugby player. Shit soft now.
'I'm sorry, Dom. I know, I'm really sorry. But it'll stop it from
coming out – something about the roots. It's done now.'

I say, 'Helena.' I never want her to see my face like this. To
see me like this.

'I know, Dominic. Don't worry – I'll get her for you, soon as
I can. Where's the fucking ambulance?'

At last I close my eyes.

My eyes were closed, but I could hear the knocking. I'd only
just fallen asleep.

'Helena?' Knock, knock, knock. 'Helena.' I opened my eyes.
'You have to get up. There's been an incident, an accident.'

'What?'

'It's young Oliver. Dominic.'

I jumped straight out of bed and down to the phone.

'Helena, it's Dixie. You're the first person I've rung. Dominic's
been beaten up. We've just arrived at the hospital and he's been
asking for you.' He sounded odd, very distant.

'Is he all right?' Stupid. Predictable.

'I think he will be. They're just looking at him now. It was right beside the house. A one-off attack, I think. I was walking Sam home, thank God. We didn't even know it was Dominic at first. Sam got your number while we waited for the ambulance.'

'Which hospital are you in?' He rattled off the name and address. I had no pen, and no memory suddenly. Stupid, stupid. 'Sorry, Dixie. Tell me again?' Uncle Mark saved me, writing the address down as I repeated it.

'I know where it is, Helena. We'll go now.'

'I'll see you in an hour or so, Dixie.' An hour. Unbearable.

It was a grim journey. At least Uncle Mark didn't try to chat, for once.

'I don't even know what's wrong with him, how badly he's been hurt. I didn't ask.' Stupid, stupid, stupid.

'We'll be there soon, Helena.' At least the Crying Cavalier, like Uncle Mark, was reliable.

'He's got his Legal Practice course next year, his party in a week . . .'

Would we ever get there?

They told us at the entrance desk which ward he was in but when we found it Dixie was waiting outside the door in the corridor, for me – the first shock. His face was greyish and he was spattered with blood. Had he been crying? He looked more dishevelled than usual. Serious. Everything was suddenly even worse, black now.

'Helena, sit down,' he said.

I dropped on to a hard chair against the wall of the corridor and felt Uncle Mark's arm go around me.

'How is he?'

'Well, one tooth is loosened and his mouth's a mess, and his eye. They've x-rayed him. They don't think anything's broken. I saw the bloke's face, Helena – he was a real case. Dominic's lucky it wasn't even worse.'

'I want to see him.'

I gestured to Uncle Mark to stay where he was. And then Dixie and I walked through a door into a little side room.

'It's Helena, Dominic,' Dixie said, pushing at my back as we entered the room.' The back of Dominic's head reminded me of the first emerald Saturday. Then I moved to beside the bed, to where I could see him.

Shock. Total shock.

His skin was a mass of colours. The wrong colours. Automatically, I turned away from the bed and stepped a pace back from him. Part of me was absent and my ears sang. Then I felt Dixie's arm around me. 'Come on.' And he sat me back down.

'Dominic?' I just stared at him. A new Dominic. Then I touched his forearm. That seemed okay; he didn't flinch. But he kept his face turned away. I could see some of it anyway. His lips were massively swollen and bloody, starting to scab over. He wouldn't be able to eat anything, or maybe even drink, I thought. And his eye – the skin around the eye near me was a shining plum of pain, livid red and purple, and the eye itself was sickeningly bloodshot. The bits of his face that weren't bruised or swollen were an awful whitish-grey. My soft-scarred angel. 'Dominic.' Against the very white, tight hospital sheet at his waist, his chest was darkly bruised and clotted with blood. It was one of the worst moments of my life, and his, I'm sure. Neither of us spoke for a minute.

I turned to Dixie eventually. 'What happened to his chest?' I almost whispered.

'A brick. That's how I got him off in the end – I used it on him, the other bloke. Sam jumped on his back. I saw his face; she didn't.'

The place where he'd smeared my blood, just a week or so before. I desperately wanted him to talk to me. 'Dominic?' Nothing. What could I say or do? I took hold of his hand. He didn't pull it away, but he didn't move his fingers either. Ice Man. 'Dominic, tell me how you're feeling?' How could I reach him now? How could I heal him? 'You know I don't care how you look, Dominic.' Stupid thing to say. Stupid. He did pull his hand away then. I loved how he looked; he knew that. How many times had I stroked his head, his eyes, his lips?

'I don't want you to see me. I really don't.' A voice that was as different as his face.

Until I looked in his eyes, nothing would be right. I remembered. 'Dominic, you know when I was sick, after the balti house, and I didn't want you to see me? You said you didn't care about "mess" – about how "appropriate" it all was.' I knew he was listening. 'Remember how you took care of me? How you wanted to take care of me? How you carried me back to bed?' I touched a good bit of his face, very, very gently. 'I'll never forget. I felt like you'd saved my life. You didn't mind about a few scabby old bits of sick, did you?' I touched his hand again and he didn't pull away now. 'You loved me properly. Why should I care about a few . . . some marks on your face? I've seen inside you – really inside you.' I wasn't shy about Dixie being there – Dixie, who'd saved my Dominic; Dixie, who might have been crying, who wanted to protect Dominic now.

'Remember what you said just last week? I can remember every word, I wrote it in my diary.' The first time I'd mentioned my diary. '"If I can see your eyes, I'll be able to understand, to see you inside, to feel your feelings inside."' He moved slightly. I whispered, 'Dominic, don't shut me out.'

He turned then, and I saw right into all of the pain, and fear, and deep humiliation that he felt; I saw the emotional scars in his eyes, as clearly as a series of fleeting images on a cinema screen. I was with him, inside the film, inside his soul. Joined. Part of his nightmare. My breath caught and my eyes prickled, but it was what I'd wanted to feel, what I'd wanted to share, exactly. 'I know, I know.'

There was a new voice to understand now as he tried to speak. 'Tell me again, darling,' I said.

He breathed in and started again, laboured. 'Control, Helena. He took my control.'

'It hurts to breathe,' said Dixie, from his corner.

Nodding, I squeezed Dominic's hand and he squeezed back briefly at last, saying, 'He could do anything he wanted.' I nodded again. 'I did fight.' His head turned away. 'Why did he do that? Why?'

'I wish I'd been there. To help somehow.' Dominic shook his head, hard, but this hurt and his bad eye winced. How could I have helped? 'Do you want me to get your things?' I asked. He nodded. 'What do you need?'

'Anything.' His eyes looked fixed for a second.

'Are you tired?' I asked him. One nod.

Dixie came back to his side and sat down, saying quietly, 'I think the painkillers are pretty heavy.'

'Good. Sleep then. We'll stay here a while. You sleep.' I stroked his bare shoulder, his skin. 'I love you, Dominic.'

Closing his eyes, despite the mangled mask of his face, he wore an expression of such utter trust that my eyes prickled again. Shining inside. He slept at once. I was relieved, pleased that he was out of it and that the recovery process, the restoration, could begin. I wished that I could control his dreams, fill them with deep lochs and night skies, and take any nightmares into myself so that I could really share in what he'd been through on his own.

'Helena.' I turned away from Dominic, to Dixie as he spoke. 'He really has had a bad time.'

'I know,' I said, nodding my head.

'Really bad.' He was trying to tell me something else. I looked at him, asking with my eyes, but he shook his head, just once. 'I can't put it into words, but trust me and trust him. It might take him a while for him to get back to normal.'

'I understand.' Sort of.

The door opened and the stink of a very clean man made me turn my head. Aftershave and cleaning solution. I was still holding Dominic's hand, so it was Dixie who stood up.

'Mr Oliver.' Dominic's father. Of course. Dixie motioned him to a chair, saying, 'I'll swap with you.' He nodded at the bed. 'Dominic's asleep now, fast asleep.' There was the slightest trace of a warning in Dixie's voice. Then he retreated as Dominic's father sat down beside me. Not a good way to meet him, I thought. Then, I've got no make-up on, before I could edit it all. In fact, I felt cold towards his father. How many men wear suits at midnight, anyway? Armoured man. Cardboard man. There was something about his clinical cleanliness that disgusted me (and something that was the direct opposite to his son). I thought back to my conclusions about Nick Oliver, drawn from tiny scraps of conversation with Dominic. He dealt with lots of poor people, people he thought of as dirt (he specialised in compensation cases and most of his clients needed legal aid). But he was absolutely distanced from dirt of all kinds. Dominic's slightly offbeat scruffiness suddenly seemed so appealing, so human, in the face of that chemical cleanliness.

I was still looking at my sleeping darling's face. Then I looked all of a sudden at his father's and remembered instantly my own initial reaction on seeing Dominic's mouth, skin, eyes. I saw it all there – the shock and the pain that I'd felt, Nick Oliver felt now. But there was something else: an airbag of guilt, exploding against the inside of his chest – enormous, violent, almost overpowering him. He looked at me for the first time. His eyes were grey. Dominic had his father's big bones, but the face and the features were very different.

'That house, that area . . . I told him to get a house in a better area. I would have paid.' He looked again at Dominic's face – his son's face. Do you care now what degree he gets? I thought. Cruel. He looked beaten. 'Why wouldn't he let me pay?' I thought of one of Dominic's last comments to me: 'He took my control.' But I said nothing to his father; I thought that he was saying it all to himself. He sat there for a full minute, his own face working against itself, and then he seemed to remember me. He arranged his face deliberately before he turned.

I flinched a Leeched Dry smile. 'I'm Helena.'

'I thought you were. I'm Nick Oliver.' His eyes flickered. 'Well, you know that. Dominic talked about you the last time he phoned me. You were at St Mary's Loch with him, weren't you?' I nodded. He lowered his eyes to Dominic's face as he continued, 'He was really happy when he talked to me.' I nodded again. More guilt stained his face.

Time to go. 'I'll get Dominic's things and come back later,' I said to his father, and he nodded, deliberately keeping his face turned away from me. I kissed Dominic's cheek and whispered in his ear, 'See you later, Dominic.' Letting go of his big, sleeping hand was the hardest thing of all. I wanted to join my flesh to his, to graft my skin to his, so that my blood could flow through him until he was able to be strong again alone. But I had to go.

I turned around briefly at the door and saw that his father had taken Dominic's hand and was resting his brow on it. I heard him say, 'My son,' just once, very quietly, and I hoped that my darling could hear that too, through the painkillers.

* * *

I slept heavily last night, because of the painkillers. I hadn't realised I'd got so battered, like, until I got home.

The funny thing was, I started to feel something for him after that. Really feel it. I thought I was through with all that, after Helena let me down. But no. First of all, we'd shared her – Helena: we'd both seen her beauty, both loved her, both shed her blood. One blood. Triptych – three frames, one story.

Then there was the fight; it was a bit like being in a Roman arena. My arena. Dramatic. Erotic. My world, and I'd pulled him into it, part of it. Part of me. Two gladiators, locked together. And he'd put up a reasonable fight, Dominic, all things considered. Not as strong as me, like, but still.

And when he had that brick in his hand – my dad would've bricked my face in if I'd done that to him, might have killed me. But he didn't – Dominic, I mean. It was a weakness, like, obviously, but it was more generous than anything a woman's ever done for me. And I'd been generous to him. Hadn't really hurt him. Don't think I even broke his teeth – couldn't get through his arms properly.

And then, thinking of him like that, like he was at the end . . . It always gives me a hard on. All curled up, dirty blond hair messed up, red lips, open, pouting, swollen. Waiting. A crimson cushion for my cock. I liked that. I kept reliving that bit, loving it. Ready for me, screaming for it. My own Dominic.

I sort of lost my own virginity, something I didn't expect at all. I mean, I'd never even thought about blokes much before, not like that. Not really, like. But lying in bed now, whenever I think of him, Dominic, I think of my cock and his face. Together. A cushion and a cock.

And the best bit is that I know he's waiting for me. In hospital.

Visiting time soon – it's the last thing I think as I drift down into sleep.

Uncle Mark, Dixie, Sam and I drove around Edinburgh that night, looking for the things that Dominic would need (I was desperate to do something for him immediately, even if it was only buying a few things) and we found a shop that stayed open all night. Not looking at Uncle Mark's face, the first thing

I picked up was a bottle of Lucozade. Then I bought tins of sweets, chocolate, magazines: baby things to spoil Dominic, just like he'd spoiled me when I'd been ill. When we went back to his room, I collected some books I thought he'd like to read, his emerald, some clean clothes, our photograph and, when no one was looking, the cream that I knew he needed for his skin. A few open pores seemed less relevant than ever to me now but I knew, purely from the fact that he'd never once mentioned it to me if nothing else, that Dominic was really sensitive about his skin.

Later we drank coffee and talked – what the doctors had said, the ins and outs of damaged ribs, bruises, loose teeth, black eyes, discovering bits of medical knowledge amongst us that had never been of any use or interest before. We lived and re-lived the attack, trying to make sense of it all. And then we slept (Uncle Mark on the couch and me under the mousey quilt) so that we would be fresh to go and see him the next day. Only the knowledge that Dominic would sleep heavily because of the painkillers allowed me to slip into sleep myself, breathing in his nightsmells from the quilt.

So this morning, I was up and ready. Not early, I've got a fair bit of damage to recover from myself, but I was up at 10, adding the new script to my file. My back's a bit sore and bruised, I mean, I've been in the wars. But I need to see Dominic. I'm not going to speak to him, necessarily, but I don't want him to forget me either. Strike while the iron's hot.

I go straight to the hospital nearest where he lives. Got it in one. Then I'm at reception, acting the part, with my rehearsed voice and speech and my worried mask. 'Jason Oliver, brother of Dominic Oliver. Came in late last night – badly beaten up. Some damage to his ribs, I believe.' Nice woman directs me straight to his ward.

But when I get there, he's already got company. Standing in the corridor, I can just about hear some of what they're saying to each other. It's more than a bit familiar.

I can see straightaway that it's his father. He's that age, like, and the same build as Dominic. And while his dad doesn't look as much of a bastard as mine, he doesn't look a barrel of laughs either, or sound it – that's one more thing we've definitely got in common. The type of argument is different – more of a middle-class subject, like – but I can see Dominic hasn't got the golden boy existence that I thought he had before either.

It's more his dad's tone of voice than anything else, harsh, like, when it's obvious that Dominic's having a hard time.

'Cancel it? We were all set to fine-tune the arrangements when we spoke last week. If you could even just make an appearance – I'd do everything else.'

'Leave it, Dad.'

Dominic's voice sounds strange. Does he think of me, every time he moves his lips? Soft lips. Cut lips. Breakable beauty. He's black and blue and a few other colours besides; anyone can see that the last thing he'll feel like is some kind of a do.

'Leave it? After all the time I've put into organising it, all the work I've done?'

There's more along the same lines – I can't hear it all. And then my attention is taken up with something else. Someone else. Obviously I'm keeping an eye out. I don't think any of them had got a good look at me in that alleyway, but if Rasta man or the purple girl make an appearance, I'm making myself scarce, like.

I hear footsteps, take one very quick look over my shoulder, and stare straight into Helena's eyes.

Electricity. Like the click of a light switch. It's the third time I've seen him but the first time the wires have touched.

Uncle Mark and I are walking down the corridor to Dominic's side ward, chatting half-heartedly. My mind is one-third on Uncle Mark's conversation and two-thirds on Dominic. How will he be? What will I say to him?

Then I look up at *him*: eye to eye, one bright shot. Freeze frame – one shot that changes my mind more than any whole film ever will again. One shot. Because I know exactly what I'm staring at.

He was the cut-out at the window. He was the dummy on the train, with the black-eyed, white-faced, rag doll girlfriend. And now I've got a black-eyed, white-faced, rag doll Dominic lying in bed while *he* is here in the hospital. It was all *him*. The Stone

Man. I know him. And I know in that second that I've really come of age. That sooner or later, I will have to act.

Coming of age. Alone.

In that one second, I know – she knows me – she knows what I've done. What I am. And she knows what I can do, and she's frightened of me. A reaction.

I turn away from them at the door, quick, before she can do anything about it, and I'm off down that corridor, straight into the main ward, as if I was visiting someone down there. Escape.

Then I'm off down the stairs at the other side and straight into the car park to wait for daddy. Because I can be a lot of help to Dominic.

Who could help me? Who could help me? Who could possibly help me?

I ran through the list. Uncle Mark would be too difficult to convince, without 'hard evidence, etcetera'. He was more likely to believe that I had an adolescent mental problem than a definite hunch, not to mention he was pretty obsessed with Lisa, just then. What could he do anyway? Ditto police. What evidence did I have? Absolutely none. Dominic? Definitely, but not at that point, not in the state he was in. So what should I do? And what did the Stone Man want with me, with us? What would he do to us? What would he do to us?

All of this was in my head. Uncle Mark was in one ear and something else was in the other: Dominic's father, on the other side of the door, talking. Keeping me out. I started to listen to what he was saying. It was a pretty one-sided conversation.

'Your degree results will be out soon. It's all planned. The timing's perfect.'

'Perfect for you, for your plans,' Dominic said, slowly.

'My plans for you – to show everybody how proud I am of you.' There was a response I couldn't quite hear and then his father spoke again. 'Of course you'll get a first. You're an Oliver, aren't you? You won't have to do a thing – just turn up. You'll be feeling much better by then. We have to show the profession that you can't keep the Olivers down.'

Again, I couldn't hear Dominic's reply, but I'd heard plenty by then. It looked like the father had a much quicker recovery rate than the son; but then, he hadn't been subjected to the rag doll routine. Nick Oliver suddenly seemed like a very small fiend in comparison to the Stone Man with the stare. Enough.

My make-up mask was in place, my hair was combed and my social skills were well honed: I was ready to make my entrance. I sailed in, very bright and breezy, as if I'd only just arrived there.

'Mr Oliver, how nice to see you. Have you been here long? We came earlier but Dominic was too tired to see anyone.' A lie. 'The doctor said we were to expect him to be very worn out for a few days.' I was rewarded by a look of instant contrition on Nick Oliver's face. I took charge of Dominic's bedside table then, emptying my bag and arranging his books and things, making little comments about what I'd brought as I went along. As I expected, his father stood up.

'Right, Helena, I'll leave you to it. I've been here a while anyway.' And then, to Dominic, 'I'll see you later this afternoon then. Anything else you need?' Dominic must have shaken his head because I heard, 'Right. Think about what we were saying, then. Take care.' And he was off through the door, exchanging professionally polite and inappropriate greetings with Uncle Mark in the corridor outside.

If only the other demon was as easy to dispel.

Brothers under the skin – his dad, my dad, his girl, my girl, his skin, my skin. One blood.

I watch the old bastard get into his big BMW, then I follow him in the Bundymobile – right across to the other side of Edinburgh. He's in such a strop, stupid wanker, tooting and hooting at people: I'm sure he doesn't notice me at all. Too wrapped up in his own fucking ego to see what's right in front of his eyes.

It's all big Victorian houses where he lives so I can't get an address. Can't see a street sign, would you believe? Detached. Par for the course. But I reckon I could find it again easily enough, like, with my orienteering skills. Then he goes back to work, parks in his own little parking space, his own little world, looking all important and blown up with himself – past the flash bastard brass plaque on the door:

> # PORT OLIVER LEGAL SERVICES
>
> ## Portman, Oliver, Rumney and Tremain

Next, I see his head appear at a ground-floor window. (Bet his secretary is in for a bollocking. I make a mental note to give her a ring, some time.) His office is all modern, glassy and sharp, with big, glossy prints on the walls to match. That's what gives me my idea – instantly – for my own next work of art, *Alchemy Four*, something altogether more Damien Hirst.

It's like the click of a slide in a projector – the whole image falls right into place.

I clicked my chair towards Dominic's bed, back in my rightful place, just as I'd pictured myself before. I slipped back into my normal, non-cheese-and-wine persona and smiled at him, taking his hand in mine.

'How did you do that?' he asked, smiling his first hospital smile. Even that must have hurt.

'Easy. I just pretended to be as insensitive as him. It works with a lot of Uncle Mark's friends. It's one of my Leeched Dry survival techniques.'

I grinned at Dominic. The swelling of his face was still grotesque, and the colours more spectacular if anything, but he looked better in himself – stronger.

'How do you feel?'

'Like shit.' Very Dominic. I laughed.

'Well, I think you look a tiny bit better than yesterday.'

'My chest hurts.' He drew breath. 'And my ribs.' He paused. 'My dad was being an arsehole.' Every breath was laboured.

'I know. I heard. If you don't want to go ahead with the party, then don't. You don't have to.'

Dominic touched his skin. 'My face.'

'I know, I know.' I tried to send some healing power to him

through my eyes, and my fingers as I stroked his hand. 'Do you know when you'll be able to come out of here?'

'Tomorrow, I think.'

'That's quick. But Dixie said it might be that soon.'

'Can you stay?'

'Of course I can.' I stroked his hair. 'Uncle Mark is going to stay at Cromwell Street tonight as well, so he can ferry me to and from here and pick you up tomorrow. Then he's going to get some stuff for me from Leeched, so I can stay a while. He's been brilliant.'

'I didn't know he was here.' Of course – Dominic hadn't actually seen Uncle Mark.

'Yes, he's just outside. He's finding Cromwell Street a bit of an experience.' I laughed. 'He's bought you a loo brush for the bathroom, some Jif for the kitchen, and some fabric cleaner for the settee he had to sleep on.'

Dominic smiled again. I missed his strange, energetic bark of a laugh, and went into an Uncle Mark impersonation of my own. '"I can't believe this is Nick Oliver's son's house. Nick Oliver's kitchen is all steel and granite."'

Dominic closed his eyes. 'The food museum . . . He hasn't been in there?'

'Once. He couldn't even bring himself to use his Jif. He had to come out; I think he felt faint. We've been eating takeaways from the cartons, "to lessen the health and safety risk" etcetera.' I rolled my eyes. 'I don't imagine your dad went in for steel and granite when he was a student, anyway. Or Uncle Mark either, come to that.'

'My dad went in for steel and granite nappies.' Dominic paused for breath. 'That's if he ever needed nappies.' He smiled the strange, swollen smile again. How could I make him feel better?

'I've tried to bring your favourite books. And some magazines and sweets. Oh, and I'll leave this here.' The emerald. 'I'm glad you'll be out soon.' A new concern. 'What about food? What will you eat?'

'Nothing. I can't.'

'But you'll have to eat something or how are you going to get better?'

Dominic shook his head very slightly. 'Too sore.'

'Maybe I could buy some thin soup? Or some of those health food drinks?'

'Later,' he replied. I would have to have a word with the nurse, like a real woman, a wife almost, before Dominic came out.

It was amazing but just that short conversation seemed to have tired him out – or maybe it was the longer 'conversation' with his father that had preceded it. I could see the change in his eyes immediately.

'You're sleepy, aren't you?'

He nodded slightly. 'Painkillers, I think.'

'Rest then. You need to rest.'

But he made his creased green eyes stay open. 'Don't go.'

I kissed a pale bit of cheek and squeezed his hand. 'No. I want to watch you sleep. I want to stay with you. Don't worry.'

One slow smile and then the eyes did close. I stroked his fine, fair hair. I wanted to lie down on the bed beside him (but not with Uncle Mark just outside). My soft scarred angel.

Fear of the Stone Man lay heavy in my stomach. What on earth was I going to do?

I thought hard for most of that afternoon, preparing for when Dominic came out of hospital – trying to ease his way, like. And I was full of *Alchemy Four*. The finale had to be something really special and so did this one, being the middle one, like, the crux – the centrepiece, so to speak. So it was three scripts, one soft sculpture and three more pieces, I'd decided. Between them, a tribute to every one of my heroes.

I didn't know what sort of a do his father had in mind but that didn't matter. I knew all about people making you do things you didn't want to do, and ignoring how you felt all the time, blind bastards. So I was the man to stop it. This was a crux for me as well, like – generous in the extreme.

Now what I've got in mind wouldn't bother my dad that much – apart from the waste of flesh, like – he's a hard bastard. But I've seen 'Mr Oliver', all clean, crisp and confident. And I've heard his voice. He'd have damaged Dominic much more than I had over the years, and with much less cause. All's fair in love and war, and my love has shifted. I'll protect Dominic a bit, now. He seems a soft, middle-class shite in some ways – the old man. And I know something about the kind of things he likes, which makes it pretty easy to work out what he'll hate. So it doesn't take me long to work out how I can disgust him the most. I know exactly how to prepare it. All it takes is a visit to a supermarket, a visit to a card shop and a bit of concentration.

A film isn't the appropriate medium this time – I'm not sure how it's going to land, for one thing – but I wanted a permanent reminder of my art for my records and myself. So I typed a review of my sculpture into my computer last night as part of my preparation, my fine-tuning, and put it in my file with the shooting scripts.

Then I put a copy of the review on the wall, alongside a photograph of Damien's sheep: The Funeral Follower, my inspiration. Shock art. Have a look at the review if you like.

Alchemy Four
The Party's Off
This highly creative and disturbing piece of work by Adam Ramsden was commissioned by his friend, Dominic Oliver, as a gift to his father, Mr Oliver, Senior, following Dominic's stay in hospital.

The vividly evocative soft sculpture consists of an ingeniously selected and prepared display of offal, which includes a lamb's heart and an entire lamb's lung. (Dominic Oliver recently sustained chest injuries, and was suffering from breathing problems at the time he commissioned the sculpture. He has since fully recovered.)

In addition, Adam included some of his own semen as part of the exhibit which, he explains, is a reference to Mr Oliver, Senior's public school upbringing, and the effect that this has had upon his relationship with his son. (It is common practice in some public schools for adolescent boys to pass pieces of liver around dormitories, each boy masturbating in turn on to the meat before quickly passing it on.)

The sculpture was designed to be assembled at Mr Oliver's house in an almost haphazard heap. This form of ad-libbing is a recurrent feature of Adam Ramsden's work.

The title refers to a 'Thank you for your invitation to a party' card which sits on top of the assembled offal, completing the sculpture. The message inside the card reads, 'The party's off': a witty pun, which refers to both the cancellation of Dominic Oliver's party and the pungent state of the one-day-old offal (which was deliberately kept in a very warm place in order to create the desired aroma).

This is a brave and innovative piece of work by young Adam Ramsden, the centrepiece to his collection of seven inspired, and connected, works of art.

The whole thing is one big laugh, like. (Apart from the bit with the raw liver – that was fucking heroic. Perverted public school wankers!) And here I am, all ready to deliver it now. (Did you spot that one? I'm quite getting into these arty farty puns.)

It's fairly early in the morning. There's a wall around the house and plenty of room around that, so nobody sees me jump across with my carrier. It's all heavy and slopping around in the carrier bag – just right. Stinking.

I can see through the letterbox that the floor of his hallway is marble: black and white, pristine, the perfect frame for my dead meat. What a contrast! And it's a red hot day – Lady Luck again. It'll ripen up nicely in there. It's already sweating away nicely in its bag, all seven pounds of it – one for each hero and all for Dominic. Four for a boy. I shovel the lot through the letterbox with a kid's plastic spade (I don't touch it myself, of course) and take a photo quickly of the bloodied letterbox – to make the connection with *The Parting of the Lips*. Then I wipe the letterbox with a clean cloth. What I'm really hoping is that he'll stand in it, unsuspecting, like. Give it a more personal dimension. I drop the card on top of it all, and I'm away.

I sneak a look through his living-room window as I make my escape. Maybe I should create another piece called *Movement against Minimalism* in his lounge? Bowel movement. I'm quite getting into this. Everything in his house is black and white. Dead classy, of course, but no life in it. And no death – until now.

It's the most selfless thing I've ever done, I'm thinking, as I walk back to my car, and I have to say, I enjoyed it. I've got a feeling I'll be coming back to the father again at a later date. Lots of work to be done there and I'm just the one to do it.

*   *   *

I thought long and hard about how I could please Dominic the most and so I spent most of the afternoon preparing for when he came out of hospital. His room was a work of art, considering its original state. I'd put all of his law stuff (carefully) into a big box underneath his table, and arranged a selection of books and magazines in its place. Sam had let me borrow the TV from her room and that was there too. This was Dominic's leisure area, I thought.

The table to one side of him was his snack bar: I'd put big straws on top of it. (The nurse had said he would be able to drink soup and stuff with those soon, when the swelling went down. Soon? He'd already not eaten for thirty-six hours. Dominic – who normally ate like he breathed.) Plus some cold drinks and a little menu with all of the soups and juices and drinks I'd bought for him on it, so he could choose what he wanted.

And the table to the other side was his healing table, with Lucozade, his tablets from the hospital, some vitamin pills and a topaz on it. (*'Inspires an abundance of health by giving powerful assistance to tissue regeneration and strengthening almost every organ and gland.'*) For myself I'd bought pyrite, as a prayer to myself for *'a more positive outlook on life'*. *Crystal Health and Wealth* assured me that, *'This one gives off sparks.'* I knew that I needed energy of my own to beat the Stone Man. Giving off sparks was about right.

Dominic's bed linen was all clean, and his clothes. I'd even sprayed my perfume over his sheets – like Lady Macbeth and her petals, preparing for the king's visit in the Polanski film. (Not sure if that was a good idea or not – a bit on the pungent side, maybe.) I'd tidied up and hoovered (they had one next door) and I'd even cleaned the bathroom. This was the most (almost the only) housework I'd ever done in my life, so I was feeling really selfless and good.

One interesting thing I'd found in the middle of all of this was a little old diary, navy blue, from the year before. The diary was tucked away in the middle of all of his clothes. I was dying to read it, but I knew how I'd feel if Dominic read mine so I left it. It can be easy to get completely the wrong impression from diaries, can't it? I knew that better than anyone from some of the things I'd written in mine at one time or another.

I couldn't wait for Dominic to come home so that I could look after him, protect him. Make him all whole and healed and perfect. My soft-scarred angel. And when he was feeling better – to protect him further – I would have to tell him what I knew about his attacker.

All of the time I was preparing for Dominic's home-coming the next day, I was also working out how to protect him from his father's pressure as well. His exam results were due out in three days time, his party in five. So I was composing a blazing letter in my head, obscene almost, to be honest, to his dad, meaning to slip it through his steel and granite door at some point. I revised it until it was word perfect and wonderfully hard-hitting. But I only thought about it; I never actually wrote it or anything. Just as well probably, don't you think?

At 8.30 the next morning we were ready to bring Dominic home in the Crying Cavalier. Uncle Mark walked towards the car in ambulance driver mode, sort of stiff and proud and terribly important. Dominic was pretty damaged – bruised everywhere (not least his Lion King's pride), but he managed to get into the car, just, and he certainly seemed pleased to be leaving the hospital. I had to pretend I didn't see him as he was struggling a bit to get into the back of the Cavalier. Uncle Mark took his things and then I jumped into the back seat beside Dominic, a bit energetically, which made him flinch, but he didn't say anything.

'We'll be there before you know it, young Oliver. Home and dry.'

Dominic flinched again, an expression in his good eye that made him look almost his normal, wicked self.

Dixie, Sherry (of course) and Sam were waiting at the door of Cromwell Street when the Crying Cavalier crawled solicitously up the road, and they all made a tremendous fuss of him. Sam and Sherry had even bought presents for him – a bottle of wine and a book, going by the shape of the parcels.

I felt Dominic try, and succeed, to ignore the alleyway, to avoid looking over to the left-hand side of the house as he walked through the doorway. It seemed as if the actual ground there had absorbed some of the violence and he was drawn to it yet afraid of it. I associated Cromwell Street with fun, friendship, love, lust and Dominic. His memories of it now would be damaged, I realised, and I felt sad. The end of his student semi-childhood. Then Dominic was in the house, opening his presents (wine and a book) and soon he was catching up on the Cromwell Street gossip. Jen had gone home for a while; Sam and Doug had had a row (for a change) and Eric was still being Eric. Dominic talked a bit about the police interview he'd had at the hospital, saying that they didn't hold out much hope of catching anyone, because there was only the description and no other evidence, which was pretty much as I'd thought. He turned down some of Sam's chicory coffee with his usual ease and smiled, slowly, several times. Almost back to normal in other words.

Waving Uncle Mark off always took at least twenty minutes and that day was no exception. His elaborate three-point turn (punctuated by a window wave at every one of the three points, plus a few more besides) was his trademark, and it painfully delayed the delicious sigh of relief we all shared when his car finally disappeared from view. Uncle Mark was probably the most relieved of all – Leeched Dry's faraway antiseptic cleanliness was a siren to his tortured senses, not to mention the Avon-like scent of the fragrant Lisa. I was staying at Cromwell Strect for a while. Dominic said he was tired and, leaving the others, we went upstairs to his room.

Dominic's shoulders dropped by inches as he entered his own lair and he said simply, 'Nice to have peace,' before sitting down on the bed, sniffing suspiciously and coughing. I showed him all the magazines and books that I'd got for him and the menu. He lifted his eyes to the ceiling. 'I don't think I'll ever want to eat again.'

'Well, just tell me when you want to try. Do you want the telly on?'

'No, I don't want the telly. I don't want food. I don't want anything.' Pause for breath. 'What have you been doing to these sheets?'

Ow! I thought for a second. 'Is it seeing the alleyway? Is that what's upset you? Maybe it would be better if you moved.'

'Jesus, Helena, you're worse than my dad,' he snapped. Hardly fair, but fair isn't always the point. 'Just because I've been beaten up once doesn't mean that I'm a complete wimp, you know.'

'I know that.'

'Well, stop talking about moving then!'

Stopping talking altogether seemed the best solution, so I did. Dominic sat on the bed, a mass of stiff, limbs and stubborn pain. Then he turned to me and let out some breath as he looked into my face. 'Not your fault, I know. I'm sorry.'

'Whose fault, then?' I asked, and waited.

He exhaled further. 'Guess?' Averting his eyes from mine, Dominic looked inside himself for the right words. 'He's taken something away from me, Helena. Forever. I know now that anyone can do anything they want to me.' He paused for a second. 'That's what this has hammered into me. I never knew it before. Hadn't a clue. You're not in charge of your direction the way most people think they are. How *dare* he do that to me? How fucking *dare* he?'

This was Dominic's longest speech since the attack and he breathed hard for a minute as his sore chest recovered, giving me time to work out how to counter his feelings of helplessness. 'Dominic, you *are* in control of your direction, your life,' I said. 'You fought him, didn't you? And Dixie and Sam fought him for you. That was all taking control. It's just that he was the one with the brick, at first.'

'Yes, at first.' He shuddered. 'If I had the chance to fight him again, it would be totally different. I had the chance to beat him, Helena, I really did, after I got the brick. But when I looked at his face, and saw that his skin was exactly like mine, I didn't want to do it.' Another pause for breath. 'It would have been like hurting myself. But later, when I saw the look in his eyes, I felt like I was facing pure fucking evil. If ever I have to face him, face *that*, again, at least I'll know what I'm up against from the start.'

'He's gone now, Dominic.' Was I trying to protect him or was I too much of a wimp myself to face the next stage? I'll leave you to answer that one.

Dominic cleared his throat. 'And you were right about the alleyway. I sensed him when we drove past there before.

'And the strangest thing was when I was in hospital, talking to my dad, while he was going on, I got a sort of replay of the whole thing, this sense of evil and a feeling of unreality, of being in a film, all over again. Just before you came in.'

Dominic had sensed him then, the Stone Man, had known that he was near. A wave of energy left my body, lifting my hair. The perfect time to tell him. I turned my eyes towards his, just as his head fell forward and he looked down towards his knees.

'God, Helena, I'm tired.' He handed me a get-out clause.

'Too much talking. Do you want to be on your own?'

'No. Lie with me.'

Bliss. Bliss and ease. It was exactly what I wanted to do as well, and I swallowed my feelings of guilt, of copping out.

We almost undressed, then lay down together, and I held him carefully in my arms, feeling as if I could pass my energy to him as he rested. I looked at his face and his eye, and examined the various scabs and bruises all over him as he slipped into sleep, getting to know and love the new version of him – a slightly different person forever, maybe. Loving scars. I put the topaz underneath his pillow and dreamed awake for a while as Dominic dreamed asleep beside me.

Resting was mainly what he wanted to do, and the rest of the day passed uneventfully until Sam called upstairs at about seven o'clock.

'Phone call – for Dominic, next door.'

'Thanks, Sam.'

Dominic was asleep, so I ran downstairs.

'We give next door's phone number to family and so on, just for emergencies,' Sam explained. 'They don't mind.'

'I'll go and see who it is.' And I was off into the house next door, which was a mirror image of Cromwell Street, only clean. The young couple gestured towards the phone and I picked up the receiver.

'Dominic?' a voice barked.

'No, this is Helena. Dominic is asleep,' I explained. 'This sounds like Mr Oliver.'

'Yes, it is.' His tone softened slightly. 'How is he?'

'He seems a bit better, actually.' I chatted about Dominic's progress for a few minutes, assuming that that was why his father had rung, then began to wind the conversation down.

'Hold on, Helena. Do you know anything about, shall we say
. . . a delivery made at my house today?'

'A delivery?' I immediately thought of my mental (forgive the
pun) letter, but no, it was safely stored in the post box of my
mind. 'I don't know what you mean.'

He thought for a while. 'Are any of Dominic's friends art
students or whatever?' There was an odd sort of scorn in
his voice.

'I think a couple of them are media students, but I'm not really
sure. Why?'

His father tutted. 'Some student prank. Anyway Helena, tell
Dominic that as far as he's concerned, the party really is off. My
secretary will ring all of his friends to explain, and I'll use the
food and the marquee – turn it into a purely legal do.'

'That sounds like a good idea.'

'Are you sure you don't know anything about a . . . package?'

I was genuinely bewildered, and slightly irritated by him now.
'Absolutely not.'

'We'll leave it at that, then. Pass on the message about the
party if you would, please. Oh, and tell Dominic to ring me when
he gets his results.'

And he was gone. I thanked the neighbours, swapped houses,
and ran upstairs to Dominic to tell him the good news.

12

'The crab's sensitive nature is covered with a hard shell'
– Linda Goodman's Sun Signs

Dominic's results. He wouldn't even get out of bed at first – barked at me all morning, and *not* with laughter. Dixie was dispatched to the University alone, to wait for the posting of the results on the notice board. Meanwhile, Dominic sat in bed, changing channels constantly, brooding, his eye an alarming yellow at the edges of its bruise and his mood almost visibly black.

Sam cajoled him downstairs eventually and he was frowning at a cup of chicory when Dixie arrived back. He walked straight into the living room, absolutely overtaken by smiles, and looked directly at Dominic, who jumped to his feet. 'A 2:1 and a first, mate – my 2:1, your first.'

Dominic tilted his head back and shook Dixie's hand, held it almost, then put his other hand on Dixie's shoulder. 'Brilliant, Dixie. Well done. Brilliant.' A kind of spark passed between them; Dominic's hand stayed around Dixie's for seconds and I felt, not for the first time, that I didn't know everything that had happened that Sunday night.

The moment passed, the handshake broke, and Sam and I both kissed Dominic at once, one on each cheek (quite a stretch for Sam). He'd have been a hero to me if he'd got a pass degree but I was delighted for him. I noticed that he didn't rush to ring his father. We celebrated with extra hot chicory (at first) and then began to make plans for a very different graduation party altogether.

Ten days after receiving Dominic's results, it was party night at Cromwell Street – a twenty-two-year-old's party rather than a middle-aged lawyer's party. His birthday had fallen into the recovery period and we'd decided to celebrate it later.

The house's name and reputation had given us the theme for the party: it was to be a horror party, with guests appearing as characters from their favourite horror film, book or song. I worried that this was a tad tactless, bearing in mind what Dominic had just been through, but he was undaunted – maybe laughing at horror was one way of recovering from it – so preparations had gone ahead and the night was upon us.

The house had been 'Cromwelled up' as Sam called it, in lots of different ways. A friend in fashion had brought several mannequins and we'd half buried them in rugs, going (pretty unsuccessfully) for the 'buried bodies' look. The light bulbs were all red, which helped a bit. The toilet had been left especially streaky for its star appearance, and handcuffs and chains were attached – suggesting the worst torture imaginable (and one that I could personally identify with, unfortunately).

There was a witches' cauldron of soup, prepared by Dominic, and green bread, cooked and hand-coloured by Sam's fair hands, using some food colouring left over from when her hair had been bleached and lawn-striped, and she had also made a Devil's Blood Punch, with peeled 'eyeball' lychees bobbing glassily around in it. Black plastic and dry ice made smoking, hellish tunnels of the corridors, and Dominic's sister's candelabra was out in flame again. The tapes were done – theme tunes from *The Hunger*, *The Omen* and similar. Cromwell Street was ready; there was only ourselves left to prepare.

Eight o'clock, and Dominic and I were in his bedroom. Dominic was ineptly smoothing white theatrical make-up over his still colourful face, 'drooging' himself up for the evening as *A Clockwork Orange*'s own Alex, while I was strategically cutting bits away from an old black dress. I don't expect Cathy's ghost (from *Wuthering Heights*) normally had slashes in her skirts up to the tops of her thighs, but then, the Brontës themselves didn't have much fun, did they? All that coughing and those tiny little shoes. I reckoned I was allowed my own artistic interpretation of the character, after all, so I'd gone for wanton, abandoned hair, very raggy dress and one well-lacerated wrist – stage blood, of course (all that to-ing and fro-ing through the window with Lockwood).

Dominic's bad eye was dramatically encircled in false eyelashes (Sam's again) and he was just posturing proudly in his bowler hat and Crombie, working out the most flattering angle for the hat. I was quite frightened of him myself. He caught sight of me hacking away at my hem in the mirror. 'What've you got on there?'

'Well, I'm meant to be a waif – it's got to be all raggy at the bottom.'

'What's underneath the raggy bottom?'

I laughed. 'Some of the sexiest underwear unknown to nineteenth-century womanhood. Especially selected with my own Heathcliff in mind.'

Dominic rolled his eyes. 'Shit. I'll have to keep Jem in line all night.' A thought distracted him. 'Did you move those stockings, the train stockings, when you sorted my room out?'

'I don't think so.'

'Well, I haven't seen them for ages.'

'I must have, then.' I walked up to join him at the mirror. 'Do you want to see these ones?' We hadn't made love since his hospital visit and I'd been reluctant to initiate it. Dominic touched his face. There was a strange, waiting presence about him, somehow, that night.

'I'm not exactly a silver screen heart throb, am I?'

Actually, he looked pretty fierce in his black clothes, with the remnants of his bruises showing through the make-up, but I kissed him anyway. His lips were getting back to normal, at least. 'You're getting there.'

I reached back to the little bedside table and pulled out a parcel from it. 'Happy birthday – a bit late.' He grinned and ripped the wrapping paper off. A heavy, plain, silver chain lay coiled in his hand. 'I want you to wear it all of the time,' I said, and ran my fingers across his healing chest, 'to touch your skin when I'm not there.'

'I love it,' he said, and kissed me with real feeling before drawing away and putting it on immediately. Then he ran his hands right up my legs, stopping short at skin level. 'You feel gorgeous.'

'Good!' I wanted to tease him. 'I'll finish getting ready, then.'

Banging doors a few minutes later told us that the first people had arrived, and we ran downstairs. It was Sour Sherry, a critical look on her face and some smiling friends at her side.

'Helena! You look like a face from the grave in all that black.' Followed by a complete face-change. 'And Dominic, looking gorgeous as ever.' Sherry was a natural as Edward Scissor Hands, hair and make-up more or less as usual and kitchen knives attached to her hands. Bliss. She and Dominic wouldn't be able to touch each other for blades.

Death stumbled in, offering drinks. 'Welcome to hell! Have some Devil's Blood.' Sam, in a sort of black fencing mask. Once at the Devil's Blood herself, Death discovered that she couldn't drink through the mesh, so one of the mannequins took Sam's place as Death, although she kept her scythe, using it to jab at any unfortunate man she found vaguely attractive, later. Dixie appeared next, looking shy, with 666 'tattooed' below the dreadlocks and a ridiculously angelic expression on his face. Then a whole coven of brightly painted witches arrived, covered in stockings and suspenders, and all making the most incredible fuss of Dominic: returning hero, birthday boy and first-class bloke all round. They soon had white make-up smeared all over their cheeks as well. The cauldron was stirred, the music was on, and the party was underway.

As more and more people turned up and the noise built, I had a bit of time, curled in an armchair in the corner, to think about the past week. I kept thinking I could see the Stone Man, hidden beneath various people's masks and hats. Where would I find the strength to face him, and to tell Dominic? I'd never had to deal with anyone like that before, and I wasn't in a hurry to start. Would I ever have the courage? Was I really that small, inside? I hated my weak, sneaky, silent self.

And why was he targeting us? The attack on Dominic obviously had something to do with me. But what? I remembered those eyes on the train that day, the eyes in the window, eyes trained on me. Evil. Evil and something else. Lust was too kind a word for it. Part lust, part hate – totally terrifying.

I'd been so worried about Dominic, and force-feeding *him* that I'd lost even more weight. So I was feeling skinny, cold and light-headed by that stage – just right for Cathy. And I kept thinking more and more about *Wuthering Heights*, about Heathcliff and Cathy: his sadism, her hysteria. Their passion. And I thought about Cathy's diary in the novel – the one that Lockwood was reading, prior to the laceration scene. Thought about how much of Cathy's life and character were tied up in those few pages. Intriguing. A picture of a little blue diary kept returning to me, tapping like a tree's branch at the window of my mind.

Swooping arms picked me out of my chair and shook me out of my mood, making me squeal – a very dramatic, bald and bold Dracula was carrying me in his strong wings. 'Helena!' he shouted, as he paraded me from room to room.

'Get *off* me!' Complete stranger.

He held me like a prize. 'I know you: Helena Bonham-Carter. It's the Pre-Raphaelite hair – absolutely irresistible!' He tried to nibble my neck through the mass of my hair, while I tried to restrict everybody's view of my legs and all the other bits. 'Our characters were meant to be together: it's fate.'

'It's really corny. Put me down!'

Eventually I was upright and relished a glare of pure jealousy from Dominic in the midst of his adoring, cosy coven. Released, I escaped Dracula, and rushed past Dominic into the kitchen for a drink.

By midnight, a few of the monsters were mating. A repentant Doug – almost humbled as *Misery*'s nurse – was wooing Sam. Meanwhile Sherry had discarded her blades to throw her arms around Hannibal Lecter. A match made in heaven. I walked past a stringy-haired Carrie (it was all in the eyes) in search of my own prom date. I hadn't seen Dominic for at least half an hour and those witches worried me. I dashed upstairs and tried his bedroom.

Sure enough, there was a figure there, sitting on the bed, a bald figure, who rapidly spun round. 'Helena!'

'Dracula.' I rushed to leave but his bat-winged body was at the doorway before me.

'Don't go!' Bat-blocked, I had little choice. 'It's mad out there. Just come and sit here for a few minutes.'

'It is a bit manic!'

'A bit! Sit here then, and enjoy the peace.'

It wouldn't be very peaceful if Dominic walks in, I thought, but I sat down anyway, gingerly, poised for a bat-like flight of my own, if necessary.

'Who are you then, specifically?' he asked, sitting beside me on the bed.

I pointed my slashed wrist towards him. 'Can't you tell?'

'Suicide blonde? No, wrong hair colour.' He looked at my whitened face. 'Vampire victim? But I always go for the throat first: no marks there. Yet.' He grinned. 'I give up.'

'Cathy. The first one.' He looked blank. '*Wuthering Heights*,' I explained.

Dracula shook his shiny head. 'That's cheating. That's not a horror story, is it?'

'It is for the people Heathcliff lives with; those who aren't Cathy.'

'Ah. I can imagine.'

'He's a real spaniel hanger.'

Dracula laughed, an inviting laugh. He had nice, even teeth, and smooth features underneath the make-up. 'You're at Uni with Dominic, then?' he asked.

'No.' Why didn't I want to say I was his girlfriend? My instinct was leading me on a maze of a journey that night. 'What about you?'

'I'm Eric's brother. Eric who lives here.'

'No!' Amazing! 'Really? Is Eric downstairs tonight, then?'

'Oh yes, he's down there. He's a character from a Thomas Harris book. When he opens his mouth, there's a plastic butterfly inside.' Dracula laughed again. 'That's probably the best-kept secret of the night.'

'I still don't know who he is, then – there are millions of people who aren't dressed up: he could be any of them. I'm never going to meet him,' I moaned. 'Damn.'

'You've met me, I'm the closest thing there is, a blood relative, so to speak.' Wicked, vampirish grin. 'Andrew, or Eric Senior, whatever you like.' Slow handshake. And he didn't let go.

I stood up, pulling my hand and myself away. 'I'd better be off, actually.'

'There's no rush.' He stood up too, lopsidedly.

I pulled the shreds of my dress down. 'I must see what's happening downstairs.' Music boomed up through the floorboards, heavy music. Maybe Eric was doing a bit of DJing. I headed quickly for the door, the bat fluttering behind me, and felt the whisper of a wing on my thigh. Dominic, I thought, help, as I grabbed the handle.

Dominic! Bang. Charging into the room as quickly as I was charging out of it. 'Helena!' Twisting at the waist, he grabbed my arm and lost his bowler.

'This is surreal,' said Dracula. 'She's not really Helena Bonham-Carter, is she?'

'Who the fuck are you?' Dominic's head snapped back around.

'Eric's brother. Andrew. Or Dracula, whichever you prefer.' Dominic stared at him incredulously. 'Look, pal, nothing happened.' Dracula lifted his arms in a peaceful gesture, made more theatrical by his wings.

'Get out, *pal*!' Dominic stamped out the words with thuds to Dracula's chest.

Dracula dropped back. 'All right, I'm going.' And he backed away, the door closed and Dominic and I were alone. The room was quiet apart from the background thumps of people and music.

He spun around to me and I could see in his eyes that he wanted to hit me. His voice was cold when he spoke. 'What were you doing with him?'

'I was looking for you. I came in here. We talked.' I tried a shrug. 'That was all.' Dominic's lash-lined black eye glared at me hard. 'Don't you believe me?'

'Did he touch you?'

'My legs. He touched them. Then I left, looking for you. That's when you came in.' My words were slow.

'He touched your legs?' Dominic's tongue spat out the question.

'Yes – no.' Terrible. 'I mean, he didn't know we were together or anything. How could he?'

'How could he? Is "I'm seeing Dominic" so hard to say?' Satanic yet sad, Dominic drew back from me, turning away his strange, cracking mask of a face. I was aware of the bruises underneath. 'You wanted him to touch you.' A statement. Green eyes turned to mine.

'No, Dominic. I wanted *you* to touch me.'

'My fault, then? We don't make love for ten days and you let *him* touch you.' I sat down on the bed and pulled him down beside me. 'I'm sorry, Dominic. I want you. I think that's what I've been trying to get through to you.'

Dominic's face returned to me. 'You want me?' A question now rather than a statement. I looked deep into his eyes, seeing through the make-up, and nodded, slowly and definitely. 'Helena.' The look on his face made me bite my lip. He looked at me, touched me between my legs, just once, then pulled my tiny black knickers down.

It was the quickest and one of the most intense of our love-making experiences. The condom was on within seconds and Dominic was back, circling both of my wrists with one hand, holding them above me while he touched my clitoris. The gentle downward pressure of his hand on my wrists was matched by the upward movement of my hips, rising to meet him – violently meeting each other again – trusting each other within the private and magical circle of energy, within the extremity of our need for each other. He was inside me in one, two big thrusts, making me feel incredibly excited. His fingers were still on my clitoris, and I moved my body up and down to his touch, his penis, filled by his strength, my control inside of his control, very much connected. His pushes were deep. My Dominic. I think I said his name.

The climax was almost too harsh, too sharp, too urgently needed, and I heard a very real, animal cry, which brought Dominic's lips to my ear.

'Gently. I love you, Helena. Gently now.' He was gentle himself, now, but I had felt the strength of the spasms of his climax too.

'I used him. I used him to show you, to show you I wanted you back. It was you I wanted, always. You wanted me all of the time at St Mary's Loch. And then afterwards, nothing.'

'I want you now. I always did want you. I just needed a bit of time to . . . get myself back together.'

'Don't go.' Mine. I fingered the silver chain.

'I won't go. You know I won't. I'll hold you until you go to sleep. Then I'll have to check that *this* Cromwell Street doesn't get demolished.'

Thuds and music. My Dominic. All around me still. Sleep slipped around me. All around me. Still.

My dreams were strange that night, when I eventually got to sleep, when the usual dull thudding of our house and all the houses around it eventually died down.

The forces. The armed forces. I'd always loved those words. Forces of energy. Macbeth's soldiers in Macduff's castle, surprising his wife and babes, so to speak.

Armed forces, between soft, white, kicking female legs. Army hard.

Hard reality. The next day, the house was rancid. Beer smells and smoke (and the odd, sweet whiff of illicit substances) were seeping through the ancient carpet, re-activating the older smells that lay beneath like grievances.

Dominic was surprisingly bouncy and pleasant, appearing at the foot of the bed at about 10 with a tray. I relished the hot coffee and picked at cereal and fruit as he sat at my side, chatting about the party and the horrors of various sorts to be found in the rooms that morning. I got the feeling that he was building up to something and sipped my coffee, waiting for it to emerge. After about five minutes, out it came.

'Helena, do you remember that night after you were sick? When we met Dixie and Jem and the others in the pub – they were all vicars and tarts or something?'

'Yes. Sherry had her legs out, I remember that.'

'That's right,' he laughed. 'Do you remember Dixie talking about travelling around France in a camper van?'

'Vaguely.'

'Well, he was going to go with a friend from home, but it's fallen through. And I haven't done anything about a summer job so far – with this and everything.' He touched his face now, thankfully, cleansed.

'Right.'

'Dixie's asked me to go with him.'

'What exactly has he got in mind?' What did I care? My Dominic, wandering around France with Dixie. Without me.

Dominic's shoulders lifted as his head angled towards me. 'He's got some work lined up on a family friend's farm, in the Charente area, for a few weeks. They grow grapes. He's going to drive down there, spend a few days in Paris, a few days in the Loire Valley and then four weeks or so on the farm. All last night he was talking about it; it sounds great.' Excitement filled his voice. 'Dixie reckons we can earn enough in those weeks on the farm to pay for the whole thing. We can sleep in the van if we're desperate, or stay in cheap hotels. There's accommodation there when we get to the farm. He's stayed there before.'

'All planned out.' My voice sounded empty.

'A good way to make me forget all this.' Half nodding, he touched his chest this time.

'Yes.' Hollow.

'The only thing is, what about you? You've been brilliant lately. And I'd really miss you. A month. It was bad enough when I couldn't see you for a week at a time.' He paused, and I looked away from him. 'We could go away afterwards, together. What do you think? I would really miss you, I know that. I won't go if you don't want me to. I've told Dixie that already – said I'd talk to you about it first.'

Cosmetic exercise. Plus, he did need a break – to recover from his degree as well as all the rest. Backed into a corner, I went for Leeched Dry grace and style. 'Sounds like a great idea, Dominic. And it'll give me time to concentrate on my driving. I think Uncle Mark's got some work lined up for me provisionally, anyway.'

'Great.' Big smile. 'I'll ring Dixie.'

And I still hadn't told him about the Stone Man.

'The truth is rarely pure and never simple.'
– Oscar Wilde *The Importance of
Being Earnest* Act I

So Dominic was gone, exploring the Loire Valley and the Charente with Dixie, while I explored the inside of a solicitor's office in the Borders with Uncle Mark. Wonderful. Dominic left me the emerald as protection, and a guilty smile as a goodbye gift.

For the first week I heard next to nothing from him. There were two brief phone calls but no letters arrived. His voice over the phone was relaxed and happy: he was visiting the big châteaux, I don't remember their names. Apparently the history and the myths connected with the places fascinated Dixie. They'd visited the castle that Perrault had had in mind when he wrote *The Sleeping Beauty* and quite a few others.

Meanwhile I was comatose with boredom temping for Uncle Mark, covering for his holidaying staff: making coffee, typing letters, sorting post, etcetera. Waiting once again for my prince to come. The second time Dominic rang, he told me that his face was completely healed and free from marks. My Leeched Dry poise had left me: I felt completely abandoned. I was also acutely, bizarrely, jealous of Dixie – to think that he'd been with Dominic during both his crisis and recovery. I was glad that he was better and glad that he was safe from cardboard men with suits and bricks. But I felt cold and cardboardy myself, as well as thin, tired, neglected and angry. I missed him so much.

The third time he rang, he'd been away for over a week, and had just arrived at the farm.

'It's fantastic. There's a brilliant crowd of young people working here as well. They're all about our age, so there should be plenty to do when we're not working.' Tactful as Sam. What if I lost him now? I couldn't keep the bitterness out of my voice when I replied.

'Sounds great. Just don't forget me.'

'As if I could.' His voice was low, private, my Dominic for a second. Then I heard shouting and he returned to his public persona. 'I saw a portrait when I was at Azay-le-Rideau. The woman really reminded me of you – Gabrielle D'Estree, she was called.' I memorised the name. 'I'll show you when I get back. Dixie's bought loads of books.'

'I'm fed up here. The weather's foul, I'm freezing cold and Uncle Mark's office is so boring I'm turning into a female version of him. It's deadly.'

There was an awkward pause. At least Dominic didn't laugh. 'I know. I can imagine.' And, quietest of all, 'I'm sorry.' I relished the guilt in his secret voice. 'Look, why don't you go over to Cromwell Street at the weekend? You've got a key. Take Diana – have a bit of fun, do the town.' Like him? 'Sorry, Helena, I've got to go. It's chaos here, and we haven't even unpacked properly. I'm writing to you.' At last. 'You should get a letter soon. I've started writing it, honestly. I'll be back in just a few weeks. I love you.' The last was whispered very quietly and very quickly. And the phone clicked.

Why didn't I feel loved, then? And why couldn't I stop the thought of his old diary from tapping at my memory, over and over again?

I knew exactly why I was heading for Cromwell Street three days later. The Crying Cavalier was my carriage and Uncle Mark my coachman. Even (especially) his inane chatter couldn't keep my mind off the blue diary and its contents. 'Open the book, open the book, open the book . . .' The movement of the car seemed to rap the message out.

Diana had already organised a night out with another friend, so we'd arranged to meet in Edinburgh the next day instead. Nothing then lay between myself and the sheets of the diary. And there was also the appeal of sleeping in Dominic's bed that night, dreaming of when he would be back with me. As my coachman (and his carriage) departed, with a crack of his clichés – 'Young Dominic will be back before you know it. Still, you can paint the town red with Diana tomorrow' – the place I most needed to visit was definitely Dominic's room. Before Uncle Mark was around the corner, I was up the stairs and sniffing at the mousy old quilt, almost enjoying the familiar thump of Eric's heavy metal music muscling its way through the doors. Everybody else was away and there was a forlorn dankness about the whole house that sank into me at once.

I unpacked my night-clothes and then took the few bits of food I'd brought with me down to the food museum, planning to have a snack later on. The pretence of a normal visit continued as I watched television, wandered around Dominic's room and then watched television again. I even went through the charade of a diverting stroll through Edinburgh's insalubrious streets before returning to Cromwell Street for (more) television and a dismal snackette: some low-fat cheese and crispbread. By the time I'd experienced this riot of entertainment, the diary had assumed the proportions of a visit to Venus.

The door was locked and the diary was opened – little, dog-eared and frail in my hands. Personal. Irresistible. The combination of insecurity, neglect and curiosity easily unlocked the diary's pages for me (and allowed me to ignore the guilty sense of betraying Dominic).

The reality was disappointing at first. There was lots of stuff about law (that I flicked over with the same ease as I showed when I closed my ears to it in conversation), and some stuff about parties, pubs and clubs that was a bit more interesting. (What was a 'Two Sex Sleepover'? Was it a male/female sleepover, or did you have to have sex twice in the course of the night?) And then, something else. Someone else. One word, spotting pages and pages of the diary. Emma. Emma, Emma, Emma, Emma, Emma.

'She's very sweet and very Scottish – a midwife, or training to be one. Lovely, dark, wavy hair. She seemed so quiet that first night, maternal almost, but she's definitely got a wild side to her as well.' Sweet Emma.

'Emma is convinced that she's fat, like all women. But I love her breasts – warm, round breasts. A woman's breasts.' Round Emma.

'She's older than me – by just a year. I love her soft, brown eyes. Her dark warmth. My lovely Emma. Hard work to make her believe how I feel for her.' Wild and warm Emma.

Wild Helena. I was too angry to cry, but there was worse to come.

'We had a row about something and nothing and she was upset. I told her I loved her. I really meant it. The first woman I've ever really loved.'

Enough. It was my own room 101, my own cage of gnawing rats, yet it was also exactly what I had been looking for. Proof that I wasn't really loveable, in the end.

I ran to get my own diary, to read the words I'd recorded there at Tibbie Shiel's.

'I love you. I love you. That's how I feel.' Bastard. And then, *'Everyone wants to fall in love like this but it gives the other person so much power over you. Gives you so much power, Helena.'*

I understood fully what he'd meant now. Bitterness was a new and unwelcome emotion to me. Then, *'I love your lips, your eyes, your hair, your gentleness.'* Emma's soft brown eyes, warm, round body. *'I've never felt like this about anyone before.'* Dom's romantic enthusiasms. *'We're both virgins then.'*

Well, I'd been extra-virgin. Until now.

Of course, I'd known he'd had sex with other girls, and I'd guessed he'd had several other relationships. But I had thought I was his first love. *'I've never felt like this about anyone before.'* Liar. My Dominic. Not my Dominic. Emma's Dominic.

I put the diary back inside its cotton nest: so small, so dangerous, just like his words – tiny beaks that would bite into my brain for good: 'Curvy Helena' and *'Warm, round Emma'.* I hated him. I would never ever forgive him.

But Dominic *had* wanted me – had always found it so difficult to make his body wait long enough for me. He'd been so tender; he'd always made me feel so special. My trust in him had been almost complete. Had he cradled Emma to him after their lovemaking, gentling her, calming her, reassuring her? Had Emma been able to make him come, just by whispering his name? Had he worked away at Emma's secrets, moving into her mind and heart as he'd begun to move into mine?

I missed him so much now. Now that I would never believe in him again, trust in his magical eyes again.

Surrounded by smells of him, I lay in his bed to sleep, but I knew that sleep just would not come. I flicked off the light and began to make my plans there, in the dark.

Dominic, meanwhile, over a thousand miles away in his bunk-bed nest, was making his own plans by lamplight.

---

*Helena – Places to visit in France with her (when I **finally** get some money)*

- Paris – Musée D'Orsay, Impressionist paintings, Degas, etc, shops, Montmartre, restaurants, literary trail, cafés
- Loire – Langeais, little shops, castle
- Azay-le-Rideau – paintings, castle, moat
- Usse – Sleeping Beauty, Perrault
- Charente – Cognac, vineyards, fields, walks

Dominic added a few more notes to his journal, doodled one of Helena's eyes on to his notepad, sighed dramatically (half hoping to waken poor Dixie) and then flicked off the lamp.

As he turned his head on the pillow, he looked straight ahead into the darkness, Helena's face in his mind. He searched for ease, for rest and for her. All three eluded him.

When morning opened its one grey eye my plan was ready for it to read. Exit.

Because I knew what I needed in a man: I needed a family, a father, mother, lover, brother and sister all rolled into one. And all rolled into me – me and me alone, past, present and future, always and absolutely. And I couldn't get that from Dominic now. I listed the case against him in my head.

> **One** – the big lie. I wasn't his first love.
>
> **Two** – the big freeze. He'd gone to France with Dixie, and had barely contacted me at all, even though he knew how much I was missing him. The letter he had said was (finally) on its way was just a further source of pain now.
>
> **Three** – the big bully. He'd bullied me, teased me about my weight, when he'd obviously been perfectly happy with a relatively rounded Emma.

I was meeting Diana at 11 o'clock so that morning saw me in action at 7, packing my clothes, creams and assorted treasures, lifting them from the places where Dominic had so carefully put them months ago. The objects felt heavy and unwilling in my hands: I knew that I was removing myself from his life just as deliberately as I was removing my things one by one from his room. My fingerprints were smudging themselves into place beside Dominic's for the last time.

By 9 o'clock, I was desperate to escape from the old house, my old dreams and my new gloom. I decided to walk down into Edinburgh to look at the art gallery and brood nastily there for a while before meeting Diana. The mention of the Gabrielle D'Estree painting was intriguing me despite myself and I was keen to unravel this one last puzzle set by Dominic. The solution could lie in the art gallery's bookshop. So I set off from Cromwell Street, feeling as dull and heavy as the sky above me.

As I walked down the hill, I formed a kind of superstitious pact with myself about the painting, like the pacts you make with yourself about the messages on Loveheart sweets when you're little: if the image that had reminded Dominic of me was true, beautiful, or special in some way, then perhaps there was a chance – somehow – for our relationship to survive. And if it was meaningless, cruel, or ugly in any way, then I was right to end it as I planned.

The answer to my Loveheart dilemma lay in a hard-backed book in the corner of the bookshop. Appalling. Gabrielle D'Estree had skin and hair of my colour but apart from that she wasn't in the same *species* as me: her breasts were pomegranate pips, while the rest of her body was lumpily and frumpily plump; her eyes were narrow and mean and her mouth was about half the size of mine, and thin. Did Dominic really see me in that way?

But there was worse to come. In the background, yet vital to the picture, was an ominous-looking, dark-eyed, very rounded woman, a child suckling at her womanly breast. Emma. Fury. The pips and the pendulums – four breasts painted side by side together. Indelibly. The hideously unattractive expression on 'Emma's' face was little compensation. Blackness. Dominic was welcome to her, and his self-satisfied-looking, angelic Gabrielle. My picture book replacements.

I left the bookshop and the art gallery at speed – mad rather than sad – and stalked out into the street outside. Suddenly – thud! A tangle of arms and I was inside someone's jacket, breathing heavily at him. 'Sorry. I'm really sorry.'

He smiled, a dark man, laid one hand on my shoulder, shook his head and moved on.

I caught a glimpse of black hair, a faint but definite male scent and the flash of a dust-jacket smile. Will Jackson. And he hadn't said a word.

14

*'Like the March winds, your Pisces girl will have many a mood.
She's terribly sentimental, and when her feelings are wounded,
she can cry buckets . . . If the fears go too deep, she'll shut herself
off from others, then wonder why she's lonely'*

– Linda Goodman's Sun Signs

Waiting for my exam results was even harder now. What did it
matter if I went to Edinburgh or York? Who would care where I
went? My future was bottomlessly black – the watery underside
of my vision that first day at St Mary's Loch.

And waiting for Dominic's phone calls was the worst bit of
all. Because of course I did still wait for them, even though
I'd definitely decided that it was over between us. Uncle Mark,
meanwhile, had been given steely instructions that I would *not*
speak to Dominic under *any* circumstances. Ever. Ever, ever,
ever, ever. Really ever.

'Well, the course of true love never runs smooth. Especially
young love.' So far, so Uncle Mark. Then he surprised me.
'Can't say I'm disappointed, Helena. Since you've been with
young Oliver, you've been a shadow of yourself. Thin. Worried.
Time to start looking after yourself now.'

Was he right? Or was the thinness, the shrinking to a shadow,
something I'd done to myself? Because Dominic had loved me
– I'd felt that for certain. I knew it. What was Uncle Mark on
about now? 'A few nights out with Lisa and me will have you
feeling as right as rain.' And how did rain feel? It was certainly
starting to pour. And when Diana mentioned 'girls' nights out'

I'm sure I heard lightning strike.

Twice, Dominic rang from France and Uncle Mark told him that I was out. Then, a few days later, the letter arrived. I'd waited for a letter during the whole of the first part of his holiday – and now, when it was too late, here it was. But I had to read it, naturally, so I hid up in my room and opened it up.

My Darling Helena,

I've managed somehow to find an hour spare from cleaning equipment, checking gauges and picking grapes to write to you. I bet you've been wondering why you've not heard from me much but there's just so much work here when it's light, and at night we're all knackered – though there's been a fair amount of drinking the grapes in the evenings, I have to say. And we've taken over the local sports bar (or 'Sports Bra' as one of the girls insists on calling it) in the village a couple of times as well.

Helena, all the time I was in the Loire, I was thinking about you. Loads of the châteaux were surrounded by moats, or were next to rivers, and I kept thinking about you and St Mary's Loch. When I make some money (if I ever finally qualify) I'll bring you to the Loire with me. You and your sexy rope of hair, you'd be really at home in all those castles. You'd love it all – more than me, probably. (Dixie's a bit of a buttress bore, to be honest. They all start looking the same, after a while.)

In the Charente here, it's just so fucking hot, you wouldn't believe it – too hot to work, definitely, but it would be great if you were on an ordinary holiday. The countryside is amazing, massive sunflowers everywhere (big petals, big black centres – Helena eyes).

I do feel a bit guilty, more than a bit, thinking of you suffering with Leeched Dry, the mousey quilt and, worse, Uncle Mark's office, while I'm having such a brilliant time here. But it honestly has helped me to get over my exams and everything else. It's been great working with my body for a change, instead of my brain. I've got really strong and brown – you'll be impressed, I'm sure, Helena. (It nearly fucking killed me at first.) It's great feeling used up and worn out at the end of the day. After a hard day at the law books, your head's still packed with ideas and facts, whereas here I can totally relax after the work is done. Sometimes, we walk down to the river with some bread, wine, fruit, beer and cheese and have a picnic at the end of the evening. You would love it. Dixie's enjoying a fair

---

amount of female attention here – I don't think the French girls are used to dreadlocks, and they're queuing up to stroke his head – Dixie-paradise. He hasn't had a passionate affair or anything, though, so we've had plenty of Dixie-type heavy discussions in the middle of the night, putting the world to rights, or trying to.

Around the time I get back, you'll get the results from your highers and you'll be deciding about university. You must talk to me first, before you make your final decision. I've rung you a couple of times lately and spoken to Uncle Mark, who tells me, with his usual clarity, that you're 'otherwise engaged'. I'm glad you're having a good summer, anyway – with Diana, I guess. I'll be back really soon and we'll have plenty of time to spend with each other before university starts, weeks, in fact.

I can't wait to see you, to touch you, to talk to you. I hope you've been looking after yourself while I've been away.

Sleep with the emerald under your pillow and remember that I love you.

Dominic

The emerald was, at that second, resting on a white sheet of paper in the blue bed of a book, open at Emma's name.

15

'Cancer man

'He'd rather lose a claw than let go'
– Linda Goodman's Sun Signs

The phone rang much more frequently after Dominic got home. I was starved of his voice but, being me, I wouldn't let myself eat. Eat at the trough. Instead, I listened as Uncle Mark became increasingly irate. The third time Dominic tried to ring me was the worst, and the last.

Uncle Mark was holding the phone away from his (manicured, believe it or not) ear, when I walked into the kitchen that morning. I sat at the shiny pine, elbows on the top, and heard events unfold. The conversation was concluded pretty quickly.

'Well, she doesn't want to speak to you, Dominic,' was the first thing I heard Uncle Mark say. I could imagine Dominic's response and hear some of it. Then, 'Perhaps if you'd been a bit more attentive when you had the chance, Helena might be looking a good deal healthier than she does now and you could be having this conversation with her instead of me.' I cringed and scowled at him. Uncle Mark recoiled following the next blast, then, strongly for him, 'Please don't ring again. Your telephone calls are not welcome in this house.'

I wasn't surprised that I could hear Dominic's reply without the aid of the receiver. 'Pompous old bastard!' Poor Uncle Mark hung up – a first for him. But I noticed that his hands were shaking and his shoulders drooped.

And that was that. There were no more phone calls.

First the letter, then the phone calls, and then – of course – the visit. The inevitable visit.

Still, I was shocked when I saw Dominic standing outside Uncle Mark's office one lunchtime. For a start, he looked so well – much sturdier, like a big, strong tree – while I felt leaf-frail and frazzled, no make-up on for one thing and no breasts for another. A long, brown branch grabbed me before I could get away, and I twisted my green-stick of a wrist back against him, as hard as I could. Not hard enough.

'Helena, you've got to talk to me.'

The girl I'd been about to have lunch with backed away, embarrassed. 'I haven't *got* to do anything,' I said, throwing the words over my shoulder as I tried to pull my hand away from him, but he held on. Chinese burns.

'Well, you've got to listen, at least: I'm not going to let go of you. It's just a matter of whether the rest of the street hears as well.'

'I'll see you later, Helena.'

'Nicola? Nicola!' But she was heading down the road, fast. 'Right. Ten minutes in the café around the corner, then I'm going straight back to work. You've got the length of time it'll take to drink a cup of coffee.'

Dominic nodded. But still he gripped my arm, right until we were inside the café and sitting down. Luckily for me it was waitress service – I think he'd have handcuffed me to the counter if we'd had to stand in a queue.

Dominic didn't wait for the arrival of the coffee-timer before beginning his speech. 'Helena, I never told you about Emma because I didn't want to hurt your feelings. That's all. I never intended to lie to you, to mislead you. I *didn't* lie to you.' The tumble of his words showed how much he had to say and how long he'd been dying to say it all.

I said nothing, felt a lot, mainly an ache in my chest. I loved his voice, loved the sight of him, but how much had he loved me? Two cups of coffee arrived below my nose and I swirled my cup around an old circle of a stain on the table. Round and round. Round and round and round, in silence.

'I did love her, but not in the same way that I love you. There was nothing like the same intensity. And I never said that you were the first person I'd loved. What I felt for Emma was nothing compared to what I feel for you.' He gripped my wrist again, shaking it for emphasis. 'I can't manage without you. There's no point to anything.' His ear turned slightly, waiting for a response, and then he carried on anyway, less certainly. 'It's really special with you.'

Taking a big sip of my coffee, I refused to bow when I burnt my mouth. The burn just made me glare at him even more as I rubbed my reddened wrist. I wished I'd worn make-up. Did he really mean what he was saying? Dominic tried another tack.

'I know you didn't really want me to go to France, but the trip came along at the perfect time. I really appreciated your support while I was ill. I should've written more, rung more, I know. The longer I left it, the worse I felt. The farm was busy, and I felt so bad about going away without you, I suppose. I'm sorry if I've been selfish. You have to let me make it up to you now.'

Well, he could still read my needs, then; he'd just got more efficient at ignoring them. I was surprised that he wasn't annoyed with me for reading the diary, but then I remembered how nosy *he* was. I knew I couldn't afford to look in his eyes, I had enough pain of my own, so I looked downwards and started to ring the stain again. Spirals – the sun contracting, according to the Celts. My throat hurt. I took a long drink of cooling coffee, as if it was gin and I was a ruined mother, and then I did look up at him. I saw the silver chain around his neck and felt the tug of a chain at my own throat as I heard Dominic's next words. 'Helena, I'll *make* you see it my way.' The wrong thing to say.

'You can't *make* me see things your way, Dominic. You make me diet and then you try and make me eat. You make me wait for you to phone me and then you try to make me forgive you.

'Remember what you said after that night in the alley? "He took away my control." Well, I'm taking my control back. I'm sick of waiting for you – waiting for you to decide that I was old enough for you, when we first met; waiting for your exams to finish; waiting for you to phone me, to write to me from France. Waiting for you to mention Emma, to mention that you'd been in love before me.' I took a long, cruel swallow, hurting myself as much as, more than, I was hurting Dominic. 'Your time's almost up. I wrote three letters to you at that farm, for you to read when you arrived. You wrote to me once – by which time it was too late.'

'Never too late. Don't say too late.' His eyes were fixed on me, trying to persuade me. He was close to desperation. I looked away. 'Don't ignore me. You're not the only one who hates being ignored, you know.' He almost spat it at me. I enjoyed ignoring him more then, looking away more dramatically. 'And we talked about the dieting. I didn't know you were still losing weight!'

My eyes snapped back at him. Black sunflowers. Full of seeds. 'I'm not losing weight now.' The sun contracting all the time. Tracing the old stains, the old marks.

'Yes, you are; it's obvious. And you look fucking awful, Helena, if it's any consolation.'

Enough! Gentle Helena. I threw my last inch of warm coffee in his face. 'It's definitely too late,' I shouted, as I pushed back my chair. He did spit then, involuntarily. Big brown beads of coffee covered his face.

When Dominic grabbed my arm this time, I wrenched it away. 'Get off me!'

He snatched his hand back and I was off. I charged down the street, back to the dull safety of Uncle Mark's office, leaving Dominic wiping his face at the table and glaring through the window at me as I went.

Should I have forgiven him? He had a point in that he hadn't actually said I was his first love – more, that was how I'd interpreted his words. But had he lied by omission?

What would you have done?

I only had one choice. I'd lived most of my life with a small sort of love, the love of a kind 'Uncle' rather than that of my own parents. I just couldn't accept a small love in my relationship – plus Dominic hadn't told me the whole truth; he'd put himself first too often; he'd not loved me enough. The case against him recited itself insistently enough in my head.

And, worst of all, he'd gone away. I needed to test Dominic's strength and his will to return to me. It was as if all of the intensity of trying to heal him had turned into a huge well of need. My own need. Yes, I was right to send him away.

So why did it feel so wrong?

And why didn't he come after me?

16

> *'Ask and it will be given you*
> *Seek and you will find*
> *Knock and it will be opened to you'*
> – Luke, Chapter 11 & Verse 16

Edinburgh or York, York or Edinburgh? I still couldn't decide. I had a free choice, having just scraped the necessary grades. The degree I'd opted for at York appealed to me most, but part of me clung to the original idea of Edinburgh. Part of me clung to the original idea of Dominic. So I was stuck.

Uncle Mark, predictable and predictably, was no assistance. 'Both excellent universities, based within pleasant cities, full amenities, etcetera. On balance, a business degree may be of more use to you than an arts degree.'

'But I'd be bored stiff doing a business degree.'

'Ah, but you won't be bored stiff with the lifestyle that may follow it, Helena.' Animated, Uncle Mark waved his arm around the palatial peach Dralon splendour of Leeched Dry. 'Always go for the most practical option.'

The grey staleness of moderate wealth and respectability held no appeal for me, probably because I'd had such a thorough experience of it at Leeched Dry.

Diana was also keen for me to go to Edinburgh: that was where she was going. 'What does it matter about the course? We'll have a brilliant time – out every night, sharing a flat together. You'd be miles away in York.'

But I felt I'd partly done all of that student stuff through my Cromwell Street connections. And I'd just passed my driving test, so I could get to York easily enough, by road or train.

My father had set up a fund for me until I was twenty-two, out of which Uncle Mark supported me. When I left Leeched, I was to be given the money directly, to spend as I wished. So I didn't need my £300,000 inheritance until I graduated, really. But I did, desperately, need some advice. I could hardly ask Dominic's opinion and I was sick to death of asking myself.

I went to Uncle Mark and I asked him for my letter. And I thought that I might as well have the cheque that went with it too. Yes!

Uncle Mark left me alone with my letter immediately this time and, in fact, I didn't want to open it inside Leeched Dry so I took the little envelope out on to the patio. I let the warm scents of the summer stocks and the rushing traffic noises wash over me for a few minutes. Then, when I felt calm and ready, I opened the dry little package and focussed on the blue pages in my hands.

My darling Helena,
I love you, I love you, I love you, I really love you. That's the main thing.

And here's the cheque. Enjoy it. Sometimes I've earned it by reciting beautiful words to rows of respectful middle-class faces. Other times I've earned it by chuntering on about baker's chains, biscuits and frozen vegetables to bored people ten yards away from the screen in their kitchens, making coffee. That's how it's the size it is – I wanted it to be fairly dramatic and life-enhancing in itself. And, as you know, this is the only cheque. So I hope that you'll be frivolous, creative, materialistic, careful and careless with the money – as appropriate, if that makes sense. Listen to your instincts. Explore all of yourself. Make yourself, spoil yourself, but look after yourself too.

Decide on your wishes and shape your life, especially at the times when life is trying to shape you. And be persistent. Ask, seek and knock and, as Luke says, 'it will be opened to you', whether it's an envelope, a pair of arms or a secret box. Picturise what you most want, clearly, and you will find it.

> *And remember that wishes are renewable, renegotiable – that you usually (but not always) get more than one chance to make them come true ('Ripeness is all'). Remember the ending of Brigadoon when Tommy goes back for Fiona and the village rises miraculously out of the mists? (I don't expect you're quite as keen on that now as you were when you were six!) So use the cheque and don't forget that magic and love exist everywhere. And they don't die either – only change, as people change.*
>
> *Somehow, keep a place for me wherever you live (a room, maybe, but that will depend on your plans). Mark will carry out my final piece of earthly magic for you there. And the third and final letter will be there too. When you need me, go to that place.*
>
> *And always know that I love you.*
>
> *Dad*

I only had one big wish: a mountain and a quarry rolled into one. St Mary's Loch.

And so the long-awaited moment had arrived. And my father's feeling for the dream, the heart (following, as it did, years of Uncle Mark's concern with the head) absolved me from guilt as I planned to spend – some of – his money lavishly. I started with a few mental pictures.

My first wish was to look gorgeous. Dominic's comment, 'You look fucking awful, Helena, if it's any consolation,' had stuck in my brain, because in a weird way, he was right: it *was* a consolation to look ill. The part of me that was on self-destruct wanted to look as fragile outside as I felt inside. But now I had some instructions and some wishes to carry out. My wishes. My anger towards Dominic was the perfect spur, so plan one was ready – the clothes, the hair and the car.

Diana helped me with the first bit, a more sophisticated image. 'Long lines, dark or neutral colours, natural fabrics,' was her advice, and Edinburgh's shopkeepers were as happy as ever to supply. Plus I was easy to dress – a moving mannequin, with my long legs, breastlessness, hard hips and fat purse.

Next was the hair. I wanted to keep it long, but Rapunzel had got boring. I visited a good hairdresser (recommended by Lisa) who 'redesigned' it for me. She cut lots of curls off the length, allowing it to fall just below my shoulders. I felt new, exfoliated, like a snake that's shedding its old self, as I saw the crispy crescents of my dead hair gather around the chair like dry, dead snakeskin. The hairdresser showed me different ways to style it – sweeping parts of it up into smooth, conkery curves to lift my eyes and cheek bones, making them look larger than life. Best of all, she introduced me to a special diffuser, showing me how to make my hair look thicker, wavier, wilder. Wild Helena.

So at last I was ready, with Diana's sense of style and Uncle Mark's car magazines, to choose my car. My dream car. I opted for a high-powered, soft-topped BMW, and Diana (who had finally been let into the secret of my money) and I drove to the garage to pick it up in her £500 Metro. It was a gleaming, girly, curvy red treasure, instantly named Red, stylish enough for the Piscean girl yet powerful enough to take her wherever she might want to go. I'd gone for black leather seats, and as I sank down into the driver's seat and drank in the liquoricey, male sort of scent, I was pleased with my choice. Diana – the ultimate shopper's companion – was equally enthusiastic. 'Mmm. Smells gorgeous. What a totty magnet!' And we were off, leaving the little Metro behind, looking very sorry for itself on the garage forecourt.

Red whirled us both around the local streets first, and then I couldn't resist heading for Edinburgh, 'You look fucking awful,' in my ears and a vision of scattering coffee drops before my eyes. Secretly, I was speeding towards showing Dominic my remodelled self – still sleek but hardly half-starved. There was no sign of him as we drove through the busy roads of the city and I certainly didn't want to go anywhere near Cromwell Street. I'd rather have died than given Dominic the impression that I was looking for him, for God's sake! Diana, on the other hand, was thoroughly enjoying herself, sloping her magnificent blonde head and ship's prow breasts this way and that, at every nice-looking man on the street. I was concentrating on my driving – naturally – when a dazzlingly artificial red head jumped right into my line of vision. Red veered left, making Diana's head tilt more dramatically than usual as I pulled into the kerb.

'Sam!' And louder, 'Sa-am! Sam!'

She was staggering under the weight of three desperately depressing-looking carrier bags. Her face split into a smile, though, when she saw it was me.

'Helena! Christ crapped – where did you get that car?'

'I just picked it up today – it's a long story.' I rushed around to the passenger side of the car to speak to her. 'This is Diana. And this is Sam from Cromwell Street.'

'It goes with my hair – even wilder than usual!' It was true – her hair was blazing. Glints? Glows, more like. Glares, even. It was a very brave or a very foolish choice, depending on whether or not you liked Sam. Very Sam altogether. 'You look like a real woman, Helena,' she was saying, her eyebrows raised in shock.

'Is that good, or bad?'

She thought about it. 'Just different.'

In the face of Sam's legendary lack of diplomacy, I reckoned that I'd got off pretty lightly. 'How's Doug?' I asked.

She pulled a face, saying, 'Putrid. Full of gas, as usual.' I laughed. 'Aren't you going to ask how Dominic is?' The pavement fascinated me suddenly and my smile shrank. 'He misses you, Helena.' Sam's blue eyes looked startling beneath that flimsy red fringe. 'He's been *unbearable*. Fucking unbearable. I haven't had a civil word out of him since he came back from France. Anybody would think that *I* was torturing him.' Torturing him. The spikes of the emerald pushed into my guilt-riddled mind. And the knowledge that poor Sam was living with the Ice Man brought my eyes reluctantly back to her face, just as she asked me, 'What on earth happened between you?'

Relaying the bare bones of the scene in the café, I concentrated more on the comic effect of the spilling of the coffee than on any real spilling of the truth and Sam snorted in all of the right parts. 'That explains it. Doug accepts insult and attack as part of the price he has to pay for female company. Dom's just a bit less easy-going.'

'He did deserve it.'

'Oh, I know Dominic can be a moody, selfish, awkward, arrogant shit-headed bastard . . .' Sam lived each separate insult slowly, with relish '. . . but he's suffering for it now. He never comes out of his room – makes Eric look like the ultimate party animal. Even Dixie can't cheer him up.' Dixie, who'd been through so much with Dominic. Mean, but I couldn't suppress a glimmer of satisfaction. 'At least he's got a job: he's working for a friend of his father – semi-legal, office-work stuff.' Sam glanced at her watch. 'He'll still be there now.'

'What about you, Sam? What're you up to?'

'Still unemployed and unemployable – the arts graduate's lament. I might have to do another course to turn me into something useful. I'm still thinking about it.'

'Do you want a lift back to Cromwell Street?'

'In the dream machine?'

I laughed. 'I'll stick your bags in the boot – you'll have to squeeze in beside Diana. And duck your head if you see a policeman.'

'If we see a policeman, you just unravel your legs and we'll be all right,' Sam laughed. 'I think Jem misses you more than Dominic does!'

I walked around to the driver's seat. 'I'm sure Jem'll survive. They both will.'

Sam was duly squashed into place and we all headed for Cromwell Street in my purring new pet, knowing that we could deposit Sam safely without having to face Dominic. But as I pulled up at the pavement, I felt a real pang. I thought of Dominic's room as it had looked when I'd left it, with that Judas of a diary holding the emerald in its nasty little pages. My face must have dropped, because as she spilled down from Diana's knee into the street, Sam bent towards me, saying, 'I'm not sure that he will actually, Helena.'

'Will what, Sam?'

'Will survive. Dominic. With all of his best bits intact, that is.'

She grinned and changed her tone as I moved to the back of the car to help her unload. 'Keep in touch, Helena.' Bon Jovi boomed down into the street through the upstairs window. 'Look after the beast.' She patted the car's bonnet. 'Keep it red!' Cromwell Street's musky swampiness swallowed her, as she waved and sank inside.

So if Dominic wasn't surviving, if he did – just maybe – love me enough, then why exactly wasn't he ringing?

* * *

That was the bottle bank summer, cracking glass all day and wanking away my wages all night: clear, brown, clear, brown, clear, brown – crash here; fisting, femdom, latex, lovelines, backyard, barnyard, double trouble – click here. Sex. Solo sex. Sex and chips. It was ringing all around my head whenever I slept. Peek sex, magazines, meek sex, gas and teens, Greek sex, anally, speak sex, verbally. Freak sex. Solo sex. Sex. Just me and a fucking glass screen. Skin to screen. The empty clicking of the keyboard. Shit-shagging bitch of a mother made me pay the phone bill. I was draining my juices into the sheets when I should have been doubling myself with Helena.

My mother had used all the influence of her pathetic connections to get me a job for the summer, sorting out bottles and generally clearing up the area. A real fucking intellectual challenge. Half of the filthy gets didn't even wash the bottles properly, so you were stinking by the time you got home. Almost made me wish I'd finished some of those essays at school, except the poor bastard standing next to me had, and he still ended up stinking like a pissed-on pub carpet at the end of the day, just like me. I was tempted to put him out of his misery, like, with a crowning connection between a broken bottle and his jugular – gave me something to think about – but I decided it wasn't worth the hassle. Green, white, brown; green, white, brown. Crash here.

At least it meant I could get the car back on the road and I patrolled Gadsby Street a few times, but I never saw Dominic. He was probably living it up in Florida or Las Vegas or something, courtesy of daddy. Copper-arsed old fucker must have some uses, like.

Then, one day, when I'm just about to give up on him, I see her: Helena. Looking very different – very Kate Moss. *Very* thin. But she's lost that neglected look from her eyes and there's something else there instead: a spark of electricity, anger maybe. I don't know, but it suits her, and it sparks some electricity off in me. The old chain reaction at work again.

She's in a brand new BMW, soft-top, bit of a girly shape but a lovely six-cylinder engine, black leather seats. A proper shagging wagon, the lads at school would have said. And she's had her hair done – shorter, but still classy.

So has old red head, who she's dropping off. What a fucking state: her hair's like a matchstick on top of her head. Makes me think of school again, of how the lads used to set the ugly girls' hair on fire in the back of the bus, just now and then, like, for a laugh. (Bastards set fire to mine once – and half of my neck. One scar I never talk about.)

Good job I've got my sunglasses on, for camouflage as well as protective purposes. Very delicate, the eyes, you know. I wind my window down and earwig a bit.

I only catch a couple of scraps of sentences, from old matchstick head, mainly, just before the carriers make their appearance. But it's enough.

'. . . Not sure if he will, actually, Helena.'

'Will what, Sam?' My Helena, looking worried.

'Will survive. Dominic. With all of his best bits intact, that is.'

I wind up my window and move off. It can only mean one thing.

Split.

Electricity.

Every day in Uncle Mark's office was like spending a month inside Dominic's bore drawer. And I reckoned that the way I felt about the two universities was a bit like the 'torn between two lovers' syndrome: if I couldn't decide between the two of them, then I probably wasn't in love with either of them. So I deferred my place at Edinburgh for a year, just in case, and decided to find a job.

What did I dream of, then? What did I love? What should I *do*, for God's sake? Difficult? Impossible! I tried writing it down – maybe that would help.

LOVES	HATES
Lochs, seas and rivers	Smoke
Mirrors, spirals	Measuring, squares
Velvet, rich colours, softness	Dralon, greyness, hardness
Food	Calorie counting
Clothes, costumes	Uniforms, suits
Novels, poems, letters	Text books, graphs, computers
Paintings	Essays
Ideas	Exams
People, dogs, animals	Grades
Shopping, spending money	Numbers, counting money
Travelling, dreaming	Instruction, diagrams
Stars, skies and moons	Bricks, cardboard and stone

Pathetic. Painful! I hoped, for once, that my father couldn't see me. What a career plan – I mean, accountancy was definitely out! Still, I'd made the right decision about university, looking down the hate list. The computer programmes at school had been even less help, suggesting everything from shoe designer to fishmonger. Something in the arts field was my conclusion. And I went to the Situations Vacant columns with that in mind.

Uncle Mark, of course, knew someone. I've told you about his killing passion for art galleries, haven't I? Well, he had a friend who was involved in running one. How did I fancy working in the bookshop there? Yes!

The job had just been advertised and his friend would be on the interview panel. The pay wasn't fantastic, but topped up with my allowance, I reckoned I could live life to the max without touching much more of my cheque. And I'd get myself all of the gloss of the arts without any of the grind of the essays. Pictures of myself arranging shiny, coffee table books into elegant displays sprang into my mind, my hair wound into a sophisticated chignon, chatting over the paintings in my lunch hour. Perhaps progressing to organising exhibitions, doing some drawing of my own.

Perfect.

Within three weeks the job was mine.

I've got my work cut out from this point on. Because now that he's split up with her, I reckon he'll be waiting for me – looking for me, like. Whether he knows it or not. So I look for him. Harder.

I'd seen that he had a computer in his room, like me; I still had her letter as well, and that helped a lot. And then I'd got his e-mail number from his revision sheet. I had two machines to help me in my work – the Bundymobile, and my computer, obviously.

The angry feeling she's been giving off is the last piece in the puzzle: she'd been the one to finish it, like. Definitely. That's just enough.

Like my father had said, there's usually more than one way, one chance, of making a dream come true. My next wish was easy. Diana and I went house hunting, and I'm sure you can guess where we began.

Red, Diana and I zoomed up to the loch, and I treated Diana to lunch. We sat in the little dining room at Tibbie Shiel's, where I'd sat with Dominic, and a stubborn, strong ache hurt my heart. Diana distracted me.

'It is gorgeous here, Helena.' She squinted at the menu. 'You don't think you'll find it quiet, though? If there is anywhere to buy, that is.'

'Not really. And, I mean, I'll be in Edinburgh every day, at the art gallery.' I steeled myself to look at the familiar menu, then looked more closely at Diana's face. Waited until it was almost too late to say it. 'Also – I was wondering if you would be interested in staying with me? We could go into Edinburgh together sometimes, when you start at the University.'

Diana thought for about one second flat, then grinned. 'Sounds great. About a million times better than a student house like Cromwell Street.'

I laughed. 'With my housekeeping skills, it mightn't be much better.' The waitress came up with her pad to take our order. 'Anyway, we'd better get eating and then we'll see what we can find.'

The little red car vroomed us down the Tibbie to Moffat road, the Tibbie to Selkirk road, the Tibbie to Traquair road. Nothing. Or nothing that captured our imaginations, anyway. So we were back at Tibbie Shiel's again, looking to Uncle Mark's favourite James Hogg statue for inspiration. I plucked a green leaf from a hedge, lazily, hopefully, and turned it over in my hand. A road wound out from behind James' head, upwards and outwards into the hills. I'd never noticed it before.

Brigadoon.

'Look, Diana – let's drive up there. There'll be brilliant views of the loch from there.'

Red wound her way up the curling grey ribbon of a road and, after climbing for a couple of minutes, reached a tiny village of old, stone houses. Heathery purples painted the land around us. It was a sort of Scottish Monet. There were about twenty houses, one old church with a very big bell, and a low-walled field in the centre on which some children were playing noisily. Sure enough, there was a direct view of St Mary's Loch glittering up from the bottom of the hill.

And a dilapidated tower-house at the edge of it all, smiling straight down over Diana and me.

We swapped one look. Then we jumped out of the car and ran up to the house.

The garden was small, overgrown and walled; it was filled mainly with herbs that'd gone to seed. Fennel stems the size of trees swayed, the afternoon sun squeezing out a strong, aniseedy scent from their old, yellow seeds. There were strange insects everywhere, with thin wings, dancing in the lights of the sun. Diana and I pushed through the insects and the aniseed scent, and crushed a carpet of thyme to sneak a peer inside the house. It was half-finished – part-house, part-building site – the walls covered with grey plaster. As we stared through the thick, dusty windows, I remembered a game that my father used to play

with me when I was six or seven: he would create enormous
– global, really – bubbles from washing up liquid, and I would
smile at his face through the see-through, rainbowy shimmer.
Gazing through the bubble glass, it was almost as if I could see
his face inside the tower-house, waiting for me to join him.

As my fingers stroked the soft, yellow-coloured walls, gritty
grains came away in my scrabbling fingernails, reminding me of
sandwiches spiked with sand. Fuchsia fairy dresses and conker-
shelled cups. I knew that I could be a child and a woman in
this house, a lover or alone. It needed me to love it, and I did.
Completely. The inglenook crooked its finger at me, inviting me
to fill it with fire and life. There were nooks and crannies all
over for my candles and my oil burners. And when I'd warmed
it, wooed it and loved it, it would love and protect me in return.
No one could wave a wand at me and take my security away
from me again, ever, I thought.

My fingers curled around the new green leaf in my pocket
and I turned to Diana.

'I've got to have it.'

I had to have him. I knew he was waiting for me, was connected
to me, was fascinated by me, but he probably didn't know it
himself. Yet. It didn't take me long to write the e-mail, and I
even let him have some of my letter as part of it. I kept it short
and sweet. My own little net.

Hi,
I bet you're surprised to hear from me. How can I start? It's always
so difficult to begin, especially today.

I wonder how you're feeling as you read this. Did Sam tell you
that I saw her and gave her a lift back to your house? It started me
thinking about you again, and wondering if there was any way that
we could sort something out.

Can we at least meet to talk about things?

I will wait outside the Holly Bush for you at 7 o'clock next
Tuesday night.

I can't wait to see you.
Helena

I got the other bloke from the bottle bank to let me send it from his computer, just today, so it's untraceable. The Holly Bush is just around the corner from his house – and right beside is this very dark, very deserted car park.

The most intimate section of *The Parting of the Lips* is about to come alive.

Uncle Mark's reaction surprised me. The grand affair with Lisa seemed to be progressing speedily, so I was expecting him to be pleased that the squawking cuckoo was about to fly the Dralon-lined nest. But he was wary overall.

'What if the position at the art gallery turns out to be unsatisfactory?' He looked really miserable, not like Uncle Mark at all. He usually really enjoyed quizzing me. 'Or what if you fall out with Diana? Why don't you travel from here for a while and see how it goes?'

'Because it's obvious that it won't be long before you want Lisa to move in here, with you. She already spends half of the week here.' Uncle Mark flushed a bit, so I moved around the shiny pine to sit beside him. 'You're entitled to your own life, Uncle Mark. And I love the tower-house, love St Mary's Loch. If I buy it now, we could be in there in time for Diana to start at the University, or near enough.'

He still looked crestfallen. 'Helena, you're very young.'

'But you didn't think I was too young to leave home and go to university – as far away as York – and I'd've been even further away from you there.'

'That's true, but you'd have had more people around you there – a more protected environment.'

I thought of when I was really little, when I used to say my prayers: *'Matthew, Mark, Luke and John, Bless the bed that I lie on.'*

I used to think that the Mark in the prayer was Uncle Mark. And it was really. I softened. 'What I really need is someone to help me buy the tower-house and make it into a proper home. I don't even know who owns it or if they want to sell it. I'll need loads of help to do it up.'

Uncle Mark stroked his big moustache and smiled. 'Planning permission, land registry, rights of way, etcetera, etcetera, etcetera.

Could be very tricky.' Uncle Mark's own, very individual, idea of paradise. A man with a mission.

I was on my way.

'Cancer man

> 'It's hard to slide away from the grip of the crab. You probably
> won't want to, of course. Lots of girls are looking for a moonlit
> world like his to dream in, where someone will hold them tightly
> and protect them from the big bad wolf at the door'
> – Linda Goodman's Sun Signs

So most of my wishes were sorted! My car was in the drive, my image was in gear, and the art gallery was waiting for me. And the tower-house was being (extremely thoroughly) looked after.

In fact, I didn't need planning permission (Uncle Mark was almost disappointed) because it had already been – mostly – turned into a house. The previous owner had run out of cash before completing the conversion and had handed the keys back to the building society, hence the state of the place. They'd been just about to advertise it when Uncle Mark put an offer in for me, which had eventually been accepted.

So that left just one wish. Guess what? Dominic. Dominic, Dominic, Dominic Oliver. Obsession.

I hadn't seen him for weeks, forever, but I missed him so much. Uncle Mark was still under the strictest instructions that I didn't want to speak to Dominic. But there had been no more letters, no phone calls, no visits. I was aching for him, but aching just as much at his betrayal, his half-heartedness. This was one test that he could *not* fail.

Surely there was some way that Dominic could find of letting me know that he loved me? Really loved me. Loved me more than he'd loved Emma, more than he could ever love anyone else. Loved me as I loved him, because that was what I needed. Loved me enough to pull me out of a fire before himself. Before his parents. Before his children. Nothing else would do. Dominic. Where on earth was he?

My messages flew to him in many different forms. I prayed to my father, asking him to send me my Dominic back. I filmed his return in my head, over and over again. I clutched my crystals, trying to make him think about the emerald. I read and re-read my astrology books, trying to find a page that said, 'The crab will crawl back to you.' Guilt about my silence regarding the Stone Man tormented me. Three times, I drove past Cromwell Street in my shiny red car, dressed to impress. Nothing. Three times – nothing, nothing, nothing.

And then, one very ordinary morning, God listened. I'd just stopped working at Uncle Mark's office because I wanted some time to myself before my art gallery job began. I was looking at magazines and books about houses, and picturing my own, beautiful, tiny castle – and Dominic – when there was a very loud knock on the door.

The second I opened the door, he was in the house. Dominic. There, with me, inside.

'Helena!' His face, his movements, were all energy. Electric. 'Thank God you're all right. I came as soon as I got it.'

'Got what?' Confusion.

'Your message.' I looked at him. 'Your e-mail. The Holly Bush. Jesus Christ, were you trying to get yourself killed? I wouldn't wait outside there alone myself.' Infuriating. All shoulders and testosterone, as usual. Wonderful. 'What the fuck were you thinking about? You're so naïve.'

'And you're bizarre. Dominic, I don't know what you're talking about.' I tried a minimalist shoulder shrug of my own. 'I really don't.'

'Your e-mail,' Dominic repeated, 'I didn't see it in time. I only use my computer when I'm at the University. I left my summer job last week so that I could do a bit of reading for my course.' He ran his hand through his hair, tugging at it in agitation. 'I switched my computer on this morning and found your message. I went straight round to your Uncle Mark's office, and the girls there said that you'd left so I came here. I've been really worried about you.'

'Well, you can stop worrying. I didn't send you an e-mail. Not my style at all actually, Dominic.' I glossed my hair back at the sides with my fingers. 'I don't even know where the Holly Bush is.' I could tell from his face that he didn't believe me.

'Well, who did send it, then?'

Crystals, candles, prayers, leaves and books, yes. Computers just didn't speak to me. 'I've got no idea,' I replied.

'Did you get my letters?'

Letters. Bliss. I breathed right in. Then it was my turn to be doubtful. 'No – I didn't.'

'I rang you but Mark would never let me speak to you. He must fucking hate me. So I wrote to you. Three times.'

A too-rigid interpretation of my affronted instructions? Did part of Uncle Mark want to keep his Dalmatian penned in forever? 'I didn't get them.'

Perplexed, I flopped on to the peach dream suite and Dominic sat down beside me at once, looking untidy, incongruous, energetic and brilliantly big in the neat little room. 'Helena, you have to listen to me now. Please. I've been miserable without you. Awful. I never meant to hurt your feelings, or to lie to you. Just let me show you how much I feel for you.' His voice dropped when I glared at him, suspiciously. 'I love you.' Emeralds, condoms, sex and tenderness. What did I want to happen next? What I'd always wanted had happened. Dominic Oliver. So what exactly did I want now? I sat quite close to him, side by side. Could I trust him? I wanted to – every single inch of my skin wanted him. 'Helena.' He turned my chin towards him with his big hand, his gentle fingers, just like he had that first time when we'd stood outside Leeched Dry. 'I've never loved anyone like this before. That day at the coffee shop, I really thought it was over. I was furious. But I just couldn't leave you, couldn't forget you. I had to have a kind of, well, faith in you.' Dominic's eyes made me know it, made me whole again; I saw the love in the greenness. My body knew. Knew that I had to trust him, knew that, magically, Dominic *really* loved me.

The answer to my prayers, if not my e-mail. His big arms wrapped me up and he was whispering into me, 'Helena, I

missed you. I missed you. I've been so worried about you.'
This is desperately unfashionable, but it's true: when I looked
into Dominic Oliver's eyes, I knew for certain that there was a
God. And I could see Him. I could see everything. I held on to
him, breathing in his smell, feeling his head, his hair. Him. My
fingers wrapped right around a handful of his hair, like that first
night at Tibbie. We stayed like that for a full minute. Mine.

Then he pulled away from me a bit and smoothed my hair
down. 'Your hair's different. Have you been all right?' I moved
my fist, and a few of his blond hairs, to his sleeve, and nodded.
He smiled, very slightly. 'You look better. I'm sorry about what
I said in the café. The way you looked that day – it was terrible.
I felt like I was killing you. No wonder Mark hates me.' His
expression, and then his head, lifted at the hint of hope. 'Which
university did you decide on?'

'Neither. I've got a job. And a car.' Brighter.

'Sam told me about the car. Where's your job?'

'An art gallery in Edinburgh. In the bookshop.'

The light shone out from Dominic's face. 'I can imagine you
doing that. Are you sure it's the right thing for you?'

'I've still got my place at Edinburgh in a year's time if it isn't.
And I think I'll like it. I start in a week's time.'

'Jesus, you've been busy. What brought all of this on?'

I took a deep breath. If I finally trusted him with my whole
self, then it was time to trust him about the really much smaller
matter of the money: Dominic, who'd rung me, written to me,
worried about me, come to see me. Borne the coffee drops, in
spite of the Lion King pride and arrogance. Held on to his faith
in me. All before he knew that I had any money at all.

'My father – he left me some money, a lot of money, and
some letters. That's how I bought the car.' Dominic nodded.
He was holding my hand tightly. Another deep breath. 'And
the house.'

His eyes widened, and then he tilted his head back and roared.
'A house?' He laughed again. 'Shit, Helena – you are amazing.'

So I described the tower-house to him, the tiny village, the
noisy children, the view of the loch. Explained about sharing it
with Diana. 'It sounds brilliant. Let's go and see it.'

'Well, I suppose I could get the keys from the estate agents.'

Dominic's hand warmed my arm. 'Helena, come to stay with me for a few days. Leave Mark a note. Soon you'll be working in the gallery and I'll be back at Uni. Let's make the most of the summer. I've missed you so much. Really.' He pressed my arm hard on the 'Really'.

Paradise. Just my Dominic and me, snug inside the mouse's nest. He kissed my lips softly, a promise and a tension there within the tenderness.

But very soon I would have to tell him about the Stone Man. Immediately, almost. A solid slab of dread weighed down my back as I paced upstairs to pack.

Dominic's Allegro was left outside Leeched Dry, decorating the drive, as a punishment to Uncle Mark for his withholding of vital information. Within the hour, we were parked outside the tower-house in Red. The estate agent had let us go alone, reckoning quite rightly that there was nothing much in the dilapidated shell worth pinching. As we left Red, I explained about my father's letters to Dominic, and pointed out the tiny turret in the back, left-hand corner.

'It's the seventh room – that's the one I'm going to leave empty, for his letter. What do you think of the house?'

'It's fantastic.' Dominic was staring up at it. 'What's it like inside?'

I smiled. 'Less fantastic. Come and have a look.'

We opened the old oak door and we were in the dark little living room that adjoined the kitchen. 'I'm going to have a Rayburn that runs the central heating,' I explained, and moved into that room next.

The 'kitchen' was actually a bare square of a room – neither it nor the bathroom was fitted out in any way, this being the point at which the last owner's money had run out. 'The Rayburn will be red, and I'll have old cupboards put in and shelves – here.' I waved. 'Wine racks here, and a little table here.' I wanted it to be a warm room, a generous room – a nourishing, healing sort of room. I was planning to paint the walls with swags of fruits and flowers from the different seasons, from cherry blossoms to rose hips and oak leaves. 'There's a dining room upstairs as well.'

We moved up the winding staircase to it. 'I'm going to have a really dramatic cast-iron chandelier over there,' I explained.

I loved the view of the village from the window. 'And the fireplace is the best bit,' I said. Heavy stone lintels bordered the old inglenook and there was a seat within it at one side. 'It'll be like *Wuthering Heights* in here, when that's lit.'

'"*Sundry old villainous guns, and a couple of horse pistols*" and all that,' Dominic laughed.

My face froze for a second. The image of the boy with the dead eyes flashed before me. I wouldn't tell him here, though. The stonework was rough, exposed and rugged, and the empty room with its bare fireplace felt cold and unloving. I carried on. 'And in the centre, a long oak refectory table.' There was a small reading room to the left of the dining room. Upstairs were the bedrooms, a big one for me at the front, overlooking St Mary's Loch of course and a space that would become an en-suite bathroom, and a smaller one for Diana (originally intended as the bathroom) that would have a shower room in its corner. The tiny womb of a turret looking over the loch at the top of the stairs completed the picture and the tour was over.

'Come on. We'd better get the keys back to the estate agent,' I said, and we started to move downwards.

When we got to the room that would be my bedroom, I heard Dominic's voice behind me. 'Wait, Helena.' And he took my hand and pulled me over to the window, holding me tight beside him as we looked over the loch. As I slipped my hand inside his shirt, I was surprised to feel a small, crescent-shaped scar on his chest. Of course – the corner of the brick.

Dominic kissed the top of my head. 'It's beautiful, Helena. Perfect for you.'

I wound my arms around his neck, and as I hid my head in the mainly bones and muscles there, I wondered how, and when, I was going to word my message to him.

Our lovemaking that night was exactly that, a creation and a recreation of our love for each other. There was also plenty of lust and energy, thank God. Clear proof, I was sure, that there'd been no one else in the mousey little nest apart from me. (I'd even sniffed it, slyly, once or twice, like a little ratty thing myself, when I thought Dominic wasn't looking.) And the emerald was still in its proper place.

Afterwards, when we were lying together, warm, released

and relaxed, the shiny pink scar drew my fingers to his chest again. 'Dominic?' The luxury of making his name with my mouth again. 'Dominic . . .' how could I put it? '. . . has anyone else seen this scar on your chest, apart from me?'

'Why?' A sharp, crabby frown transformed his previously gentle expression. 'Has anybody else seen *your* chest lately?'

Ow! The brittle-boned shell was hard against my skin now, so I split myself off, and propped myself up on my shoulder. 'You first.' A slippery fish technique of my own. The only fish in the sea, that was the deal. A breath. It reminded me of my own intake earlier, when I'd decided to tell him about the letters. What was coming next – commitment or catastrophe? Dominic had moved over to my side now, watching me warily, face to face: two even sea creatures.

'I only thought about you, Helena – what you were doing, how you were. Where you were. How to get you back.' His claws contracted again, and his eyes glittered. 'Sorry if that's boring for you. Perhaps you've had a more mixed audience, lately.'

Dominic was on his back now, shell tightly in place. But I could feel him waiting for my answer, sense his sensitivity. The bed creaked dramatically as I jumped on top of him, with great weight and enthusiasm, tickling furiously. 'I have actually. I've had a bad-tempered Dominic, a jealous Dominic, even an affectionate Dominic.' I couldn't resist winding him up even more. 'And I could have had a very insistent vampire.'

His howl was loud and sepulchral as he wrestled me, pulling me underneath him.

'And I've had offers of my own, you know, Helena. Or Cathy, should I say? You're very lucky to have me in bed with you tonight!'

'Matter of opinion. And offers from whose corner?' I wanted to hear *all* about this.

'Enough information for one night. Your head's big enough as it is.'

'Is that a problem?'

'No.' Dominic rolled towards me, propped himself up on his elbow, and kissed my brow. 'Of course not.' He thought for a second more. 'The best thing is, you told me about your dad –

the letters, and the money and everything. I mean, you're right not to tell many people, not to risk getting ripped off. But I feel great that you trusted me.' He kissed me on the lips. 'Well, you knew that I'd never rip you off.' His head was tilted right back. 'I'd never need to, would I? I'll be such a soaring success in my own right.' Bark of laughter.

Dominic, Dominic, Dominic Oliver. 'Now who's an egomaniac?' I threw my arms around his neck and pulled him to me. He spoke in the low voice that I loved and rarely heard.

'I want to impress you. Just you.'

I fingered the pink crescent again. Before I could edit it, a wicked but utterly truthful thought came into my mind. I was glad that Dominic was scarred – scarred by violence, as I had been scarred by the death of my parents. Worse, the death of his father flashed into my consciousness, just for a second, alongside the words, 'One blood.' I touched the tiny moon. We really would be one blood then. United. United in what? I actually asked something much safer. 'Back to these offers, then?'

But I didn't get any answers, not that night anyway.

Nightmare. It was a replay of that day at Beech Trees, almost. Waiting, waiting. I had my brick in my bag and everything. Half an hour I waited, and it took a lot less than that to work out the possibilities of what had happened, why he hadn't come.

- *He never wanted to see her again*
- *They'd made up before he got my e-mail*
- *She'd contacted him before I had*
- *He couldn't make it at that time or place*
- *He'd rung her to check the meeting time*
- *He hadn't had his computer on*
- *He was away somewhere, on holiday, or working*
- *He had her e-mail address, and knew the e-mail wasn't from her*
- *Something had gone wrong with the e-mail (unlikely)*

It had been worth a try, like. Still, that was a pretty long list. Must be slipping. And it's been ages since I've seen either of them.

Next time I contact them, it will be foolproof. Nothing will go wrong.

Waking up with Dominic the next day was wonderful – absolutely magical. A warm cat, I stretched my sleepiness away as I heard him get up, and I was just opening my eyes as three parcels appeared on the pillow beside me.

'What's this?'

'Presents. Presents from France. I was going to give you them the day after I got back.' A glitter came into his eyes. 'I burnt that fucking diary.'

'Good job you didn't get tattooed ever.' I tried to lighten the mood. 'You'd have barbecued your arms.' Carbonadoed.

Dominic laughed once, quickly, and then reflected. 'The difference is, if you wanted your name here,' he touched his chest, 'I *would* get tattooed.' He laughed again. 'I think I'm quite safe there. Not your style, really.'

'Don't be so sure. Some of those Celtic ones are quite nice.' I touched his wrist. 'Maybe a little chain around here? Could be quite erotic.'

'Maybe not!' he said, pulling his wrist away rapidly.

I sipped my coffee. 'Do you have to work today? You said you were getting ready for your course.'

'God, no, Helena. Not with you here.' He thought for a second. 'That was part of the problem last term, I know – putting my exams before you the whole of the time. No, I'll do the work later. I want to spend the whole week with you, if that's what you want.'

'The only things I need to do are related to the house. I need to check that the legal side is moving along, but Uncle Mark's doing most of that for me anyway. I want to work out how it will look, how I'm going to furnish and decorate it and so on,' I explained.

'Edinburgh's the perfect place, then. I'll help you. But not today.' Dominic stroked my cheek. 'Open your presents.'

Bliss. Shiny, emerald earrings, a slim, silver bracelet and two little wisps of underwear.

We barely got out of bed all day.

'I can daydream for hours, and pictures fall in just like slides,'
– David Sylvester, *Interviews with Francis Bacon*

Whole, healed and renewed the next day, I was ready to drag Dominic around every shop in Edinburgh to find new treasures for my beautiful house. I'd decided on bronze, gold and russet colours, to celebrate the daily flipping of the old penny of the Scottish sun that I'd see from my bedroom window at the tower-house, and the seasonal changing of the trees.

An antique French day bed was the first gem I unearthed. I pictured myself lying in my bedroom, looking over the view to the loch through my bubble window. A soft, golden throw, in which to wrap the day bed or myself, depending on temperature and mood, completed the picture. And I went for heavy, theatrical curtains as well, to frame the tower's windows' dramatic views. The number of candelabras that I bought made Dominic complain that the house was going to look like something out of *Carrie*. Several huge mirrors and sconces were essential purchases, to reflect the candles' light.

Shopping for the kitchen was my favourite bit. I bought solid, glazed terracotta Spanish cooking dishes; bright Mediterranean crockery (Dominic shaded his eyes theatrically to protect them – 'The food will cook in the heat of the colours, save electricity!') and heavy cast-iron pans and griddles. It was a definite advantage that Dominic could cook. And they looked good. I also picked out an enormous Belfast sink and a cheery, cherry Rayburn. Flashing my own plastic felt good, not that I hadn't always enjoyed using Uncle Mark's, of course.

Dominic's favourite part was the choosing of the bed – Lion King-sized, of course. In his own, inelegant yet arrogant, half-crab, half-lion way, he stretched himself out on one after another of them, before pulling me down, roaring (him) and squealing (me), into his own den-cum-seabed, which I bought. He insisted on buying a quilt and some bed linen for it saying, in front of the bored girl on the till, 'Now, just make sure you wash this lot this time, Helena!' in an almost uncle-esque reproving voice.

As a shopper's companion, he wasn't a patch on Diana and we were both ready for a bath and a drink by six o'clock.

My mood changed when we got back to Cromwell Street as I busied myself in the bathroom. Because I knew that I was going to have to discuss the Stone Man with Dominic. I'd already put it off for a dangerously long time.

Parts of Leeched Dry were stained with the memories of my childhood traumas as clearly to me as if the carpets were marked with bloodstains. So I had to select the spot thoughtfully where I would tell Dominic about the Stone Man – I didn't want to further soil either Cromwell Street or the tower-house with his mark. I suggested a visit to a new pub that night. I chose a fairly quiet corner of the Art Deco-style bar, where reddened light streamed in through the stained glass windows, and I waited for Dominic to bring over the drinks. I was finally ready to spill out my news and launched right in as soon as he got back from the bar.

'Dominic, do you remember when you were in hospital – you said once that when you were talking to your dad, you felt a sense of evil? An evil presence, really?'

'Yes, I know. It was a weird feeling.'

And I was about to recreate it for him. My Dominic. I held my hand up to the candle on our table, watching the flames pink my skin. Big breath. And then I began. 'Well, I think I know why.' My palm warmed and I breathed in again, trying to get rid of the wobble of my voice. 'I saw the boy – the one who attacked you – I saw him outside your hospital room. The boy with the dead eyes . . . I saw him.' His chair legs screeched as he moved towards me.

'What? How would you know? You weren't there.' Glower of concentration.

'I know,' I said, 'but I've seen him before.'

And I told him at long last about the staring eyes in the face of the window, the dummy and the rag doll on the train, and the final shocking recognition. 'I know it's him.'

'Why didn't you say something before?'

'Because you were in such a state. And then you were in France. These last few days are the first time I've really seen you since.'

'Bastard! What does he want? What does he want from both of us?'

'Well,' I looked away from him, 'from the look on his face that day on the train, he wanted from me what most men want from women. Pretty basic.'

'Fucking pervert.' The pub table quivered under Dominic's assault. 'I knew it. I had a feeling about the train that night. Why didn't you tell me?' But he wasn't listening; he was thinking. 'It was planned, then, the whole thing.' He went quiet for a few moments. Then, 'Tell me what he looks like?'

I described the slight yet strong frame, the burning eyes with the dead blankness behind them, the skin. The thought of him made me shiver. The candle flame was hot against my fingers but I left my hand where it was. Dominic nodded. 'Sounds like him, though we can't be certain. And what does he want from me?' He kicked the table leg. 'I don't get it – he watches you, attacks me, wants you then . . .' He seemed to stop himself, with a swift glance towards me. 'So why?' Another thought flashed into his eyes and he pulled my hand away from the candle, holding it tightly between both of his. 'Shit! All the time I was in France, and afterwards, you were here on your own – with him on the fucking streets.'

'He doesn't know where I live.'

'How do you know that? He knows where I live and he obviously knows we're together.'

An awful thought. 'Dominic – that e-mail – I really didn't send it.'

Dominic saw my face and understood. 'Christ, he was going for round two.' Another screech of the chair. 'Let's go back to the house and have a look at what it said exactly.'

The e-mail lay between us on the bed at Cromwell Street. My mouth opened as I looked at the first sentences. Very familiar. 'Do you remember that letter I sent you when you were in the middle of your exams – the one you never got?'

'Yes.' He nodded.

'He's got it. That's exactly how it started.' I read on. 'He's been watching us both all that time. He must have seen me with Sam as well.'

'And he's been to my pigeon hole at the University.' Dominic shook my arm. 'Helena, you're not to go anywhere on your own from now on, anywhere at all – really.'

'Do you think we should tell the police?'

Dominic considered. 'Well, we haven't really got any new information for them, have we? I mean, it's hardly illegal to watch people or to send them e-mails, is it? Or to travel by train and stare. Might as well try though there's not much for them to go on. But we've got to be really careful. Especially you.'

I felt as if he might be outside the house even then, under a street lamp or in the alleyway again. I felt as if he was injected into my skin, making me dirty almost. Safe in Dominic's room, we went over the facts again and again. Several times I'd tried and failed to find the house where I'd seen him that first time, scouring Scotland's streets on my own in Red. We fine-tuned our description of him together. But we couldn't come to any new conclusions so finally had to concede defeat. We got ready for bed.

Dominic folded his arms around me tightly, just as he had on the night of the puking incident, his face nuzzled into my hair. 'We're together. Tomorrow we'll make a plan. Sleep now. You're safe with me, Helena. I'll make certain of that.'

It was a promise he couldn't keep.

Despite our closeness, we both stared into the darkness alone, cold, sour fear in our stomachs, before we slipped separately into our dreams.

I often have to wait for sleep, wait for the scorpions in my mind to die down a bit, so to speak, before sleep will come. But dreams aren't something that happen to me – they're something I work, direct, re-direct.

I play computer games all day and I carry on with them all night, chasing little characters over the massive computer screen of my mind. I'm a khaki cross on the screen, a khaki cross against a red background. A khaki cross that can fire bullets, hard, and eliminate. Control. Camouflaged.

I prayed for a flying dream that night, like the dreams I used to have when I flew above St Mary's Loch.

But instead, I dreamt of men – of dead men, slow men, following me. Gaining on me, however quickly I ran and however often I turned.

'I want you to be a brave girl.'

Decision time. I could hear one man behind me, breathing uniformly, could feel his stare on the back of my head. For the first time, I turned around and looked at him – looked right into him. Knew who I was dealing with. And then I ran at him anyway, so fast that I flew. Flew right above him, right over him, right past him, until he was an insignificant dot in my past.

I knew then that I could do it. I could do anything I wanted to – anything. It was just a matter of realising it.

Freedom.

Everything was very clear, with the clarity that only darkness can release. I woke Dominic as dawn lit the walls of our room.

'Let's get up. We've got an e-mail of our own to write.'

The bottle bank boy passed it on to me. Guessed it was mine, like.

Filthy sheet of paper. Full of threats. Bastards. I haven't been able to think of anything else since I got it – cracking glass. Bits of it keep clashing through my brain. 'The police have a detailed physical description of you.' Middle-class wankers. They'd getting their fucking faces re-decorated around here for that. 'We know where you live.' She'd driven past my cousin's house, once. Once. 'The police are investigating the incident thoroughly.' I'll investigate their arses thoroughly, with a hard object, and that's a promise, not a threat.

And finally, 'Do not contact us again.' They've turned nasty. Terrifying. Ha-fucking-ha. They've got no idea what nasty means. Who they're dealing with. What they are dealing with. That e-mail changed everything.

She thought I was the underdog. Under. Dog. Time to show my canines.

Army hard. Time for a campaign.

Once we'd faced him, I was ready to face the rest of my life and the rest of my world as well – ready to put him where I preferred, in the back of my mind, although he would never quite go away.

Dominic and I decided to contact a few people and organise a meal, to celebrate the re-erection of the tower, as Dominic insisted on calling it. The walls were still grey, but the Rayburn was installed, the central heating was in place and the bathroom was on its way. We had some furniture, and lots of candles, so I felt that it was time to name the day and plan the action.

About a week after sending the e-mail, I was ready to start. 'Right. So who should we invite?'

'Dixie, first of all. And Sherry,' he said. I kept my eyes averted; I'd never admitted to Dominic quite how much I disliked Sherry. 'Oh, and Sherry's new man.'

Much better. 'And Diana,' I said, adding her to the list.

'Doug and Sam (who were 'just good friends' again at that stage), and Jem, and Jen.' Dominic continued. 'What about Eric?'

'We could try,' I decided.

'And Matthew.' Matthew rented Jen's old room, Jen having moved out to somewhere more civilised when she started work as an education officer in a cinema. 'That'll do, I think.' Dominic was probably considering the catering – definitely his province.

I totted up. 'That's twelve, including us.' The dining room's refectory table and candelabra were in place, and just about nothing else. The table would seat twelve comfortably. 'That's about right. I'll design some invitations and send them out, if you organise the food.'

'Right. Make sure that you stick a note in to tell them to return the invitations here, though, Helena. Just tell them we've had some trouble. I don't want anything appearing in my pigeonhole. I've blocked it up, anyway.'

'Good. If I send them out today, they'll all have a week to get sorted out.'

And it was done.

Now I've got something I can really get my teeth into. Get my toolbar into.

Even as I'm walking up towards his pigeonhole, I know there's a message for me there. His slot is blocked, so to speak, by a box-file, so he knows I've been there before. But pinned to the box-file is a little envelope – like an invitation to a children's party, which is exactly what it turns out to be.

Even under cover (darkened hair and eyebrows, little round glasses, well-meaning, stupid, academic face) I've got to be quick. It's getting more and more dangerous all the time – but I'm getting more and more strong and clever, to manage it, like. Looking vague and nonchalant, I just pick off my 'Dominic Oliver' envelope, walk out of the room and into the Bundymobile to read my post.

All it is is a little sheet, with a sort of chained Celtic border to it, and a map and a date, a time and an address underneath. The Tower House. It stinks of Helena. They've bought a house, then. Having friends around. More friends than they realise, like. On the back of it is scrawled:

> **Love to come,**
>
> **Love, Sherry**

Mushroom face. Some friend. Thank you – love to come. Mushroom soup – I'm having some of that.

Saturday evening 'supper'. Wankers. Three days, then, to prepare, to get everything just right.

*   *   *

The setting was perfect: the dining room looked just how I'd imagined it, the cast-iron candelabra casting shadows on the long table, silver sconces on the walls and wide open orange and yellow lilies in the centre of the table. The dark plaster of the walls looked eerie but dramatic, heated by the flickering of the candles and the flames of the fire. Dominic had brought his portable CD player from Cromwell Street and some CDs that echoed the mood that I was after, somewhere between needing and getting, sour and sweet. He'd also shopped, chopped and prepared Chinese food.

All I had to think about now was my clothes.

I've got the set just perfect now for *Alchemy Five*. It'll be a short, sharp, spunky shoot, before the glory of golden *Six* (which I'm working on already, something really special for you). I've got no intentions of approaching Helena and Dominic for *Five* and I don't feel like it, after their betrayal. So *Five* will feature a minor character. Shame. But there's more than a bit of poetic justice in my selection. And I've really gone to town on the preparation and the set. I hope they'll have some decent women there who'll be worth the trouble. I certainly don't fancy old matchstick head.

I know for certain that none of them have ever seen the Bundymobile – I've been very careful about that. And I've carried out a reconnaissance mission, located the tower-house and examined the environs. I reckon I can tuck the Bundymobile into a little corner just around from the house. And this will be a night-time operation, of course.

The inside of the car is just as Ted would have wanted it. The front passenger seat has been taken out and there's a silver chain, a sheet and my brick on the back seat. (The brick is a recurring image in the series now.) There are some candles, for aesthetic, erotic or practical purposes; I'm not quite sure which myself just yet. I know Helena likes candles, and I've still got quite a soft spot for her, so to speak (not that it's soft very often), despite everything she's done to me. Best of all, there's a triangular bandage in the glove compartment. And there are big black screens to block the light out and the view in. The set owes a lot to the Legal Eagle, but not the content – the content will be pure, hard Adam Ramsden. A complete original. No sneak previews, this time! Not yet, anyway. Masked balls. As Ted said, 'I'm in charge of entertainment.'

All I have to concentrate on now is my clothes.

Everyone had replied as requested, apart from Sherry who had rung, and Eric, who had pushed a patchouli-scented note under Dominic's door, saying, 'Can't come'. So the table was set for eleven.

When Diana finally descended, I was outside, planting candles on long sticks into the soil alongside the skeletal fennel. She was halfway through the process of moving into the tower-house that week. Her cleavage shone in the dusk. 'Any decent men coming tonight, then?'

'Well, there's Dominic's new flatmate, Matthew, I haven't seen him myself yet. And Dixie – John – who you know. And Jem, who you don't. Oh, and Doug, but he's sort of Sam's always.'

'Jem. Describe.'

'Tall, thin, with a green nose stone . . .'

But that was enough – she raised her hand dramatically at the mention of the stone and shuddered. Her chest seemed to deflate. Still, at least she might be of some use to me now. 'Here, Diana, stick the rest of these in, will you?' And as she poked one in half-heartedly, at a rakish angle: 'Artistically!' She curled her lip and continued.

Dominic was wreathed in steam in the kitchen. The main courses were his job and I had prepared the pudding – platters of fruit (very Cézanne) and an arrangement of cheese (very Braque) were waiting on the kitchen table. I'd started at the art gallery that week. Dominic's preparations looked a bit more complex and he kept shouting, 'Bastard!' at the pans, as one or the other of them boiled over, tipped over, burnt dry or spluttered to a halt. The Rayburn bore the black smear of a rubber-soled kick and I guessed he hadn't quite got the hang of it yet. Time to go. I kissed his heated cheek. 'I'll just get some drinks and take them outside for when the others get here.'

Most of me was squeezed into a short, black dress and I was wearing a necklace of glittery red stones. Dominic was wearing the usual ancient, ripped jeans, plus a new T-shirt that I'd just bought him, so it was very *Lady and the Tramp*, a little jokette that I didn't share with him. But as I left, he caught my eye and grinned, rolling his eyes. 'Don't work too hard, Lady Penelope!' Then he said, 'You look great,' before returning to his stirring, snarling and swearing.

I escaped into the night outside with my still cool face and my drinks tray, which Diana generously lightened for me. The moon was high, full and pale as yet and the sun had almost disappeared. The gloamin'. It was great to see the tower-house lit up and in action. 'Looks a bit different from the first time we saw it doesn't it, Diana?'

'It's looking better every second.' Her voice was charged with a definitely non-decorating-related energy.

Turning, I saw Sam with Jen at her side, looking very blonde and appealing. Two men were in their wake. Diana's prow lifted. 'That must be Matthew.' He was as tall and blond as Doug was dark and stocky, then Sam was in amongst the fennel seeds, crunching freely and gesturing towards the tower with her elbow.

'Helena – this looks fantastic.' She swept a glass from the tray. 'And so does this!' She downed half of her cocktail before introducing, 'Matthew – our new man.' Her eyes flickered towards Jen, and Doug pushed out a hand to Diana.

'Sam has the manners of a pig, as always. Ye must be Diana. Ah'm Doug and this is Jen.'

But Diana kept her eyes fixed about a foot above Doug's head, somewhere at the point of Matthew's face. Matthew's eyes, meanwhile, were a good foot below Doug's head, exactly on Diana's chest. A perfect fit. Then the second car snarled up, and Sour Sherry and *her* new man were heading for the cocktail tray, Dixie (looking matted) and Jem (nose stone twinkling at the moon) bringing up the rear behind them. I kicked against a tree stump, the frill of a hundred, white-edged mushrooms at its neck – dressed for the party, I thought, as I waited for the carful to reach us. Dominic emerged from the kitchen just as Sherry advanced, extending her tongue towards me. 'Helena, nice to see you. You've put on a bit of weight. Suits you.' Ow! It was just like being back at a

Leeched Dry occasion. Before I could speak, Dominic stepped forward.

'Do you want a cocktail to dilute the acid, Sherry?' Loyal Dominic, normally so immune to her chemical output! What was going on? His voice was quiet and I felt his arm go right around my shoulders. Sherry's eyes shone blackly, while her companion looked muddy and dull. Anyone could see it was an escort agency job – just proving she could get a man. And anyone could also see exactly who'd been after Dominic in my absence! I caught Diana's eye and she gave the tiniest nod. I winced and passed around the margaritas, pointing the one with the saltiest rim in Sherry's direction.

The night had begun.

Smoke and change charred the air. Fall. We drank outside until the moon sharpened, the night smells rose and the darkness thickened, then I went inside, to light the candles there, while Diana began to blow out the torchères, her glinting eyes on Matthew's as her lips approached the flames and her breasts approached the light. Then it was all noise, movements and perfume smells as everyone seated themselves and Dominic and Sam charged up and down the stairs with one steaming dish after another: crispy spheres of chicken and a separate red sauce; piles of noodles; fluffy, yellow rice; a glossy, yellow pepper dish and other treats. Bliss. Something about the way that Dominic cooked – everything about the way he cooked – always reminded me of that miracle with the loaves and fishes. Sam dipped her fingers into just about every dish and advised on their content as she 'served'. I was pouring wine, and all of the others were drinking it, shuffling against each other and talking loudly. The candles' light flickered in the silver sconces, like the shimmering of the loch below us, and there were pools of burning oil in glass bowls in every corner of every room.

'Helena,' Sherry's voice again, 'this all looks positively funereal to me.' She fingered a lily, nipped off the head and put it behind her ear, the orange bloom violent against her blackened hair. 'I wish . . .'

'It's the Last Supper, Sherry,' interrupted Jem. 'And I wonder who will betray who before the crowing of the cock?'

Or who has been betrayed already, I thought, settling into my

seat and scowling at Sherry as I did so. I put crowing cocks out
of my mind. Jem looked down at Jen – he'd engineered a seat
beside her. 'Gentle Jen, a Virgin Mary of a girl.' Sam and Jen's
crackling laughter seemed only to inflame Jem more. 'Jem and
Jen – a pair of priceless jewels.'

'Priceless fools more like, Jem,' said Sam, before grinning a
'Sorry, Jen' in her friend's direction.

Dominic arrived with spoons which he dropped unceremon-
iously into the centre of the table as he squeezed in between
Dixie and me. Diana was on my left, mooning at Matthew
shamelessly. 'There's loads for everybody – just help yourselves,'
Dominic said, which they all did, very swiftly, sloppily and
enthusiastically.

As Dominic talked with Dixie, and laughed, and ate, I thought
about him as I watched. Not only was he beautiful to me, but
he actually *was* beauty – the thing itself. He looked so relaxed
and confident, his fair hair touching his brow and his shoulders
pushing expressively towards Dixie as he spoke. His complete
confidence came from his trust in Dixie: I thought of the
alleyway. (He was relating the latest Stone Man news.) And
I trusted Dominic. Leeched Dry girls don't fight for anyone –
scabby knees soil clothes and reputations – and certainly not for
themselves, but I thought then that I would fight for Dominic.
If I lost him, there'd be no point in anything: my plans, my job,
even my tower-house. So I was finding a spine that I'd never had
before, that I'd never needed before. I had everything to lose –
that was my strength. The moon stared like an eye through the
window and I knew she was watching the loch below me too.
I turned back to the conversations around me.

'Dominic, have you got any more of that gorgeous beany
stuff?' Sherry's greedy beak was wide open, as usual. Smiling
absent-mindedly, Dominic pushed the dish in her general direction and it landed about a foot short. It was an unintentional
stab (twisted when he turned to me immediately afterwards)
and Sherry's face was more than usually white and bloodless,
suddenly. Her partner, eventually introduced as Ewan, looked
bored again, and I felt a first pang of sympathy for her. No
wonder she hated me.

'Have you got enough?' Dominic asked me. 'You didn't

listen to that weight rubbish, did you?' He blindly deepened Sherry's wound. Still, I reckoned she could look after herself so I concentrated on him.

'I'm fine. The food's brilliant. How's the kitchen?'

He grimaced. 'Less brilliant. Good job you haven't decorated yet. It's a bit Jackson Pollock in there, you could say.' Dominic rolled his eyes, yawning theatrically. 'Here, just eat a bit more.' He arranged spoonfuls of food on my plate.

'How is the art gallery, Helena?' Sam cut in.

'Glossy,' I replied, distracted. 'And gorgeous. I've got plenty of time to read some of the books as well.'

'And Dominic gets to do all of the cooking,' hissed a battling beak.

'Brilliant!' Sam steamed guilelessly on. 'Matthew, do you think this set-up would work in our house?'

'If you like toast.' He smiled.

'I love cooking,' Diana pushed in, nipping me hard as my jaw dropped incredulously. 'There's no need to go hungry, Matthew.'

In fact, he was looking extremely replete and well fed, if a bit squashed, mainly because Diana's chair was inches closer to him than it had been when I'd set the table earlier. Shy as he seemed, he was getting the message. It was funny, he had that sort of look on his face – as if he thought no one could see him. As if he were a beautiful spider's web, invisible until the mists hit it. Well, the mists were certainly coming down now, because Diana definitely liked what she was seeing.

'I'll get some more wine,' Sam offered, then leapt down the stairs to the kitchen and returned with a bottle in each hand. She busied herself with filling everybody's glasses and then returned to her seat, inexplicably leaving Jen's glass empty, with the remnants of the bottle nearby. Jeremy bounded up at once, 'More wine, Jen?' and artlessly bowed towards her, saying, 'A thirsty virgin just won't do,' as he refilled her glass. Sam caught Jen's eye and they were laughing again as Jen spluttered her wine down.

'I'm driving home, Jem. This'll have to be the last,' she said. Plus, it would take a lot more than two glasses of Bulgarian red to make Jen see Jem through wine-tinted glasses. Still, you had to admire his stamina.

My mind drifted in and out of different subjects, as I drifted up and down the stairs with Dominic, clearing the table: my new bath, with its wonderful little feet, Sherry's legs and how much Dominic had seen of them, the eyes of the boy with the rag-doll girlfriend. Then, before I could flick the switch, I put the last two together – Sherry's skinny legs and the dead man's hungry eyes. Maybe she deserved it for trying to take Dominic away from me.

Thank God it was just a thought. Still, as I reached over her to pick up her half-full plate, guilt chilled my fingertips – they were icy cold.

My fingers are as cold as ice as I sit out here in my car. Autumn is coming around again and the cycle is almost complete.

The first sign that anything interesting is happening is Helena, fiddling with some torch things in the garden. She looks such a very different person from my autumn girl of a year ago, and my plans for her now are very different as well. They're a pair of self-satisfied bastards, the pair of them, in their cosy fucking tower-house. Then another girl comes out – long blonde hair, big tits – must be a guest. They all arrive then – clitoris allsorts – and it's drinks in the garden time.

It was mushroom face's waxy skin that had given me the idea for *Alchemy Five* in the first place, that and Ted, of course. And she had handed the invite to me – poetic justice. (One of my strong points, that.) Not to mention, she'd be the easiest to see when it got darker – that white face against the black hair. Reminded me of voodoo, sticking pins in wax dolls. And she looks such a slag, with her skirt up to her arse and her lips jam rag red. Waving a red rag at a bull, so to speak. So I don't need to think about hurting her; she's already been well used. Not a lady, like Helena – a lady and a babe. I know all about women like Sherry, and all about how to treat them.

This piece is my most extreme yet. I've got nothing to lose and that's always been my strength. People like them, sipping drinks in their tower-house, are easy for me – greed, and what they need to keep, keeps them, keeps them meek.

Meek for me. Stops them taking things to extremes, like I can.

Anyway, see what you think of this one. It's a full playscript, this time – the first piece with extensive dialogue.

Alchemy Five
The Silver Chain
Adam Ramsden is a man in a hurry. He sits in his 'specially adapted Volkswagen Beetle (a shining tribute to his hero, the American Legal Eagle, Ted Bundy) outside a Scottish tower-house, a picture of impatience. A striking-looking young man with slicked back, darkened hair and piercing eyes, he taps the fingers of his left hand restlessly against the dashboard of his vehicle (from which the passenger seat has been removed). Adam's right arm is heavily plastered and he wears a sling. On the back seat of the Beetle is a brick, a clean white sheet, three candles and a heavy, heavy chain. The night darkens, and it becomes clear that Adam is waiting for the inhabitants of the tower-house to leave. The atmosphere within the shadowy interior of the car is powerfully sinister, contrasting dramatically with that of the cheerily lit tower-house, from which the sounds of music, laughter and lively conversation can be heard, drifting over into Adam's car. The moon shines hard through the glass of the windscreen, and the night wears on.

At around midnight, the first of the party-goers begin to leave and Adam's muscular body is a study in pure animal tension and suspense as he poises, ready for his task. Three, four, five guests leave, and then a white-faced figure dressed in black walks, waving and alone, from the house. Adam suddenly makes his move, his lithe body springing from the car like a panther, despite his weighted arm.

Adam: I'm very sorry about this. (He smiles.) My name's Adam. I live in one of the houses opposite, and I need to get something out of the glove compartment of my car – a bit difficult with this thing on my arm (indicating his plaster cast). I can't get my hand in. Can you possibly help?

Sherry: (her face concerned, yet mildly impatient) Yeah, sure. Which one's your car?

Adam gestures towards the Volkswagen and leads the girl

towards his car. He holds the passenger door open for her with his left arm, and then points towards the glove compartment.

Adam: Could you just reach inside and get some keys for me, er . . .

Sherry: Sherry.

She smiles, her darkened eyes and painted lips an open sexual invitation to Adam.

Sherry: Just let me have a look.

Sherry bends deep into the car and feels around the glove compartment in the shadowy interior. She emerges, holding a single, black stocking, and turns grinning towards Adam, about to make a joking comment. The smile dies on her lips as she sees his expression, and she looks again at the stocking in her hand, the truth dawning, before trying jerkily to pull out of the car.

Foolishly, she has reckoned without Adam Ramsden's speed, strength and skill. He whips his muscular arm out of its sling and catches her an expert, beplastered blow to the back of the skull. She is dazed but still conscious as he seizes her body and bundles her into the car, gagging her swiftly with the stocking as he does so. The car door shut, he enters from the driver's side and chains her arms above her head in supplication before wrapping her breasts, waist, legs and ankles in the heavy, silver chain. Five for silver. Sherry moans through the gag at the pain caused by the blow to her head, and Adam picks up the bloodied brick from the back seat for the first time. He holds it close to her face.

Adam: Quiet! Or I might just forget I'm a gentleman.

Silence. The girl's eyes are full of fear – fear and something else. Respect.

Adam drives with speed and skill to some deserted woodland, about twenty minutes away from the tower-house. Sherry's face is the essence of terror, the eyes doll-like and wide within the whitened mask of her face. Adam parks the car down a narrow dirt track and, reaching behind him, puts the brick, candles and white sheet into a large, canvas sack, which he had stowed beneath the back seat. He slings the heavily chained woman effortlessly over his strong shoulder, clasping her thighs to his chest with his chalk-white right arm. The night is black and the moon is high in the chilly, Scottish sky, a silver coin above their heads. Sherry begins to whimper, fearing, rightly, what *lies ahead of her. Adam strikes her buttocks hard, once, with his large, open palm.*

Adam: I'll tell you when you can and can't make a noise, when you can and can't move, when you can and can't speak. Just stay still and keep it shut.

Sherry is silent, her body limp and submissive over Adam's strong back. Adam heroically carries Sherry into the wood, his step sure and confident and his back straight, despite the weight of his burden. After ten minutes or so, he reaches a small clearing in the wood, lit sharply by the moon, as if by a bare, overhead light bulb. With Sherry's thighs still pinned to his chest, Adam prepares his operating theatre: the sheet is laid flat on the ground, the candles and the brick in the top right-hand corner of it. He lies Sherry on top of the sheet, the black clothes making her a clear target in the moonlight, a dark petal against the dazzling whiteness of the sheet.

Adam (kindly): Now, in a minute, Sherry, I'm going to remove your gag. I don't want to make you any more uncomfortable than I have to.

Sherry's eyes are huge in her face as she listens obediently to Adam's words.

Adam: However, if you issue a single sound, except in answer to my instructions, you will force me to silence you, and to complete the operation while you are unconscious. Do you understand me?

Sherry's eyes follow Adam's eyes to the brick, which lies near her head, and she nods, swallowing a response.

Adam (mercifully): If you remain silent and follow my instructions, you will not be hurt. Is that clear?

Sherry nods her head quickly, eager to please now.

Adam: Good girl. I'll take the gag off now, then.

Adam bends down to the terrified girl and removes the gag deftly. Crazed by fear, Sherry immediately and unwisely begins to scream, shrilly. Adam's reaction is characteristically swift, decisive and strong, and his palm meets the girl's white cheek with a slap that rings out in the silent, dead night. Sherry's lips are silent and stained with blood now, black against her skin in the moonlight. The sheet is similarly spotted with the red juice of her body.

Adam: That was very foolish, Sherry, very foolish indeed.

He lifts the brick to Sherry's staring face, and grazes it down the skin beside her left eye.

Adam: Can I count on your co-operation now?

Sherry nods, sobbing, and Adam replaces the brick and begins to issue his instructions.

Adam: You may answer me when I put questions to you directly. Is that clear?

Sherry (her voice quiet): Yes, Adam.

Adam: Good girl. Now, I am about to loosen some of your clothing so that I can gain access to your vagina, anus and breasts. Is that clear?

Sherry's head twists away, her stained face an agony of humiliation.

Adam: I repeat, is that clear?

Tears roll down Sherry's doll-like face, mingling with the blood, which ran on to the sheet from her lips.

Sherry: Yes . . . yes, Adam.

Adam (smiling): Excellent. Now, lie still and I won't hurt you. Otherwise . . .

His eyes are on the brick again.

Sherry: Thank you. Thank you, Adam.

Not really hurt.

Curtain down.

It's got lots of different endings at the moment, depending on my mood and there are several ways to use the various props. Sick, isn't it? But I bet you read every single word. What does that make you? The same as me, in thought if not in deed. Just a bit less active. We've been to the woods together, you and me. And Ted, can't forget him, of course. Credit where it's due.

Notice, I don't have to actually touch mushroom face, not with my bare hands anyway. Don't go thinking I fancy her, will you? More the opposite. And I don't enjoy thinking about this one as much, because of that. It's just my way of getting back at Helena and Dominic for their betrayal, like. I have to hurt her, to show them how much they've hurt me. Let them know how much I hate them and let them know the calibre of the person they're dealing with. I don't want to do it, you know. Nice touch of irony too – I'm helping to keep those two together by pulling Sherry apart – I'm sure she's been playing away with Dominic – and I'm sure she's had worse than that done to her already. Once again, Dominic and I will be connected through the blood – but not love, this time – of a woman.

Part of me still loves Helena, despite everything she's done. I'll be glad to return to her in *Six*.

I look through the window of my car and in through the window of the tower-house. I can see everything, the moon is so bright, and I've had a little stroll, like, just once or twice. There's a tree stump, just outside the house, covered in filthy fungi things. One of them's broken off and dozens of flies are sucking at the bit where it dropped off the tree's throat, like filthy leeches. And I can see Helena's sitting down again, between Dominic and the blonde with the big funbags. The candles flicker between her face and mine. She doesn't see me. She can never see me, that's the whole point, the whole fucking problem.

She looks as if she's about to speak.

'Would anyone like a coffee? Or another drink?' The elegant white candles of the early evening had dripped down hour by hour into lumpen, skin-like forms, reminding me of deformity. It was after 11 o'clock, but it was unlikely that anyone would want to leave for a while. Matthew would be lucky if he got out alive (although he looked pretty cheerful about it).

'I'll get more wine for everybody.' Sam's lips were stained dark red with wine already, giving her, alongside the neon hair, a supernatural look.

'And I'll get some coffee for the drivers,' said Dominic, glancing towards the drooping Ewan. Jen, deep in shallow conversation with Jem, smiled and nodded at Dominic.

'We'll have to be going soon.' They were almost the only words that Ewan had said all night and I guessed he wouldn't be in a hurry to take Sherry out again.

'Is it all right if Sam and me come back with ye then, Ewan?' asked Doug. 'Ah've got a football match tae play tomorrow.'

'I could do with a lift as well, mate,' said Dixie.

'Living dangerously,' scowled Sam from the door, bottle poised. Then, something about Jen's expression distracted her.

'Almost as dangerously as Jen – escorted *Home Alone* by the unchivalrous Jeremy.'

Jen snorted. 'Thanks, Doug.' She pointed at Jem. 'Just remember, you'll be in the passenger seat. Any more "virgin" talk and you'll be treading trainers!'

Jem smiled sweetly, his nose stone gleaming above his teeth. 'I will be the very soul of discretion, Jen, as ever.'

'As never,' cackled Sam. 'Make sure you've got your knuckle dusters ready, Jen.'

Five minutes more and Ewan was released, taking a sulky Sherry, Sam, Doug and Dixie with him. Diana and Matthew disappeared into the kitchen, and very shortly afterwards disappeared up the stairs to Diana's bedroom, Diana wearing an expression that could only be described as victorious. Which left Dominic, Jem, Jen and me. Dominic began to clear more of the dishes and glasses from the table and Jen fell into helping him, chatting about Sam and Doug as she did so. There was a generous smear of sauce on the T-shirt. I pulled my chair back from the table and breathed out, relaxing – unwisely forgetting about Jem for a second, until I heard a tortured, theatrical groan. 'Helena, whatever you do, don't wave those legs at me. I might just forget I'm a gentleman.'

'I'm not "waving" them at anyone, Jem – they do have to carry my body around. I'm not a doll, you know.'

'Oh, yes, you are, Helena, a living doll. A perfect living doll, china skin and long, long legs.'

A shot of the ventriloquist's dummy and the rag-doll girl clicks into my mind, and a second frame, of Sherry's black and white face, her big eyes wide with fear, follows it involuntarily. Superstitious, I know, but I walk across to the window and stare outside, full of guilt that I had, just for a second, wished the very worst on her earlier. How would I feel if I couldn't have Dominic? But it all looks fine outside – their car is gone, the moon is round and bright, and the night quiet. Peaceful. All safe at home, apart from Jeremy's usual jibes. I turn my face back towards the interior of the room just as Dominic walks through the door. 'I think we'd better go, Jem,' says Jen, lifting her eyebrows almost indulgently at him. But Jem can never resist the opportunity to wind Dominic up.

'And Helena was just warming to me nicely.' He jerks his head towards me and grins. 'You don't want me to go, do you, Helena?'

Jen saves me. 'Of course she does, Jem – you're a complete pain in the neck.' Her smile takes the sting out of her words.

Jeremy sighs. 'I've got a date with the bath tub on legs. At least somebody wants me.'

'Jem, we'll be here forever!' Jen grabs her coat. 'I'll go out and open the car up. I'll see you in a minute.' She reaches up to kiss Dominic gently on the cheek. 'Thanks, Dom. The food was brilliant.' And, turning to me, 'It's been an excellent night, Helena.' She heads for the door just as Jem, grumbling half-heartedly, heads for the stairs.

Dominic binds me in his arms as we hear Jem stumble his way up to our en-suite bathroom. The seventeen or so glasses of wine he's had seem to be impeding his progress slightly. 'You were lovely tonight, Helena.' Dominic's hands move around to the back of me and his palms cup my bum beneath my dress. 'And you look superb in this.'

'Dominic!' We're standing right in front of the window, with the tower-house lit like a lighthouse.

He laughs at me. 'There's nobody there. It's getting on for midnight. There's not a soul around.'

Then Jem comes clattering down the stairs and Dominic crosses over with him to release some of his own Bulgarian red and beer. A slight noise outside in the street makes me turn back to the window, calling, 'Dominic,' as I do so.

'I'm having a piss, Helena.'

I look outside. God, no! A slight man, with his arm in a sling, is bending down towards Jen and, as I watch, pulls her towards him. Shock. His hair is greased back, and he looks different, but I know him from the inside out.

'Dominic, it's him!' I shout up the stairs.

'What?' Dominic calls back.

'Chill out, Helena,' advises a drunken Jeremy.

Jen's scream lets me know that there's no time to talk, know that *I* have to do something, something harder than I've ever done before. Now. I clatter down to the kitchen, grab a greasy knife from the sink – me, gentle Helena – and run outside into the dark, Jeremy stumbling along behind me.

Jen is twenty or thirty metres ahead of me. 'Jen!'

'Helena!' She's trying hard to pull away from him. He turns towards me in a flash, still holding her wrist. We're all three in a horrible, slow dream, his dream, as he unfastens the sling from behind his neck, lets it drop and lifts Jen up into his arms. It looks awful – so wrong – the broken arm and the strength, him and Jen, him and the tower-house.

Stepping out of my shoes, I run faster, glad of my long legs. Jeremy, behind me, is tripping over my shoes and swearing, and God knows where Dominic's gone. The Stone Man is at his car in seconds – a black Volkswagen Beetle. Trying to open the door with a plastered arm and a struggling Jen slows him right down and I take my chance, remembering Dominic's one possibility with the brick last time.

'Leave her alone.' I jab at his side, ineptly, with the knife. Action. Trying to frighten him but not hurt him. Useless. Then nightmare. A moment of utter dread – the car has no passenger seat in it. What on God's earth is he planning to do to Jen? I jab again, almost shutting my eyes, as the knife hits his jacketed shoulder.

In a second, Jen is on the ground and his hand is on my wrist, twisting it violently. He stinks of whisky. The knife drops just as Dominic and Jem run in behind me. The Stone Man picks up the weapon and stares over my shoulder for seconds. I can hear Jen crying, breathing hard and swallowing. The point of the knife comes over towards my breast and he twists it, as his eyes twist into a sort of smile. His first words: 'Any time I want, Helena.' I hold my breath. Then the knife moves and he looks past me towards Dominic again.

Dominic speaks quietly. 'Not like this.'

The plastered hand moves towards the handle of the door, and the blade flashes in front of me. 'Don't risk your life, Helena,' he says. His eyes are completely sincere and very cold now. He opens the car door, steps over the empty seat and into the driver's side. The car starts first time and he's gone.

'Again.' Dominic kicks the wall. 'Not a-fucking-gain! I got his number, though,' he says, searching through his pocket for a pen. He writes the number on the back of his hand. Then, 'Shit, Jen. Are you all right?'

'What was he going to do?' She's still crying. 'Did you see inside the car? What was he going to do with me, Dominic?'

He puts his arm around her. 'I know. I know, Jen.'

'That's when I really fought. You know Ted Bundy – the American serial killer? The one who defended himself in court?' She just stares ahead for a second. 'That's exactly what he had – a Beetle with the front seat removed.'

'Christ,' says Dominic.

'Jen.' I rub her arm. No one speaks for a minute.

'Dominic.' Jen sways suddenly, looking deathly. 'I don't feel well.'

'All right, Jen. Just sit down for a minute, lean against the wall.' He leads her over to the stone wall and kneels down beside her, his arm around her shoulders. 'Just breathe properly and relax. He's gone; he can't hurt you. He's gone.' Jen turns away and vomits once, violently but almost neatly. Poor Dominic, I think, always cleaning up sick. Then, poor Jen. 'Jeremy, get a cloth or something from the house, will you?' says Dominic. He turns back to Jen. 'Just stay there until you're feeling better. You're safe, that's all that matters.' She shudders and rests the side of her face against him for a minute as his words sink in, her cheek on his T-shirt and her eyes shut. Dominic lifts his head and looks into my eyes with anger and pain in his. I know that he's thinking. Not another fucking rag-doll. A downcast Jeremy hands Jen a cloth and she wipes her mouth.

'I feel a bit better.' Then she remembers something. 'He said his name was Jason Oliver. Weird. That's what made me suspicious from the start. That and the smell of whisky.' Dominic and I exchange stares.

'Can you walk?' Jeremy is exceptionally subdued. Not Jeremy.

'Yes, I'm sure I can walk,' Jen replies. Almost Jen.

Jem holds a hand out to her, pulling her up, and we all begin to step back towards the house. 'Jen – did he touch you?' Jem asks. Maybe he takes lessons from Sam.

'Of course he touched me, Jem. You saw him, didn't you? I thought he was going to kill me.'

'But did he . . . ?'

'Shut up, Jem,' says Dominic.

'Rape me, do you mean, Jem? While you were on the toilet? No, no. He just dragged me along and picked me up, like some stupid toy.'

I wonder if Jem is blushing in the dark. He puts his arm around Jen, brother rather than lecher for once, and then his jacket.

Dominic squeezes my arm. 'Helena, I would never have dreamt that you could do that,' he says. 'Are you okay?'

'I lost my shoes.' I laugh, oddly. 'And the knife. Stupid.' We let Jeremy and Jen walk on a little and then Dominic turns me towards him, rubbing my shoulders. 'I'm really proud of you.'

'My shoes,' I say again. Now I'm being a rag-doll. Stupid. I straighten my back, and point into the road at them.

'I'll get them for you.' Dominic lopes into the road and picks them up. 'Here.' I'm not crying, don't even feel like it, which is strange, but I know I'm looking a bit Catherine Earnshaw (*after* her death).

'He got the knife.' I'm so angry with myself.

'*After* you got him off Jen,' says Dominic. 'God knows what would have happened otherwise. And you went for him, Helena – I mean, you're normally so . . .' he looks for the right word '. . . sensitive. You must have been terrified.'

'No, I wasn't actually. That was the thing. I just thought about Jen, but,' and this is important, 'I have to get even stronger. I have to fight him, face him, for me. Myself.'

'*I* wanted to fight him for you. I can't believe he got away again.' Dominic spins around, full of redundant adrenaline.

'With a knife. What could you have done? And you got him to leave, got through to him.' I think back. '"Not like this." What did you mean?'

Dominic sits down on the kerb suddenly, holding up his arm to pull me down beside him on the hard pavement. 'I don't know, really.' He looks into my face and strokes my hair down with his hand. 'Christ, you look terrible now.' He looks down and rubs my hands, warms them. 'I just know he didn't want to attack you like that – like a cornered animal. I think he's felt cornered for half of his life. He needs his dignity.'

'His control!' I say, remembering. 'So that's why he took away yours – and Jen's, tonight.'

'I know. He likes to plan. To attack.'

'To rape?'

He holds my glance steadily. 'Definitely. I should have warned you about that.'

My expression is fixed. 'I knew really, Dominic.' I curl into his arms and hug him. 'And he's connected to both of us, somehow.'

'Why did he use my surname?' Dominic looks puzzled.

'Thank God he's gone.'

'At least for now.' He looks grim. 'Let's see how Jen is.'

Jen is nestled into a chair, pale, but sipping hot chocolate, and Diana and Matthew are on the scene when we get back to the tower-house. Jem is about to phone the police. 'At least we can give them the number of the car,' he says, 'and a better description. Was it definitely the same bloke?'

'Definitely,' says Dominic.

'Right. I'll give them a ring, then,' Jeremy says.

It seems like hours before the police come, the police question, the police go. They listen to the description of the car, and him, say that they'll check out the registration number and get some photographs together for us the next day. When they give me the third degree about the knife, Dominic is so infuriated that *he* almost gets arrested. Then the police are gone, and Jen and Jem follow them and Diana and Matthew disappear upstairs.

At last Dominic and I are alone. We make sure that the door is locked before we go to bed. Dominic helps me to undress and then he goes into the bathroom. As he is undressing himself, I see his eyes fix on a sicky bit on the front of his shoulder, right where Jen had leant against him. He doesn't comment though or even (as I would have done) wrinkle his nose up or wince; he just pulls the T-shirt off and flings it into the wash basket, then goes into the en-suite and wipes his shoulder clean. I just love it that he is *so* unsqueamish, so accepting, of physical things, human things. And mental things too, I hope.

We lie in bed together, Siamese twins of need, and I whisper to him in the dark before we fall asleep, 'Tomorrow. I've got things I need to tell you. Tomorrow.' New mess and old dirt, all stirring up together. Making a new dream from my oldest nightmare at last. Tomorrow.

Driving into my dreams.

Driving back, I think, That was it then. We're even now, the big bastard and me. A tooth for a tooth so to speak (and he seems to have kept all of his). Next time it'll be different.

The worst blow of all was the car: it was the best thing I'd ever owned, like, the thing I loved more than anything. Mine. And I'd have to get rid of it. Now. Because they'd know it, definitely. The numberplate was neither here nor there, because that belonged to a long-'lost' TWOC model of my mate, who'd sent it deep into the sea somewhere near the Mull of Galloway. The car that is. The numberplate he'd given to me, to use on top of mine, as and when it was necessary.

I knew straightaway that mushroom face was out – she was the first to leave and she was very firmly embedded in a foursome, shall we say. I never fancied her anyway. My standards are high. Then old matchstick head left, looking as pissed and as rancid as a fart (and just about as fanciable).

I stayed in the car, washed my mouth out with whisky, and felt the spirit of my father seeping right inside me. And I waited.

Ten minutes later and she's there, on her own, little and blonde, a bit shy-looking even. A bit like Vikki. Little tits, rounder face. Not as classy as Helena, you understand, but still perfectly acceptable. Maybe I could be a bit gentler with her, a bit more artistic, like.

The first part of the routine goes fine.

'I'm very sorry about this,' my borrowed smile, 'I'm Jason Oliver. I live in one of the houses opposite and I need to get something out of the glove compartment of my car. A bit difficult with this thing on.' Waving my stump, so to speak. 'Could you help at all?' She listens to it all but the little bitch has no trust, right from the start, like.

'Could you just wait a minute? My friend'll be out any time. I'm sure we'll be able to help you then.'

Oh, yes, I'm sure. A quick glance towards the house shows no sign of him, or her, and the door is closed. No friend. I've got a minute, then – and a surge of energy, of pure adrenaline, washes right over me. I take her arm – army hard. 'You'll be finished by the time your friend gets here.' I practise my warm smile – try charm. 'Do your Good Samaritan bit, er . . .'

'Jen.' She smiles, relaxes a bit. 'It's Jen.'

'Come on then, Jen.' I tilt my head towards the car and look into her eyes. Tighten my grip, a mistake.

'No, I don't think so.' She turns back towards the house, tries to pull away. 'I'll wait.'

No time to wait. I pull harder, really hard. I know I have to get her into the car, pronto. I've got it all ready. I drag her and she makes a high scream, really girly, like. Gives me a hard on straightaway. Then a real yell. I move her a few feet and then I hear the click of heels coming from the house. Helena! Is she the friend who'll help? Two birds in one, two for joy. The little one is bait now, a worm to fetch Helena. Mouth man. Meat sandwich. Maybe I can get them both in the car? The chain's long enough. I'm definitely not going home empty-handed. I pull my sling off and lift the little one up (heroic and easy, my favourite combination) and run with her to the car. Can't get the fucking door open, with my arm in plaster and everything. Bastard. The blonde is only little, but she's struggling like fuck to get away.

Then Helena is there, right there, with a knife. Girls and knives – only fucking hurt themselves. Two girly jabs and a 'Leave her alone!' Just like being at home. But it hurts me that Helena would try to touch me like that. The knife is mine in a twist of the wrist. I actually touch her on the breast with it – very artistic. Threaten her. 'Any time I want.' Sincere. An improvement on the script.

The men arrive – Dominic, and some toxic waster with a nose stone. Me and Dominic, gladiators, face to face, eye to eye, skin to skin. But I'm unfairly outnumbered again. And he catches my eye – makes me think I owe him from last time, with the brick and everything. Still, I might have had a go at him anyway but he clinches it. 'Not like this.' He knows, knows that this is my work, my art, and my world. I want to do it in my own style. Total control, that's the deal. I've had enough of being boxed in, limited.

I can always move, that's the point. So I'm off inside the Bundymobile for a dramatic exit, a hero's exit. 'Don't risk your life, Helena!' Saved her.

Then I'm gone, driving into the night.

'Cancer never feels really secure'
– Linda Goodman's Sun Signs

Dominic was up early the next day, ringing around security firms, and by that afternoon a very sensitive security system was installed.

Meanwhile, a visit to the police station in Selkirk had made *me* feel very sensitive – and very insecure. There was no one like the Stone Man in any of the photographs they showed us; possibly he didn't have a record. The car with the registration number that Dominic had noted down had been reported missing almost a year before. They didn't seem to be able to help us at all. But I was advised against 'brandishing' kitchen knives, as I had been 'extremely easy to disarm'. That sounded about right. Still I was glad I'd faced him at least; the 'ineffectual' jabs had had an effect on me if nothing else.

Fencing lessons, scythes, guns, boiling oil and atomic bombs were Dominic's chosen weapons: the security system was definitely a poor relation. His enlightened and perceptive feelings of the night before had turned into something altogether messier and less pleasant. He insisted on instructing the security firms about equipment, the police about descriptions, and me (in great, listed detail) about tea. By the time we began to think about preparing the food, my confessional needs had all but evaporated.

The oil finally boiled that evening. Diana was out for the evening with Matthew, and Dominic was cooking a ham (off the bone), mushroom (cep), herb (coriander and parsley), cream (*fraîche*) and garlic sauce to go with some pasta (*tagliatelle verde*, fresh). Naturally I was at his side, preparing a side salad, which I had been allowed to organise myself: lettuce, cress, tomato, vinaigrette and one crowning mushroom.

I didn't really want to go near any of that steam in his corner, so I'd placed myself at the square kitchen table, away from the stove, while I very happily, and quite slowly, worked my artist's palette of ingredients into a petalled picture of a salad. I love knives, and clean slices of food, so I'd chosen one of those marvellous silver half-moon things, with a big, black handle on each side, to swish silently through the lettuce with. Dominic had his back to me and was simmering or stirring or something, I'm not sure which. My head was full of William Morris prints and the patterns I was forming with my fingers, when suddenly Dominic was in front of me.

'Helena, for God's sake, get that thing out of your hands. It's like giving a baby a razor blade to teethe on. Put it down.'

'What do you mean? You've nearly turned the house into *The Towering Inferno* more than once, but I haven't tried to belittle you.' I punctuated my points with swinging swoops of the knife. (Dramatic but safe, as Dominic was keeping his, equally dramatic but safe, distance.) God was watching: a wet dollop of sauce hit the hob, hissing, as I spoke. 'I'm perfectly okay.'

Dominic lifted his eyes to the ceiling suddenly, and then he lowered his head deliberately. He scraped a chair out and sat on it. 'What the fuck are we doing? We're arguing about a pasta sauce and some salad.'

I dropped the knife. 'No, we're not. We're arguing about that.' The silver half moon blade caught the light. 'And last night. And him.'

'Look,' Dominic said, 'you got him off Jen, I got him to go and I got his number – even if it was useless. And we saw him properly. And he didn't really hurt anybody. All of that's a lot better than it was last time. We did what we could. But we've got to get cleverer again, and faster, and stronger. Much stronger . . . Shit! The sauce.' He jumped up and lifted it, bubbling and spitting Sherry-like from the heat.

'I could go to self-defence classes. I bet Sam and Jen would go with me. Maybe Diana too.'

'And I've always fancied kick-boxing,' said Dominic. 'I could drag Dixie along with me. Or Jem. I don't expect he's feeling that great today.

'And we've both got to get smarter. Knives are his sort of weapons. We've got to suss him out, not let him manipulate us. Suspect *everything*.'

'Except each other,' I said.

'Except each other.' Dominic took my hand. 'Except each other.' Bending down, he kissed my hair. 'Now, should we eat in here or in the dining room?'

'Here!' I wanted a different atmosphere from that of the night before. 'I'll get the cutlery out.'

Put the sharp knives away.

20

'The fish is mutable always'
– Linda Goodman's Sun Signs

'Things you need to tell me?'

We were halfway through our meal when he lowered his head and focussed his eyes on mine. 'Last night. Before you fell asleep?'

Finally.

I knew I trusted Dominic, at last. But this was something else altogether. *Complete* trust. I took a huge swallow of wine, followed by a huge cough. Spanish plonk. Dominic smiled and dragged his chair around to my side of the table, rubbing my back and my shoulder with one lovely, big hand and circling my arm with the other. 'All right. It's all right, Helena. Just take your time.'

'Eleven years.' A lot of time.

He nodded, still rubbing, but more slowly now. 'I know. Take it easy.'

Not easy at all. Almost impossible, like crying sand. I took a smoother, smaller swallow, and then Dominic took the wineglass out of my fingers and put it on the table. What I had to say was so big that however I chose to express it would minimalise it somehow.

'The words won't be enough.' Even that sounded ridiculous.

'Don't worry. I'll hear it – it doesn't matter about the words you use. I already half know somehow,' said Dominic, his heavy head nodding and his eyes on mine.

I had to start.

'I don't remember much about my mother from when I was little. I was just young when she died – about four. What I do remember is just pieces: a birthday party with a three-shaped cake; rocking on a duck toy in front of her; falling off a bike, and having my knee plastered up. Little stupid things. Just bits.' He nodded. It got a bit harder. 'When she was pregnant with me, she found out that she had cancer – breast cancer.'

'Right.' He looked sad but I carried on mechanically.

'Somebody told me later – they didn't know what had happened to her – that if you get cancer when you're pregnant, your cells are reproducing so quickly because of the pregnancy that the cancer spreads much faster than it would otherwise. Is that true?'

'I don't know, Helena.'

'Anyway, by the time I was born, she was riddled with cancer – consumed, Uncle Mark used to say. She should have been making milk, and blood, and new life, and she was making tumours.' I thought of the candles of the night before. 'She refused to have a mastectomy because she was worried about how it, or the anaesthetic, might affect me. So I grew, fed from her, inside of her,' (like another lump, I thought, but some things were still too ugly to say) 'while she shrank. She hardly put any weight on during the pregnancy at all. But I was seven and a half pounds when I was born, and she had two tumours then, not one.'

There. I had told him. Told him what I had never told anyone else before. I didn't look at him but took my biggest sip of wine so far, not flinching this time.

Dominic didn't speak for at least a minute. Then he looked at me. 'It was what she wanted, Helena. She wanted you. And none of it was your fault.'

I ignored him. 'After I was born, she was just over seven and a half stones. She had the diseased breast cut off. She's not ill – in any of my bits of memories, she's not ill. She's not ill at all. I wasn't aware of it. I must have just fed. Grown.'

He pushed his chair away and knelt by my side, so that his eyes were close to mine, forcing me to look into his face. 'No, I'm not having that, Helena, I'm not. All babies feed. All children. It's

natural. She would have liked it, loved it, to see you all healthy.'
I looked hard at him, just as he looked right inside of me, his
greenish eyes full of feeling.

'It's disgusting.' I'm disgusting. I am disgusting.

'It's natural,' he repeated. 'It's survival. I'm glad that you
survived it. You have to be glad – it's what she wanted, what
you have to want. You have to celebrate your survival, your life
– otherwise, what was the point of what she did, the point of
delaying the operation?'

'Apparently she had one operation after another after that.
Secondaries, Uncle Mark said. If you don't get rid of cancer with
the first lump, then it's difficult to get rid of it later. She had
radiotherapy. Eventually it spread up into her spine.' Another
kind of rag-doll. 'She had chemotherapy then. It still spread.'
I stopped for a few seconds. 'It was everywhere, really. It was
amazing that she lived as long as she did, Uncle Mark said.'

Dominic nodded. 'I understand. I understand loads of things
better. The trouble you have with separations. The way you are
with food.' I'd never thought of that. It was like when we first
sort-of had sex – the funny feeling that he understood me better
than I understood myself. 'The way you are with yourself,' he
carried on. 'You have to forgive yourself, heal yourself. You
have to.'

'I do remember my first day at school. And I remember she
cried. It was the only time I ever saw her cry. I cried as well,
but only because I didn't want to go to school.' My voice was
uneven, fourteen years later. 'I never saw her again. When I
got back from school, my father answered the door, which was
unusual. He said, "I want you to be a brave girl, a very brave
girl." And then he told me that she'd gone. She was in hospital.
I never saw her again.'

'Oh, Helena.'

I hardly heard him. 'She waited until I was old enough to go
to school, until I was old enough to manage. She sort of gave
me her strength, her life – herself.' And the worst bit. 'I hated
her for leaving me. And him. I still do sometimes. How selfish
is that?' I turned away from him and tried hard not to cry, my
face twisted away, my awful, ugly greediness. Always hungry.
And then always alone.

'Helena, no, no. Come on, now. No.'

'You wanted to know; I didn't want to tell anyone. It was you – you wanted to know.'

'I know, I know, sweetheart.' He was trying to cuddle me but I couldn't let him. And I had to cry, with hard spasms of my body and a hurting throat. 'Helena, don't.' He stood up, twisted around, and then came back to me. 'Don't. This is my fault; I shouldn't have pushed you all of this time to tell me.'

I managed to get out the words I knew, through my twisted mouth. The real words. Ugly. 'I'm disgusting. I disgust myself.' Unloveable.

'Jesus. I never dreamt it was as bad as this.' Dominic didn't know what to do. And then he did. He bent down to me, picked me up out of my chair and carried me right through the kitchen and into the living room. When he laid me down on the settee, he lay right down beside me himself, exactly like that first night at Cromwell Street. He tried to smooth the sharp angles of my body, the hard edges of my distress, whispering, 'Shhh, I love you. I love you. I can heal you. You can heal yourself; you can start again – you already have.' I cried still. 'It's not good to cry like this,' he said. 'You'll make yourself sick. It's my fault – all the shock of last night and now this.' Standing up, he lifted my curled, hard body up from the settee. 'I'll take you up to the bedroom.' I didn't care where I was but I clung to his neck, loving the feeling of him lifting me, taking away the responsibility of my stupid crying, my stupid self-hatred, my stupid self. Taking it all away from me.

Upstairs, Dominic laid me on the new day bed, took my things off and wrapped me in his big towelling dressing gown. He wiped my face one last time, trying to restore me, to piece back together his Tiffany vase. Could I ever be beautiful to him again, now that he knew the truth? But he was looking out over the loch – St Mary's Loch. 'Remember when you bought this house? How you felt?' He did look at me then. 'If I had a child and it was a choice between suffering cancer myself, and the child suffering cancer, I would rather suffer the cancer myself.' Dominic turned his face back to mine. 'Your mother preferred to lose her own life to the cancer, the disease, rather than lose her baby's. *You* are what she wanted. That's the truth, the centre of you, if you like:

you're never on your own. You and she are connected. Always connected.'

Through the window the moon showed the hills reflected in the depths of the lake. Two of everything. Not alone now.

'Separate but the same?' I said to Dominic.

'Separate but the same,' he repeated, and lifted his palm up to mine, palm against palm. 'Mothers who love daughters, men who love women. Separate but the same. The loch and the stars. The moon and the seas. It's all essentially the same.'

'Me and the loch?' I felt tired and tiny.

'Especially you and the loch. You and your mother. You and me. Everything.'

I felt calmer, emptied, foetal, and curled myself into the day bed, looking down at the moony beauty of the loch. Then I felt the hairbrush on my head. 'You stole it from Cromwell Street!' I turned around to him.

Dominic laughed, with a tiny tilt of the head. 'I don't think anybody missed it very much. Do you want me to clean your face?' I nodded, and he went to the bathroom, and then patiently rubbed the cream into my face, cleansed and wiped. This time, I felt cleansed inside as well, felt that I'd lost a black and messy part of myself, felt white, inside and out. Reformed.

'Come to bed now, Helena.' His voice was so gentle.

'No. The last part – I have to tell you it all now.'

'No, you've had enough already.' He shook his head.

'It's easier to say it all in one go – now that I've started.'

'You're sure?'

'Sure.'

He tucked the big, white (off-white, being Dominic's) dressing gown around me and, stroking my hair with his fingers, said, 'Go on then.'

'My father had a heart condition – his father had had it before him. My father had two by-pass operations when I was really tiny, and he knew after that that his situation was dangerous.

'He looked after me when my mother died. He was still acting.' Bakers and biscuits, I thought, and smiled at Dominic, who was still stroking my hair. 'That's when Marie lived with us. She used to brush my hair for me, like you do sometimes.' I stopped. 'There's not much to say really.' There was one nice thing. 'I remember waking up once in the middle of the night, and I couldn't see, my eyes were all glued together somehow.'

'Conjunctivitis, probably,' Dominic explained. 'Kids get it.' Doctor Dom.

'I shouted for my father. He came into my room. He wiped my eyes with cotton wool and said, "There, you can see. You could always see." And I could.' I smiled. 'I felt like he could do anything.'

The last bit. I looked over the loch again for a second before I finished my story. Circling stains. 'Uncle Mark can't have known, obviously. He was good friends with my dad. I'd seen him at the house often enough before.

'And then, one day, when I got back from school, there was no Marie. Uncle Mark opened the door instead. He took off my coat – he was smiling, uncomfortable. And he said almost exactly the same thing as my dad had. He couldn't have known, could he? He said, "Now Helena, I want you to be a brave girl."'

Dominic's hands stilled in my hair but the warmth of his palms on my scalp made it possible for me to carry on, automatically almost. 'And that was about it – until the letters. The rest you know.' Leeched Dry.

'There.' Dominic exhaled. He touched the thin skin around my eyes with his long fingers. 'This has been eating away at you.'

But there was one last point. 'That's how I feel, I know, that I can face him. Because I've faced that – twice. He's my third wall, the Stone Man. My third trial.' A trial I could face?

'No trials now. No walls. You need to rest. I'm going to get up in the morning and ring the art gallery: I'll tell them you're not well enough to go in. There's no need for you to face people or anything else, just now.' Lifting me, lifting me away from the responsibility of myself. 'I'll go and make you a hot drink then you can sleep.'

I lay back and heard him go downstairs. I loved lying on the day bed when I could hear him moving about below me. The loch was glittering slightly in the moonlight. Separate but the same, separate but the same. It spoke to me in its way – it had always spoken to me in its own way. Separate but the same. I was almost asleep.

*   *   *

When I came back with her drink Helena was fast asleep on the day bed, just as I'd left her, but the eyes that had been fixed on the loch were closed. It seemed as if she'd used up every ounce of herself that was available, and then a few more. I put the cup down silently, curled my arms underneath her legs, her arms and lifted up her slender body, holding her soft heaviness to my chest, carrying her towards the bed. I'd always loved lifting her, holding her, and I'd always known how much she needed that.

Now I knew exactly why.

She woke up as I walked across the floor to the enormous bed, but she just put her arms around my neck and burrowed into me like a baby. She needed to be a baby until she was back to herself, until she'd come back from reliving everything she'd just told me. But when she did come back to me, she'd be healthier, more whole. I hoped. That was why I'd pushed her into talking about it.

Helena's eyes opened again when I laid her on the bed. She had beautiful eyes, very wide and alive – dark blue. Amazing. She was all eyes, really. She'd been somewhere really dark, and she'd brought some of it back in her eyes. I understood the pictures in her eyes so much better now. I took the drink across to her and she sat up.

She drank six or seven sips as I held the cup to her mouth, then she lay down as if she were drugged and fell deep into a healing sleep.

I swam down into my dreams that night and they were fresh but turbulent waters to me. I swept through the stirring, salty water, through the churning depths of the sea, and right down to the seabed. I thought it would be Dominic I was in search of, Dominic, Dominic, Dominic Oliver.

But no. The faces that I found there, the strange and swimming faces, didn't belong to Dominic. The distorted, watery shapes beneath the sea were dark and foreign, coming and going with the dipping waves. Strange and shadowy. Only one face emerged as slightly familiar, encircled as it was by the silky, floating Chinese hair around it. Will Jackson. Even the water seemed charged and warm. But I enjoyed the beautiful, liquid surge of the waves and the feeling that came from his eyes as I stared right through the blue. The warmth built more as I turned and turned in the sea in front of him. Right in front of him.

A sound in my ear. 'Helena . . . Helena.' The bed was hot, and the sheets were twisted. 'Helena!'

'Dominic.' I was uncomfortable in the spiralling sheets. It was pitch black and very late. And the heat between my legs was teaching me, teaching me to drink life in through my body, a feeling I had never felt so intensely before. In the shadow, everything was clear. I needed to push myself into life, like a baby pushes itself into its own fresh air from the warm encircling fluid of its mother's sac.

'Helena, you were dreaming.' Dominic's fingers touch the dampness of my brow. I need him inside me so that I can move right outside myself.

'Dominic.' I grip his shoulders and he wraps his arms tight around me, burying me inside his limbs. I feel him harden and grow dramatically, as I soften and melt against his skin. Pushing. For once, there's little foreplay. He slips one arm around my waist beneath the dressing gown and strokes me between the legs with the other hand, as I press myself against his chest, soft breasts to broad breast. Heat, life and sensation connect us. Humanity. My fingers press to the rooted base of his cock. 'I need you to be strong.' Strong enough to partner me. He grows even bigger, groaning and throwing his head back, as his body pushes more firmly against me. He slips a condom on and his rigid cock pushes into the soft skin around my sex.

'Helena.' I guide him into me, there and then, and he pushes up, saying only, 'Helena, Helena,' again. My hands are tangled in his hair, and I move my hips hard and hold him inside me, our muscles straining as the tension builds. Mine. I love him inside me. My legs ache as the spasms come. Mine, mine, mine. Oval purple marks remind me of birth, and rebirth. And death.

When Dominic comes, seconds later, he's working against himself somehow; he makes a noise that sounds like pain. 'Dominic?' He holds my head to his chest, breathing hard. 'Dominic?' Silence still. It's ages before he speaks.

'Don't leave me, Helena. Whatever else you do, just don't ever leave me. Not after this.'

I never thought I would.

All night long, he's murmuring, murmuring to me in the dark, like a spell. 'We're stronger than he is, much stronger. Stronger together than apart. Because I'll never let anyone hurt you. I'm ready now. He's got his rage, his rage and his loneliness. His emptiness. But how can emptiness compare to what we've got?

'We're connected now – connected to each other, and connected to everything else. Mine now. You're mine, and I'm yours.'

Angels.

And I've never felt so alive

The nights had always been hard, and they were getting harder. During the days, I got more and more strong, fine tuning my body and mind, as I worked towards *Six*, my plans heightened and intense, more so because *Six* was devoted to Helena and Dominic again, and to my sort-of-love for them. And the heroes helped. I was reading a lot of Joseph Kallinger. The Poet, I called him. There was a family man for you, a man after my dad's heart.

But the nights would have finished a weaker man – the thought of him with Helena, them together, and me outside; it fixed my intent. It was the way they'd left me. It was the way they'd taken my car away from me, taken themselves away. And the way that they had everything: their middle-class friends, their fucking tower-house. Each other. The way they didn't trust me. I'd mastered them but they still didn't respect me, the way my dad could master me but not deserve an ounce of my respect.

Surely they know how strong a man is when he's got nothing to lose? A man like me. And getting stronger all the time – apart from the ache in my balls. But maybe that's what drives me on the most. It joins with all the other hates and all the other aches from the times before.

Aching hatred. Aching, aching hatred. Aching hatred.

And love.

Summer had cooled into autumn and I was working towards two things: the next time with the Stone Man (and I knew there would be a next time) and the third letter – the third letter in my father's room.

Uncle Mark had his own key to the tower-house. He and Lisa had helped me to furnish it and had arranged all of the structural work, and we were just finishing the decorating. And I knew that, bit by bit, he must be getting the seventh room ready for whatever my father had planned for me. Then, after that third letter, my third meeting with him, I would never have any communication with my father again – he'd made that quite clear. Three letters. How would that feel – parting with him for the very final time? Leaving him, or being left. Forever. I hoped I'd be strong enough to face whatever had to be faced before I turned to that last letter, and strong enough to face life alone again afterwards.

It was strange but as I waited it was almost quiet, uneventful, Mariana and the moat all over again. Do you ever leave anything completely? I hope so and I hope not. I worked on my house, worked at the art gallery, worked on my body.

In the end, Sam, Diana, Jen and I all went to the self-defence classes. Sam wore her purple and yellow leggings with great pride, and Diana wore her chest. Sam was hopeless. At first, she was always being picked out by the instructor to demonstrate how a woman of just 5′ 2″ could throw a 6′ man over her shoulder every time, using the right techniques, of course. Only she couldn't – couldn't throw anyone over her shoulder at all. There would be a protest, another protest, and then an attempt – using exactly the wrong techniques. And the instructor, or partner, always remained firmly on his feet. Sam would give up, with a red face and a grunt while the instructor remained serious and humourless. Sam was a bit of a challenge, a real challenge, and finally an embarrassment. And she threw no one around, unless she was paired with Jen or me: we'd fling ourselves to the floor like judo victims, to try and build her confidence up, but that didn't help much either.

We always went for a drink afterwards, 'Just to top the calorie levels up,' as Sam put it, then Dominic or Doug would collect us and make sure that we got home absolutely safely. Despite Diana's increasingly dramatic displays of strength, we were more careful than ever about our safety in general. And however hopeless we were, we went to those classes every week. We never said it out loud, but it was a symbol of the fact that we had a fight to face – and that we might be facing it together.

Dominic was working hard on his course and becoming increasingly reluctant to leave the tower-house for the glories of Cromwell Street. He wanted to be with me. Despite the fact that we were building other, more suitable, defences, he was haunted by the memory of me walking out into the street alone (save Jeremy-the-Neverready) with a knife in my hand. I knew that what really frightened him was the thought that I might be alone when the next attack came out of the dark. So he watched me carefully, and kick-boxed vigorously, with Dixie and sometimes Jem as well.

I loved my work at the art gallery at that time – it was just exactly as I'd imagined it would be. And twice, now, I'd spoken to Will Jackson.

It was a quiet day in the art gallery shop and I was reading a two-day-old Sunday supplement featuring the Pre-Raphaelites. (My manageress encouraged me to follow media coverage of the arts, to help me 'to understand and anticipate fluctuations in book sales'.) I was so absorbed that I actually jumped when he spoke. 'You look calmer today!' Black hair and very white teeth. Instant recognition.

'Yes. Sorry about that. I was in a bit of a rush.'

'And a bit of a state as well.' He looked down at what I was reading. 'And you've lost part of your Lizzie Siddal look.' How could he possibly know about my favourite, old Ophelia pose? I stared at him. 'The hair.' He laughed, and touched it in explanation. 'You've lost a few inches of your Pre-Raphaelite womanhood.' Yes, I tried to look glossy rather than girly in the gallery, and I was wearing a plain, green shift dress and a smooth hairstyle.

'Oh, I finally outgrew my Rapunzel waves, or some of them.'

'And you're working here.'

'Yes.' I indicated the area of floor space allocated to me. 'This section is mine, from Impressionism to Realism. What are you doing here?'

'Today I'm just having a look around. I've had a couple of exhibitions here in the past.'

'Boxes within boxes. I know.' I smiled. Secret roses. 'You're on my bedroom table, holding my earrings for me.' I didn't mention the condoms.

Just as Will grinned suggestively (as if I *had* mentioned the condoms), I was called away by my manageress, with an, 'Over here, Helena!' When I looked around for him a couple of minutes later, he'd completely disappeared.

The afternoon was dragging a bit a week or so later; the mists were down and I was feeling less than lustrous. I was restocking the cards when I became aware of a presence behind my shoulder. A customer, I thought, and I spun around with a, 'Can I . . . ?' on my lips.

Will. Will Jackson.

'Can you?'

I laughed. 'I thought you were a customer.'

'I am, Helena, I am.' It felt really strange, hearing him say my name in his deep, dark voice. He seemed much older than me. 'I need a card for a friend, a woman friend, and I can't decide which one to choose.' He thought for a second. 'Impressionism to Realism. Which of these Impressionist ones do you like best?'

'Well, the colours of the Monets are gorgeous, of course.' Long purples again. 'And I've always loved this.' I gestured towards a card featuring a print of a girl working in a café, her face the soul of listlessness and longing.

'I was thinking of something more personal.' He had a girl-friend, then. He fingered a nude, dipping Degas figure. 'Something that celebrates the female form.' I smiled, continuing with my work, as he plucked out the card and walked towards the till with it.

The card arrived at the art gallery two days later, with: *'To Helena, in celebration of the female form, Will Jackson'*, written inside it. Corny, but I kept it (equally corny). And I certainly didn't mention it to Dominic.

Just as Dominic worried about slice two of the knife, so I worried about a repeat performance of the alleyway incident, especially as the nights darkened. He spent an awful lot of time at the tower-house with me anyway, and I began to think about asking him to stay there with me all of the time, to live there with me – me and Diana (and Matthew quite often), that is. A big step, or was it?

I rang Uncle Mark to ask him what he thought. 'Well, Helena, I've been expecting this conversation actually, anticipating it.' Desperate – he had a speechette especially prepared. 'These are the problems as I see them: one, you are giving young Oliver access to your property. You need to be very careful about which bills he pays, etcetera. We don't want him believing he enjoys any rights over the property.' That was no problem: Dominic was far too Lion King to try to sneak anything away from me like that. Uncle Mark was moving down his list. 'Two, you need to think of your reputation. Living over the brush may be more acceptable than it was, but it is still not acceptable in all sectors of society, particularly the upper echelons.' Ridiculous. Lisa was at least halfway over the brush at Leeched Dry; I could hear her hoovering in the background as we spoke. And none of the 'upper echelons' I'd ever met at Leeched would have lost any sleep over brushes.

'And thirdly,' Uncle Mark continued, 'what if the relationship doesn't work out? It could be very messy, Helena, very messy indeed.' Yes, that was the one that was genuinely bothering me. But what had Dominic said that day, the day of the bloodstain? 'We're big, we're complicated, we're messy.' Part of being a human being. And what had my father said? *Work out your three wishes*. My biggest wish had always been Dominic. Once again, Uncle Mark had clarified things beautifully for me.

I rang Dominic and gave him the good news.

21

'Cancer man

> 'First you shiver under his freezing glances, then you get smothered
> with devotion'
>
> – Linda Goodman's Sun Signs

The view from the dining-room window that Saturday was the best ever: Dominic, bounding up the path, with a box in his arms and a huge bouquet of roses balanced shakily on top of it. I rushed to open the door and he dropped the lot, to give me a very dramatic, bent over backwards, kiss. Utterly Rhett and Scarlett. 'How have you resisted me for so long, Helena?' His heavy head was thrown back, half-Lion King, half-Victorian villain. He almost dropped me, then pulled me up and picked up the roses, pressing the enormous bouquet of dark red, velvety heads into my arms. 'Colombian.' He lifted the bouquet slightly, so that the blood red petals (and some of the prickly green foliage) touched my cheek. 'Perfection.' This from the man who had seen me at my thorniest, my muddiest: exactly why I loved him.

'Ridiculous!' I said. He gave me another Rhett and Scarlett snog, then he was off outside, unburdening the Allegro of his belongings.

Soon, Dominic's accumulated cache of Cromwell Street belongings was nestling up to my natty tower-house treasures: his chipped cafetière nuzzling my new espresso maker; his sticky non-stick pans rubbing alongside my cast-iron creations, and his entire selection of well-worn T-shirts hanging loose amongst my elegant (I hoped) art gallery attire. It didn't take long. 'I've left my computer and a few basics at Cromwell Street – I'll move the rest at the end of the month or before,' he said. 'Sam's got another friend moving in then. The Allegro can only take so much.'

'Fine.' We were just finishing off in the bedroom. I fingered one of the threadbare T-shirts on its hanger, a jade green horror that had probably been bottle green years ago. 'Maybe you need some new clothes.'

'Maybe I always need new law books.' Dominic pushed me backwards towards the bed. 'Don't try to change the strange and unique combination of factors that make me into the masculine creature you adore, Helena. Imagine if I lost my essence – my pure, animal magnetism. How would you survive?' he roared, and shoved me on to the bed.

'You sound like Doug – "pure, animal magnetism"!'

'Would Doug wear that T-shirt?' Doug was immensely proud of his stylish, smooth dress sense. I thought of his expensively and extensively perfumed chest, pressing against the faded cotton of Dominic's prehistoric T-shirt.

'Definitely not!' I decided.

Dominic started to pull my clothes off, flamboyantly, and then his own. 'Exactly! Just thank God you're the lucky girl who's in bed with me today,' he tore off the antique bluish number he was currently wearing, 'with or without my impeccable clothing.' He threw the sea blue monster over his shoulder.

We had much more interesting things to think about than his dress sense.

22

'Cancer man

> 'A taciturn expert at circumlocution he is'
> — Linda Goodman's Sun Signs

The Ice Man's first visit to the tower-house followed. I was in the garden, hacking back the bones of the herbal skeletons when he came out, slamming the door behind him with an, 'Awkward bastard!'

'Sorry?'

'Not you, obviously.'

'Oh, right.' I threw a shroud of black-limbed leaves into a plastic bin liner, on top of the fennel dust that lay at the bottom. Dominic began to move the debris away alongside me – crisp packets, sweet wrappers, stiff old plants. There was a rare silence for ten minutes. Then the frost melted a bit.

'My dad.' I'd guessed as much – the weekly telephone call. Letting Dominic phrase the problem in his own way was a difficult but essential business, which took five more minutes at least. 'He's just worried about my career. My legal career.' There was another pause and then he looked at me shiftily. 'He says it's better to have a base in Edinburgh, better for the purposes of professional contacts,' he explained. 'Occasionally he arranges a lunch, or that kind of thing, with someone with a growing legal practice. He's always setting me up with people who might help me later in some way.'

'You can still get into Edinburgh easily enough.' I didn't like the way this conversation was progressing at all. 'Have Allegro, will travel, don't you think?'

'Well, the other thing is . . .' Dominic was being unusually hesitant '. . . he says that in legal circles,' a swallow and a sideways glance, 'marriage is the norm.'

'What? Not in this century, surely?' Dominic was irritating me now. 'Uncle Mark said exactly the same thing.'

'I told him that he and my mum had put me off marriage for life.' Guilt creased the skin around his eyes.

'So what are you going to do?' I asked.

'Clear weeds, and then think,' he said, bending down to begin.

'What is there to think about?' I asked. 'I'm not getting married because Nick Oliver thinks it's a good idea. I'm not. Plus, I didn't take any notice of Uncle Mark – didn't even mention it to you.'

'Uncle Mark doesn't pay my bills and I don't think my dad was seriously suggesting that we get married.' Dominic's voice was terse.

Ah. 'Well, I could pay your bills,' I offered.

'No, thanks,' he said, with a toss of his mane.

'Do you think that your dad would really stop your allowance?' I asked. 'Could you manage?'

'I've already got a student loan the size of Everest. And he's been pretty generous so far about money.' He pulled a face then, wrinkling his brow. 'He always is – unless you do something he doesn't like. I've told you, he's a bit of a control freak.'

The words 'control freak' brought a different face to mind – bad skin, staring eyes and a starving mouth. Guess who? I started to feel quite icy myself. 'Surely you can cope with your father and his games? I mean, he's not exactly the biggest problem in the world, is he? Can't you talk him around?' I was stung by the fact that Nick Oliver didn't seem to want Dominic to live with me – the implied criticism – but I didn't want to admit to that. It gnawed at me, though. And why was I never invited to Nick Oliver's house with Dominic? My work rate rose as my discrimination ebbed: I was now removing roots and shoots and stuff that might otherwise have had a chance of rebirth later on, in the spring. I'd stopped looking at Dominic and he was no longer at my side. A juicy sedum squashed beneath my toe. When Dominic finally spoke, the Ice Man had returned, and this time was addressing me directly.

'Sorry to interrupt you with my minor problems. I'll leave you to your cull.' Damn. And the door shut again.

Punishing the now pretty bare garden and punishing Dominic and myself took about another hour. It was the first time in a while I'd made a list. Obviously you can have a look at it, and, equally obviously I was much too busy composing it to share any of it with Dominic.

DOUBTS ABOUT DOMINIC

Did Dominic's father criticise me and did Dominic stand up for me?

Will Dominic put his ambition and his legal career before his personal life, me, forever? Is this a kind of test?

Does Dominic's father envisage some sort of an awful Leeched Dry marriage between Dominic and myself, in which I prepare complicated meals and smile at women like Sherry, only twenty years older and twice as powerful?

Does Dominic's father disapprove of his son living with a girl who hasn't got a university degree?

How much does Dominic want to live with me?

How much notice does Dominic take of his father?

That last one was really the crunch. This was proving to be more of a trial than the Stone Man. Almost. Thinking of which, I noticed that the moon was full and the sun was fading, plus the garden was pretty decimated. I decided to go inside.

'Helena, I was just coming out to get you.' Dominic had two glasses of wine in his hands. 'We can't fall out about this. Can't I keep you and my dad happy at the same time?' He handed me a glass, bending his head to look into my face. 'What if I tell Dad that I'm staying at Cromwell Street and leave a bit of stuff there? Sam's friend would find somewhere else to live. I could still spend all of my time with you here. I mean, I don't want to leave you on your own anyhow. How does that sound?'

I took a swallow of wine. 'Fine.' Except it didn't answer any of my questions at all. I hated his father at that second and that led to the worst question of all.

If I hated Nick Oliver, what chance did my relationship with his son stand?

23

'He crawls into his convenient shell (the one he carries with him at all times), safe for a while from his own emotions'
— Linda Goodman's Sun Signs

My fantasies about Will Jackson really began to mount then. As I'm sure you've seen, I'd been fascinated by him from the start, from before I'd even known him, and now that Dominic seemed to be turning into Old Nick before my horrified eyes, I kept thinking of Will Jackson's admirable qualities, as I perceived them.

Perhaps the most appealing one, in the face of Dominic's new Nick Oliverness, was Will's background as a paramedic. Paramedics are so much sexier than doctors, don't you think? So much more 'hands on'. Wonderful. And so heroic, charging down the roads in those big, blacked out boxes of vehicles, to face God knows what every day, rescuing people over and over again, rescuing all kinds of people, just because they're people. So much sexier than lawyers with their clean suits, white bills and obscure words.

And because most of the Doubts About Dominic implied criticism of him, his father, or both, it was impossible to discuss any of them with him. So I was pretty silent with Dominic, but as Will Jackson came into the art gallery more and more, I was chattier and more open with him. You can see what's coming, can't you?

Events shortly came to a head with Dominic. As he'd promised, keeping the room at Cromwell Street was just a ruse: he rarely spent any time there. But one night, he came into the living room after a phone call from his father, looking more sheep than lion. Two secretive glances in my direction warned me that he was dreading the conversation to come, but I was buoyed up for it by the fine-tuning of the Doubts About Dominic list I'd effected over the last few weeks. When I met his third glance, he spoke. 'Helena, I'd better stay the night at Cromwell Street on Thursday. My dad's arranging a night out with the man who's offering me a traineeship for next year and he's going to pick me up at Cromwell Street. He'll think it's weird if he doesn't drop me off there as well.'

'Dominic, *I* think it's weird that you want to stay there – that you go along with this farce at all. Why don't you just tell him that you live here?'

A lawyer's answer. 'What harm does it do? Look, I'll talk to Matthew and make sure he stays here on Thursday night; you'll be quite safe.' He saw my frozen face. 'Okay. I'll drive back here afterwards then, if Matthew isn't going to be around.' No reaction. 'Helena?' He was testy now, but so was I.

'First, you have to go along with what your dad wants, so that he'll still pay your way. Then you have to meet with and impress this man so that you can do your traineeship with him. What about what *you* want, Dominic?' Do you actually want to live with me? I thought. And when you're used to living with me, will you expect me to try to impress your legal contacts, your father?

'I just don't see what all the fuss is about.' Dominic went to the bottom of the stairs and bellowed up to Diana's room. 'Matthew? . . . Matthew!' Trundling footsteps followed, and then Matthew and Diana were with us in the living room.

'Dominic?'

'Are you going to be around on Thursday night? All night, I mean.'

Matthew looked puzzled, and Diana stared at me question-ingly. 'This Thursday? I think so.'

'Can you make sure that you definitely stay here? Helena doesn't want to stay here on her own, or just with Diana.'

'Dominic!' I was really embarrassed and annoyed.

'Yeah – that's no problem,' said Matthew.

'Dominic, you're missing the point completely.' I spun round to Matthew. 'What about tonight, Matthew? And tomorrow night? Will you be around then?' He looked at Diana and nodded his head. 'Right then, Dominic. You've got all week to impress your legal colleague.' Dominic's face was livid. Diana, noticing, pulled on Matthew's arm.

'Let's get something to eat,' she said, dragging him into the kitchen after her.

Dominic looked so furious that I was nervous, suddenly, though I wouldn't show it. He came across towards me and his voice was crackly with anger. 'Why did you speak to me like that in front of them?' he asked. I averted my face mutely. 'Do you want me to go?' The low voice was full of a horrible coldness and my own voice was quiet when I replied.

'I haven't come all this way for an adult version of Leeched Dry.'

'And I'm not your fucking Uncle Mark.' He spat it at me. 'Surely you know that?'

Yes, but are you a younger version of Nick Oliver, do I know that? I thought. Thought, but couldn't say. So I ignored him completely.

The final straw. 'I'll get my things.'

And he was gone.

24

'Pisces woman

'She's sometimes a bit deceptive when she practises her art of wrapping you around her emerald earrings'
           – Linda Goodman's Sun Signs

Will Jackson's visits to the art gallery had become an almost daily occurrence and the next day I was lighter and brighter than usual – a mixture of defiance, lust and curiosity. So when he asked me out for a drink the following evening, I said yes.

Imagine how I felt that Thursday night, getting ready? Guilt, guilt, guilt, guilt and more guilt. Dominic Oliver. If I loved him – and I did – then why was I going out with someone else? Getting back at Dominic was an important part of it. (He hadn't rung.) Also, a very dangerous part. There was even a chance that we would see him or his friends in Edinburgh that night. But the other part of it was that I was just eighteen and, although I loved Dominic, I'd never really been out with anyone else before. I didn't have to kiss Will or anything, I reasoned. Not if I didn't want to. But the combination of that paramedical background and those secret roses was a seductive one. I wouldn't betray Dominic by starting up a full-blown affair with Will, I thought, but I wouldn't betray myself either, by denying myself the experience of a night alone with a man like that.

Dressing, I opted logically for the professional image rather than the artist-in-waistcoat look that Will himself affected. Diana helped me to get ready. 'Now, we'll keep it simple – the cream silk top with the mandarin collar for a start. You won't *do* anything with this man, will you?' Holding the blouse up to my hair, 'Nice contrast with the chestnut mop. And black trousers,' going to the wardrobe to get them out. 'I mean, remember how hard I looked before I found Matthew? There are some real horror stories out there. And high black shoes . . .' She deliberated over which was the best pair. 'He'll probably be smaller than you . . . Will, I mean, not Dominic, obviously. And you do like Dominic. More than like.' She paused for breath. I opened my mouth to speak. Too late. 'I'll get you some of my new perfume – drives Matthew wild.' She moved a pace back and then stopped. 'There again, maybe these clothes are more Chanel No. Five.' She squirted me thoroughly with an ancient bottle (bought by Uncle Mark) which now smelt of aged talcum powder. 'I know Dominic's got a temper, but you don't want to go out with John-boy Walton, do you?' Even Diana had to breathe at last.

'The temper's not the problem,' I said. 'Or even the arrogance. It's the doing-what-his-father-says thing. I mean, I need a big Dominic, not a little Nick.'

'But he killed himself to get a first.' Diana's voice was almost pleading – pleading for Dominic. 'Of course he's going to use it. Then he can tell his dad to get stuffed . . . if need be, I mean.'

'But will he, Diana? Where is he now?' I asked. 'Why is he still renting that room? I could pay his living expenses for this last year, easily.'

'Helena, men don't have testosterone so that we can "pay their living expenses", now do they? Thank God! Think yourself lucky. I know Dominic's a bit King Lear, but you don't want to wake up beside Oswald either, do you?' (As you can see, Diana had just started a degree in literature.) 'Speaking of which, if Dominic sees you with Will Jackson tonight, it's going to be more like one of the most tragic bits of *Othello* than anything else.' She punctuated her words with a savage buttoning motion, a vicious Emilia lacing up Desdemona's corset.

'I thought of that. And I've told Will, not quite in so many words, it's to be a strictly hands off affair – he knows that. I think I'll suggest somewhere noisy or young or something.' There was no way that I would risk that particular meeting.

'Good idea. Anyway,' Diana stood back, 'you look just right.

The hair's a bit tousled, but that's the only thing that'll pick his chisel up.'

'Charming!' I laughed, grabbing my bag. 'I'll not be late, and I'll toot my horn before I leave my car for the house.'

'Fine, but no other toots!' Diana waved her finger at me as she spoke.

And she watched me, waving from the window, as I walked towards Red and drove away.

Will and I were meeting outside Jenners, central and safe, and I was glad to see him already standing there as I rounded the corner on to Prince's Street. His spine was hard against the glassy front of the store and his eyes were on the jostling street; I saw him watch several people pass by before he spotted me. He moved forward, kissed me smoothly and gracefully on the cheek, and said, 'You look neat.' Neat? He took my elbow and steered me along the street. 'There's a new bar/restaurant, just opened tonight, a tickets-only do. Very sharp lines, very understated. A friend of mine designed the atrium. You'll love it.'

I smiled wanly at him. What was an atrium? And would Dominic and Co. also have acquired exclusive tickets? Though 'sharp lines' sounded absolutely Nick Oliver, not at all Dominic. Guilt nearly overwhelmed me at the thought. Dominic, Dominic, Dominic Oliver. I would have to make quite certain Will knew that I wasn't available, I thought.

Within minutes we were uncomfortably seated on metal chairs inside the atrium (a kind of mega test tube-cum-bell jar thing, full of plants – and therefore probably insects). I felt like another trapped insect myself as we talked. The restaurant was off to my right, full of frighteningly trendy-looking groups and couples. We chatted about the art gallery, his work, various artists, and eventually we got on to the Edinburgh social scene, at which point I sensed a chance to introduce the subject of Dominic. Sipping my bone dry wine, I slipped in as casually as I could, 'It's really nice to be out in Edinburgh, actually. Dominic and I often stay around the Borders lately.'

'The boyfriend?' Will knew then. I caught his narrow gaze. 'Oh, I did some research at the art gallery.' The silky, polished-looking hair moved closer to me. 'The current boyfriend, I should say.' He sat back, spine like a steel rod against the metal chair.

'Don't worry, I'll be the perfect gentleman.' I thought of Jem and felt distinctly nervous, sipping my wine very quickly. The aphid in the atrium – horror story! Good job we were in a busy spot.

As we chatted for the next hour or so, my eyes kept flickering over to the doors. How embarrassed would Dominic be if he walked in with Mr Traineeship and Mr Oliver, Senior? How furious? How upset? Guilt. That would take some careful handling and possibly some of my new self-defence techniques. So I couldn't relax.

I was acutely aware of the glass-trapped plants at my side. I mean, some of Will's stories were very impressive, peopled as they were by local sculptors, architects and so on, but it was a bit like being at work after a while, so during a pause I pounced. 'Why did you leave the ambulance service, Will? I mean, I guess you wanted to spend more time on your furniture and carvings, but did you miss it?'

At first he gave me the spiel I'd already seen on the book jacket: soothing qualities of wood, etcetera, etcetera. Then he said something that really surprised me. 'Of course, people are beautiful – some specimens more than others.' He cocked his head at me a little as he said this. Unfortunately mention of 'specimens' coupled with paramedics, combined with the sense I already had of sitting inside a test-tube, only brought images of urine samples flooding into my mind. 'But wood is so clean. After all the blood and guts, the dossers stinking of drink, their dribbling lips . . .' He shuddered. 'My work is so calm now, so precise, so ordered. Perfection. I can aim for perfection. That just wasn't possible as a paramedic – all those damaged people.'

Loving damaged people. I thought of Dominic, holding the Colombian roses to my cheek – his Rhett and Scarlett kiss and cracked cafetière. Perfection. Wiping his friend's sick from his shoulder, and my tears (or worse) from my face. Perfection. Scores of tatty T-shirts in my wardrobe and scores of ordered lecture notes on his computer. Perfection. Dominic, Dominic, Dominic Oliver. How hurt exactly would he be if he knew what I was up to – or nearly up to – at that second? Too much guilt altogether, I decided.

There are sexy, human lawyers and there are clinical, cold artists. 'Sorry, Will. I have to go.'

*   *   *

Autumn was really starting to bite and I sat in my precious car outside Dominic's house for almost an hour – for the last time, if I had anything to do with it. And then he was there, stepping out of his father's boring BMW.

'Dominic!' I ran to him and wrapped my arms around his neck, practically knocking him flying.

'Helena! What's wrong?' He held me to him for a second and then sniffed suspiciously, his hands on my shoulders. 'And why are you wearing Uncle Mark's talc?'

'A long story.' Which I would adapt in the telling, or risk Desdemona's end. 'Are you coming back to the house?' A sudden hoot made me jump – his father. I'd forgotten about him completely. But he only waved genially and pulled away. He looked almost human. Dominic was speaking again.

'Are you all right?' My face was cradled between his lovely, clumsy, uncrafty, sexy Dominic Oliver hands. 'I was annoyed with you and I needed to think. About what you said, partly. But I was stupid to leave – really stupid.' Dominic stroked my hair, shaking his head at his own mistake. His face was so close to mine. 'I've been ringing you tonight – all night. I'm glad you're here.' He kissed me softly, then we both remembered the Stone Man at once. Damn. 'Just come inside for a second. I'll get my stuff and we can go.'

Yes.

Deep into the night we talked, getting closer and closer to the centre of everything. We were lying in bed, candles lit all around us, with the curtains open so that we could see the stars through the window. I was luxuriating still in the size and the comfort of the bed, the closeness of the bathroom (we'd just shared a bottle of wine!) and the size, comfort and post-coital closeness of Dominic Oliver. My Dominic. Back again.

'It was when you asked me what I really wanted,' he was saying. 'I mean, for a lot of the time, studying law's been a slog for me – you know that. It's been hard to make some aspects of it stick at all because it's so fucking boring half the time. Criminal law, for example. And you were right – there I was with a meeting all set up, Dad on one side, traineeship on the other, and me bang in the middle. Just doing what I was told, really.' He looked down at me and kissed my brow, then nipped me with his claw and laughed wickedly. 'That's partly why I was so pissed off with you the other night – because I knew you were right.

'So I stayed at Cromwell Street, stewed in a mood for a couple of nights, and gradually worked out what I was going to say to my dad and his friend.

'Mr Hallshore took us to a casino – not to gamble, just because he's a regular there, and he knew it would be quiet enough to talk. And all the time he and my dad were talking, I watched the chips flying below us and thought, How much of a gamble is it, really? Either I do what Dad wants, do my traineeship, use his contacts and make a lot of money squeezing legal aid clients and employers on compensation cases, becoming a sort of imitation Nick Oliver . . .' I waited '. . . and a living/dead Dominic Oliver eventually. Or I become Dominic Oliver right from the beginning. From now, anyway. Not that I want to starve.' He looked at me, smiling, and touched my temple. 'But you're not meant to live someone else's life. That's not the point of it all, is it?' I shook my head.

'All the time we were talking,' he continued, 'I kept looking down from the bar/restaurant bit of the casino to the gaming tables on my left. I've been in there before with Dixie and the others. They do free food – loads of students go, and we normally have a really good laugh there, or a good talk. Anyway, all of the fat bastards were there tonight, half of them lawyers probably, moving piles of plastic and paper around. Dissatisfied. Meaningless. Work and leisure, just moving pieces of paper and plastic around. And people, of course. As if it was all the same, dead material. Dead tissue.

'On my right some bloke was trying to impress the woman he was with. He was telling her all about his parents' money – how much *they* were worth and how much *he* would be worth, and how he was trying to get them to take steps to avoid inheritance tax later on. It was pathetic.'

Dominic's whole life has been one long inheritance problem, I thought. But he was still talking.

'Anyway, by this time, I must have been quiet for ages, because even my dad eventually noticed and said something about it.' I laughed, and touched his fingers with mine. 'So I just told them both. I was very grateful that they were both willing to help me to shape my career, blah de blah, but I'd decided to go off in a slightly different direction.'

He looked across at me and the skin around his eyes crinkled. 'I've never sounded so smooth-and-sincere, "I-hear-what-you're-saying" Nick Oliver in my life! Told them I planned to specialise in medical negligence cases.' He lifted himself up on one elbow and looked directly at me. 'And guess what? Mr Hallshore's practice handles medical negligence cases sometimes and one of his contacts also does. Between the two of them, I should be able to get enough experience.' He dropped on to his back and laughed. 'Not a gamble at all, really.' His head twisted until he was looking at me again. 'What do you think?'

'I think you think you're great!' I said. Dominic roared, all signs of the sheep gone. He tickled me through my (his) T-shirt. 'And so do I,' I laughed. 'So do I.'

I nuzzled into him, and at last began to feel tired.

I thought deep into the night before I turned the light out because I knew they'd get the letter the next day. I'd worn my surgeon's gloves to write it. Had to get some wear out of them, like. I knew she'd know it was from me straightaway – recognise my style – but I fancied keeping a bit of the suspense and illusion going. I wouldn't let them see all of my work in one go, either. Have a bit of a play, like. At the same time, I was sure I was getting nearer and nearer to it – the centre of darkness, the secret.

It was all getting more acute now, so to speak. Autumn had swung right back and it was time for action; the spiral had almost rejoined itself. I'd set a web to snare a fly – two flies. Maybe even more than two. So many times they'd ignored me when I'd been there, waiting for them. Dishing up my dreams for them. And I'd watched them several times lately. Had all their movements charted on to a massive map, with a secret key, above my head in bed. I was really looking forward to this one. This time they'd think of me for days, for weeks. Maybe forever. They'd fear me all the time, whether I was there or not, fear me and feel me. Know me. See me.

And sometimes I'll be there for them, I think, as I slip down into my dreams and out of my own skin.

The dream director. Dominic was happy as he switched out the light that night, in full control of his life and its direction. He fell asleep almost at once, in his rightful place inside the tower, beside me.

But the longer I stared out into the night, into the square box of stars that was the window on my left, the stronger was the sense of fear that built up inside me, until I felt that someone, or something, was going to come staring out of the darkness right back into my soul. I tried not to think of it during the day, although it was there all of the time, but at night the fear just wouldn't go away.

Because I knew that I was climbing nearer and nearer to that tiny room at the top of the house and its store of secrets. I felt that if I dared to look at my fingers in the thick blackness, a jewelled key would appear there, sparkling in the darkness like the dagger in Polanski's *Macbeth*. And where would the dagger lead? What would I open up? The third letter was on its way.

Then I thought of Dominic's 'gamble' earlier that evening. What did I have to lose but my fear, my smallness? My worst self?

I climbed out of bed, my skin lifting with tension and suspense (plus it was a chilly Scottish night) and knelt on the day bed, my back to the bedroom and my eyes to the white-rimmed box of the window. The stars, the moon and the loch were held in the window's square, and the milk of my mother was in the water of the loch; the soul of my father was in the silver of the stars. Separate but the same.

I pressed my palms, a metre apart, to the mirroring glass of the window, and felt as though a charge was passing through all three of us – the stars, the loch and myself. Essentially the same. A trinity of light. Electricity.

I walked back to bed, not frightened by the shadows now, and curled myself into Dominic's warm and generous body. Soft, soft skin. Fealty.

The third letter was about to be exchanged and I could face whatever secrets lay within the crackling box of the envelope.

25 ∫

'Here in the hall of plenty there is nothing now.
Just you
Lying under my hands,
With shadowy figures approaching.'
         – Brian Masters, *Killing for Company*

I knew it was from him immediately – before I even opened the envelope, I think. Maybe I could smell him by then. Or maybe I could smell my own fear.

I always got back first on Fridays – did he know that? I had every Friday afternoon off, in return for working every other Saturday. So I'd dragged myself, grittily and unglossily, into the art gallery for my three-hour stint (after about three hours' sleep) at the Expressionist display, glad that I had the following day off. No Will Jackson – so far, so good. The three hours crawled past and then I was off.

Shopping on the way home involved picking up two chilled meals and some bread, wine and salad ingredients. (As you'll have guessed, I was cooking that night.) Then I headed for home, for an afternoon snoozette. Dominic had now moved in officially and he planned to secure a multi-storey student loan later in the week.

So Diana, Dominic and Matthew were still at the University when I let myself into the empty tower-house, switching off the burglar alarm as I walked in. I put the food in the fridge, made myself a coffee, and curled up on the settee to read my post: two circulars (did I want a personal loan or a stair lift?), one postcard from Uncle Mark (living it up in Venice with the lovely Lisa) and an innocuous-looking envelope – no stamp – which I immediately realised was not innocuous at all.

I breathed in, flicked it over and opened it up.

Darling Helena,

I've organised a little autumn glory for you – a Friday afternoon treat – to start off the weekend with a bang, so to speak.

If you turn to www.dom-ol.uk on the Internet, you will see that I have set up a web page dedicated to you. Don't wait for me to get back from the University before you seek it out. Enjoy.

Love, Dominic
XXXXX
XXXX
XXX
XX
X
X

Really creepy. So to speak. Thank God Dominic had insisted on us both having mobiles. What with everything that had happened over the last few days *and* his University work, dedicating a web page to me would be the last thing on his mind. Plus he knew that I ignored computers whenever possible, unlike a certain other person.

I made sure that the door was locked, then I picked up the phone.

Fuzzy line.

'Dominic?'

'Hi, Helena. I'm just having a coffee with Dixie in the library. I'll be back in a couple of hours.'

'Dominic, did you leave a letter for me this morning?'

'No – should I have?'

'Or write a web page for me?'

A penny-dropping pause. 'It's him.'

'That's what I thought.'

I heard him conferring with Dixie for a minute and then he was back on the line. 'I'm coming home. Dixie's coming as well.' Split the chilled meals – still, that was the least of my worries. 'Don't look at it on your own, Helena. And make sure everything's locked.'

'I have.'

'Right. I'll be as quick as I can.'

Click.

Forty-five minutes later (a record), he and Dixie were at the door.

Dominic's computer was happily settled in a corner of my bedroom by then, so that's where we headed. The three of us were cramped around the screen, Dominic on the chair and Dixie and I standing behind him. Dominic was so impatient that finding the page seemed to take forever.

But when the words finally appeared, I hardly dared read them.

An Early Christmas Present

'O. Henry wrote 'The Gift of the Magi', a story of two lovers who sacrificed for each other their greatest treasures. She cut her long hair to buy her lover a watch chain. He sold his watch to buy her combs for her hair. In acts that might seem foolish, these two people found the spirit of the Magi' – Christmas card from Ted Bundy to a friend

Hi! My name's Dominic Oliver. Pleased to meet you.

And I want to tell the World Wide Web how I feel about a very special girl – this web page is dedicated to my partner, Helena, the most beautiful girl in the world.

For the worldwide entertainment of all you webbies, I have a series of scripts and other art works, which I'm sure you can't wait to read. Enjoy.

The Alchemy Series of Seven

- Click here – Tease on a Train
- Click here – The Bandaged Bride
- Click here – The Parting of the Lips
- Click here – The Party's Off
- Click here – The Silver Chain
- Click here – Trinity of Blood
- Click here – Slice of Life

I hope I've well and truly captured all of you sea-creatures out there in my nerve-tingling net of fantasy. (Or should I say fact?) Pieces Six and Seven are still being fine-tuned – no peeking now – they'll be released to you soon.

I'd like to finish now on a serious note, with just a few little hints from Alchemy Six – once again, dedicated to the beautiful Helena: 'Her beauty had a potent alchemy'.

The Trinity of Blood

- I need you
- I will come to your home, my wings renewed
- I know when you are alone
- Have no fear – you will not be hurt
- I will wrap my rings of need around your flesh, a daisy chain of love about your body. Open mouths
- I know that you will understand, will share in, my hunger. That is why I have chosen you
- We will exchange sacrificial mementos of our love. Six for gold

Perfect
Fade

My mouth was dry. ' "My autumn girl". That's when he first saw me – autumn, last year,' I explained. I felt cold.

' "My wings renewed by force".' Dixie thought about it. 'He's had to change his car after his last go and he's pissed off about it.' We were all silent for a minute.

'Let's have a look at these *Alchemy* things, then,' said Dominic. He clicked on *Tease on a Train*, but '*Denied Access*' appeared on the screen.

'That must relate to when he saw me on the Edinburgh train,' I said. 'Try *The Bandaged Bride*.'

This time we did gain access.

'Jesus!' said Dominic. 'Thank God he never tried that one out. What the fuck are *Six* and *Seven* going to be like? Don't worry, Helena,' he turned towards me, twisting away from the screen, 'you just won't be left on your own. I won't let him touch you. I don't want him to touch you ever.'

'Me neither.' That was definite. I paused then. 'But I was thinking, he seems to feel untouchable himself – all those bandages, screening people off from himself – disgusted and disgusting.'

Dominic looked right into me and a shot of comprehension ran between us. 'He disgusts himself,' he said in a low voice. 'But his disgust goes right outside himself as well.'

I thought for a few seconds. 'I've barely even looked at him.'

'That's not the point.' Dominic shook his head. 'He's definitely looked at *you*.' He bit his lip. 'He's got no right, no right at all. Fucking animal! Why? Evil? Neglect? Fun? All three?'

I shook myself, shook off Dominic's anger. 'Let's see what's in *The Parting of the Lips*.' It allowed us access, and we read it through silently – amazed. No one knew quite what to say when we had finished. 'It's awful, isn't it, seeing it all down in black and white like this?' I said eventually, inadequately. 'All planned out. Seeing how he intended it to end.' Dominic and Dixie exchanged the tiniest but sharpest of glances. Something Dominic had said the night of Jen's attack flashed into my mind: '*I should have warned you about that.*'

'What exactly happened that night, Dominic?'

'Well, I'll put it this way – I knew what he had in mind,' Dominic said quietly. My face felt frozen. Dominic squeezed my hand and continued, 'But he didn't touch me – not in that way. And he's not going to touch you like that.'

I laid my chin on top of his big, blond head. 'You should have told me.'

Dominic side-stepped with his usual crabby speed. 'Jesus, do you think anybody else'll find this thing?' He made a revolted sound in his throat. 'They'll think I'm absolutely perverted.' The script was still on the screen. 'Let's look at number four,

The Party's Off,' he suggested. 'My graduation or birthday party? What could he have had to do with either of those?'

Quite a lot, as it turned out. I couldn't stop myself – a snort of laughter escaped my lips. 'Your poor dad! Imagine his tiles.' The mess. At least I understood that 'art student' phone call now – Dominic and I had had a couple of conversations trying to work out what his dad had been on about that night.

He shook his head. 'It's weird, the way he switches. Makes his actions harder to work out,' he said. 'We can never relax, Helena; he can just switch.'

'In a way,' I said, willing myself to believe it, 'I'm the safest of us all.' I shuddered. 'All of that stuff about not really hurting me.'

'But it's you he really wants,' Dixie pressed. 'It's you he's watched from the start; you he dedicated the page to. And his idea of not hurting people is a bit different from ours.'

'Surely the police will be able to help us when they've seen this?' said Dominic. 'He's given us some real clues into how he thinks, how he feels.'

'But no more evidence,' said Dixie. 'Maybe you should move out, Helena, for a while at least.'

'Where to?' I asked. 'Cromwell Street? Besides, I love the tower-house, and it's mine.'

'The security system here would have kept Princess Diana in the palace,' said Dominic. 'And he doesn't use weapons – apart from that brick. He didn't even use the knife when he got it.' Dominic stopped himself. 'No, all of that's beside the point. His whole mind, his whole body, they're weapons in themselves.' He waved at the computer screen. 'And this is one of his weapons. Let's see the last ones.' But we were denied access to the rest. 'Hardly a surprise,' said Dominic. 'I'll ring the police and update them.' He switched off the computer and I sat on his knee, trying unsuccessfully to warm our fears away with a cuddle. Matthew and Diana clattered their way into the house. 'And we'd better update them as well,' said Dominic, lifting his head from my hair.

And that's what we spent most of the rest of the night doing.

I watched the police come and I watched the police go. Cat man.

They'd had their warning but what they'd never expect, being a bit slow themselves, like, was that I would move so quickly, or that I'd make my move when they were all around. Fooled them there. It all added to the excitement, the urgency.

And where do you think I was watching them all from? Fooled you as well, I bet. The turret at the top of the house. The seventh room. The only room, I'd noted, that they never used. It's full of electrical equipment. Electricity. God knows what she's got planned for it.

My chance had come after she'd rung them. When Dominic and the dreadlocked dosser arrived, I knew they'd go straight to the bedroom to look at the computer there. And I hoped that they wouldn't think to lock the door. Fucking university students – thick as pig shit. Alarm off, door open, Adam in – very quietly. Mars man, looking at the moon. All I have to do now is wait. When I'm sure they're asleep, I'll go and get the front door key from where they leave it. They've been chin-wagging all night. Chin-wagging about me. At last.

I'll try and get a bit of kip before the fireworks begin.

The click of the door and then the click of my eyes. Open. Electricity. Him. I can sense him, smell him, and feel him in the darkness all around me. Now.

I'm lying on my front and Dominic is beside me, fast asleep. Waking him will mean noise, slow reactions and even more danger. I am rigid beside him. Think. Now. I stay still, and in the stillness hear his feet padding very, very slowly, very, very softly towards the bed. Think. I can hear his breathing – it's charged up – then I hear him breathe in sharply, like a spasm. Now. Move.

Attack.

A real attack. I jump at him, fly at him with a bellowing scream, guessing at where the soft parts of his face are, his eyes, his lips, the inside of his mouth – especially the inside of his mouth. Then he screams, and I feel one hand and something very hard damaging my face, knocking me off him and on to the floor. Nothing hurts and then the light clicks on. There's blood everywhere, all over him, and my face is wet when I touch it. My blood or his?

Weird gloves sheath his fingers, like condoms. There's a cloud of whisky all around him. And dead eyes stare down at me – he is dead and alive, bloodied and bloodless. Excited. Very excited. But unreachable. I stare back.

'I wasn't going to hurt you. You wouldn't have felt anything. You shouldn't have done that.' He has a bloodied brick in his hand, a voice that doesn't sound like he uses it very often, and his hips are pushing to a slow sort of rhythm. Coiling. Coiling.

I shrink back.

I spring forward.

That's when I really do become his brother, when I join in all of his rage, hatred and emptiness, when all of the rage from the rest of my life joins with this one – this biggest one.

The sight of him, with his need, his greed, and his brick in his hand – and my Helena, with blood all over her face – clicks on a switch right inside me that I've never been aware of before. And despite all my words following Jen's attack, it's his weapons I'm using: my hands, my legs, my kick boxing, but most of all my rage. My own rage and emptiness. Pure, fucking evil. My energy darkens, and hardens into another thing altogether, like the blackened old sea purse in Helena's bedroom. I'd always heard that mentally ill people have super-human strength. I'd always thought that mentally ill people were somebody else. It's the nearest I've come to flying. My hands are round his throat and I'm shaking him, throttling him.

'My brother. Is this what you mean by brotherhood?' His face, bulging at mine, my dad's face, Helena's body, Helena's blood, my blood, all essentially the same. His blood, my blood. One force of energy. I'm completely outside of myself. Dead and alive.

Free.

'Dominic . . . Dominic!' It's me who has to be pulled off him, by Matthew; it's him who has to be saved, by Matthew; Matthew, who is surprisingly strong, who has to forcibly twist my arms away from him. Matthew who saves me, really. I am the mad man now, baring my teeth like an animal. Snarling. It's me everybody is concentrating on while he is padding his way towards the turnpike stairs still clutching that fucking brick. Matthew is holding me, concentrating on me, but he lifts the brick to the back of Matthew's head as he walks past us to the stairs – I know he'd use it, given the chance.

And then he's out of the front door.

'He must have opened it in the night, must have been waiting here all that time,' says Dixie, who's just come up, too late, from the first floor.

'Dominic, I've never seen you like that,' says Diana. 'You were nearly the one who ended up in court there.'

Dixie takes hold of my arm. 'Calm down, Dom.' My breathing becomes more normal. I start to come back into myself. He got a few good kicks in as well. My legs hurt.

'Helena.' And then everyone becomes aware of her, crouching on the floor, with dark, enormous eyes and blackening blood caking her face, her neck, her T-shirt.

I'm shivering, shaking with fear: fear of him and fear of Dominic. I've never seen him like that before, never seen anyone like that before. He needed to be like that, for our survival. Basic. But what's happened to my face?

What on earth has happened to my face? It is stiff with drying blood.

I'm covered in it – from my mouth and my nose, I think. I guess he was right; that was partly what I had meant when I'd thought of us as brothers, partly what I'd wanted to do – push him to my extremes. Push him into proving that he was like me, a part of him at least. A well hidden part.

It wasn't as picturesque as the script had been, not as artistic. I feel a bit sad, like, when I think about some of the wasted images – the beautiful daisy chain of bites I was planning to make; the patterns I could have formed on her body. The hair. The pennies for her mouth. The closed, closed eyes. Still, it was exciting enough and all three of us had been fully involved. And the first thing I saw when he switched on the light was his scar. My scar. Half moon. That's why I didn't use the brick. My brother. Mercy.

The main thing was, I enjoyed it. (Not the only one either – Big Dom.) And they've got my watch; I dropped it at their door. And I got something in return. I reach beside me into the passenger seat, pick up my brick and press it to my face. A strand of her hair touches my cheek; I got some after all. And blood. My blood, Helena's blood and Dominic's blood, all together on the brick. My blood and Helena's blood on her face.

'Let's get you cleaned up.' Matthew is leaning over Helena.

A last surge of electricity goes through me. 'Nobody touches her! Nobody touches her but me. That's the whole fucking point.' Matthew backs off and stares at me. Christ, what am I saying? And Helena starts to cry; huge tears fill her amazing eyes. She's only got a T-shirt on, and some little knickers. I want her, sharply, in that state. Especially in that state. Is it really this basic underneath? Underneath everybody or just me? Me and him.

'Sorry, Matthew. Sorry, mate.' I kneel down and hold Helena's shoulder. 'Sorry, Helena.'

'I want my dressing gown.' Her voice gentles me.

'Of course you do.' I go and get her mine, and put it around her shoulders. 'Matthew, will you get me a bowl of warm water from the bathroom? And some cotton wool?' Then I say to everyone, 'I'm sure that's the last time. He got most of what he wanted there.'

'Sorry, mate,' says Dixie. 'Seven for a secret never to be told, remember? Then he'll go. Let's have a look at Helena's face.'

But I don't want to move. I feel safe on the floor. It feels like we've all gone mad at once. Then Dominic pulls his dressing gown around my body more tightly and lifts me up on to the bed. He holds my hair away from my face and Dixie speaks again. 'It's nasty, Helena. It's all cut and grazed. And it'll be bruised, later.' He turns to Dominic. 'Maybe we should go to the hospital, Dom.'

'I don't want to go to hospital. I want to stay here – now that he's gone.'

'Did he hurt you anywhere apart from your face, sweetheart?'

'No. I heard him come in. Then I heard him stand over us, knew he was going to hit me with something. So I jumped at him all at once, tried to give him a real shock and get at his face. Somehow, I got hit with the brick and he pushed me. I'll have some bruises but nothing like he intended – with the brick, I mean. I think he was going to knock me out with it.' I look at Dominic. 'Maybe he was going to knock both of us out with it.' I lie back against the bed head. My face is so sore now.

What I am thinking, but don't dare to ask, is, Will I be scarred?

Will I be scarred, will I be scarred, will I be scarred?

Even the car seems to question me as I drive home into the night, from the deep, black night of the tower to the dead, grey night of my own house. The tips of my scissors are digging into the skin of my back.

And at last I am back in my own grey box. I walk upstairs, switch on the bathroom light and look at myself in the mirror. Electricity. A black eye, a bloodied nose and lips, and red marks all around my throat. I didn't get my daisy chain but that would be quite a necklace. Best of all, a deep, deep cut, running down into the side of my mouth. Did Helena give me that with her nails or was it Dominic? I hope it will leave a mark, a permanent mark, like borstal spots on knuckles or a medal on a chest. Cut here. Heroism. Army hard. And I'll be able to adapt and reinvent the scar stories in public.

But in private I am going to create my very own, intimate, mark: a half moon-shaped scar on my chest – brothers in arms, brothers in scars. Mouth man, meat man. Masochist.

I go to get a needle and some black ink.

Helena's got such soft skin; such beautiful, fine, china white skin. I want to clean her up, to help her, to mend her, but I'm too terrified to look at her closely. There's blood everywhere.

I take her hands and look into her eyes for a second. Nobody could look into her eyes without loving her, I'm convinced of it. Without seeing her. But she's questioning me with her eyes now. I can't answer her, side step instead. 'I'm just going to clean your face up. Is that okay?' She nods. 'Dixie, will you get me some antiseptic from the bathroom?'

'And we'll go and make some hot toddies for everybody,' says Diana. She and Matthew start to walk downstairs and I start to wipe the blood, as gently as I can, from my darling's face.

*   *   *

Dominic couldn't tell me what I needed to know most when I asked him with my eyes so I have to watch him very closely for my answer. My face is hurting and I can feel some swelling around one eye. He wipes away for a couple of minutes and then his face relaxes and his eyes crinkle. 'Grazes, really. Not deep cuts.' His eyes darken again. 'Sore, though. And you won't be able to go to work for a few days.'

'I can live with that.' I smile at him and feel a cut crack. 'No stitches?'

'No stitches. There was a lot of blood, but it's surface damage. Maybe some of it was his, even. There's hardly any bleeding now.' He turns to Dixie. 'Will you get me some fresh water and cotton wool?'

I look down at the bowl as Dixie reaches across to take it away and see that it is full of very red water now, with blobs of cotton wool bobbing on the top. Looking at it, I become liquid, bobbing on the surface – water, between earth and air.

It's the first time I've ever seen anyone's lips actually go white. Shit. Maybe I'm wrong about how badly she's been hurt. 'Helena . . . Helena!' Her eyes close for two seconds, and when they open again they are empty, washed blue and white.

'Get her to lie down, Dom. It's just the shock, and seeing her own blood like that,' says Dixie.

Right. One arm beneath her knees, one arm around her shoulders, and I ease her down the bed so that the blood can flow back to her head. Her chestnut hair on the left is clumped with dried blood and her mouth sort of lolls. Broken. Whose autumn girl now? Her eyes are closed. Shit. I can't cry in front of Dixie – not a second time. I try to keep my jaw in the right place, try to keep my face hard. I try to blink the tears away, and as I do, her eyes blink open.

He's crying – Dominic. I've never seen him cry before. His face is all red – twisted up, misshapen. But I feel too awful to do anything about it. I just lie there. Water. Then the energy, the warmth, the body, gradually comes back. 'Dominic.' My mouth is dry. 'Do my face. Get it over with.' He nods at me, and then at Dixie, and Dixie goes to get the clean water. Cleansing, healing water to soothe the burning feeling. And soon there is no more blood to wipe away.

The worst bit of all is when it's time to put the antiseptic on, because I know how much it will sting. My fingers hover over her skin, knowing that I'm going to hurt her. But it should be me who does it. I wish it was my skin that was all cut. And she shuts her eyes while I finally do it, like a child. I try to be as quick and gentle as I can, but still it's sickening. I feel pretty ropy myself before long. I remember the alleyway and Dixie's fingers in my mouth – the pain and the same sort of gentle clumsiness. He looks at me just at that second, and half smiles with his eyes, and I know he's remembering it as well.

Then it's all done, and I feel better, sit up even and put the dressing gown on properly. And Diana and Matthew come in with a big tray of hot toddies and some biscuits.

'You look much more normal.' Diana is so healthy, she even makes me start to feel it. 'You're going to have a pretty dramatic black eye there, though.'

'His trademark! I'll get you an ice pack in a second, to reduce the swelling,' says Dominic. 'How do you feel?'

'Better. Okay really. Just bruised. It was that bowl – it was disgusting.'

Dominic's first smile of the night. 'No, you're just squeamish.' Then, no smile, and I remember his face before. 'You looked like you were dying for a second. Do you want to see a doctor?'

'No, it was just all that blood. I need a drink.'

'Okay.' Dominic hands a glass to me from Matthew's tray. 'I'm not ringing the police until the morning either. You need some rest.'

'Well, they haven't been much help to date, have they?'

Dominic jumps up. 'I'll go and make an ice pack.' He kisses my cheek, the lightest of touches. 'You drink that. And don't move until you're feeling much better.' He runs downstairs, heavily and fast. I don't feel like moving anywhere.

'Here,' says Diana, 'I'll do your hair for you. It's a real mess.'

'Thanks.'

So she brushes, and I sip, and I sip, and she brushes, and by the time that Dominic comes back with the ice pack (ice cubes and a tea towel) I'm almost restored – well, enough to enjoy the attention, definitely. He smiles at me, a really radiant smile, then sits beside me on the bed and waits until Diana's finished her grooming and I've finished my drink.

'Hold your hair back and shut your eyes. I'll just press this over your face,' he says.

'We'll go to bed then, Helena. It's after five o'clock,' says Matthew. 'We'll be around tomorrow, if the police need us for anything.' Diana kisses me on the cheek (much less gently than Dominic).

'See you tomorrow.' And they're all gone, Dixie ambling off after them to his quilt on the floor.

My shoulders drop as they leave; it's a relief to be on our own again. All at once I'm just so tired. My neck feels too small to hold my head up. Dominic puts the ice down and sits on the edge of the bed, looking almost grey with exhaustion. He wraps his arms around me, sort of slumps against me, and we hold each other, entwined. Trust.

'One blood,' he says quietly. 'Helena, I wish it was me who'd been hurt. I've never felt so close to killing someone. Thank God you're all right! Not that I would care if you were scarred, but you would.' I nod against his hair. 'Are you sore?'

I nod again, saying, 'It feels more like burns than grazes.'

'They're bad grazes, but you'll be better. Really soon.'

Dominic touches me like a man who understands pain and changes.

I won't ever feel the same, not after this. I sit at my computer, fingering the raised scabs that run down into my mouth, feeding me, inside, just like I need to be fed. I'm marked now forever – everything has changed. And they are marked too, whether they know it or not. Truly not virginal now, either of them, so to speak. I rub my big, hard cock. Perfect.

We're on a different level now, the three of us. We've fed from each other in the night. Fed on blood. And *Alchemy Seven* will be different altogether: seven for a secret, never to be told. But brothers have no secrets from one another, and I'm about to involve my brother in my next work of art. Directly involve him. Because I've finally seen that he is up to it now. Extreme, like me.

I finger the skin around my mouth. Scarred. Raised. Heightened. Changed forever. United.

Helena lies down in the bed, in just her nightie now, and I squeeze the ice tightly inside the towel and press it against the swollen tissue around her right eye, trying to press as much of the damage and pain away as I can. Then I go downstairs, check every single lock in the house, every single room and every single window, before getting some fresh ice and heading back upstairs to her again.

As I walk at last to the staircase, I see his watch out of the corner of my eye. I shudder, remembering his web page, and pick it up, using a piece of clean paper. Maybe that'll help the police later – tomorrow. Everything is safe now.

Even after all this, she is so trusting, opening her arms to me as I come back towards her on the bed. All of me wants to protect her, all of me.

'Shhh. Just let me do this once more, then you can sleep. Everything's safe.' She closes her eyes, ready, and nods.

I fall asleep to the sound and feel of him pressing the hard, wet ice against my numbing face, again and again. The Ice Man. I smile, but I'm far too tired to tell him why.

The sound and feel of the keys clicking quietly against my fingers calms me, hypnotises me almost. Because I know I that I won't be able to sleep until I've finished preparing it all for him, until I've perfected it for him – *Alchemy Seven*. Seven for a secret, a happening on a very grand scale. The Bard helps me the most. Climax.

It's in the post and on its way before I go to bed.

We spent most of the rest of the day with the police – four hours, about two of which were spent listening to a lecture about not calling them earlier. They took the watch, but he'd wiped it clean of fingerprints (those creepy gloves). And they took endless statements. Photographs too. Dominic wasn't very pleased about that – neither was I really, not exactly looking my best. (I hadn't braved the mirror yet.) Still, maybe it would all help somehow.

Then we went to Dixie's flat to stay for the rest of the weekend. His flatmate was away, and we felt safer surrounded by the whole of the rest of Edinburgh. None of us wanted to do very much – the Stone Man was a bit of a hard act to follow, really, and we were all pretty worn out, so we talked, ate pizzas, that sort of thing. Watched a lot of videos.

I chilled, mainly, over the weekend. I knew that they wouldn't get the letter 'til Monday, but it was good to know it was on its way. Watched *Un Chien Andalou* again, to fine-tune my plan (slice that ball – an image that's always haunted me). Of course, I had some real-life experience too – it was a little something I'd tried on my own, deceased *chien* (before my mother interfered). You'd be surprised how resilient I found it to the blade, pretty tough. But I was tougher. Poetic justice, I think to myself, over and over again. Scarification. They'll be delighted, enthralled, appalled by it. All three.

26

'Aries man

'His beautiful iron faith is pure'
— Linda Goodman's Sun Signs

Red was zooming towards the tower-house, bright and fresh on Monday morning. There was no art gallery for me and no University for Dominic. I *had* braved the mirror at last: I'd definitely made the right decision about Will Jackson – I was certainly a less than perfect specimen now. Diana and Matthew were still there, had been all weekend, and there had been no sign of *him*.

But there was a letter – addressed to Dominic, this time – sitting importantly on the table. He opened it up and laid it flat for us all to read.

Alchemy Seven
Slice of Life
(1) A Dedication
To my father, from myself, Iain Banks and Salvador Dali
(2) A Riddle
What's almost round and sharp and slices eyeballs?
(3) An Answer
A flying Frisbee with a razor blade wedged inside it
(4) An Image (or three)
An eyeball deflates like:

> *A boy's football*
> *A teenager's testicle*
> *A man's ego*

> *Followed by:*
> *(5) A Promise*
> *You're about to see it happen*
> *(6) A Happening*
> *Is on its way*
> *(7) A Final Clue*
> *Seven for a secret, never to be told*
> *But can you work out who the message is aimed at, brother?*
> *Fade*
> *To black.*

'Yuck!' Diana's was the first response. I touched the white envelope that had enclosed this latest threat and thought of bandages. I fingered the skin around my eyes, then looked into Dominic's.

'Blinded? Dominic . . .'

'Nobody's going to be blinded, Helena.' He gripped my hand. 'I'm ringing the police now, then we'll try and work this out.'

We reckoned it would take ten minutes or so for them to arrive. The black and white threat of a razor blade sharpened our perceptions as we waited, and as we tried to see what he was trying to tell us – apart from the obvious.

'Well, the Salvador Dali bit's easy,' I said. 'It's related to the razor blade. It's a reference to the Bunuel film, *Un Chien Andalou*. There's a very gruesome shot of a razor blade slicing an eyeball.'

'And he thanks Iain Banks for the Frisbee and the razor blade,' explained Diana. 'That's one of his numbers.'

'But what's the secret? And what does the reference to me as his brother mean now?' Dominic was puzzling it out.

'And why is it dedicated to his father?' Matthew asked.

'Brothers and fathers.' Diana's voice was low and slow as she pieced it together. 'And eyes. *King Lear* . . . It links to the spermy one, *The Party's Off*, of course! In *Lear*, the father who is blind to his children, Gloucester, is blinded himself; the father who doesn't understand his children, Lear, has his understanding removed.'

'The mad characters are the sanest, bringing messages to the more powerful characters,' I continued.

'And one son, Edmund, stands by while it's decided that his father will be blinded,' Diana finished. I don't dare look at Dominic. I think of that one, thoroughly regretted, second when I wished for his father's death, wished for it so that Dominic would understand me better – Dominic, who understood everything. I close my eyes, feeling that he'll be able to read within them what I had thought that day. Then I hear his voice.

'He'll be in his office by now. I'll ring him.'

I rarely ring him at his office – it's one of his rules. All the time I'm waiting for him to answer, I'm also straining to hear the police arrive. At last he picks up.

'Dad, it's Dominic.'

'This is Nick Oliver's personal assistant. Can I help you?'

Of course. I've met her socially a few times. 'Look, Mrs Mackay, it's Dominic Oliver. Can I speak to my father, please? It's important.'

'Hold the line please, Dominic.' Fuck, fuck, fuck!

'Dominic!' His voice. 'I hope this *is* important? I thought we'd agreed to disagree about your living arrangements.'

Irritating bastard. The temptation to hang up lasts for one second only. 'It's nothing to do with that, Dad. We've had a lot of trouble since I was beaten up that time and on Friday the same person broke into the tower-house. He attacked Helena.'

'Why on earth didn't you tell me?'

Because you never fucking listen. But that's not the point now. 'After you visited me in hospital, you found a mess of blood and offal, in your hallway, didn't you?'

'I always wondered what you . . .'

'Me? Shit, Dad! It was this same bloke, the person I'm talking about. And he sent us a letter today, threatening something similar.'

Dad's voice pumps up an octave. 'Childish rubbish. I won't be . . .'

'Threatening something worse.'

'Threatening what, exactly?'

I look at Helena, desperate for support. It's obvious I need to be more direct. 'Razor blades. And eyes. The police are coming here. Stay in your office; I'll send them over as soon as they get here. Or you could ring the Borders police from there. Detective Ashworth has been dealing with it mostly.'

'I'll keep my eyes peeled, Dominic.' Dad actually laughs his dry, cold laugh. 'I suppose you're right to be cautious. You're absolutely sure it's not a student prank?'

Can teeth chip against themselves? 'Just don't go out. I'll get across there as soon as I can.'

The insensitive bastard didn't even ask how Helena was. I look into her soft yet scabby, broken yet beautiful face. 'You stay here with Diana and Matthew, and the police.'

'I'm going with you.'

'Stay here, Helena. It's what I want. I meant what I said before – it was worse for me when I saw you hurt than it was when I was attacked myself. When the police get here, I want you to stay with them, explain where Dad's office is and what we think this bloke's intentions are. Better still, ring them now and tell them what we think. That's how you can help most.'

She thinks for a few moments, then nods.

'Right,' I say, 'I'm going to his office.'

It's vital that I get to the office before Dominic, just before him: the timing is crucial with this one, like. So I'm parked way out of sight of the tower, with my binoculars going, and I see the two of them go into the house. I reckon it will take them a few minutes to work it out – just the few minutes I need to get ahead of him on the road to Nick's place, where the fireworks can really fucking blast.

I'm driving as fast as I can – faster than I knew I could. He's an awkward, arrogant, shit-headed old bastard, but he's still my dad. When will he realise that I'm not still a child? The most awful thing is the thought of Helena, pulling me back all the time. Stupid, but I wish I'd brought the emerald with me. I really didn't want to leave her – but I know she's safe.

And he is already on his way to my dad's office. The message is as clear and definite as the ringing of a phone.

Mrs Mackay answers. I knew she would: I've had a few nice

chats with her before, like; and I've had a few, inquiring, legal sorts of conversations with Big Nick himself as well, which I've always enjoyed. But neither of them would remember any of that. So I put my Dominic Oliver voice on – it would fool her, but not him.

'Hello. Look, Mrs Mackay, I need to speak to my father. It's urgent.'

'I'll just put you through, Dominic.'

'No, no. Could you just give him a message? I'm in the car outside, the Allegro. Can he come out and meet me, please? Now.'

Spot on. Live entertainment. Dominic just makes curtain up. There he is, just as I promised Old Nick – young 'nic in his trusty Allegro. And just a few cars away is mine. I feel the raised line on my face, the red marks on my throat. I shiver when I touch the new scar on my chest. Get a hard on. Young Adam, waiting. The Alchemist, with a sharp, silver razor blade between his smart, sheathed fingertips.

About to turn it into gold.

The first person I see is Detective Ashworth, in an ordinary car, parking right in front of Dad's office. I'm just going to go up to his car when I see an Allegro – exactly like mine, only with shaded windows – about six cars away. Of course! I look again at Detective Ashworth and he lifts his hand, discreetly but definitely. Leave it to me. He's obviously sussed the car connection, brother link, because he nods, just once, in the direction of the Allegro.

Leave it to me.

Just the three of us, then, just how I like it. At *my* invitation this time. Perfect. My brother on my right, my Frisbee in my hand, and my father walking out of the brass-plaqued door in front of me. A winner, a loser and an audience. Family fortunes. The Mouth Man would have approved – spin the wheel. If Dominic plays the hero and jumps in front of him, I'll have to invent a few new rules, ad lib a bit, like. Dominic knows that: he can either walk over to his dad and take a chance there, or he can take his chance by walking over to the car. Or he can always just watch the fun. Typical family sport – choose pain, pain or non-participation.

I've always opted out – opted for control. What will Dominic opt for?

I should never have let him go like that. My soft-scarred angel. Some things you have to face alone, I thought, so I let him go. But I knew as soon as he left that I was wrong. Even death couldn't part Dominic and me, not permanently. So why did I let him go alone?

Will I ever have another chance like this to prove my love for him?

I have to save my dad, I have to save myself and, I realise, I have to save my sick 'brother'. I have to stop him – I know how he thinks, know what he feels. How much he feels. I think of his front teeth – one grey, one crowned. Broken. I know how he hates being trapped, sense the poverty of the choices he's been offered in his life, and there's no way I can do that to him – get him locked up. Not when I remember so clearly how easily he reduced me to using his methods, his fury. His face will be marked now, and his throat. Marked by my hands. Reluctant brotherhood. I have to start to forgive – and this time, it's all or nothing.

I'm totally on my own, with just seconds to act. Quick, quick, quick.

I put all thoughts of razor blades away, put a middle-class, academic sort of expression on, and walk towards the unmarked police car.

'Detective Ashworth!'

Loud and clear.

Shit. Bastard police. Time to go.

Wasted gesture. They're all over the car within seconds, before he can even start the engine up – so many of them. And only one of him, the poor, sick bastard.

I didn't realise there were so many. Stupid bastards. I throw the Frisbee in a bin – give some stinking, scrounging, mongrel-touting *Big Issue* get a surprise.

Pity I've got to leave another good car, though.

He's not in it! Incredible. He really isn't in it. He must have been watching secretly somewhere, from a distance, silently, as always.

Seven for a secret, never to be told. So much damage. So many of his secrets, never to be told.

Thanks for the warning, brother. Thanks for the warning.

27

> 'What we call the beginning is often the end
> And to make an end is often to make a beginning.
> The end is where we start from'
> — T. S. Eliot, *Little Gidding*

And that brings us right up to the last chapter of my girlhood.

How much had I learnt? There I was, waiting and waiting for Dominic to ring again, wondering if he thought I'd let him down, wondering if he was hurt. Wondering if he was coming home. The forty plus minutes felt like Jesus' forty days and nights in the desert. And why had I hurt him so much in the past? Then almost wishing this on his dad. Was I like Matthew, web-like, not realising that I was really visible, that I could have an effect on people?

When the phone finally rang, it sounded deafening – a clear message. I knew suddenly that I needed the final letter from my father. Then I answered the phone to Dominic, with Diana and Matthew for an audience.

'It's over, Helena. Really over. He's gone – he got away. The series of seven is finished.'

'How's your dad? What happened?'

'Untouched physically, but almost shocked out of his complacency, his Big Nick Oliver thing. The police had arrived before me, just as his PA was taking a message from someone sounding like me, telling him to come outside.'

'Him?'

'Yes. And the police hadn't had time to ring Dad to warn him not to do anything. But they knew, you'd told them, that I had. So they were as shocked as I was when he started to walk outside.

'Dad says he just didn't think, didn't take the whole thing seriously. Maybe if I'd talked to him more about the whole thing, he would have done. The police found the razorblade contraption in a bin nearby. Dad actually apologised for not listening to me then.'

I could tell Dominic was pleased, but he had something else to say and his voice dropped. 'Helena, I gave *him* the signal that the police were there.'

'Dominic!' I was amazed.

'There wasn't a right thing to do, Helena, there just wasn't. God knows what was the right thing to do. You decide.' Dominic sighed, the weight and difficulty of his decision still bearing down on him. 'That's what puts me off some aspects of the law. You saw me that night in our bedroom: I was as mad as him. Evil. But it would have been him who got locked up, or a record, or whatever. Not me. Because I'd acted in self-defence. Because I'm Nick Oliver's son, even.

'And whose son is he? I dread to think. Do you think our children would have that terrible look in their eyes? All of those fantasies about open mouths? Can you just picturise his life?'

'I can't,' I said, but I could hardly argue – I was still stamped with guilt following one or two little fantasies of my own concerning Dominic's dad in the past. I thought of gardens, of a flower and a thistle. Which had more right to be there? And I really couldn't picturise his life clearly at all. Everything I knew about him, I knew from his eyes, and had done from the start.

Dominic's tone brightened up suddenly and he continued. 'And Dad asked how you were. Listen, I'm going for a coffee with him now, then I'm coming home. I'll tell you all about it later.'

The reunion was blissful and sweet – I'll spare you all the details: I'm sure you can imagine them. And then we talked, and talked, and talked.

Before we went to bed (for the second time) I rang Uncle Mark and gave him a very reduced version of events over the phone.

Then I asked him and Lisa to come over to the tower-house the next day.

I was finally ready to go into the seventh room of my house.

Going home gives me plenty of time to think, to think, back on the train, where the series of seven began, and where it ends today. Except I'm not going home: it never has been home – my dad saw to that. But I'll put all that to rest now. Start to forget. Hacking a few layers off old Nick Oliver's ego, with or without the razorblade, has helped to even that score.

And I'm getting tired of kids' things – I've moved from computer games to people games. So what's next? Back to the bottle bank, the dole, or some shitty part-time shop job? Back to my room?

No. I've shown I've got more potential than that. More options, like. I've played with the best of them and I've won. No question about that. And I reckon I built up a bit of a bond there with Dominic. Taught him a thing or two, definitely. And I've got him to thank for *Seven's* happy ending. The fights were pure electricity, the sex was good (if solo) but it's time to move on now, just like the old bastard always did. Put the Frisbees behind me. Time to say hello to Hollywood, search for the hero inside myself – serve my King and country. Pictureyes my future. King Adam. Army hard.

Time to visit the recruitment office.

Uncle Mark visited, for the occasion. He clucked over my face for a while (he'd brought his Germolene with him) and inspected the security system approvingly. Then he pulled Lisa to his side.

'Helena, Lisa and I have some news for you. Good news, this time.' Dominic and I exchanged glances: we'd been expecting this. Uncle Mark beamed jovially at Lisa (who, much less jovially, fiddled with the Germolene tin). 'Lisa has agreed to become my wife.'

Surprisingly, there were tears in my eyes. I blinked furiously and kissed Lisa – her cheek smelled of talc. Desperate. She'd have to spend the rest of her life listening to him on the loo through the cardboard walls. Maybe it was bearable if you loved him.

'Congratulations, Lisa,' I said. *I* loved him too, in my own way. 'And Uncle Mark.' The bristly moustache brushed my face as he gave me a big bear hug.

'And don't worry, young Helena, there'll always be a room for you with us, if you need it.' My smile stiffened – still, I was glad he'd said it.

'At our *new* house,' Lisa said, very firmly. 'We're looking for a house together at the moment.'

No more Leeched Dry? I stared at Uncle Mark, astonished. He looked crestfallen. 'I can keep my furniture, or at least some of it.' He brightened. 'And my barbecue. It'll be a delicate operation to shift it, though.'

I laughed. 'I'd better move that mountain of old toys, then.'

'Oh, no. We can easily move those to the new house,' said Uncle Mark, before Lisa could speak.

'Well, maybe I'll thin them out a bit.'

'I'll just go up to the room, Helena, and make my final adjustments,' said Uncle Mark. Lisa followed him upstairs to help him in his last task at the top of the tower-house.

I was feeling very nervous now. One last message. Dominic came across and held my hand, slipping something into it as he did so. The emerald. He kissed my temple. 'I kept thinking about it yesterday, as I was driving to my dad's office, over and over again. Why did I leave it?'

'And I kept thinking about you. Why did I let you leave alone? I'll never do that again.' My eyes looked up towards the top of the house, inviting him. 'Will you come with me?'

He squeezed my hand, emerald and all. 'Of course, Helena. I'm really glad you've asked me.'

'One blood.'

'One blood.'

Uncle Mark and Lisa came clattering down the stairs. 'Just a bit of tidying and rearranging, Helena,' Uncle Mark said. 'It's all ready for you.'

'Me and Dominic.'

Uncle Mark and Lisa exchanged glances. 'And Dominic, of course. We'll make ourselves comfortable down here.'

I nodded, and then I turned and nodded to Dominic. We headed for the stairs.

The third letter was pinned to the door. I pulled it down and opened the door, holding the envelope in the same hand as the emerald.

The small, circular room held a video player and a television screen so huge in comparison to the size of the room that it seemed as if Uncle Mark had installed a full-sized cinema screen. In front of the screen were two chairs. We sat down, side by side. I looked once at Dominic, then tore open the letter, holding the blue pages between us so that he could look at them too. This also felt larger than life: opening the other two letters had been such intensely private experiences.

The wonderful, loopy handwriting welcomed me for the last time. With the sheets of paper between us, Dominic and I read the words together.

Helena darling,
I really, really love you, whatever horrors you've committed, faced or embraced on your way to adulthood. I love you.
Your mother and I made a film for you of some of the video highlights of your childhood. It was meant to be a part of your 18th birthday present, part of the celebrations. Watch it now as a celebration of your life, watch it over and over again, and let it prove to you how deeply you were loved, how deeply you are loved. Helena, death must have dragged me away from you, never doubt that. But there you are now, the survivor. Celebrate that.
Be safe, be strong, but be wild. Be happy. Most importantly of all, be yourself. Helena Edwardson. Is a parent ever ready to say goodbye to his child, even when the child is an adult?
My Helena, go towards your future with pride and with all of the love of both your parents,
Dad

For my whole life I had searched for my mother's eyes, and now, when I was just about to see them, my own were blinded by tears. Dominic passed me his handkerchief, but his eyes looked a bit full themselves. 'They did love me, didn't they?' I said to him.

'Of course they did, Helena,' he answered, and held me for a minute, then he took the hanky back off me and blew his own nose. 'Are you ready to watch it?'

I pushed my chair to join his and cuddled into him, foetal almost. I nodded my head and he started the machine.

The sound of the old Eurythmics track started the video off, *Sweet Dreams Are Made of This*. My father had used it as a backing track to his film. I thought about the boy, that first day, and then I forgot about him as memory after memory came to life for me.

Her memories were alive again, and they became my memories instantly. I was a part of her past: Helena's mother, no older than me, playing with a tiny baby with reddish hair; Helena's parents, laughing together, young and lively, at Helena's birthday party, watching a curly-haired, cherubic Helena, fumblingly cutting her thickly iced, three-shaped cake; Helena's mother, rocking a sleepy Helena on her lap, cradling her, loving her. And lastly, terribly, Helena's mother, very thin, waving a highly polished little Helena off to her first day at school.

Helena was crying her eyes out by the time the short film ended and I wasn't much better. 'I love you,' I told her. 'I'm your family now.'

Not quite, I thought. I was strong now. But I was silenced.

The strangest thing was that, despite the efforts I was sure Uncle Mark had made technology-wise, the video crackled so loudly with electricity that it felt as if they were actually there. I could feel the energy of their bodies, their spirits, their lives. Neither of us had turned the video off and it crackled still in its black, plastic box.

The other shock was the way that both of my parents looked. My dad was so young and relaxed and happy, not more than thirty. And my mother's eyes were exactly like Dominic's. They were Dominic's eyes, green and loch-like. Enchanting. Creased and laughing when she was watching me struggle to cut my cake, and tender and beautiful, smiling, when she was reading to me. And in the film she was about Dominic's age. Except when she was waving me off to school. She was a different age altogether then and her eyes were in a different place.

She'd waited as long as she could.

I thought of my sea purse for the first time in ages. Nature had given me my very own sea purse, and I reckoned that that was what had been guiding my energies so far. But I realised now that my father had given me another one. I had everything I needed in the world and I still had a pretty big chunk of my cheque left. How many lives could that create, or recreate, if I used my imagination, if I used myself? Encouraged the artist within myself, rather than dreaming about other people and their art? Put the restlessness I'd wasted so far into my own adventures, my own journey?

Annie Lennox's voice winds its way into my head, singing *Sweet Dreams Are Made of This* to me. I've survived so much. And I know there is so much more that I can do now that I know what I'm capable of.

Dominic and I look right into each other's faces and the film crackles away in its electrical box.

'My Helena, go towards your future with pride.'

Now read on for the first chapter of Margaret Burt's *new novel, SLEEPLESS IN NEWCASTLE* coming soon

The Street

'Angelo, touched by the angels.'
'Sit down here with me, look into Angelo Paulillo's eyes, and you
will fall in love from your armchair.'

This is a story of the night and it is night now, brightened only by
my lamp, my torch, and the words inside the petrol-soaked square
of paper that I turn over with the matches in my hand. Midnight.
Flakes of blood-red rust fall down onto my skin, while the wind
sings like a siren through the cracks in the walls, then spits rain
onto my hair and howls. The stench of petrol has seeped into my
clothes.

I *miss* her. I miss them both. And I really want to tell you
about it.

I roll my story back for you like a Turkish rug at our feet. The
pictures of my life, my loves, of my converted church, the casino,
Christina, me and Mic, are hand-knotted into the rug, and I stare
into the figures in the half light, working out the words to tell my
tale to you. My dark red love story. I see the rug so clearly in my
mind. I touch it and its redness touches me – the redness of fire,
women, blood, and blooms and heat.

Its redness touches me like Christina touches . . . touched, me.
Please, let me tell you about it. I don't know what else to do.

*Well, when you hear about some of the experiences that we had, some of
the dreams that we shared, I know you'll think it was strange. Weird, then.
But you weren't with him. You didn't see his eyes and you didn't see through
his eyes. Sit down here with me, look into Angelo Paulillo's eyes, and you
will fall in love from your armchair. Because Angelo was bitter chocolate
dipped in cream. Rich. You will not want to move from your armchair,
once you've felt what I felt. Hot, hot, hot. But at the same time, he was*

as cool as a tooth-screaming iced Coke to a woman finishing a power-walk.
Iced cream. And this to a girl who'd just run a sticky marathon!

I was more than thirsty for him. You get the message?

But from the start, there were so many points that I couldn't be certain
about. Why did he step in that first day like that, when nobody else dared
to, for one thing? Did he even see me that day? I didn't know at first.

I only knew that I'd seen him, for sure.

That first time I saw her, I didn't actually *see* her, not properly,
I mean. But she saw me. Let me make out those first few patterns
on the rug for you first. The meeting.

I was just walking through the Town (Newcastle is a city, but
everybody calls it 'the Town' or 'the Toon') on my way to work.
I'd turned a tarot card over that morning and found the Six of Cups
staring at me. 'Don't let the past detract from the present' was the
message – one message I should definitely have listened to.

Anyway, I was on an early that day and I had a couple of
shirts to get from the shops before my shift. The town was fairly
buzzing: pubs, shops, people, noises and jostling everywhere. Then
I stopped short. I had to. There was a gigantic crowd in front of
me, a solid circle of backs blocking my way, wind swirling around.
Intrigue. Scuffling noises and jagged, raw breathing were at its
centre. Evil.

His voice came first, between breaths. 'Bitch. Fucking bitch.'
Male, metallic and angry. Half mad. I stretched up over a ginger
girl's head so that I could see what they were all standing watching.
Or who.

He was wellying her, kicking down into her, hard, a young bloke
and a dark girl. 'My cross. You've lost my cross.' His breath was
going; he was wearing himself out on her ribs. 'My fucking cross.'
She was curled up like a bean, like a baby on the pavement, with
her arms up over her head and some straight, brown hair sticking
out. All the rest were just watching in this great circle, watching like
it was some sort of a sick wrestling match. *'You could do nothing to*
help?' Her voice came first. *'You could do nothing?'*

And then Mic switched into my mind. Mic. I could never, *never*
let it happen again.

I pushed through the audience and I wrenched boot boy's arm
back, but hard. Really hard and sudden. That was my first sight

of his face in front of mine, of his great eyes, glaring, his greasy hair and the slaver all around his mouth. A chemical smell was coming off him, rising off his clothes, his breath. Dangerous. Deadly dangerous. Quick.

'I'm a copper, mate,' I said, quiet, but I was aiming at a grip like a mastiff's jaws on his wrist. 'Off duty.' His head kind of twitched towards me. His eyes sussed my eyes out, timing the stares, then narrowing. I wished I was anywhere else at all, but I couldn't weaken. I spoke again. 'Just leave the girl alone.' I sounded like a macho character from some corny, 1940s, 'Get out of the city!' type gangster film, but it did the trick. My eyes won. Five seconds passed and his just edged away.

Still gripping his wrist, I noticed that some girl, I just got a shot of long blonde hair and some CK One, had some guts at last, and she was pulling the curled-up, beaten dog of a girl off the pavement, pulling her away from the man (if man's the right word) with the big boots, away from the crowd. The bloke's wrist dropped and some of his energy went. Listen, I swear I could see it coming off him in waves. The shoulders went down, the head went back and the beaten girl was gone. I dropped the hard man's arm.

The audience split to let him through and he was off, giving out, 'Bastard, bastard,' over his shoulder as he swaggered off his stage. I breathed, like for the first time, and headed off in the opposite direction, in the direction of work. As I got further away, I could hear him, shouting, with his voice full of dirt and tin. 'Fucking probation. Fucking bastard could have fucking ruined my probation, man.' Then, 'Bastard,' but harder, now that the distance was safe. 'Fucking bastard.' I turned around to give him the stare.

The popcorn crowd had left the ring and I saw that he was standing there with the dark girl; she was right next to him, just waiting for him to finish, glaring at *me*, shaking. Puce face, trying not to cry. Jesus. I just walked away. What else could I do? Some hero. Some hope. Film noir, I thought. *In a Lonely Place.*

It's funny, but when I was younger, I'd always thought that it was women that were connected to the hardest things in life: birth and madness, blood and death. Mess. I'd always thought that it was women who led the men into the darker, the uncharted places, like Eurydice, tempting Orpheus down into Hades to find her. It often is. But that wasn't the way it was between us, between her and me. I realise that now. Because that was just the first time that I led her into a dark place, a *dangerous* place, though I didn't mean to.

I was shaking as well, but not because of boot boy. All I could think about was Mic, and what happened to Mic. Why there was no one there for him that day.

Where was my big, heroic act that day?

I was shrivelled *with nerves that day, absolutely shrivelled. Dead scared. So I spent the whole morning on my mask. I hardly dared leave my flat for the Town. Wimp City! My interview at the casino was for half one, but I made sure that I was heading for the Town before half twelve, dressed like I guessed a dealer in a casino should be dressed. The last thing I wanted was to be late.*

My footsteps were stamping out my tables as I stamped my way down through the Bigg Market. 1×17=17, 2×17=34, 3×17=51. Just in case they asked me, like. 4×17=68. And then out of nowhere, I stepped out of the Market and over to a circle, watching with the crowd, like I was at a baseball game, or in one of those gigantic Roman arenas from Ben Hur, *or* Spartacus, *you know, the ones you draw diagrams of at school. The Colosseum. The lion's den. Gusts of wind pushed me to my place in the ring. I'll spare you the description – I'm sure you know the sort of scene – and just before this, I'd found myself alone in a theatre of war with a pretty big-mouthed lion myself. Bad news. Some Geordie men really know how to make a show, but it's not often that a* real *hero steps in to help. Spectacular. It made me braver than I knew I could be as well. I thought of Rose, going back down into the bowels of the* Titanic *to rescue Jack, before that choppy bit with the axe when Jack risks his wrists. But wouldn't you risk the water, the depths, for the lovely Leonardo or the corsetted Kate? One look at Angelo's face was enough to make up my mind.*

And he even sounded like the hero out of a really classy old black and white film. Dead strong. 'Just leave the girl alone!' Deep. 'I'm a copper, mate,' he said. Seemed more like a fire fighter to me, all cool and collected in the face of emergency, not to mention the sooty-black hair. But his eyes were the first thing I noticed. Gorgeous. His eyes and his strength shone out with that sort of burning *glow that he had. Magnetic, totally magnetic. What with the jet-black hair and the dark, dark eyes, he didn't look like he belonged in Newcastle at all – Italian was my first thought. La Vita e Bella! He never looked like he belonged anywhere and it was hard really* to work out how he felt, at times (though he was sharp enough at rooting out other people's thoughts). He hardly spoke, action was more his thing, but when he did speak, the accent was Geordie, but soft, like, for a lad, that is. Have you ever noticed, their accents are usually worse than ours? Well, his was softer than mine. And his voice was sort of still and cool. But you knew not to cross him, and you knew he meant what he said, straightaway.

That's why I was so surprised by what, or who, I found when I finally got to the casino for my interview (feeling a bit calmer by then). I was sitting in the reception area, waiting, my head back into my tables. (Jonty's top tip, the tables – he'd joined the last training school. Said the interview was a 'piece of piss', naturally, for a genius like him.) Doing the splits, bets covering two numbers. 5×17=85. Doing the splits, like the dancers at Sun City. Then black eyes appears all of a sudden, cool as anything, walks right down the massive Gone With the Wind staircase they've got there, right past me and over to the receptionist. Dead casual. I couldn't believe it. And I couldn't stop looking at him.

This might sound stupid to you, or it might even sound familiar, I don't know, but right from the start, he seemed to have this edge of light all around his head and body and a darker edge inside that. My eyes were fixed on his face and my breath went. Why wasn't everybody in reception staring at him the way I was? Stop it, I said to myself. Stop, stop, stop. He looked right through me and walked over to the reception desk.

'Message from above, Paula?' he asked, looking up at the ceiling and doing a tiny, a really slow half grin. The girl was all polished up – sports car red lips, smooth white face, painted-on black hair. Dead professional she looked, at first. Until she spoke to him, that is, then she couldn't resist a dig.

'Mr Andreas wants a large tray of ham sandwiches and some home-made shortbread taken up to the office now, Angelo.' Then she turned and whispered in his ear, so quietly that I had to strain my head towards them to hear. 'As if the miserable old pig isn't well porky enough to start with.' She laughed, and she flickered her eyes across the reception towards me, all mischief. His eyes, Angelo's eyes, were dead steady; they always were steady. Only the minutest twitch of the lips on the left-hand side of his face showed me that he thought this was funny at all, which made old Porsche Lips laugh even more, poking his arm, flashing her shiny eyes into his face and flinging her hair back, all flirty.

One nod in her direction and he was back off to the kitchen.

Angelo. Touched by the angels, I thought, followed by 6×17=102. 7×17=119. I felt dizzy, disorientated. Vertigo. I felt like I was staring down at him from this endless Jacob's ladder of lust. Is that why they call it falling *in love, then? Talk about physical! Then a stuffed-looking old suit showed up at the desk, so I stood up to shake his hand, walked through to his office and concentrated on my numbers, smiling and leg swivelling for the next thirty minutes. I really hate interviews, don't you?*

Not a policeman at all, a waiter. Always did look like an Italian waiter, only taller. Much taller. I thought about him all the way home, racking my brains to work out what I knew about Italy. The Old World. Milan, Turin, Florence, beautiful Venice, resting in its salty, salty lagoon, the Bridge of Sighs. Big beautiful Angelo Paulillo, dead salty, and little ordinary me, Christina Rae, all sighs. Four hundred bridges in Venice meant four hundred chances to connect, to connect one island to the land, him to me, man to woman. The New World was normally more my scene, but I did a massive *sigh in real life – practically blowing some poor old woman off the pavement with the draught – a sigh for him, for Angelo and Italy. Little cafés, big gondolas, humpbacked bridges and dark, dark men. Brilliant. Of course I fancied him, more than that, right from the start, Jonty or no Jonty. But you've already worked that one out for yourself, haven't you?*

I'll only say this to you once, I can only stand *to say this once to anybody, but it's a really big part of Angelo's story and mine: Angelo is better looking for a man than I am for a woman. Definitely. Desperately! No point in dwelling on things that you can't change, but it has to be said. It's important. And I knew from the start that he would hurt me. Did that put me off? Not for one single second. Do you think it should have done?*

Angelo. Touched by the angels.

Looked right through me.

I was knackered when I got home, partly because of running round after weak-minded, fat-bellied punters all night, but mainly because of that business with the young bloke and his damned cross. I'd thought about it all day. Thought about Mic all day. So I wasn't surprised to find a message from him waiting for me on my answer phone when I got back to the church at ten o'clock that night.

'Ango, message from your brother.' The old woman, wheezing her filter-tipped words down the phone line as usual. 'Sez he was impressed by the "pig impersonation". Mek any sense to ye, pet?

I'll see you at the weekend, son, all being well.' One big cough and a clatter and she was gone. Pet. Son! She was a real pain.

And impressed? Mic? Not usually. Not by me. Not by anybody much.

Maybe if I'd had someone to talk to when I got home, it would have been easier. If I could even have rung someone up, sent out a message, instead of receiving them all the time, on my own. Still, the old church didn't seem as lonely that night as it could do. At least I had the notebook.

And I knew I'd be hearing from him again in a few days' time.

I went straight back to my flat after my interview, couldn't afford any more time in town, with all those shop windows blinking at me, bars of silver-wrapped chocolate twinkling at me from every till and me with no money in my pocket, as usual. Typical. So I curled up at home with a coffee, wondering whether there'd been enough leg-swivelling, fake smiling and number-spinning to win me a contract at the Casino Club. I'd know soon enough: they were going to give me a ring at the weekend, after they'd finished all the other interviews. Jonty was on a late, so I knew there'd be no sight of him to disturb me; he got fed at the casino. Time for some peace.

Except there never was any peace in that flat, anyway. I know that in London, the West End of the city is where it's at. Swish and smart. Newcastle's West End is a bit different. Dangerous dump. My flat was near to Benwell: try typing 'Benwell' into a computer and it won't understand you, keeps turning it into 'Bengal'. Pretty perceptive, I'd say. Who's going to be left in the North East in twenty years' time? Only people who can knit, crochet, remember ration books and suffer, or who do every depravity going.

And property developers. Loads of developers had bought the flats around mine as investments: you could buy one of them for four or five grand, it was that rough an area, but it was right in the city centre. So these developers had bought the flats at auction, boarded them up and had a bet with themselves that the house prices would go up in the end. Losers. The whole area was dead. Dead depressing. At least you could have some fun, spending your money in a casino, I thought. (I thought then.) I mean, that night was typical. Just about the only light on in the block was mine, one lit window, reminding me of the last rotten tooth that poked out from my great auntie's gums for twenty years until she died. A pickle stabber, my mam used to call it, neither use nor ornament, she used to say. So what if it fell out? Only got in the way, anyhow.

I got up to stir some more sugar into my mug. At least you were never lonely in the flats, always plenty of conversation around to keep you going, plenty of action altogether, what with the voices from every side, and the buzz of the traffic from down below. And the views out over the town were fantastic, as good as the views from the Quayside flats or St Peter's Basin any day. (Five grand would barely buy you a bog seat down there.)

What I liked best of all about the flats (apart from the rent, like) was being right up high in the sky with the stars. The gods. If you stuck your head out far enough, you could see all the people rushing around down below, like they were in a tiny world of their own. You were right up there in the blackness, on your own, like a bird. High. You saw the wind pushing the clouds past, the seasons change, and then at night you saw all the stars and the ins and outs of the moon. You felt like a star, watching the Milky Way and the Plough, the Big Dipper, and thinking about what your own path right up to the skies, or across the seas, might have to offer.

Recognising magic is half the trick. Great Expectations. *When I was really little once, I saw a bat, all curled up on the pavement, and everybody else thought it was just some piece of rubbish, like to everybody but me, Angelo was just a policeman or a waiter. No. I knew this little lump on the pavement was a bat that could fly in the night and squeal, all dramatic, like a ghost, and that deserved to be protected because it was so magical and special, just like Angelo. And I always knew my flat was special. Honestly, the whole block seemed to sway around you, sometimes, and you were right up there with the bats and the birds and the whole night. Dead tall. That was even better than hearing the ins and outs (and there were plenty of those) of all my neighbours' goings on!*

I stuck the telly on. A caged bird. Dead small. Best not to think about the casino job either, I decided. Jonty'd said they'd had loads of applications and I was hardly your prime candidate, was I, one of the notorious Raes, with my two good GCSEs, my crappy work history and my scraggy, shaggy hair that hadn't quite grown out of its perm? That had been the last thing that Jonty had said to me, the last time I'd spoken to him. 'For God's sake, Teen, get your hair sorted before you go. Other girls'd be seein' a counsellor over hair like yours.' Well, I'd had a trim. I wondered if he'd put in a good word for me.

I filled in my diary, but I wasn't holding out great hopes that night.

> SMALL DREAMS
> Get a hairstyle that suits
> Get the job at the Casino Club. If not, get more hours at the
> Dunston Club, or sign on
> BIG DREAMS
> Casinos, America, Las Vegas, New York, Los Angeles
> and Chicago, Angelo, stretch limousines,
> white wine, chocolate, lots of money and heaven in general

Those first ones are pretty inspiring, eh? Bet you're seething with jealousy there. And the second ones are ridiculous. Bette Midler chunked pineapples, you know, and Sean Connery polished coffins! But Bette could sing; Sean could act. What exactly could I do? Things like being a dealer, in a casino, exciting things, never happened to people like me: that's the last thought I remember from that night, before the telly did its usual anaesthetic bit. I had no idea then just how exciting things were going to get.

It was pretty hard to get through those next days at the casino, when I was waiting to hear from Mic the whole time, waiting for something that much more important than getting Mr Andreas' sandwiches ready or watching the other waiters spitting in the most miserable punters' coffee and stirring it in. Great. Only three months ago, I'd been at university. Some people would have said I was letting myself down now, people that didn't understand me, that is, which was most people. I just kept my head down, my brain clear and myself busy. Felt like I was between things, that I needed to get some energy back. Renew. After that I could travel, study, read and work in the way I'd always planned to before. In the meantime, I was glad of the peace, the normality, after all the commotion I'd been through before. And all the commotion I was about to go through with her, if I had but known it then.

Commotion and more. Much more.

Well, just how wrong can you be? Christina Rae, the Queen of Chance. The phone woke me up a few days later. (I always did sleep more when there was nothing going on when I was awake.) I picked it up.

'Miss Rae?' he said. I nearly squealed out. I knew who it was the second I heard the voice. Dead formal, he sounded.

'Speaking,' I said. I made my voice all posh and calm.

'This is the Casino Club . . . Mike Turner. I'm happy to say that we've decided to offer you a position, Miss Rae. You were very impressive at interview.'

Impressive? Me? I wondered which bits had impressed? Brilliant! But I kept my voice dead cool, tried to pretend I wasn't a Geordie (because Mr Turner wasn't, hardly) more of your Las Vegas, or your Cockney, type. 'Thank you, Mr Turner. How kind of you to say so.'

There was a bit more of the same, some information about when the training school would start, and expenses, and contracts and so on. You don't get paid until the six-week training school is finished, but I knew that already from Jonty. Six more weeks of pensioners' discos and singing along to Going Loco, Down in Acapulco with people pretty much like me, who'd never been across the Tyne Bridge. Six more weeks of beer-sticky shoes, pulling pints for men with hair cream and appetites like Elvis (grease is the word), before listening to that woman in the long dress who pretended to be all different birds, doing her turn. Or was that having a turn? Not to mention the act where the hair-gelled wonder tears chapatis up into the shape of whatever country his audience has asked for. Fantastic! Six more weeks with nothing to look forward to but the Dunston dawn chorus singing their hearts out in the Dunston, not-so-many-of-them-are-working-now, Working Men's Club.

But it would be different now. I felt like I had a ticket to step into a brand new world. And which part of Disneyland are you most interested in seeing, Miss Rae? Whose autograph are you going to sign first? It was a massive leap. I could choose my future now: a little casino in Newcastle at first, and then maybe one of the bigger ones, in London or Birmingham. After that I might try the liners, cruising the Caribbean or the Mediterranean or the Scandinavian fjords even. Next stop, Los Angeles, City of Angels.

Who knows what it could lead to? I'll let you in on a bit of one of my very favourite (and very private) scenes. Dream on, vision one. Hello!

Christina Rae's Pismo Beach Home

Halfway between San Francisco and Los Angeles lies the beautiful Pismo Beach, a classic Californian beach town. It was here that Rudolph Valentino filmed *The Sheikh* and Cecil B. De Mille is reported to have buried the set of the *Ten Commandments*. This is one of the only beaches in the States on which cars can be driven.

Christina Rae walks between her enormous, beachside house, with its works of art, and its walls of glass overlooking the coastline and the sea, laughing, two beautifully-dressed, cherubic children holding her hands. She looks over her shoulder and smiles at the startlingly attractive, dark haired young man who is smiling and waving to her from the house.

Christina looks remarkably like the young Julia Roberts in her *Sleeping with the Enemy* heyday . . .

. . . only happier. Because my version was Sleeping with the Lover, *a wonderful, family-orientated love story, rather than some horrible, gloomy thriller where you get all your make-up washed off and there's a load of battering and boring fuss about a few old towels. Wide screen vision. Glossy. Miramax, megavision, megavoice – forget about* Little Voice, *LV, altogether, I said to myself.*

I'd have to get some contacts and grow my hair.

It would be like stepping inside a film.